T0367597

Build a Hurricane Business

An unexpected love story!

Michael Kelly

Order this book online at www.trafford.com
or email orders@trafford.com

Most Trafford titles are also available at major online book retailers.

© Copyright 2009, 2011 Michael Kelly.
All rights reserved. No part of this publication may be reproduced, stored in a retrieval system, or transmitted, in any form or by any means, electronic, mechanical, photocopying, recording, or otherwise, without the written prior permission of the author.

Edited by Marilyn von Qualen. mvq@corselan.com.
Illustrations and sketches by: Mr. Rob Hay. robertbhay@hotmail.com
Cover artwork: Mr. Michael J. Schwartz. info@halodezign.com
Designed by: Michael Kelly
Photography by: J. Gailliard Photography. photography@jgailliard.com

Note for Librarians: A cataloguing record for this book is available from Library and Archives Canada at www.collectionscanada.ca/amicus/index-e.html

Printed in the Unithed States of America.

ISBN: 978-1-4251-3221-7 (sc)

Trafford rev. 06/02/2011

Trafford PUBLISHING® **www.trafford.com**

North America & international
toll-free: 1 888 232 4444 (USA & Canada)
phone: 250 383 6864 • fax: 812 355 4082

To my beautiful wife Rose,

Thank you for allowing me to tell your story in an honest and forth-right way. You mean everything to our family and The Kelly Team. You are greatly admired and even more loved.

Thanks to Mr. Stephen Marshall for saying during our company's National Sales Rally a simple quote that shaped my thinking...

"A lot of loan officers don't get it;
it's about the service, not the sale."

What Would You Really Commit To Do?

When you first entered your profession, you made a commitment to do business a certain way. It was at that beginning moment your commitment was unchallenged and at its zenith. But what you say upfront and what you actually end up doing can sometimes be different. Why? The simple one word answer is "answers." More times than not, the altering of your commitment is due to a lack of business-building answers. But what if you had those answers? That presents an interesting situation, doesn't it? Such a situation would mean your initial commitment remains unchallenged because there is no knowledge impediment. Now, what would you really commit to do? Having the business-building answers in hand moves you from who you say you want to be to who you actually are. Get ready to read those answers and reveal yourself as a businessperson.

Here are some things to think about if
you bear the responsibility of building a business...

Referral

Its dictionary definition is simple, but the service industry will never know a more powerful or complex word with so many meanings. Why is it powerful? The output is greater than the input, given that the financial gain from referrals outweighs the cost of service to generate them. Why is it complex? It takes a well thought out and highly executed business model to receive referrals. What are its meanings? If you are talking about business, it means conducting business at the highest level. If you are talking in personal terms, it means being a professional businessperson. If you are talking about industry, then it means being a member of a proud and prestigious industry. If you are talking about clients, it means trust. And if you are talking about business partners, then it means entrust. The confluence of so much under one auspicious word has rightfully earned Referral its place in the pantheon of words by being the pinnacle word in the service industry—universally recognized, highly sought after, and respected by all. As such, for as long as you are alive and long after you are gone, people will continue to build businesses in the exclusive quest to receive referrals.

The Third Question

It's the question you should have asked yourself right after you answered the two questions of what profession to join and where you work. It's not an obvious question, but it is a profound question. So much so, it would have determined the work you did. And it would have determined how people perceived you. And it would have determined how you perceived yourself. And it would have determined your success. And it would have determined how you achieved that success. And it would have determined your lifestyle. And it would have...stop with the ands. What's the third question? "How do I lead and serve others?"

Dual Education

There are jobs that require an education, and then there are jobs like yours that require a dual education. The determining factor between the two jobs is in the level of personal responsibility one assumes. Both jobs will require an education in required technical ability (conduct transactions). But where some people only have to conduct business for somebody else, you must generate business for yourself. This distinctive feature is what makes the second education necessary. And what is the second education? It's the other half of a business—the service side. It's an education not to be overlooked by you, for it's what puts your technical education to work.

Don't Ask That Question

You are excited and eager, excited to be starting a new profession and eager to learn. It's just what you need to be because the challenge in front of you is daunting—build a business. To get off on the right foot and on the road to success you earnestly ask, "What do I do?" Wrong question! Such a question unexpectedly places you on a long and winding path that eventually leads to being a follower of others. Instead, ask, "How does a business work?" and "Why do I do things?" When you know the how and the whys, you'll know what to do. It's a level of learning that provides answers, not directions. Answers that will empower you to build a business reflecting your individualism while becoming the leader of your business.

One Simple Word

The success of service can be told in one simple word. Even when you consider the breadth of service, you can still measure success with this one simple word. As such, never has so much been done for so little a word that means so much. So what is the told word? It is a word that will cause you to spend hours upon hours building a level of service that is uniquely individual, all the while knowing your pursuit is unsure, for service is nothing more than a subjective opinion. But you pursue it anyway because it is the most coveted word to hear in the same breath whenever your profession is mentioned. So what is such a compelling word? It's a word that unequivocally conveys trust and loyalty, which makes it the origin of repeat and referral business. Such a word is simply known as "My."

Success

If success is simply defined as a result achieved, then why is it so personally desirable? Because before you can achieve it, you must first pass a character test. A test so difficult you would swear the word itself is conspiring against you. The inevitable awaits you on your way to success...struggles, obstacles, self-doubts, fears, failures, and maybe even thoughts of quitting. And all for the purpose of judging if you have the character needed to handle success. That is why it's so personally desirable; it tests you before it rewards you. You must first prove you can handle the many challenges of achieving success before you can achieve success itself. But when you do, you are rewarded both professionally and personally. Not only do you achieve the highly sought after result you desired, but you are a better person for doing it.

Purpose

Every activity you accomplish in your business has a reason behind it. That fact is what allows you to make sense of your business. The answers are there if you seek out the purpose for doing things. So much so, the implicit simplicity of a business is revealed when you understand its purposeful actions. But purpose takes time to learn. It's not the "just do this" answers but, rather, the acumen answers. When you seek out purpose, you are demanding an education, not training. Where training taps into the discipline of the human mind, education unleashes its creative spirit. So when is purpose necessary? It is necessary when you have the personal responsibility to build a business, and you are uncertain of the many purposes of its interlocking, interdependent pieces.

Curiosity

At no other time in your life did you learn more then when you were curious as a child. You wanted to know the answers to all sorts of things and so you asked, maybe to the point of annoyance. You had an insatiable thirst for knowing that needed to be quenched, and it was the instinctive way to learn. Then you grew up and you naturally outgrew what you thought was the childish act of curiosity. You thought there must be a more mature way, so you stopped asking questions, and you settled for being told what to do. Something you loathed as a child. It's time to get curious again—to learn once again—this time about a business.

Contents

Introduction xv

The Argument For 1

My Inspiration 7

Lost Opportunities 13

The Other Half 19

Out of the Clear Blue Sky 27

Clear Skies 35

Tropical Depression 37

Tropical Storm 41

Hurricane 43

The Truth Be Told 45

The Defining Moment 53

The Psychology of it All 57

The Pentagon Effect 63

Just Two Questions 69

The Scientific Proof 85

It's More Than Just Geometry 89

You're Not Alone Anymore 93

The First of Two Essentials 99

And the Last Essential 109

Gotcha! 123

Where the Rubber Meets the Road 133

Why Isn't Your Hurricane Rotating? 147

The Passion Moment 151

Making a Difference Begins 161

Become a Manipulator 169

Do What You're Told 183

You Better Say It 189

Everybody Needs to Get Mad 199

Get the Branding Iron 205

Prepare For the Moment 211

Just Thinking About You 221

Get Some Fresh Air 229

The One Thing You Must Do 239

The By-product 249

It's a Journey, Not a Destination..255

The Bud Effect 271

The Sand Has Sifted..277

From a Revolving Door to a Front Door 285

Our Client Service Today 291

A Hurricane Business 305

The Bowtie 311

I Have My Fingers Crossed 317

Some Final Thoughts 323

Introduction

HAVE YOU EVER WONDERED how to build a *powerful referral business*? It's an intriguing question—and the particular question the author asked of himself after retiring from the United States Air Force and joining his wife in the mortgage business for a year. To his complete surprise (he never had any intention of writing a book, and he wasn't an aspiring author), his simple three word answer of "I don't know" set him on a mentally challenging journey for over a five year period to try to figure out the answer.

What was the reason that drove him so hard to try for so long? It was his deep love for his wife. This book is about their uncommon business journey together, their successes and failures. As such, it is not a story shouted from the top of the mountain but, rather, a personal business story about a wife and a husband from two totally different worlds, business and military, and how they came to realize in the end they were both from the same world. It is a world that is tightly bound together by a core competency.

This book makes the assumption that the reader is both technically competent in his or her chosen business field and professionally conducting transactions in it. Therefore, requisite profession competency and required technical service that directly supports a transaction are not the focus of this book. And personal motivation is not the focus of this book either. Instead, the information herein is simply intended to help entrepreneurial type business people in the service industry who have a choice regarding the level of service they provide, work with clients and business partners, and are dependent on repeat business and referrals for business success. If these three criteria are the elementary business principles at work within your business, then this book will have beneficial meaning to you, regardless of your profession. In other words, this book is for business people who are responsible to generate their own success.

Although this book addresses the subject of a powerful referral business in a somewhat unorthodox manner with unconventional wisdom and unique perspectives, it might very well help business people who are at all stages of a business career. The information is adaptable enough to where it has applicability to business people who are just starting out, struggling now, want to take their business to the next level, or who have perhaps failed in the past.

The love story told here intertwines a personal business story against the backdrop of the author's views, insights, and concepts—along with his mad scientist-like ideas. He even includes the reader in the story. Altogether, it makes for a page turning read.

A thought-provoking and powerful read, this book directly takes on the two most difficult and seldom addressed questions in business: "How does a business work?" and "Why do you do things?" They're the *headwater questions* of a business—from them flows the acumen answers. Such acumen answers (interesting and uninteresting, obvious and unobvious) will formulate your business model thinking by showing you the *beginning knowledge* required to build a powerful referral business. Such knowledge has every type of answer in it—blah, blah, blah; yeah, yeah, yeah; hmm, and aha!

The idea of beginning knowledge represents a novel way to learn about a business. Not only is it an innovative approach to learning, it empowers business people in many different ways. Learning such knowledge results in the following: It brings perspective to every aspect of a business. It brings clarity to business thinking. It provides business-building answers. It empowers business people to make decisions across a business. It allows them to think while they listen. It brings intellectual thought to their business conversations. It makes words matter. It makes sense of their business. And it even makes sense of what other people are saying about a business. It is for all of these reasons why beginning knowledge (framework) is the focus of this book and why it is the first thing to know when building a business.

As you read this book, keep in mind that it's far more important where your business is heading than where it is. As you will see, the journey is always more important than the destination. So turn the page and start your journey of reading an unexpected love story while discovering a powerful referral business—from beginning to end.

When you have time to focus on an issue by observing and thinking, you'll surprise yourself by what you really see and think of...

The Argument For

Just thinking...
Oh it's there...you can't see it, but it's there.

IF YOU READILY ACCEPT THE CHALLENGE to build a powerful referral business, then the very first question you face is, "Where do you start?" An instinctive question that is often difficult to answer and even more frustrating to figure out. You know in general terms what you want to do, but you just don't know how to specifically do it. So where do you start? The obvious answer is at the beginning. But where exactly is that? Or you could start with the first thing if you knew what that was. The answer isn't easily discovered, but not for the reason you might think. The answer is elusive because you literally can't see it. For that reason, it's not something that immediately comes to mind.

The answer to the question, "Where do you start?" is found in the phrase, *build a business.* If you're going to build something, you have to start by building something. You need to start with the first thing—*the framework.* But will it really make all that much of a difference? It is only framework. Clearly there must be more important things to worry about or know about beforehand when it comes to building a business. Framework can't be all that important, or can it be? Don't underestimate the fundamental importance of framework in the construction of anything. It is a definite necessity that comes first. Without framework, it is structurally impossible to construct anything—to include a business.

Because framework is unglamorous and quite boring to look at, it may well be an afterthought to people in the service industry and, therefore, easily overlooked. However, if you were an architect, you wouldn't overlook it. An architect knows all too well that when it's time to start constructing something he begins with framework. He can't do his job without it, and neither can you. It may only be the skeletal structure, and it'll quickly be covered up, but from it everything and anything is possible. Framework is never showcased, but the end product it helped build is. When people look at an architect's finished work, they won't talk about the framework; instead, they'll talk about and admire what was created. The architect also admires his work, but he knows the hidden secret that made it all possible. His secret is now your secret.

The service industry is more like the construction industry than you may have even realized. Just like an architect, you will require a framework to build a business because it has the same characteristics of a structure—interlocking, interdependent pieces. And just like a structure, if your business is built without the proper framework, it'll be poorly constructed and, therefore, unable to stand up against much of anything. Such a business would almost certainly under impress, under perform, and negatively present you. It would be a business no sturdier than a house of cards.

Here is yet another reason with a different perspective as to why framework should be important to you. Within the business world around you, there are three segments that offer you possibilities. Each one is bigger than the next, more uncomfortable and challenging than the previous one, and less tolerant of you. The first two worlds help you achieve a minor level of business success because of the people you know. Those worlds are composed of family and friends. You can get by without much thought of framework in these worlds because business tends to be *given* by virtue of association. Even with that said, they are still important worlds to enter, especially when you are just beginning your career. They are the worlds that offer the best opportunity for early business success and building self-confidence. However, if you limit yourself to them alone, you limit your success. You and your business will be confined to these limiting worlds as illustrated below.

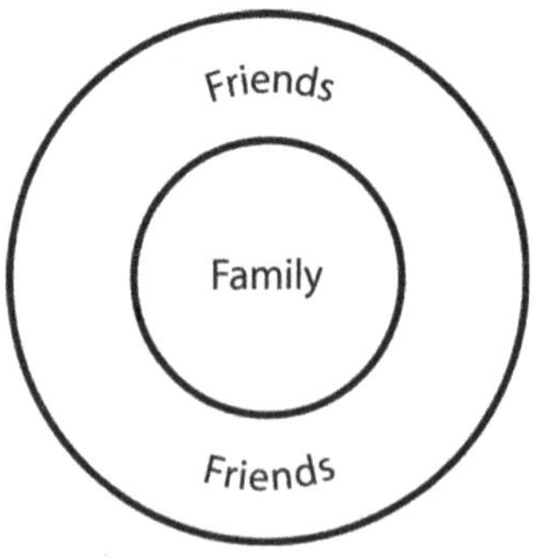

The third and last world is vast and full of opportunity, but it is unfamiliar and uninviting due to the unknown factors that compose it. Just those thoughts alone can cause trepidation and prevent you from truly trying to penetrate it. You must be prepared when you enter this uncertain, unlimited world, or you stand little chance of successfully competing in it. Not surprisingly, it is this world, and this world alone, that demands a well thought out framework. And interestingly enough, it's the only world out of the three that excites the senses because it has it all: intimidating, fulfilling, scary, and rewarding. A powerful referral business resides and finds comfort in this highly competitive world because it's *the world of success.* From a purely business point of view, it's the final and truest measure of business success; while on a personal level, it indicates your seriousness to build a lasting and self-sustaining business.

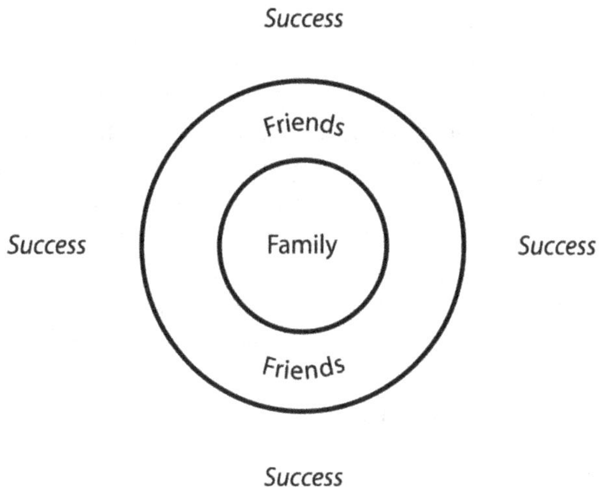

Just as the three worlds build upon each other resulting in a greater business success along the way so too does the sophistication of business framework. So much so, the level of business success reflects the level of business framework. The direct correlation is undeniable.

And here's the personal difference to recognize when it comes to the three worlds. When family and friends give you business, you are appreciative; but when you earn business on your own in the world of success, you feel successful. Only one of the ways indicates a chance for long-term success and real achievement.

The brilliance of learning the framework of a business is you can see its most basic building structure. Nothing is covered up, since everything is exposed. You can see how it all fits together as one, and therefore, it is simple to work with. In your mind you can easily take it apart and see what specifically requires improvement. Learning the framework of a business leads to a compartmentalized computerization-effect within your mind. When your brain processes in *Framework Language,* it can immediately analyze a business, identify problem areas, and provide answers. The importance of that is it empowers you as a businessperson.

Framework Language still has more to offer. When you think in Framework Language, you hear a completely different conversation when you listen to people speak because you synthesize what they say into the framework of a business. *You are, in essence, thinking as you listen.* For example, if you were attending a seminar and the speaker was talking about a business in some capacity, you could immediately put his comments into the framework of a business, thereby determining the true business impact of his commentary. It is quite revealing. The same principle applies when you read something. *It's the learning of business framework that brings perspective to every aspect of a business and clarity to business thinking.*

Now the thought of framework may at first seem limiting to you, that it will confine your creativity in some way. That couldn't be further from the truth. If anything, it unleashes your creativity. How? Picture yourself looking at a $250K and a $1M home side-by-side. What you'll see are two distinctly different homes beautifully showcasing the architect's intended work. However, if you were to take a closer look, you would realize that each home was built utilizing *the same framework building concepts.* What that specifically means to you when building your business is *framework doesn't limit you; it inspires you to build whatever you aspire to build.*

When you know the framework of your business, you know its every secret. You know its most important points, where you have to get it just right, and where you can be a little bit off. Framework is simple to see yet sophisticated to learn. When you do learn it, you know about more than just framework. Such knowledge makes you the mastermind of your business because you alone are its master craftsman. Nobody else will understand it more or do more.

The concept of framework has much more to offer, as you'll see. For all of its attributes, its most important contribution is it allows you to work your business in a steady way, every day. By doing so, you avoid the irregular and disruptive business pattern of having to surge at some later point. Why's that so significant? When you have to work extra hard to create a short period of business success, it's only natural to want to rest or take it easy after doing so, which inevitably necessitates you surging all over again in short order. Conducting business in this uneven fashion has you constantly relying on surges for success, creating a business cycle based on reaction instead of action. Your business isn't flowing, it's surging, and thus, it's not as dependable as business that's flowing. One is steady; the other quickly rises and falls. By employing the proper framework, you instill in yourself a more productive mindset rather than limiting yourself to reactions because of your own inaction.

So in the end, why does framework work? It works because it's only based on what's needed. And how does that expressly apply to you and your business? With the proper framework in place, you become effective and efficient—you are the best businessperson you can be.

Maybe without even realizing it, when you joined the service industry, you joined the building business. So put on your hard hat and get ready to unfurl the blueprint building plan for a powerful referral business.

My Inspiration

Just thinking...
Inspiration for me came at rock bottom. I had finally reached a point where it was safe to try; I couldn't go any lower.

WHAT INSPIRED ME TO WRITE this book? The short answer is I was living with a personal goal I didn't know how to achieve. The long answer embodies two compelling reasons, and I'll discuss both of them in great depth. For now, let me discuss the first one, which was my poor attitude during my first year in corporate America.

I spent twenty years in the United States Air Force in space and missile operations and missile maintenance, and I achieved success in whatever job I was assigned. I loved serving my country and will always be thankful to the United States Air Force. Among the many positive things, it put a roof over my family's head and food on the table for that entire time; and most importantly, it gave us our dignity as a family. I couldn't ask for or expect more.

Let me share with you the elegance of the Air Force. When I made my decision in February 2003 to retire the following August, I shared my thoughts with the Vice Wing Commander, Colonel Mike Selva. His first question to me was: "Was it anything we did?" It was the perfect leadership question for the poignant moment at hand. It simultaneously showed genuine concern while displaying a willingness to take action. What a first-class individual and officer. That moment reaffirmed to me what I already knew in my heart: the Air Force is about great people executing important missions that serve all Americans.

With the reading of a retirement order on August 1, 2003, I immediately transitioned from a lieutenant colonel with knowledge, authority, and responsibility for others, to an individual at the very bottom of a new profession with absolutely no understanding, no authority, or any responsibility for others. I was in the exact opposite position of an 18-year-old teenager just out of high school joining the Air Force. Where she was just starting out at the bottom, I was starting over at the bottom. Nevertheless, I knew deep down inside I had made the right post-retirement career decision.

As the sun set that evening with a huge blowout Jimmy Buffett themed retirement party (to include Polynesian dancers and a fire dancer), my military days were officially behind me. I went from wearing a uniform with a flight cap to wearing dress pants and a polo shirt with no headgear on top. Without taking any time off, I immediately jumped into an unfamiliar business world the following Monday morning and went to work (in theory) as an assistant for my wife. Rose has been a mortgage branch manager and a loan officer in Colorado Springs for 10 years and has worked in the business for 30 years. She was in the business long before we married and continued during the time I served in the Air Force.

By choosing to work as Rose's assistant, I was taking on a role I had never played before in our marriage. I was going to be the man behind the woman. Rose was going to receive the full benefit of my abilities. So how would I do in this new support role? Considering that I had achieved success throughout my military career, no matter the challenges placed in front of me, I fully expected the same to occur here. I was completely confident in myself and my abilities, and *I thought I was ready* for the work that was ahead of me.

In hindsight, it was a big mistake to come to work for Rose right away. I should have taken some time off. So what actually did happen after I retired and joined her at work? I started to grow my hair out, stopped shaving, showed up late to work, and left early. If anyone wanted to play golf, though, I was available. Sad to say, even all the rounds I played didn't help my weak golf game—I'm still trying to break 90 at the United States Air Force Academy golf course.

My days at the office were not focused on work and were, therefore, unproductive. If anybody wanted to discuss any subject other than mortgage lending, I was the man to talk too. I was just as bad in the weekly staff meeting. I always showed up with the obligatory notepad and pen in hand, and I would feverishly write throughout the meeting, but never about anything being discussed. Instead, I was doodling away: hastily drawing stars, figure eights, circles, and three-dimensional boxes. Such doodling offset my boredom.

I was basking in the sunshine of having no job or leadership responsibilities for the first time in 20 years and unabashedly enjoying it. Hard to say it, but I was the absolute worst kind of rebel one could be—I had no justifiable reason for my lack of action. I was an unworthy rebel. I was completely adrift and somehow turned into a schmuck rather quickly. It wasn't a pretty picture. No other way to put it, I took full advantage of sleeping with the boss every night!

As my first year with Rose drew to a close, the realization of so many things being wrong on so many levels all coalesced at once. I was highly disappointed in myself; I had let Rose down; I was still at the ground-level of a new career that I didn't technically understand; and I didn't know how to build a business. It was my rock-bottom moment in corporate America. I was bankrupt in every way possible. My dismal circumstances reminded me so much of a person who set low goals and then failed to achieve them. My job performance was that bad. So bad, I could only go up from here.

I was deeply ashamed of my lackluster effort after Rose had supported me throughout my Air Force career. She freely sacrificed her business career by putting it on hold at times to raise our children and to move from one base to the next while we were in the Air Force, never complaining once. All Rose ever did was give unconditional love to our children and to me. As I write this tonight, I get teary-eyed. What a colossal failure on my part. How did I fall so far, so fast? I was facing an adverse moment in my new business career that would introduce me to myself. So what did I do? I did what most people do when they are depressed—I ate! Let me explain.

The turning point for me finally came at my one-year anniversary in August 2004. I took Rose out to lunch and apologized for screwing off for a year and for not helping her grow her loan officer business. *My only goal when I came into the mortgage business was to build a business model around Rose's talent that would allow her to realize her full potential as a loan officer.* I didn't know how to do it, but that was my goal. At this one-year turning point moment, I had more guilt and love inside of me than answers. Even with this obvious shortcoming, I wasn't deterred in the slightest way. I knew my deep love for Rose would somehow produce the extraordinary effort needed to deliver the answers, thereby allowing me to achieve my goal. *I was really ready now.* This was when I started to write.

The specific business model I wanted to build around Rose's talent was a *leverage business model* of a powerful referral business. It was through this model that Rose could realize her full potential as a businesswoman, which was her most pressing issue. Her potential was far from being reached (she had so much more to offer). As such, this business model was not beyond her potential but, rather, at the cusp of her abilities. In short, a leverage business model is a combination of traits, service processes, pounce processes, and execution strategies employed to make a difference to the people who interface with or may interface with the business. What does all of that really mean? For now just realize that traits represent the personal characteristics a businessperson brings to the business, and service processes reflect the service provided. Pounce processes reflect the service effort to convince people, and execution strategies entail how it's all executed.

Not to be overlooked are the resultant people dynamics of a leverage business model. First, through providing service, a businessperson can both *connect* clients and *attract* business partners to the business. And second, through a set of clearly defined *expectation standards,* clients and business partners make a difference across the business. The end point of it all is when a business first cares about people, the people will then care about the business. The resulting mutual respect creates a business that works hard for the businessperson.

A powerful referral business looks at a business through *a people lens.* It is through the leveraging of people (clients and business partners) that a business will achieve its greatest success.

Let me get back to Rose. Rose has always been very talented, but she'd never had the time available to develop and build a *business model* that would bring her the success she so richly deserved. I feel that's chiefly because she puts her employees and management responsibilities first, never herself or her business, which is the right thing to do in a leadership position. Her branch manager responsibilities always took precedence over her personal business.

During lunch I told Rose I was not the assistant type. Truth be told, I was a horrible assistant—and she knew it. I didn't have to, but I explained we needed to hire someone to do the administrative work I was absolutely miserable doing. I was ready to wholeheartedly focus my talent on what I do best: *applying common sense to a problem.* I was, in essence, telling Rose that I needed to stop thinking about business and instead start thinking about a business. She readily agreed, so we took a leap of faith and hired an assistant to relieve me of the administrative responsibilities of her business. We were excited at taking the first step to start moving Rose's business from a tropical depression to a hurricane.

But excitement alone wouldn't be near enough. To truly start moving her business forward in such a way, I would need to have a complete understanding of both people and business and how they fit as one and work together. Only when I had this knowledge could I make sense of her business, thereby allowing us to move it forward together. Being a visually-minded person, who tends to think in pictures, I imagined the difficult challenge ahead in the context of an hourglass. When you bring people and business together in a purposeful way, over a period of time, the combined-effect will settle into a powerful referral business as illustrated below.

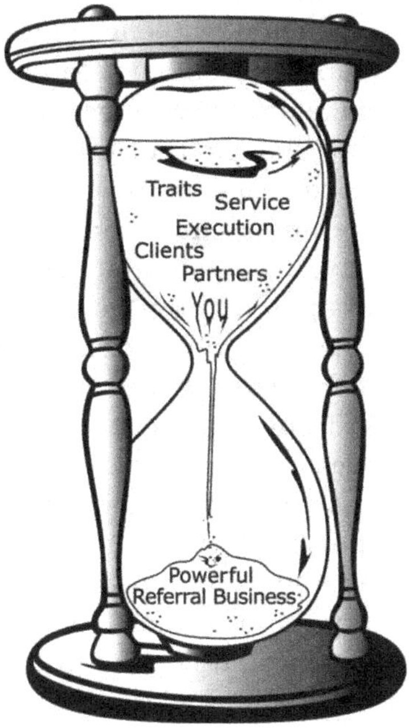

All that the hourglass really shows is that I figured out the easy half of the answer—I figured out what I needed to know. Now the hard work began, trying to figure out the many details of what I figured out. The key to building a powerful referral business was to understand the individual roles of the people and the dynamics of a business and how it all interlocked. I didn't have the answers, but it didn't matter. I had a direction to head in, and that was all I needed to start my journey of *how* and *why* in earnest. Being a curious person, I was looking forward to the long, thoughtful journey ahead.

More specifically, I was looking forward to the *critical-thinking.* In my twenty years in the Air Force I had used thought to solve all kinds of problems, but never to this extent. I didn't know the exact dynamics it would take to effectively think at such a deep problem solving level for so long a period of time. I did know that I'd have to think on a level that was far beyond the reach of everyday problem solving. I would need to someway, somehow develop a kinetic-like mind if I was to have a legitimate chance to effectively think across an entire business. Even with this very steep mental challenge, I was still hopeful that at the end of my long, thoughtful journey I would both understand a powerful referral business and the coalescing dynamics behind critical-thinking.

There was yet another mental challenge ahead to acknowledge. I knew full well when I embarked on this thinking journey that I'd eventually ask Rose to make drastic changes to her way of business of so many years. I had no illusions that this would be easy for her, and therefore, I fully expected her to show signs of uneasiness, be resistant at times, and even have the occasional if not frequent disagreements with me. I have to admit that these negative thoughts gave me a slight sense of apprehension going forward. What would see us through these uncomfortable and contentious moments and help me get over my apprehension is we both knew her potential as a businesswoman was far from being reached. She herself knew she had to make major changes across her entire business if she was to fulfill her potential. It was this realization on her part, along with her knowing that I had her best interest at heart, that would eventually get us through the toughest of moments.

The one thing I was not apprehensive about was working with her. It's easy to assume that would be a far greater concern because one spouse working for another can easily lead to just trying to survive each other. Rose and I had successfully been through the many rigors of an Air Force career, all the while raising three boys and everything that comes with it. Somewhere along the way, through it all, we shared enough difficult, wonderful, and everyday moments that we became one. I don't know the exact day or time it occurred; I just know that we eventually reached the point where we couldn't imagine life without each other. This experience gave me confidence that our transition from a military journey to a business journey would only serve to further strengthen the close bond already between us, no matter what happened.

Lost Opportunities

Just thinking...
Growing up can be difficult, even in business.
Learning brought with it the realization of past lost opportunities.

I KNEW WHEN I RETIRED from active duty service I wanted to work for Rose instead of pursuing a follow-on career in the military defense contractor world. Her unwavering support of me throughout my career had made me a better Air Force officer, and now I hoped to return the favor by helping make her a better businesswoman. After twenty years, it was time to put Rose first and for me to support her in her career. When I finally joined her in early August 2003, I didn't understand the technical side of the business and still don't to this day. I have yet to learn how to pre-qualify a client, one of the easiest and the first required technical activity you conduct when helping someone acquire home financing.

What little I did know about the mortgage business was primarily learned from reading service-related magazine articles, company training that focused on service ideas, and observing Rose. The extent of my knowledge pretty much involved thoughts about service. It was what I was most comfortable and familiar with. The technical aspects of the business went right over my head. I didn't know it at the time, but I was subconsciously filtering out technical matter and absorbing service matter. The only other things I had going for me were common sense and 20 years of serving in the military, both of which turned out to be very helpful in building a leverage business model. Not only did the military allow me to proudly serve every day, it also turned out to have *widespread application* in the business world. There was even a shared core competency between the two. Who would have thought?

Over the many years Rose had been a mildly successful loan officer. Her annual production numbers were not great, probably just a little bit above middle of the pack. Her technical talent, however, was on par with the best-of-the-best in the business. She could easily structure the most challenging loans. It was amazing to watch her mind work so fast and yet be so right. Interestingly enough, it was for this precise reason she became the perfect *case study* and inspiration for this book. Rose was near the top of her profession technically, while her actual business success was slightly above average. Clearly something was awry, but I didn't know what or why.

This was confounding for me. Conventional thinking initially led me to believe there was a direct correlation between technical talent and success—that they were somehow directly linked to each other. Still, as I watched Rose over time, I could see this wasn't true. They were links in the equation of success, but technical talent and success were not necessarily linked. It wasn't long before any notion I had about technical talent being the only key to success was dispelled. Yet, there was a link that connected technical talent to success—and that link was a business model. It was what Rose was lacking, and it was the simple equation of success.

As I observed Rose interact with clients during appointments in her office, a clear pattern of conduct emerged. Simply put, she was brilliant in so many different ways—courteous, warm, professional, caring, and intelligent. She easily connected on a personal level and was silky smooth. Clients could immediately sense a truth about her and would gravitate toward her. STOP! Think about what I just said about Rose. How could she not be successful? Outside of required technical talent, she never really brought anything more to her business other than a pleasant splash of her endearing characteristics and her beautiful personality, which quickly faded with time. She was dipping into human dynamics, which is what a powerful referral business is all about, but not to the sustained level that was necessary.

I remember a story about a young couple for whom Rose closed a home loan a while back. A significant amount of time had passed since Rose helped them, and quite frankly, the clients had forgotten her name. They needed to refinance their home and were working with a loan officer from another company but felt very uncomfortable with what he was telling them. For whatever reason, at that moment, they remembered Rose. They called her and came in for an appointment. During the meeting the husband said, "Rose, we will do whatever you tell us to do." It was a compelling trustworthy moment—they had complete trust and confidence in her. At the end of the meeting he stood up, walked over to Rose and tightly hugged her, saying, "Thank goodness we found you." It was another wonderful comment, but more importantly, it was a telling business moment. It was only five words, but it told Rose's business story so well. Here's how. She would caringly and professionally help clients with a home loan but then allow them to walk away from her business. It was up to them to find their way back to her, which, thankfully, some of them did. But for the majority of them, they moved on. It was hard to watch and even harder to understand.

It's important to take a moment here and go into more detail on how Rose would serve a typical client couple. When they came into her office, she was very cordial and engaged in small talk to connect on a personal level. It wasn't long, though, before she would delve into the number-crunching portion of the meeting and get down to business. It was what she was most comfortable doing—primarily focusing on the transaction. She was chiefly a single-minded businesswoman. When the clients left her office, they felt very confident with Rose and had no doubt she would take great care of them, which she most certainly did.

From this moment on, it was typically two to four weeks before their loan would close and they could move into their new home. During this time, Rose would interact with the clients on an interim basis, and those interactions were always pleasant, although transaction-related. She was primarily gathering required or underwriter requested documents. Rose wouldn't attend the title company closing, for she was too busy with other work that in her eyes had a higher priority. After the closing, which always went smoothly, the clients would receive a mailed quarterly newsletter and, one year later, an anniversary card. Rose wouldn't call throughout the year, nor call on the anniversary. That was it.

It's disappointing to say, there was no business model wrapping around Rose's enormous talent. She was very good on the surface, but there was no depth to her service. She was a flash in the pan—here one day and gone the next. Dare I say it? *She was a transactional loan officer.* Rose had the two hallmarks—she was honest, and *she* was working hard. And she broke Mr. Stephen Marshall's rule: "It's about the service, not the sale." Thinking back to the family refinancing story mentioned above, I had no choice but to acknowledge the countless other opportunities over the years that were never nurtured, and the business that was subsequently lost because Rose wasn't properly positioned to capitalize on her brief but brilliant contact with clients. *Rose was a businesswoman who wasn't thinking and acting like a businesswoman.*

In all fairness to Rose, I could understand her being a transactional businesswoman. She was just following through on the *natural instinct* of wanting to be in control—depending on herself for her success. And without her even realizing it, that was her root problem. A business provides a unique opportunity through its *dichotomy*—you can work hard, or your business can work hard. One way you depend on yourself, and the other way you depend on others. Which way do you think would bring you more success over time? The unnatural choice of depending on others. Why? You're thinking like a leader by trusting others for your success. It was the way Rose needed to think in her business if she was to ever achieve the success she so richly deserved. *A business will naturally let you be a follower, but it will greatly challenge you if you want to be a leader.* It's this glaring personal contrast that brings us right back to the importance of understanding a leverage business model of a powerful referral business.

There is an underlying leadership dynamic occurring within *the dichotomy of a business* to recognize. Regardless of whether a businessperson is a follower or leader in his or her business, they will still have a *leadership responsibility* imposed upon them. There's no getting around that fact. Why? A business begins as an inanimate thing that becomes animate when people become a part of it. How much animation occurs in the business, and what that animation specifically is, will simply be a reflection of the collective business actions. And because business actions are a personal choice, the businessperson gets the credit if his or her business succeeds, and if it fails. They're responsible either way. That's leadership responsibility in a nutshell.

This dichotomy and leadership discussion brings to light an interesting insight about Rose. She had a dichotomy occurring in her personal life that involved leadership. When I observed her actions as a branch manager, she was quite comfortable and very good at fulfilling all of the leadership responsibilities demanded of her. I never saw her side-step a difficult or uncomfortable moment. But when I observed her actions in her own business, she had taken the exact opposite position. It was all about being a follower. She faced no leadership decisions involving people (clients and business partners). I knew it had to be unknowingly because her natural forte was to lead, not follow. Knowing this quality about her, I concluded the only reasonable answer I could; she didn't have a clear understanding of what it takes to become a leader in her business. The legacy of her many years of training was well entrenched and holding her back, without her even knowing it.

This business observation of Rose brought to light a very interesting insight about her profession. And that is, there was a minimal focus on education. It was as if there was a failure to recognize the distinctive difference between training and education or a failure to recognize the requisite need for an education. Regardless of which one was ultimately responsible for the lackluster approach to education, I firmly believe that training a businessperson when he or she first needs to be educated *silently imposes* a limit on his or her potential. Where some professions require training for a person to reach his or her full potential, Rose's profession first requires an education, then training to achieve such an end result. The reason being is a business is a complex entity comprised of several knowledge-based and action-based concepts working together as one to achieve an objective. Here shortly, you will see the significant difference between education and training highlighted even further.

I have to admit that this situation made me wonder, if only for a brief moment, the following thought: are there other people in other professions who are facing this same type of situation. I hope not. But if there are, I know their frustration all too well.

Here is one more thing I learned by observing Rose. I realized to guard against thinking that the most technically talented people are the most successful business people. More often than not, that distinction resides with the business people who have taken the time to build a business model around their talent. Whether their talent is immense or average may not matter. Rose proved that to me. *A business model is the great equalizer in business*, for it can serve as a counterbalance for talent level. I knew we had to do something, and do it quickly, if we wanted to start tapping into Rose's vast talent base and leadership ability. It was time to get serious, to retool the way she did business.

The Other Half

Just thinking...
It was like a difficult math problem. I knew the answer, but I didn't know how to do the work. And just like in school, it was a failing grade.

IT'S TIME TO ADD YOU to our story, to bring you along on our journey. Like Rose, I'm sure you are giving your very best effort every day, so why isn't hard work paying off with client referrals? You are talented like Rose, and you work hard like she does, yet you don't have the business success your talent warrants. Does this ring any bells? You may even be like her in another way if you arrive at the office first and in the evening leave last. You know the type, turn on the lights in the morning and turn them off at night. Why isn't hard work being rewarded accordingly?

That's a question I'm sure frustrates many people in the service industry. It frustrated me my first year in the business as I shamelessly watched Rose work sixty-hour weeks, do the aforesaid things, and then achieve lower than desirable production results. My only saving grace was my observation of her helped me realize that most people don't have success commensurate with their talent, and the people who do are few and far between. I refer to these lucky few as the people who have successfully broken *The Business Code of Leverage*. You may not know them personally, but you know who they are in your business field.

Observation time was over. It was time to start building a powerful referral business, but how do I build it? As quickly as I asked myself that question and decided to try, I immediately faced a dilemma. I realized I didn't know how to be successful. It was quite a humbling moment that created an insufficient feeling inside.

I was now in the mortgage business, yet I didn't know how to build a business, let alone a powerful referral business. Like most people, I knew great service and referrals were crucial fundamentals, but I didn't know how to *specifically* get there. I didn't know how to help Rose achieve those end results. That thought bothered me because it was counter to what I had been accustomed to in the

Air Force as a missile combat launch officer. The Air Force would never allow me or any other missileer to operate an intercontinental ballistic missile system without first knowing *how it worked*. Learning such empowering knowledge is what allowed us to safely operate the weapon system on our own and handle any situation. How could I not know how to build a business? It was a *core requirement* of my new professional work—how embarrassing. But thank goodness for embarrassment because it marked the emotional point that moved me to do the things I should have done from the beginning.

The humiliation of not knowing how to help Rose build a business led me to the second and, by far, the most compelling reason for this book's inspiration. As I started to really try, I noticed everywhere I looked the next great idea was being aggressively marketed and sold. The ideas covered every conceivable subject, ranging from one end of the spectrum to the other. They were in books, magazines, seminars, workshops, classes, conference calls, and more. It was mind-boggling, and it all sounded wonderful, which it was; and at first, I couldn't get enough of it. In time, though, I came to realize the majority of the espoused ideas were just a part of an overall business, yet they claimed a disproportionate share of its success, which eventually led to my *temporary* frustration with ideas.

I had finally reached the personal moment inside where reading and hearing about the same things over and over again (ideas) became maddening to the point of eventually driving an internal question that itself became maddening to me. The more I read and heard about the same things, the more persistent and louder the question became: How does it work? HOW DOES IT WORK? The industry was deafeningly screaming out the *"what,"* while I was desperately screaming inside for the *"how."* I wanted answers, not directions! In no uncertain terms, I was longing for the Air Force way of teaching. My question was embarrassingly elementary; *I was searching for the first thing to know when building a business.*

Did you ever wonder that same instinctive question about your business while maybe someone or something you were reading was telling you what to do? If you were to try to answer the question of "How does it work?"—what would your answer be. I ask that question of you now because when you see the answer, you'll probably say, "Oh, I know that." It's exactly what you should say because the answer is just common sense. The difficulty in answering the question comes not from the answer itself but, rather, from the volume of the answer. That is my challenge ahead: provide you the volume of the answer, present it in a way that allows you to easily assemble it in your mind, and empower you to work with it.

Just curious, what was your answer and what realm was it in—the how or the what?

I had reached a point where I had accumulated all these great ideas in my head, but I didn't know how to proceed with them. The simple response would be to just do it. But do it in context to what? Too many great ideas in your head, with no business model to situate them in, can lead to idea overload and eventually business paralysis. Put another way, I'd experienced a *business idea overdose* by having a slew of jumbled ideas in my head with absolutely no way to un-jumble them. My mind had, in essence, shut down. How was that possible? Let me explain it by sharing my simple concept of *A Half Never Equals a Whole.*

By and large, the service industry is focused on marketing and selling the next great idea. It's like a race to see who can come up with the next idea that will top the last one. The field is overcrowded with entrepreneurs and companies wanting to enter this exciting race of *"what to do."* What they are doing is important and necessary because they do create the next great idea that allows us all to make ourselves or our business better. The problem is, no matter how many ideas they make available, they're only providing one half of a whole. The number of ideas doesn't matter; it's still a half. Why is that so important? A powerful referral business is the whole and ideas are a half of that whole. Look at the illustration below.

The half circle portrayed around "Ideas" on the previous page encompasses only the upper half of the circle for a reason. There's something that comes before it that complements it, and together, they make a whole. That something is, "how it works." When you only have half the answer, you are not in control and will, therefore, struggle to figure out the other half, if you can figure it out at all. Such a frustrating struggle can easily lead to a dependency on others for answers. Look at the next illustration below.

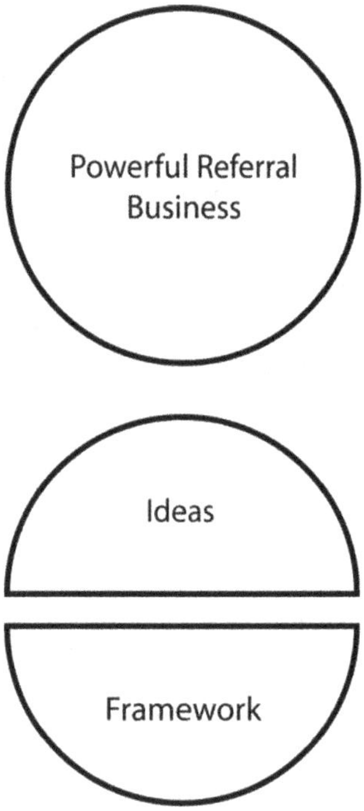

Framework and ideas together equals the whole and puts you in control. The simple drawing above perfectly illustrates framework; it comes first and ideas fit right over top of it. *Framework is the business acumen behind the ideas.* When you think of your business in these terms, you'll naturally be inclined to think about framework when you come across ideas that interest you. Ideas by themselves will not excite you but how they may fit over the framework of your business will. Together as one, they show you the simple architecture of the service side of your business.

It was time to stop thinking about or worrying about the next great idea and get back to logical basics. I needed to first understand the concepts associated with framework so I could eventually help Rose build a powerful referral business with the great ideas being marketed and sold. Why was framework so important to me? I knew it would bring structure and purpose to every aspect of our business.

Now what does that really mean? I realized I needed to be *educated* before I was *trained*. With an education (learning framework), I would understand *how* our business works and *why* we do things, which would naturally mean I'd know *what* to do. If I was trained first, I would learn what to do (have ideas), but I wouldn't understand on a deep level how our business works or why we do things. The problem with only knowing *"what"* is everything told to me or read by me would seem important. Learning *"what"* by itself would make me a follower—something I'm not accustomed doing.

Really think about those three words—*how, why, and what*—and their impact to you. They are three innocuous words that, depending on their order, will tell if you're heading down the pathway of becoming a leader or a follower. Will you take the time upfront to learn the how and the whys and, therefore, know what to do; or will you need to be told what to do because you never learn the how and the whys? It is an individual choice that'll reflect on you personally while determining if you're independent or dependent in business.

Consider the consequences of your choice from this perspective. Each method of learning, education and training, tells the tale of a different journey. When you take an educational approach to your business, you learn to think for yourself, and you, therefore, make your own way through your career. *It is a self-determined business journey.* And when you take a training approach to your business, other people do the thinking for you, and you act on what they tell you to do. *It is the nomadic business journey*—moving from one answer person to the next throughout your career.

The core decision you are making with the words how, why, and what is, "Who will be empowered?" Will you empower other people by depending on them to tell you what to do, or will you empower yourself by independently knowing what to do? That's the simple dynamic of empowerment; whoever knows the "what" is empowered. Why? They have the business acumen answers. When you take the time to personally empower yourself, you will professionally enrich yourself. I'm sure you've heard the expression, knowledge is power. When you learn the entire framework of a business, knowledge becomes empowerment, which brings us right back to the importance of learning the framework of a powerful referral business.

To fully grasp the concept of framework (the how and the whys of a business), I needed to understand seven basic features about our business:

1. *Where are we in our business model development?* It's the expected first question to ask, given that it assesses our business effort to this point and tells us what the eventual end point is.

2. *Who participates and how?* Who are the players, and how will they participate in our business to help us achieve success?

3. *What are the individual demands?* What traits do we have to adopt to build a powerful referral business?

4. *What are the aspects of service?* What's the behind-the-scenes work of service, the natural progression of service, the objectives and goals of service, and the differences of service?

5. *How do we build valuable service?* What are the specific steps we have to take to make our service the best it can be?

6. *How do we best execute what we have built?* What do we have to do to make our business work hard for us?

7. *How do we continually improve our business?* What exactly do we have to annually assess to improve year after year?

When I had the many answers to these seven framework questions, I would have everything I needed to readily incorporate new ideas into our business. An idea, no matter how great, was of little value to me until I understood the framework of a powerful referral business. It was through framework that I would be able to figuratively get my arms around the enormity of a business.

It was also through framework that the numerous concepts of a powerful referral business would methodically emerge, creating a language in and of itself. The significance of that occurring is a *language of concepts* must be present before an educational approach to a specific subject matter (in this case, a business) can begin.

The underlying reason for taking an educational approach is a business, at its skeletal level, is simply sophistication that requires creativity. To make a business achieve its intended end result, you have to first acquire knowledge (framework) and then apply creative thinking (ideas). That's what an education is at its most inner core, knowledge uniquely applied. If you discount this sequential business insight, you make yourself susceptible to an education standard you do not want to face. That is, an educated business field is unforgiving of those in it who are uneducated.

Let me take a moment here and share a personal thought about framework. I had to be at the bottom of the mortgage profession, in every conceivable way, to realize I needed framework. I had finally reached my *maverick survival moment,* in that I desperately needed to hear and know something else. What I didn't need to hear was more groupthink of *"what to do."*

From a metaphoric standpoint, I was like a tortoise in the sense I was mentally slow. I didn't know how to think about a business because I didn't understand a business. Worse yet, I'd reached the dual vulnerability point of being hopelessly dependent while questioning my mere existence in the profession. Without anybody else knowing, to include Rose, I was in silent crisis mode. My spirit was either going to be broken, or I'd emerge a renaissance man.

This precarious dilemma made me realize that my dignity within the profession rested on two successive things. I first needed to understand a business, and then I needed to help Rose build a business that not only captured her natural forte to lead but reflected her individualism as well. I have to tell you that never before had I experienced this type of ultimatum pressure. There were many important and pressure-filled moments in my Air Force career, but never to this extent. It truly is a lonely and scary moment to feel your dignity rests on trying to figure out something you don't understand, you have no one to teach you, and you have limited experience on which to draw. It is as close to hopeless as one can get.

As dire as all of that sounds, I really had a lot going for me at this seemingly desperate moment. The fear of failure, along with a deep-seated desire to help Rose transform her business would create a hypergolic mixture, igniting a long-lasting passion that would be difficult to turn off. This thought comforted me for two reasons. First, I knew I wouldn't stop until I had the answers; and second, I knew that the emotion of "love" had and will continue to push people to achieve at the very cusp of their abilities. I was determined to take my love for Rose and convert it into an energy that would push me to the very edge of my mental limit (figure out a leverage business model of a powerful referral business). If I could do it, I would figuratively add my name to the ever-increasing achievement list of people who were inspired by the most powerful emotion of all.

At this challenging moment of my still relatively new career, I didn't need to hear an oversimplification of a business, motivational words, anecdotes, snippets of a business, inspiring stories, discussion of business buzzwords, a list of things to do, tantalizing marketing phrases, etc. I wasn't interested in hyperbole in any form, on any level. Instead, I simply needed the answers that started at the very beginning of a business and ended at the end of a business.

The rest of this book is thoroughly committed to meeting that need by answering my seven framework questions—and many other business-building questions—albeit in an unconventional way. I'll do it by drawing equally on inexperience and experience. Where my inexperience in the business world will allow me to be a *free thinker*, my military experience will make me think like *a leader who serves others*. Merge them together with a lot of common sense, some creative and maverick thinking, and even a touch of madness—and get ready to read the unexpected. Why? I'm ready to be a worthy rebel.

Now what all of that really means is you need to continue to have an open-mind because in many regards your journey from this moment forward will not be familiar, but it'll be exciting as a newly named business is fully revealed to you. *You are going to see a business from a perspective that will give you perspective on everything in a business.* It's a perspective that will harness the full potential of a businessperson, the business itself, and the people who are connected to the business. So get ready to take an *intellectual curiosity journey* through the other side of a business—the service side. As you do, you will continue to see Rose's business story unfold. It'll be an unvarnished look at both her old way of business and the new way of business she recently embraced. Let's go!

Out of the Clear Blue Sky

Just thinking...
Even a lightning bolt can strike on a clear day.

WITHOUT ANY HESITATION, LET ME address the first one of my seven framework questions right now: *Where are we in our business model development?* It seems like such a straightforward question that it would beget an easy answer. Before moving on, try to answer it for your current business model development. Don't be surprised if your contemplation generates more questions than answers and ties your tongue like it did mine.

Why is it so important to know upfront where you are in your business development? You have to first know where you are, before you can determine what you need, to get you where you need to go. Put another way, you need two reference points to go anywhere. Without this type of knowledge readily available to you, it's almost impossible to move your business to the next level, especially in a methodical way that's based on efficiency. What specifically is the knowledge you need a grasp of—business organization.

This brings to light the opening problem I faced right out of the gate when I started to try. I didn't know how organized our business was today or how organized it eventually had to be. Adding to my predicament was I didn't understand what constituted the organization of a business. Why so much focus on organization? I knew success was the direct result of it.

Unfortunately, all I had at this juncture of my thoughtful journey were a bunch of jumbled ideas in my head with no real understanding of how to apply them to business organization. It was like being right in the middle of a sea of freely-floating ideas without the slightest sense of organization to them. I knew I was looking at the answer; I just couldn't visually put it together in my mind yet.

My dilemma was further heightened by the fact I knew a technical answer was totally out of the question for two reasons. First, I wouldn't understand it; and second, it wouldn't interest me. A simple man, I quickly surmised (in a way that completely caught me off-guard and surprised me) that a visual image was the only way to adequately address this first framework question of organization. Does a way exist to quickly and accurately assess the maturity of a business model? Such a method would have to make use of a familiar visual image that could clearly illustrate various levels of development. I knew a visual image of development would be worth a thousand words if it immediately communicated the *organization* of a business and a corresponding level of business *success*. That was the key. I hope you're ready because it's time for some unorthodox thinking and the first mad scientist-like idea.

With that thought in mind, I want you to briefly think about your business in terms of weather phenomena. Don't be skeptical. You'll see shortly how this clarifies where you are in your business model development today and the work that remains to turn it into a leverage business model of a powerful referral business.

Why make use of weather for the backdrop of determining business model development when other analogies could be used just as well? Weather and business share the common bond of organization. Where organization determines the strength of a storm, in the business world it determines the success of a business.

o

To effectively determine business model development through the use of weather, you'll use the visually revealing *Weather or Not Concept*. The concept is based on a simple three-step approach: identify the major components of an activity, assess the actual work being performed versus the required work to be performed within each component, and then assimilate the work results into a visual cloud formation based on the deficiencies or efficiencies noted.

The possible cloud formations that can represent the development of a business model are three distinctly different storms with three distinctly different levels of organization—tropical depression, tropical storm, and hurricane—each one more organized and powerful than its predecessor. The cloud formation created will be of a weather phenomenon that not only displays a distinctive level of weather organization, it directly correlates to a corresponding level of business success. The more weather associated with your business model development, the more organized and successful you and your business are.

The business significance of organized and success is organized shows the *focus* of a business, while success measures the *effectiveness* of the focus. Said another way, focus and effectiveness are domino business pieces, for one comes after the other. And the next domino in line to fall is—*scale.* When focus creates effectiveness, you can achieve whatever scale of business you want as simply illustrated below.

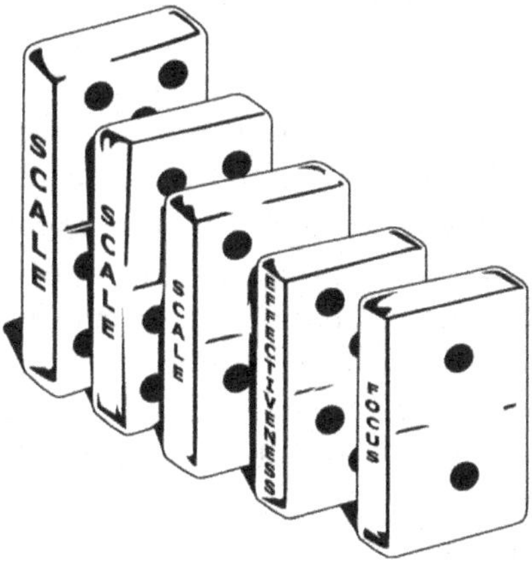

Here's the other takeaway from this illustration. The order of the dominos puts *scale of business* in its proper perspective. Business people should not be enticed by scale of business (when reading something or listening to someone). On the contrary, they should be enticed by what was specifically done to achieve that scale of business. It only makes sense; the scale number is the direct output of the many business actions. This seems so obvious doesn't it, but it was a hard lesson for me to learn. For a long time, I was drawn to marketing that focused on scale of business. The reason being is it directly spoke to my deepest desire—helping Rose achieve success at the highest level. Eventually, though, I came to realize this type of marketing was nothing more than hyperbole at its worst because it promised so much on the surface while delivering so little substance. In other words, it was never a comprehensive approach.

Let's get back to discussing weather. I hope you're ready because it's time to apply the Weather or Not Concept to what you're doing in your business to a powerful referral business. You will do it by first starting with the three major components of a powerful referral business: traits, fully developed service processes, and the strategies employed for business execution. If you recall, they formulate the crux of a leverage business model. They are also what make up the organization of a business. Next, you will simply picture in your mind what you're doing in your business within those components. And finally, you'll synthesize it all into a visual cloud formation based on the overall organization you see in your business. The more organized you see you and your business across the three major components, the more impressive your cloud formation will be.

I know this may sound a little bit far-fetched, but think about what you're assessing through the three major components. You're assessing *yourself*, the *level of service* you're providing above and beyond required technical service, and the *execution* of your business. The cloud formation represents the image of character and commitment you and your business have made to the people who interface with it and how you execute it all. It really does take you to the core of a business day; what exactly are you doing to make your business go and grow—which is compatible with the phrase, focus and effectiveness.

Keeping your attention focused on the three major components of a powerful referral business and this new way of conceptualizing your business model, we're now ready to talk about the weather.

It's during hurricane season when the television weatherperson first shows some clouds trying to get organized off the west coast of Africa, but they're all jumbled, *unorganized*, not terribly threatening...a *tropical depression*. Then that depression starts to get *organized*, further development occurs, it's much more defined, and some clouds are starting to circulate...a *tropical storm*. In due time, that tropical storm is fully developed, *highly organized*, moving forward, rapidly rotating, and powerful beyond imagination...a *hurricane*.

Think about all of the traits, fully developed service processes, and employed execution strategies that make up your business today. As you do, keep in mind the overall purpose for doing them: developing a highly organized business that creates success. At this point you're not worried about scale of business. Why? Scale is a personal choice, for it'll reflect either an achieved or desired business result of a working business model.

Imagine yourself looking at the weatherperson and the ocean on your television screen, and what do you see—an unorganized tropical depression, organized tropical storm, or highly organized hurricane? Hopefully, you don't see clear skies! With any luck, a visual image of your business model development is starting to come into view. I know when I thought of our business model in these terms it did for me. I hope it works for you, too. Remember, you're only trying to attain a *visual organized impression* of your business, not an analytical assessment, so keep it simple.

Perhaps for the very first time you're starting to get a feel for the business model development surrounding your talent. You're realizing the fullness of a successful business, and you're starting to comprehend the work ahead of you. Here's betting you'll probably never look at a hurricane update the same way!

If you catch yourself saying, "Wait a minute, how can I visualize my business model when you haven't told me what the traits, fully developed service processes, and employed execution strategies of a powerful referral business are"—that's a strong indication you're no higher than a tropical depression.

Let me share with you exactly when this offbeat but highly revealing concept came to me. Rose and I had been struggling to improve our business. We knew we wanted to grow it and provide a higher level of service, but everything we did was in piecemeal fashion. We kept latching on to the next great idea, never knowing what the endgame was. Sound familiar? One day, I was sitting in her office, in front of her desk, trying my best to convince her we needed to do something to improve our business. We passionately discussed it. I said yea and she said nay! Angst-ridden and wanting to demonstrate to her on a larger level of why we really needed to do it, I grabbed my pen, opened my notebook, and instinctively (without the aid of any forethought) drew three crude figures across the center of the page. It was an unplanned thought born out of conflict and frustration.

I can't explain where this bolt out of the blue thought came from or even why it came to me. I did know it was one of those rare moments when it's better not to question things, even if they are a bit absurd. And I didn't. As fast as this somewhat quirky concept came to me, it immediately made sense to me. Now I hoped I could effectively convey it to Rose in a way that would make sense to her.

The first figure consisted of three squiggly circles—clouds. The second depicted two large squiggly circles trying to wrap around a small circle in the middle. And the last one was a large circle with a smaller circle in the middle. I asked Rose what she thought each scribbled figure represented, but she didn't have the slightest clue. After I quickly explained it to her, I then drew a rectangular box with nothing in it and asked her what she thought that was. Once again, she didn't have a clue. When I told her it was clear skies and explained why that was, she laughed until it hurt, in part because she was greatly relieved that her business model development was beyond that level.

Rose's deep laughter told me that my visuals made sense to her. This was a profound moment for us. For the first time, we were able to visualize our business model development—we knew we wanted to build a hurricane business. Surprisingly, without even discussing it, we came to the same conclusion on where we were. And that was very important because both of us concluded on our own we had a large amount of hard work ahead of us. In our minds, we now had a charted course of sequential organizational levels to strive for that would lead us to greater success along the way. We had finally moved beyond the piecemeal fashion way of building a business.

The clouds associated with your business model are either not yet present in the sky, trying to build (like ours were), slowly starting to circulate, or rapidly rotating in unison. When you understand which phenomenon applies to you, you'll know why you're successful or why not. And as you'll see much later on, you'll know what steps you have to take to move your business to hurricane level.

Do you recollect my mentioning Rose's business was at the tropical depression level? There was Rose—an experienced businesswoman, a charismatic and caring woman, a highly thought-of expert in the profession—with a weak, *unorganized* business model continuously acting as a drag on her success.

Put another way, Rose was on the wrong side of *The Look or See Concept.* Everyone faces it. A business is either transactional or referral-based. The difference between the two businesses is one is constantly looking for new people, while the other is repeatedly seeing the same people. As such, a transactional business never really knows what it has going for it, while a referral-based business always knows. You know yourself it's much harder to look for something than it is to simply see it. When you look for something, you never quite know where it is, so you expend time and energy trying to find it. Conversely, when you can see it, it's always nearby and within easy reach. The Look or See Concept offers some insight into why business people who are always looking for business, like Rose, tend to work longer hours with less success. Her business success was based on *uncertainty* instead of *predictability*.

Through my observing of Rose I came to realize a poorly developed business model functions like a cancer. It's the hidden killer of business success. If it can happen to Rose, it can happen to anyone. The time had finally arrived to reprogram Rose's business way of thinking so she could stop being a *self-inflicted victim* of her underperforming business model. It was time to stop looking and start seeing. To accomplish this end business result would require a new business attitude so full of innovation that it would result in top-to-bottom changes. It was time to let go of yesterday's thinking.

I know that may come across as a rather harsh assessment, but the moment Rose accepted personal responsibility for her own created business model shortcomings (which she most certainly did) was also the moment we could start moving her business forward together. Blaming something or someone else would have been very easy for her to do, and she had a bona fide excuse with her branch manager responsibilities. But Rose isn't one for excuses; she knows there's no gain playing the blame game, only delay.

Let me take a moment here and expand on the *business model concept*. It is an essential concept that's not utilized nearly enough by business people, even though every type of business (transactional, referral, and powerful referral) is based on it. In a sense, it is an enigma because business people don't tend to learn at the business model level; they tend to learn at the activity level (*what* to do). That's exactly how Rose learned year after year. She was exposed to a plethora of different business activities to choose from through various means and forums. In contrast, when you learn framework, you learn at the business model level.

So what exactly is a business model? It's a comprehensive business approach based on a definition and an accompanying premise that'll tap the potential of the businessperson, the business, and the people who interface with the business. In short, it'll answer the *how* and the many *whys* of a business.

When business people don't readily have such answers at their disposal, they'll naturally do the next best thing. They will do the widely known aspects of the business they are trying to develop. It is this expected but inadequate effort that is the root cause for the following situation. The *most common reason* for inspired business people failing or struggling in business is their lack of understanding the business model of the business they are trying to develop. I know that was the case for Rose. She was a wannabe referral-based businesswoman who was transactional. I could directly tie her unfulfilled potential and her business struggle right back to her poorly developed business model.

Even though I was still relatively new to the business world at this point, I had seen enough and I knew enough to know that Rose had to change her way of learning if she was to change the trajectory of her business. There was only one way to do it. It was time for her to transition from being a casual student of an assortment of business activities to being a studious student of a business model.

This revelation presented a tempting thought to me that I just couldn't resist considering, even if only for a brief moment. I wondered what type of businesswoman Rose would be today and how much more success she would have enjoyed over the years if her choice had been between business models instead of between business activities (ideas). Surely she would have...OK, that's more than enough time to dwell on a past I cannot change.

I have to admit there was nothing that surprised me more than the widely accepted notion of first teaching at the idea level instead of the business model level. It struck me as backward thinking. The chief reason being is a business model incorporates ideas, not the other way around. One clearly is a part of the other, and only one of them shows the big picture. The adverse consequence of this teaching philosophy is business people are denied a clear-cut choice and a straight pathway regarding their business journey. I believe it is this archaic teaching philosophy that bears the most responsibility for holding back inspired business people in their profession.

Let's get back to the four weather phenomena and take a cursory look at them by examining a business model as it relates to them. As you read each one, you'll notice a distinct *marketplace impact*, an array of *business-related conversations,* and a *work phrase* that captures their individual quintessence. It is these three universal business features that clearly distinguish one from the other. The organization of your business will determine your impact on the marketplace, the type of business conversations you have, and how your success is achieved. Hopefully, you'll not only see your current business model development in one of the four weather phenomena, you'll also see if you accurately visualized it.

Clear Skies

Just thinking…
How could something so good be so bad?

JUST THE MERE THOUGHT of clear skies warms you all over. Here's the visual picture with you in the middle of it. It's the picture-perfect setting: a hot sun beaming down, light ocean breeze blowing in, tall leaning palm trees rustling overhead, miles of white sandy beach, and waves gently washing ashore. And you, you're peacefully relaxing on a lounge chair with a plush pillow-like cushion, wearing your favorite hat and sunglasses, plenty of sunscreen on, reading a fascinating book, and softly stroking your feet underneath the cool sand—paradise! The only two missing items are island music in the background and a tropical cocktail by your side. If all you were interested in was doing nothing, you have found the perfect setting.

Get up! Really, GET UP RIGHT NOW! Clear skies are absolutely the weakest situation you could be in from a business model perspective. Think about it: You haven't made a personal commitment to traits. You haven't yet developed service processes. And you have no employed execution strategies in place to help you make a difference to people or to build your business day around. The only thing you have working for you is your raw talent. In other words, yes, you are in the marketplace, but *you're not yet participating in it.* It's as if you never moved beyond your first day in business. WHEW!

If you tried to look down on your cloudless sky all day long, you couldn't do it. The glare coming off the ocean would be blinding and intensely hot. Come the breeze of an approaching storm, you would shrivel up and blow away.

As a businessperson at this level, your inquisitive mind might race along in random thoughts urgently looking for answers and frustrated in not having them. Here are some things you might say during a typical business day: What am I supposed to do? Why did you do that? I have to work harder. Besides that, what else do you want me to do? Nobody knows we're here. I don't quite understand. Why won't people work with me? Are you sure about that? I know I'm much better than this. Just tell me what to do. Maybe I made a mistake.

At this level, you are unsure of yourself professionally and personally, and therefore, it is virtually impossible to achieve success. The *complete lack of business organization* around your talent has you mired in frustrating and doubting thoughts.

If you could get anyone to work with you, it would soon become clear to them that you're all talk and no substance. At clear skies, it really doesn't matter if you're working hard or not, success will not come your way. Your talent alone, no matter how great, is still not enough to build a solid business presence in a strong market, let alone a weak one. You are extremely vulnerable, no matter how you look at it.

Think about your precarious business predicament in terms of weather. As clear skies, you might as well be on vacation because *nothing much is happening in your business.*

There's no doubt you have a large amount of work to do, but it can be done. I'm sure other well-intentioned, hard working, talented people have quit the service industry because they never figured out they were clear skies. They also never figured out that real business success is achieved when the business works hard, not when the businessperson works harder. Don't go on vacation just yet. Read on and then get ready to make major changes to the way you conduct business.

Tropical Depression

Just thinking...
No matter if talking about weather,
business, or emotion—it means not being at one's best.

PERHAPS YOU ARE NOT much better than clear skies, but there is some thought process to your business model. Could you still be on a beautiful white sandy beach, peacefully relaxing on a luxurious lounge chair, reading a fascinating book, and softly stroking your feet through the cool sand underneath? Sure you could, but your hat and book pages will be flapping in the strong breeze, you'll get occasional blasts of sand in your eyes, and the palm trees will be swaying with every gust of wind. All in all, you would stay on the beach for the time being because the weather isn't that threatening just yet, but something ominous looking is fast approaching on the distant horizon. There's nothing much to worry about here for now, just a little bit of inconvenience every now and then.

What do you have going for you at the tropical depression level? In all likelihood, a couple of traits are a part of your business day, and there are probably some new ideas you're seriously considering to help you improve your business. You may have thought of these ideas on your own; somebody you know may be working with them; or you could have heard of them at a seminar that was meant to motivate you. You may even be executing a couple of fully developed service processes on a routine basis, like Rose was with a quarterly newsletter and an anniversary card. Even a few execution strategies may be a part of your business.

The first important point is you are thinking about something else besides your talent. The other important point is you haven't yet crossed over the threshold of making a difference to the people who interface with your business. As such, you are in the marketplace, but *you're not shrinking it.*

If you looked down on your sky, and stretched your neck and squinted your eyes, not a single cloud within your cloud formation would make a circulatory movement. It doesn't matter how long you look at them; they will not give you the slightest inclination they are going to circulate. Why? Circulation leads to rotation, which directly correlates to making a difference to people. At best, your clouds are jumbled, and they might turn into something...maybe.

If you have achieved a taste of business success, you will find yourself at this level. It can be a very humbling moment because you now know you haven't come close to matching up your talent with a fully developed business model. That was Rose in a nutshell; her potential as a businesswoman was far from being reached, and her business model was just as far away from being fully developed. It was an expected result because tropical depression level (which she was at) represents unfulfilled potential. It is the disconnect occurring between a person's talent and business model development that best explains disappointing business circumstances—and tropical depression level.

At this level, you may come across as willing to do a number of helpful things, and you can probably talk a really good story. In the final analysis, though, there isn't anything of real substance around you. Your business is more about you than it is about your business. You're pretty much on your own.

This weak, *unorganized business* hits hard and hurts the most when you interface with new clients and prospective business partners. They soon find out you don't have much of anything to offer them outside of your required technical ability. And once they figure it out, and they will, they tend to quickly move on. Long-term associations may be few and far between because you're not making a difference to people. The business partners you do have will more than likely be at the same level as you. You'll see why later.

Not only that, you might well be losing out altogether or having trouble opposing rivals in your business field who have more to offer. You don't look forward to comparisons because you know more times than not you will lose in a head-to-head competition.

Business people at the tropical depression level might say some of these things during a typical business day: Did you hear about that. That is a great idea. I should be doing that. I'm going to look into that. I will get to it. *I'm just too busy.* I know what I want to do. I would do it if I had more time. Maybe I'll get to it next year. Do any of these sound familiar?

Think about it: the early seeds of success and the potential and ability to be so much better are there if you take action. In other words, you have yet to take action on the *early hard work* of a hurricane business. You'll see later what that involves. Procrastination by way of excuses can keep you at this level for a long time. A very long time. Maybe even a career! This brings to light the potential debilitating aspect of tropical depression level. Because it lets you have a taste of success, it can easily seduce you into settling for intermittent success instead of forging ahead to sustained success.

Consider your shaky business predicament in terms of weather phenomenon. A tropical depression is trying to become something. It knows what it can become, but it also knows what it's closer to being. What's really happening in your business at tropical depression level is *you're working more for less.* Success is measured in the number of transactions you created.

To start circulating the clouds within your formation, you must expand your traits, turn your ideas/partial service processes into fully developed service processes, and better execute your business. Doing so will allow you to start making a difference to the people who interface with your business. I firmly believe the toughest leap to make, but most important, is from tropical depression to tropical storm. When you do that, you demonstrate *you get it,* and you have the fortitude to go the distance.

From a business standpoint, when you make this vital leap, you leap from a transactional to a referral-based business. You have not only changed the industry you work in, you have changed who you are as a businessperson—from a follower to a leader.

Tropical Storm

Just thinking…
It is a force to be reckoned with.
For the first time, people take notice.

NOW WE'RE TALKING. You're well on your way, but get off the beach and tightly hold onto your hat and book as you hurriedly run inside to get out of the stormy weather. As you do, be on the lookout for all kinds of flying objects, to include tumbling lounge chairs, airborne cushions, and coconuts falling from wind battered palm trees. The only reading or sleeping done here will be in the comfort of the hotel room. No need for sunglasses or sunscreen today. If it's not already raining, it's coming soon; and when it does, it won't fall, it will hit you square on!

It just ruins the day when the weather is both threatening and miserable and there's absolutely nothing you can do but get out of the way; i.e., don't you love it when you force your competitors to stay inside? See the power of a tropical storm. Not only are you now making a difference to the people who interface with your business, you're starting to negatively affect your competitors by *shrinking the marketplace.*

As a tropical storm, traits are an important part of your business day. You may still have a few lingering ideas and partial service processes yet to develop, but more importantly, you have a fair amount of fully developed service processes. And you are much better executing your business with a variety of strategies. The distinguishing difference to discern between the tropical depression and tropical storm level is *you have crossed over the threshold of making a difference to the people who interface with your business.*

This level is where your get-up-and-go energy first begins to appear and momentum starts to creep in. You enjoy coming to work because your *organized business* is allowing you to experience and realize routine success. Work is both exhilarating and rewarding.

If you stared down on your sky, you would most assuredly nod your head in approval and smile. Here's the visual picture: plenty of clouds, some starting to circulate, clearly something's going to happen, no doubt about it, no turning back. This storm is getting bigger and stronger—it's an adrenaline rush.

As a businessperson at this level, here are some things you might say or hear during a typical business day: How can we make this even better? This needs to be done by tomorrow. Please review this checklist. Let's implement this form. I've already signed them. Have we contacted the client? That was a good job on that process. Did we send him the letter? I need to make a follow-up call today. We received another referral. Let's send the cards out by tomorrow. We need a new script. Make this change today. Please schedule the appointment for tomorrow. I need to make my client service calls. What time am I meeting them? Don't forget to do it. I entered their personal information in the database. It's time for the meeting.

For the very first time, you are close to synching up your talent with a fully developed business model. By doing so, you are embracing the many aspects (interesting and uninteresting, obvious and unobvious) of a business. No doubt, you are a successful businessperson. You have been through the trial-and-error phase of a business, and thus, you have a good understanding of what works, and more importantly, what doesn't work. You're effectively serving clients and business partners while adding new ones to your business. For the first time, your business is really growing.

Even with all of that, you still want more because there is more to achieve. You have witnessed the fruits of your labor and know a stronger commitment to traits, further refinement of current service processes, development of new ideas, and an even better execution of strategies will help catapult you to the final level.

At this level, you're working your business every day. It would be easy to stop and sit back, put your feet up, and rest on your laurels—and go no further. Remember, you are successful. However, if you've come this far, you understand the many advantages of becoming a hurricane, and there should be no turning back.

Think about your business in terms of weather. You are aware that a tropical storm knows what it's going to be; it's just a matter of time. At tropical storm level, your business has equilibrium. *Hard work is being rewarded with success.* For the very first time, you are seeing episodes of your business working hard for you.

You have done most of the heavy lifting, and you're ready for what's coming. You have covered all of the windows and doors with plywood; the supplies are nearby; the generator is full of gas; and the chainsaw blade is sharp. What's that loud roar I hear?

Hurricane

Just thinking...
It captures the imagination—power creating perfection or perfection creating power. Either way, it's the perfect storm.

CAN YOU HEAR ME? I SAID YOU FINALLY MADE IT! You get what this book is all about—*Build a Hurricane Business.* No one is on the beach and to hell with the hotel room. When's the next flight out? Now you have all of your competitors running for their lives. They can clearly see what they're up against, and thus, they're very quickly getting out of the way. They know they're no match against you, and therefore, they don't want anything to do with you. *They know your name!*

Several other people know your name and respect you as well. It has taken a tremendous amount of work to get here, but now your potential is fully realized. The maturation of your business model is repeatedly pulling business directly toward you at the center of the storm you have created. Your traits give you an impeccable personal reputation; your service is fully developed; and your employed strategies are executing a *highly organized business.* All of this is constantly rotating around you and positively impacting everybody important to you on a regular basis.

Rotation is what it's all about at this level. When your traits, service processes, and execution strategies are rotating, they are in constant motion, always working, and, as such, making a difference to people. The end result is *the marketplace is now coming to you.* It's not easy to reach this top level, and only the most professionally committed business people do.

If you were to stare down on your sky, the sight would be awe-inspiring. It would be difficult to take your eyes off of what you have created—a beautiful yet devastatingly powerful sight. It's the perfect storm of organization.

As a businessperson at this level, your day will be based on two things—efficiency and success. Here are some things you might say or hear during a typical business day: Good morning boss. Your first appointment is in three hours. Let's get started on the meeting. She's on the line. It's in your in-basket. It's already done. How can I help you again? It's ready for your signature. She was referred by a client. It's scheduled for tomorrow morning. It's so good to talk to you again. I have another referral for you. That's perfect. She really liked it. I can't believe you remembered that. Your next appointment is here. The checklist is complete. I knew you would take great care of her.

At this high level, you are executing a leverage business model of a powerful referral business. You are serving people by making their personal and/or professional lives better through service that makes a difference.

The difference to discern between tropical storm and hurricane level is not about adding more service. Instead, it's about creating efficiency with what you built and a period of time to make a difference to people. You're letting your business mature and grow up.

And now think about your business in terms of weather. A hurricane sets its own course and doesn't look back. Nothing gets in its way. At hurricane level, the equilibrium in your business has been replaced with *leverage*. You now work less and achieve more success. At this level, *your business is working hard for you.*

How did you reach such a high level of business? You unconditionally accepted what it takes to build a powerful referral business. And that is, it's a large amount of upfront hard work that allows your business to eventually work hard for you. You in no way shied away from this early hard work, and now the burden of working hard has been shifted from you to your business. Here shortly, you will see what that specifically entails.

For now, though, let's move on from weather phenomena and continue the journey of discovering a powerful referral business by next looking at a strong market. It is an inevitable business condition that provides business and personal insight when you look beyond its obvious attribute—increased business volume. A strong market can contrast a transactional and a referral-based business in multiple ways and then show the business results of each. And it can even teach you something about yourself and your business. Such *big picture information* is highly coveted by leaders because it provides them the opportunity to make an informed decision about something that bears great consequence. It is for that reason why it is important to examine a strong market.

The Truth Be Told

Just thinking...
Everybody eventually faces a moment of truth.
The decision made is never easy, but it will define you.

NOW THAT YOU HOPEFULLY have a feel for the maturity level of your business as it relates to weather, let's next turn our attention to what type of businessperson you think you are, transactional or referral-based? It's the logical next question to address because it'll corroborate your business model development. So which one do you think you are? A sure indication is revealed by a road sign.

You're driving along and unexpectedly come upon the following sign: CAUTION! CAUTION! STRONG MARKET STRAIGHT AHEAD. Is there really a need to be cautious? A strong market seems like such a straightforward situation, an opportunity to easily conduct a large amount of new business. But that's exactly why you must be cautious. A sign like the one above tells you more about you and your business than the market it's trying to warn you about if you look beyond the obvious.

For something that would appear to be so obviously good on the surface, a strong market brings with it a level of complexity that is often hidden and a range of emotions that can run the gamut. It has a little bit of everything in it: a real chance to quickly grow your business, a better chance to lose it; the feeling you are better than you are, the realization you were never as good as you thought; a sense of invincibility, the despair of vulnerability. Nothing you will face in your business shrieks out Pied Piper as much as a strong market. If you're not careful, it can be the most misleading time in business, kind of like a whirlwind romance. You love it when you're in it, but you hate what it does to you when it's over.

So what would you do: hit the accelerator and barrel ahead or heed the warning and proceed with caution? The answer not only determines the type of businessperson you are but indicates your chance of building a powerful referral business.

If you're a transactional businessperson, you can't get there fast enough. In all likelihood, you've seen this sign before. How many times? As many times as the market has been strong since you've been in business. It is a way of doing business you accepted a long time ago. You can't wait to see this *sure sign of success*. To you the only downside of a strong market is that it's ended. Who am I really describing? It's just one person—Rose. Numerous times throughout the years I watched her transactional business ride right along with the bell curve of an up and down market. That's what tends to happen when you don't build a business of clients who are yours. Your business is market dependent.

Conversely, if you're a referral-based businessperson, a strong market really is a time for caution. It can be a very precarious time for you and your business if you fall victim to temptation. Even a business has a temptation moment in it. The temptation you face is happily helping new people while neglecting the people already in your business. You may think you're getting ahead, but in all actuality, you're falling behind because you're replacing established and proven with new and unproven. You have succumbed to the hidden strong market constant of temptation, always lurking in the shadows for a referral-based businessperson.

That is the contrasting dynamic of a strong market—it means something totally different to transactional and referral-based business people. They are on opposite ends of the strong market spectrum. Where transactional business people see a *pure opportunity*, referral-based business people face *temptation*. No other moment in business more clearly reveals their opposing business principles.

O

Let's contrast transactional and referral-based business people as they make their way through a strong market and then closely look at their end business results. As we do, the focus will be on how they each interface with clients and business partners.

The opportunity for transactional business people is rather obvious, increased business volume. The nature of their business is conducting transactions with whomever they can and then quickly moving on to the next person and transaction. And that's exactly what a strong market offers them. It's how they excel in business.

While on the other side of the spectrum, the inordinate amount of business created by a strong market will naturally tempt referral-based business people to shift their effort from the multi-facets of their business to just one facet—the business transaction. For them, a strong market represents *the tug moment* because it tries to pull them in a different business direction. If they allow it to occur, the strong market has taken control of them by shifting what they value—from the people in their business to the transactions they conduct. So how do they steer clear of this seductive transactional thinking—by proceeding with caution!

To effectively confront this most tempting shift in value, referral-based business people have to stay true to their principles. First and foremost, they have to protect their most precious resource—client base. That's something transactional business people never have to worry about in their business—they don't have clients. Here shortly, you'll see what it takes to add a client to a business. In the case of referral-based business people, their clients have become accustomed to a level of service; and as far as they know, it wasn't predicated on market conditions. In their eyes, it's not about the market but about them. They were conditioned to think this way over time because of the recurring service they receive. The other reason for referral-based business people to continue serving clients is it allows them to serve their business partners number one priority, as you will soon see.

Next, referral-based business people need to take care of their business partner base in two ways. First, by serving their own clients as mentioned above and, second, by not degrading the level of service they provide their business partners and their referred clients. They must remember who helped get them where they are today and who will help keep them there once things slow down, which it will. No other time will afford them a better opportunity to demonstrate commitment to their business partners. As for transactional business people—this is *their nirvana business moment*—quickly conducting lots of transactions with their business partners clients (for some professions, advertising could easily replace business partners as the primary source of clients). No matter which means clients come from, transactional business people are mainly conducting business from sources other than their own business of clients. It's what their business is all about.

Once referral-based business people secure both their client and business partner bases, they have removed the temptation of a strong market, and now they're properly positioned to take full advantage of it. They will do it by adding new clients through the market euphoria transactional business people are already enjoying and by exploiting the inattentiveness of their competitors in tending to their own business partners. With new clients, the challenge is to not become transactional; while with new business partners, it's to not be neglectful.

If anything is easy in a strong market, it's finding clients, almost to the point of them finding you. Transactional business people take full advantage of this period of easy-picking business by conducting a transaction and then quickly moving on to the next one. It's the core principle their business is based on. Unfortunately for them, as fast as business is walking in their door, they're letting it walk out. As you'll see later, it is a defining characteristic of their business. On the contrary, referral-based business people also conduct a transaction but then connect the new client to their business through service. They are also staying true to their core business principle—earning future repeat business and client referrals.

One of the vulnerabilities of a strong market is some competitors are either neglecting or under appreciating their own business partners or even performing in a subpar manner when it comes to their business partners referred clients. Some obvious examples are: failing to return phone calls and/or emails, slow to respond to requests, not staying in touch, not doing what they say, etc. That's the nature of a strong market. It's something referral-based business people know all too well—it was a part of their temptation. Being personally aware of this vulnerability, they seize the opportunity to grow their partnerships by exploiting a known weakness. If they have been trying to get new partners to join their business, this is their chance for a real breakthrough. They know they will not have a more telling moment to distinctively distinguish themselves and their business. It's an unparallel opportunity to showcase their true mettle and leave no doubt in the minds of prospective business partners the level of service they and their clients will be given, regardless of market conditions. In contrast, transactional business people are still single-mindedly focused on just one activity—happily conducting as many transactions as they can with whomever they can through any means other than their own business of clients. They are riding the bell curve of an up market. Such a free-lance-approach during this brief burst of business can easily lead to sloppy transactions and/or strained business partnerships, resulting in the loss of a business partner or two. And business partners should leave—their livelihood is being negatively impacted because they and/or their referred clients are being underserved.

As you can clearly surmise from the scenario above, *during a strong market, referral-based business people think about their business; while transactional business people only think about business.* It is this contrasting dynamic that causes one to be a capitalist and the other to miss an opportunity. Here's how.

Referral-based business people protected both their client and business partner bases by remaining a principled businessperson. They increased their client base by connecting new clients to their business. And they grew their business partnerships by capitalizing on an inherent vulnerability of a strong market. It was through caution they avoided temptation, which then led to opportunity realized. *They have a business model that has positioned their business at either the tropical storm or hurricane level.*

And transactional business people—yes they did temporarily increase their business volume, which led them to believe they were taking advantage of a strong market. But in the end, what did they achieve? That's the true test result of a strong market; what was gained after the fact. Their business is right where it was when they entered the strong market—they still have no clients; they didn't acquire any new clients; and, at best, their partnerships remain the same. Probably without even realizing it, they just missed out on one of the best growth opportunities in business. *They have a business model that has positioned their business no higher than tropical depression.* That was Rose; she had *market success*, not *business success.* As a transactional businesswoman, a strong market only brought her short-term success, never long-term success.

A strong market widens the gulf between transactional and referral-based businesses. Why does it occur? A strong market provides a wonderful but temporary opportunity for explosive growth of which referral-based businesses make the most of while it lasts. While on the other hand, transactional businesses are happily misled the entire time. Here's the focal takeaway. *Where a strong market makes transactional business people feel successful, it makes referral-based business people more successful.*

Look even deeper into a strong market and it'll reveal yet another complexity that indicates if business people are transactional or referral-based. A strong market always tells business people what they want to hear, not what they need to hear. It is a friend to business people, never a best friend. It only has one message to share, and it's always the same—they're good. It's the expected message and it's delivered right on cue.

At this point every common sense indicator will instinctively tell business people to wholeheartedly believe it and go on their merry way. However, if there's ever a time that screams for a second opinion, this is it. They will find it by not looking at how much business they produced as a result of the strong market but, rather, where that produced business came from as a result of their business. Let's take one more look at a strong market but this time from the perspective of revenue streams.

When business people look at their business, they will quickly realize its financial support is primarily derived from three sources: repeat client business, client referrals, and business partners (for some business people, they could easily replace business partners with advertising). They are the fundamental revenue streams of a business. Together, they form a river of business. Another glance at the streams reveals that clients control two-thirds of them. It unequivocally confirms who the focus of a business should be.

It's quite obvious that a business will in all probability have *ancillary revenue streams* complementing the abovementioned fundamental revenue streams. A prime example of this type of revenue stream is "business associates." Here shortly, you will see them defined and the valuable dual purpose supporting role they play in a powerful referral business.

The commotion of a strong market can easily mask what's happening within the three fundamental revenue streams. Perhaps at the moment it doesn't seem important in light of business being strong. However, it's very important to understand because the flow of business within each stream should at least be steady, even in a weak market. If a business can't pass this revenue stream test, it literally has holes in it. In all likelihood, it is mostly dependent on a single revenue stream of business partners (or advertising). Why? The focal point of the business is on conducting business from outside sources rather than generating it from the clients within the business. It is a business based on the premise of money. *Thinking about money first limits the money-making potential of a business.*

Conversely, clients will partake in a business that is based on the premise of service. It only makes sense; it is a business about them. In such a type of business, clients have a dual personal involvement—they participate to first help themselves and then other people they know. When they permit business people to serve them, they trust them; and when they give referrals, they put their credibility on the line to people they know and care about. For them, it's first about individual involvement and then it's about friendships or family—which are far more valuable than money.

Thus, convincing clients to remain clients and become supporters of a business is the toughest standard business people will face. If they fail to meet it, their business is pretty much limited to business partners (or advertising) for success and is primarily positioned to thrive in seasonal or booming markets. Their success for the most part is constrained to business rushes, which makes their business vulnerable to being a bust in the long-term. They've over-leveraged their business, thereby bringing an unnecessary high risk to it. I watched Rose take this type of over-leveraged business approach year after year with her real estate agents (henceforward referred to as agents or an agent). Here shortly, you'll see the leverage business people do need to bring to their business.

As you can certainly conclude from the scenario above, *the truth be told* about a business, transactional or referral-based, is not discovered in a strong market. Such a market does everything it can to keep the truth away. If business people want to know the real truth about their business, without having to look for it, look no further than a weak market.

A weak market tears away the facade and discriminately identifies referral-based business people. The distinctive feature common among them is not luck or time in the industry but, rather, multiple revenue streams at work in their business. The telling attribute of their business is it doesn't follow trends; instead, it either leads or counters them. Referral-based businesses lead an upward market movement and counter a downward move. The reason they can do it, and transactional businesses cannot, is transactional businesses are principally market dependent; while referral-based businesses operate independent of the market. This independence is achieved through repeat business and client referrals, along with business partners (and/or advertising). Diverse revenue streams join together to create a river of business.

The true nature of a business, transactional or referral-based, is revealed during a weak market. Both types of businesses will suffer business loss during this time, but is the drop slight or significant?

That's the telling sign, which eventually results in two decidedly different emotional reactions and business outcomes.

Transactional business people *fear* a weak market because they know it tends to expose every flaw of their business in punishing fashion, which can sometimes be humiliating to the point of not being able to recover. If it happens, the weak market has mercilessly functioned as the forced exit door strategy for them.

On the other hand, referral-based business people *grudgingly embrace* such a market because they know in time two things will happen: it will force transactional business people out and allow them to increase market share. Think about that for just a moment. Every time you read or hear a news story about thousands of business people leaving a certain profession because of a weak market, how many of them do you think are referral-based business people?

Here's the bottom line on both of the scenarios discussed. Referral-based business people have a clear-cut advantage over transactional business people in both a strong and a weak market. In a strong market, they are the capitalist; and in a weak market, they are the survivor who thrives. Makes you wonder, "What's the appeal of conducting transactional business?"

Where a weak market will reveal the true nature of your business, a strong market will reveal your business soul. How you perceive a strong market—with pure opportunity or caution—will tell you if you're a transactional or a referral-based businessperson. It will also tell you if you have a real chance to build a powerful referral business. Which way did you perceive it, and more importantly, how do you perceive it now?

The Defining Moment

Just thinking...
It's the question that puzzled me and
eventually drove me to put the puzzle together.

ANYTHING THAT'S REAL HAS a definition to it—a definition giving it its own distinction and allowing it to stand on its own and be recognized for what it is. Such is the challenge I now face. I have been talking about a powerful referral business but have not yet defined it, until now. Let me start doing so by asking, "What's the difference between a referral business and a powerful referral business?" They sound like one in the same. Both are about referrals—from the macro level. It is only at the micro level that the difference is revealed. Therefore, it's important to characterize a powerful referral business before giving it a definition.

Don't think for a minute the service industry affords everybody who enters it a chance to build a powerful referral business. On the contrary, the applicable group of professions is limited. Some of the more obvious ones are: mortgage lending, real estate, home insurance, financial planning, and CPA. These five professions (the focus of this book) share a common business bond—each one of them can provide a *continuing professional service* to a homeowner. The business significance of that fact is they can *naturally partner* with each other.

In order to build a powerful referral business, three things must be present—service, clients, and business partners—in that order. That is, each one leads to the other. INTERESTING! Here's the other interesting insight about that order. When you think in such a way, you are thinking like a leader. As you continue to read this book, you'll see the significance of each one. Even with those three things in your business, you still must meet two basic but stringent criteria to build a powerful referral business.

First, your profession needs to provide the opportunity to deliver valuable service over an extended period of time to both clients and business partners. That's what allows you to first make a difference and help keep them connected to you. And second, your business partners need to be a natural extension of your profession, thereby allowing you to easily expand your client service through them. You can repeatedly refer business to them.

Just as the above criteria apply to you, they do as well for your various business partners. There is an equal opportunity for all of you to serve clients and to build partnerships beyond just a name.

With a *partnership* being such a crucial part of a powerful referral business, it's important to take a moment here and discuss its underpinnings, especially since it's probably one of the most misused words in business. *A partnership is not two businesses working together, which tends to be a prevailing thought but, rather, two stand alone businesses working together.* What's the difference?

Two businesses working together are more times than not based on one business being dependent on the other business for success. One business is primarily fulfilling a supporting role for another business. In such a case, there is more dependency than partnership occurring between the two businesses. That's exactly the type of partnership Rose had with all of her agents. Fortunately for her, it was the widely accepted way of partnering—only professionally serving their business. WHEW! This type of partnership never made sense to me...for both the agent and the mortgage loan officer, albeit for different reasons. Where one *gave up leverage*, the other one *accepted dependency*. Both conditions are counterproductive when trying to build a business that works hard for the businessperson.

On the contrary, a real partnership is based on two stand alone businesses working together to support each other. They are both generating business for themselves and capable of doing the same for their business partner, truly creating a partnership. Both businesses are growing through each other by leveraging the other one.

No matter the profession business people are in (to include being a mortgage loan officer like Rose), they can position their business through a client service experience to generate referrals for all of their business partners. Here shortly, you will see how to specifically do it. To choose to do otherwise is a personal business choice, not a limitation imposed by their profession.

Look even deeper into a partnership and you will see *The Bully-Bully Pulpit Concept.* What is it? It is a concept that resides in every partnership, and it affects a transactional and a powerful referral business in decidedly different ways. It doesn't show itself each day, but make no mistake about it, it's organic to a partnership.

When a transactional business is supported with referrals by a powerful referral business, one business is clearly stronger than the other, and therefore, what the stronger business wants will happen. The only voice that is heard and that matters is the powerful referral business. Why is it the bully with the bully pulpit? It has clients it can refer, and the transactional business doesn't. It's the strong-arm way of partnering. IT'S IN CHARGE!

Fortunately for Rose, she never once had an agent partnership that pushed the outer limits of The Bully-Bully Pulpit Concept. But make no mistake about it, she knew she was the weaker business, and therefore, she spoke with a soft voice. She knew her place. I have to admit that this business dilemma bothered me, to the point where it hurt inside a little bit. But there was nothing I could say because I knew that Rose hadn't properly positioned her business to eliminate the possibility of such a thing from occurring. In the end, it was just further confirmation that we had a large amount of hard work ahead of us.

In contrast, when both businesses are powerful referral businesses, they are capable of generating referrals for themselves and their business partner. The fact that both businesses have clients they can refer means they are equals—there is no bully. And being equals in the eyes of each other means that both businesses have a bully pulpit, a voice that is heard and that matters. It's the dignified way of partnering. MUTUAL RESPECT!

With two distinctly different ways to create a partnership, what's the preferred method? Mutual respect of course. It's the only way that guarantees each business partner makes a difference to the other business with referrals and is, therefore, treated with dignity, which brings us to the definition of a powerful referral business.

The definition of a powerful referral business comes from and is inspired by the dignified phrase, "mutual respect." Clearly stated, the definition is—*clients and business partners making a difference to a common business that is first making a difference to them.* It is a definition that is based on the premise of *service leads to sales.* This simple premise has a universal appeal; everyone loves service. With that said, don't get the wrong impression or be misled in the slightest way. Beyond its common sense simplicity is *dual sophistication.* Such a premise demands a standard of work from you and a standard of expectations from clients and business partners.

And why is it so important to have a business premise? Candidly stated, it's the basis for business success. It represents your core business belief, in that you deeply believe in it and are willing to stake your future on it. The premise of your business is the most basic thought of your business. Once it's identified, everything you do in your business from that moment forward is predicated on trying to make it a reality.

This brings to light the three interrelated fundamental problems associated with Rose's business. She wasn't operating her business under the guidance of a specifically defined—business *model,* business *definition,* or business *premise.* There was no comprehensive consideration of how success would be achieved other than working hard and being a professional businesswoman, which she most certainly is. In the end, it was an ad hoc way of conducting business. This situation reminded me of a teenager moment, doing something consequential without serious forethought. By not taking the time upfront to develop these *three guiding principles,* her success was pretty much limited to herself, which is emblematic of transactional business thinking. The focus is on the businessperson rather than on the businessperson and the business. It was the type of thinking that would never allow her to achieve her full potential as a businesswoman, no matter how many hours she worked in a day. Why? *Business potential* is based on an amalgamation of both the individual and the business itself.

So where exactly does the definition of a powerful referral business originate from, or for that matter the business definition of a transactional or referral business? That's an intriguing question, isn't it? Surely it must be a direct reflection of something, but what?

The Psychology of it All

Just thinking...
They both can't finish first...and they shouldn't.

IN THE FOOTBALL CRAZY SPORTS WORLD it's not satisfying or acceptable to see all the teams finish first. People want to see a lone winner. A team that has clearly demonstrated it deserves to be first. People love a close race with a mighty struggle, but in the end, they want to see just one team finish on top. Maybe without even realizing it, there is a similar type struggle occurring in your business—between clients and business partners. You may not think it much matters who wins, but you should. The winner determines *the psychology of your business* and so much more.

In yet another regard, it is important to briefly discuss clients and business partners. At the center of all this talk about them is an underlying issue that directly affects you and your business. An abstract power struggle is going on between the two of them to win over your mind. They both want to be first in your eyes. Therefore, you have to make a simple choice that'll determine your business state of mind.

When you do, you have started the long and arduous process of making decisions in your business. A business in its simplest form is purely based on a series of diverse yet consequential decisions that leads to actions. Together—decisions and actions—create the framework that defines your business, which brings us to the first framework building decision to be made in your business.

The fascinating thing about the moment at hand is the very beginning of a business begins with a thought, not an action. Let me say that one more time: the very beginning of a business begins with a thought, not an action. *It is thought that serves as the primer of a business.* In other words, the way to unfurl the blueprint building plan for a business, to include a powerful referral business, is to first think, not act.

What must you think about first? You must decide who is most important to your business success. The decision is either clients or business partners. It is a straightforward choice that'll profoundly affect you and your business in more ways than you can imagine. From this simple one-or the other decision will emerge the *nexus* of your business—how you think about the people in your business. The importance of the nexus is it serves as the center beam of your framework, from it the entire framework of your business will evolve and be built. The impact of this psychological decision will be felt across your business, for it will determine the traits you adopt, the service and/or marketing plan you build, and the execution strategies you employ to execute your business. No other way to say it; this is a business defining decision.

The difference between a transactional and referral-based business will in many ways come down to an either-or choice. This is just the first of many of those types of choices, as you'll see. It only makes sense; they are opposing ways of business. For example, a transactional business is focused on the transaction the client is in, while a referral-based business is focused on the client who's in the transaction. Just imagine the contrasting business dynamics this subtlety creates.

The decision you make here is so significant it will determine the business journey you travel—either the journey of a transactional businessperson or that of a referral-based businessperson. Each tells a saga of different travels that ends in decidedly different ways.

A transactional businessperson travels a journey that starts out with great anticipation and excitement. It begins just like that of a referral-based businessperson, but then all of a sudden it stops. His journey never really goes anywhere because he's constantly starting over, one transaction at a time. It is, in essence, a business of false starts. He feels like he's going to go somewhere, but he quickly returns right back to where he started. It's the safe way of conducting business, never going far away. It's a lonely journey of little experience and even less reward.

Where his journey ends, the journey of a referral-based businessperson is really just beginning. Her journey is filled with a sense of unknown, but it's still a journey that feels safe because of the clients who share in it with her. It's the clients who create the journey's many wonderful experiences. Along the way they introduce others just like them. The farther she figuratively travels with all of them, the more rewarding her journey is. It's a journey that never knows where it's heading next, but wherever it goes, there will be more rewarding moments generated. It's the rewards of the journey that keeps alive the pursuit of the journey. And interestingly enough, the rewards are not money, as you'll see.

The business journey you travel, transactional or referral-based, will be determined by the psychology of your business. That's the importance of the decision at hand.

Here's the psychological choice you face. If you believe clients are why you have business partners, then you will always serve clients because they will give you the leverage you need to attract and keep business partners. This way of thinking means you have chosen the psychology of clients over business partners. However, if you believe business partners are why you have clients, then you will attract as many of them as you can. There's no incentive to serve clients because business partners can bring them to you. This way of thinking means you've chosen the psychology of business partners over clients.

What was the psychological choice Rose made in her business? She subconsciously defaulted to the long-established transactional businessperson thinking of business partners over clients. It's the type of thinking that is systemic in the mortgage profession. By doing so, she had unknowingly transferred the personal responsibility for her success from herself to others. She was not in charge, her business partners (agents) were. *It was a dependent decision.*

Let me for just a moment delve a little deeper into this business moment. Choosing the psychology of your business is a *destiny decision* because so much of your future is determined in this moment. For example, the type of business you'll have and, as you'll see later, the type of businessperson you'll be—leader or follower. Had Rose understood the consequences of this decision upfront, she would have chosen clients over business partners. Why? Her decision completely went against who she was as a person. It just goes to show you how long-established profession thinking can compromise independent thinking. Her lack of independent thinking at this destiny decision moment prevented her from becoming a leader in her business while making her dependent in business.

So what are you really signing up to do when you choose the psychology of your business? If you choose clients over business partners, you're making a service commitment to *connect clients to your business.* One at a time. You'll see shortly what that entails. And if you choose the psychology of business partners over clients, you're choosing to *work for your business partners.* You service their business.

Each methodology presents distinctly different ways of looking at and conducting your business. As such, each one offers its own method of achieving success, but *only one gives you control of your business.* The choice should be obvious.

By making the obvious choice of clients over business partners, you not only connect clients to your business, you position yourself to create the *mini-business* dynamic. What's that? When you refer a client to a business partner or they refer one to you, that client now becomes a *mutual-client.* You both serve the client to first keep her a part of your own business and, second, to hopefully have her refer business between the two businesses. The point is both businesses are growing through repeat client business and client referrals.

The establishment of mini-businesses is only possible when you serve clients first and then choose like-minded business partners to serve their likely needs. With those two simple conditions in place, mini-businesses will inevitably pop up everywhere in your business and with every business partner.

And just for a moment, consider the actions above as to the type of business that they create. When you choose clients over business partners, you're making a commitment to build a referral business. And when you then choose to leverage client trust for the benefit of business partners, you're making a commitment to build a powerful referral business. It is through this simple mental process that the psychology of your business is created—your business intentions with a client have been established. It is also through this mental process that the definition of a powerful referral business is developed. A business definition, no matter what type of business, is just a written expression of a chosen business psychology.

Conversely, if you choose business partners over clients, what are you really building? Your focus is on attracting business partners and conducting business transactions with their clients. As soon as you finish the transaction, you're ready for their next client. Do that for however many years with however many transactions and what do you have left when you remove business partners—nothing! You have only served their business, never building yours.

That's the down and dirty version of Rose's business story and of so many other mortgage loan officers. It's a widely accepted way of doing business that in all likelihood came about simply because prospective clients moving into a new community tend to call on agents first. It's quite stunning the influence and defining-effect this one act by prospective clients has had on the mortgage and real estate professions, in light of there being so much more to a business.

For certain business people (in particular agents), choosing the psychology of their business can be an even greater struggle. Why? Advertising is so ingrained in their profession they might well have to choose between clients, business partners, and advertising. With that said, the exact same parallels can be drawn for advertising as it can be for business partners. If you believe advertising is why you have clients, then you will always advertise. There is no incentive to serve clients because advertising can bring them to you. And finally, just like business partners, take away advertising and what do you have—nothing!

In all actuality, you could've chosen numerous other things over clients (for example, marketing strategies or buying leads), and the resulting business outcome would still be the same. You're still not building your own business.

Let me put all of the choices above into the context of being a business owner. Talk to however many business owners you want and every single one of them will tell you to never give up control. Yet, when you choose business partners (or advertising or anything else) over clients that's exactly what you're doing. Can you see how nonsensical it is to make such a decision in your business?

Don't get me wrong here, clients and business partners (and even advertising) are all important, and they can all bring you business. However, the only way you can grow your business is to choose the psychology of clients over business partners (and advertising). If you do, it marks *the beginning moment of building a business.* And interestingly enough, it also marks *the beginning moment of building strong business partnerships across your business.* By choosing clients over business partners, you have positioned your business to serve everybody connected to it. You'll soon see how to do it.

At this precise moment, something else very important happens. Your choice of clients over business partners (and advertising) also marks *the beginning moment of becoming the leader of your business*. How? You'll take care of your clients. This personal responsibility for others naturally imposes leadership type decisions.

Choosing the psychology of your business not only establishes the nexus of your business, it represents the first leadership decision you make about the people in your business. And as you'll see later, when you choose the nexus of clients over business partners (and advertising), it naturally leads to three other key leadership moments involving the people in your business. Each moment is unique, but altogether they ensure the long-term vibrancy of your business. *It is through the client that you will find leadership in your business.*

Make no mistake about it; every business has a nexus. It's the chosen methodology of how success will be achieved. Where some business people make this decision consciously, most will make it subconsciously, in that they start working in the long-standing way of their chosen profession. Regardless of how the choice is made, the nexus of a transactional business is business partners (or advertising or anything else) leads to customer transactions; while the nexus of a powerful referral business is *service* leads to connecting *clients* to your business, which then leads to hiring like-minded *business partners* to serve their likely needs.

Not to be overlooked, the nexus of a powerful referral business reveals a *client-centric* business. Not only is the word "clients" visually in the middle of the nexus, the clients who interface with such a business have service on both sides of them—first provided by the businessperson and then by their business partners. Whichever way clients turn in the business, they'll run straight into service. No matter how you look at it, they are the center of attention in a powerful referral business.

Here's the bottom line. Your business journey of transactional or referral-based has now begun in earnest, and so has the type of businessperson you'll become. So which journey did you choose to travel, and what type of businessperson did you decide to be?

You know if you think about it, this is the one time when business partners should hope you put them second. And just like that, we have arrived at my second framework question: *Who participates and how?*

The Pentagon Effect

Just thinking...
Whatever it is, it has to be powerful.

NO, IT'S NOT A MILITARY THING. It's so much more important than that. In fact, your business success hinges on it. Before you start building a powerful referral business, you need to give some serious thought to what it means to have clients and how they fit into the big picture of your business. If you don't, you end up failing the two most important things to you: your clients and your business. They're that dependent on each other because each one has something of value to offer that makes the other one better. It's the one marriage you must forge in your business before you can truly enter the referral industry. Until then, you can only talk about having a referral business.

Just as it was important to pause and quickly analyze a business partnership, the same holds true for a *customer* and a *client.* They are two words that tend to be used interchangeably, sometimes in the same sentence, even though they are significantly different. I would suggest to the point whichever one applies to your business will tell you what type of business you have.

A customer and a client have two different wants that are satisfied in two completely different ways. Where a customer has a need, a client has a professional need. Where a customer likes to shop, a client likes to be served. Where a customer looks for a bargain, a client looks to be advised. Where a customer is always right, a client always wants you to be right. Both of them are going to spend money but at a different person's expense. There is no escaping the clear distinction between them with compelling business results. And there is no escaping the fact your business will attract one or the other. It didn't take long to see another either-or choice.

So what's the threshold you have to meet to have a client, and what's the purpose of having a client in your business? They're almost juvenile questions to consider because the answer seems obvious—take care of the client and get referrals from him. In reality, though, they are two crucial questions with a somewhat complex answer. I know Rose overlooked these questions in her business. However, it's essential to make sense of them before proceeding.

Just the word "client" says you are a professional businessperson and automatically suggests a level of responsibility you have to meet. A client is not somebody you conduct a business transaction with and then mention you run your business by referral as you say a parting thank you, and it's not sending out marketing pieces after the transaction is completed, and it's surely not counting how many people you have loaded in your database. If it is, then you have mythical clients. On the contrary, the standard for having a client as a part of your business is much, much higher.

You must continue to conduct three distinct activities after the business transaction is completed before you can say you've added a client to your business. The activities are: professionally manage the transaction, provide a level of service that makes a difference, and routinely ask for business. Think about how they cover the entire spectrum—your profession, the client, and your business.

There's an underlying significance for each activity. When you professionally manage the transaction, you're making the choice to advise over sell. What's the difference? Where one businessperson sells to make a sale, the other advises to make a sale. Only one of the ways puts the client first every time. And when you provide service that makes a difference, you make the client personally better in some way. Both activities introduce emotion into your business. Why is that important? When you ask for business, you are asking the client to perform an emotional act—refer you business.

Out of all the service activities you provide a client (no matter what or how many), just one will stand out above all the rest. It's *the decisive service activity*, for it gives you the best chance to connect a client to your business. The activity is professionally managing the transaction. It trumps everything else you do in service for three reasons. First, it's a continuation of the need that originally brought the client to you. Second, it directly ties into what's most important to the client—his or her money. And third, it's the only service activity that requires professional management, creating the opportunity to advise the client. No other service activity will reinforce your credibility and need in your profession more, make more of a difference to a client, or give you more justification to say you have a client.

The high standard in adding a client to your business is found in the purpose of having a client. So what's the purpose of a client in your business? The obvious answer is a commission. There's absolute truth to that response, but it's not close to the final answer. The commission is only the beginning of something considerably bigger. Just as you should be prepared to offer the client so much more after the business transaction is completed and the commission is earned so too is the client—without even knowing it. Your knowledge and deep understanding of what he can offer and how it impacts your success will bring purpose to your work and vibrancy to your business.

Think about the client and his initial contact with you. The only reason he came to you is because he's not already associated with a powerful referral business in your profession. Lucky You! Therefore, when he enters your business, his initial thought is only on closing the business transaction at hand. He's not coming to you expecting to enter a powerful referral business.

Can you see the immediate challenge you face? Not only are you a businessperson conducting a business transaction, you are also a teacher. For a very brief period, a teacher-student dynamic emerges as you explain the level of service he can expect from you, along with what you hope to realize from him. Those two words—*expect* and *hope*—perfectly capture the essence of a referral-based business because they reflect what it takes to get a referral. You are trying to make the sure thing you provide (service) compelling enough to encourage something (referrals) from him.

There's one other very important word in the above paragraph that's easy to overlook but needs to be quickly discussed, and that word is—*explain.* It is the word that draws the attention of a client to your business by formally introducing your service and the type of business you have. *Providing service is not solely based on delivery but, rather, on first explaining, then delivering.* By doing so, the client knows three things before he ever receives your service: the service he can expect to receive, you run your business by referral, and you hope for referrals from him. Taking the time to explain your service ensures he unequivocally knows the intent of your business and your intentions with him.

By explaining your service, you figuratively deliver it with a bowtie wrapped around it. The client will look forward to receiving it.

When you don't take the time to explain your service before you deliver it—it unexpectedly shows up in a symbolic brown paper bag. We all know what a brown paper bag is used for at home. Unfortunately that was Rose, never explaining her service, and therefore, the few service items she did send out rarely ever made it out of the symbolic brown paper bag. It was an expected response, for she had not placed any value on her service by explaining it beforehand.

One of the goals of a powerful referral business is to provide a level of explained service that motivates a client to become a willing and active participant throughout your business. This isn't easy to accomplish, but by doing so, you address the all important *five client tenets* of a powerful referral business.

First and foremost, *a client should allow you to continue serving his professional needs.* Out of the five tenets, this one is the most important to you because it reflects upon you personally as a businessperson. It's equally important to your business as well because it directly leads to the other four tenets. It's this activity that signals your opportunity to leverage trust. If the client won't allow you to continue serving him, you and your business model are flawed in some way, and you have no chance of having him support the other four tenets. At best, you have a transactional business.

If he will allow you to serve him, *the next thing you hope for is referrals.* A high standard must be met because you want him to put his credibility on the line to a friend, colleague, or family member. You'll see later what it takes on your part to make that happen.

Third, *you want a client to utilize your business partners for his likely needs you cannot personally serve.* It's what makes all of your business partnerships—a partnership. His taking part in this activity is crucial to you maintaining strong, healthy partnerships across your business.

Next, because your service can always get better, *you want a client to help you improve it through surveying him at various times.* No one else is in a better position to advise you of the impression your service makes and impact it delivers.

And lastly, when it's time to grow your business partnerships, *a client can be a reliable source for new business partners* if he knows someone who is already serving him like you are. It's an established mutual trust between you and him that will make an endorsement and a warm introduction possible.

Did you notice you hope a client interacts with the nexus of a powerful referral business—service, clients, and business partners? Slowly but surely, the framework is starting to fit together.

You need to pay attention to the five client tenets and build your business with them in mind. By positioning your business to encourage each one, you fully integrate a client into your business and put into place a fundamental of a power referral business. Instead of you going after business, business tends to come to you.

It's not easy to motivate a client to participate in your business. That's why it's a goal and a difficult one at that. It's what you *hope* for from every client. There's only one way to possibly bond a client to all five tenets and that's through the service you provide.

The high degree of difficulty in achieving such a lofty goal is perfectly illustrated through the use of a pentagon—*The Pentagon Effect.* As you look at the pentagon below, first focus your attention on the top—repeat business. It reflects the one tenet that must be present to achieve the other four. For that reason, it's the *cornerstone* of The Pentagon Effect. If you're able to achieve it, meaning a client has trust and confidence in you and your business, then everything is possible: repeat business, referrals, improved service, new business partners, and business partnerships where referrals flow back and forth.

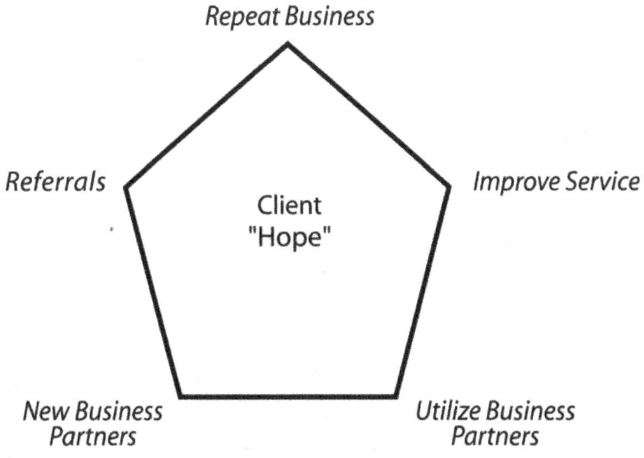

THE PENTAGON EFFECT

Look at the illustration on the previous page again and quickly think back to the three fundamental revenue streams previously discussed. Not only is the client key to two out of the three, he also plays a role in the third one as well. The client both powers your business and brings power to you—he's the *power source* of a powerful referral business.

Just for a moment, think about the preceding paragraph and transactional business people. Every time they conduct a transaction and then hurriedly move on to the next transaction, they leave behind at least two-thirds of their business, among other things. *That's the most un-businesslike move in business!*

Did you notice the geometry within the geometry? Look at the pentagon on the previous page one more time and focus on the top three activities. What you'll see are two things. First, you'll see a triangle; and second, you'll see what you hope for from a client if your business is only a referral business. Where a triangle geometrically captures a referral business, a pentagon captures a powerful referral business. In other words, your business must first be a referral business before it can be a powerful referral business.

Here's another insight. Through the client you can literally remove *single-critical business partner failure points* from your business and the corresponding stress factor associated with having them. There is a calming-effect about you and a real sense of security within your business, for you're in control. That's a rare feat in the service industry but entirely possible with a business composed of clients who are yours. Unfortunately, that was something Rose could never achieve in her business, for agents were the source of her business. And yes, over the years, she had single-critical business partner failure points in her business. And when they (agents) left her business, which they did on a couple of occasions, she had to start all over again. She had no choice; she was *dependent* on them for her success.

Just as a leverage business model allows you to confidently operate independent of the market, your clients allow the same independence within your business. Now that's real power and peace of mind.

On the surface it might surely seem as if the business transaction is where the big money is made, but that is only on the surface. In reality, the big money can only be made after the business transaction is completed. In other words, service leads to sales.

Just Two Questions

Just thinking...
If they were only yes and no questions, it would be as easy as it sounds.

IF CLIENTS ARE THE power source of a powerful referral business, then what does that make business partners? It makes them exactly what it suggests—partners. It seems like logical thinking, doesn't it? But it wasn't for Rose. It was counter to what had been ingrained in her over the years. Her way of business thinking had agents as the power source of her business. As such, this was radical thinking for her to hear. Where she was thinking like a follower, I was thinking like a leader. I was looking at a business through a *full potential lens*—what was possible. Our opposing view of a business confirmed to me Rose had a difficult mental challenge ahead of her. To successfully transform her business would mean changing what she believed in for so many years. Now that's radical.

After clients, business partners are the most important people in your business. Here's why. *Clients alone allow you to build a referral business.* If you had no one else supporting your business, you'd still be successful. It's your business. In contrast, *business partners alone make you a transactional businessperson.* Their business is your business, temporarily. Unfortunately, I know that all too well to be true through observing Rose in her business. However, when you merge the two of them, you create a *machine-effect.* Multiple parts are smoothly working together to create a power greater than the individual parts, a powerful referral business.

You probably know quite a few business people in various professions who can help your clients with a service, but not all of them can help you create the powerful machine-effect. Thus, they would not be considered business partners. They may send you referrals, even a lot of referrals, but they still would not be considered partners. Instead, they are your business associates. You don't know if your clients will ever need their services, because *business associates are based on whom you know and trust, not your clients likely needs.* It's the defining quality that separates them from your business partners.

It is important to emphasize that the characterization of business partners and business associates is not based on the number of referrals they send you but, rather, on the needs of your clients. They're both valuable business people who just happen to serve different roles in your business. In fact, it would not be the least bit surprising to have some business associates who send you more referrals than your business partners.

It is imperative to have both of them as a part of your business because when your clients have a need, you want them to think of you first. As such, your *business network* is made up of business people who can serve what your clients *might need* and what they'll *likely need.* Combined, they strongly position you to meet the total needs of clients.

There's yet another aspect to business associates to recognize, and that is they *help you* successfully conduct a transaction and/or convince people to come to your business. The work they perform is wide-ranging, which means it's important work (in varying degrees) that helps you achieve success in a multitude of ways. With that said, this work still does not rise to the level of that done by business partners. Some examples of business associates in the role of helping you with a transaction are: title company reps, appraisers, home inspectors, and even home repair handymen. And a couple of examples of business associates who can help you convince people are: a caterer who can upscale an event that you're hosting or a printing company salesperson who creates and provides your marketing materials. Here's the bottom line—business associates help both you and your clients, albeit in many different ways. They are a dual purpose business supporter.

Clearly, business associates and partners are important to your business, but they are not equals. Business partners take a vested interest in each other's business. Remember the two previously discussed criteria: both partners are providing service to each other that makes a difference, and business is flowing back and forth between the two. It's a significantly higher standard to meet than that of business associates.

It's crucial to clearly differentiate the *primary role* of business partners when it comes to a transactional and a powerful referral business. They don't fulfill the same role, even though they both share the fundamental business activity of conducting transactions. In fact, that's where the similarity ends.

In a transactional business, the *only role* of business partners is to bring you their business. You're just waiting to service it. That's exactly what Rose did for her agents for so many years. She professionally served their clients through the closing of the home loan process and then patiently waited for them to send her their next client. In doing so, Rose's success didn't come from her own hands; it was handed to her.

In a powerful referral business, the business partners perform a *dual role*. Yes, they also send you their business, which you convert into your business because you've chosen the psychology of clients over business partners. But more importantly, they serve your clients likely needs—*their primary purpose*. In such a business, a back and forth hand-off of success occurs.

Here's the significance of the difference. In a transactional business, clients emanate from business partners; while in a powerful referral business, business partners emanate from clients. It's a difference that has its roots in trust. The justification for having business partners in a powerful referral business is *they allow you to fully leverage the trust your clients have in you.*

Trust is another one of those words like Referral that belongs in the pantheon of words. It has the same qualities—important and defining in so many ways. Trust is the most *liquid asset* you have in your business because you very quickly convert it to define yourself as a businessperson. You do it with the help of a client.

When you earn a client's trust, you either consciously or subconsciously determine your intent with that trust. No matter how you do it, your answer determines the type of businessperson you are. Trust is that defining. So much so, the answer covers the entire spectrum of business people—transactional, referral, and powerful referral. All three types of business people earn trust from a client, but they all do something different with that trust.

If you are a transactional businessperson, you use client trust to close the transaction at hand but then quickly move on to the next transaction. Sadly, for so many years, that was Rose, converting her liquid asset of client trust to the lowest business form. If you are a referral businessperson, you continue to serve the client after the transaction is completed and convert client trust to earn repeat business and receive referrals in your profession. And if you are a powerful referral businessperson, you do the same thing as the referral businessperson, but you expand your referral opportunities by identifying the likely needs of your client. You then partner with like-minded business partners in those professions who can serve those needs. You, in turn, perform the same professional service for their clients. Such business thinking is the highest conversion of client trust that then naturally creates the most referral opportunities, hence a powerful referral business.

Here are the two important takeaways from the concept of trust. First, a successful partnership is not based on partner trust but, rather, on client trust, and then leveraging that trust for the benefit of the partner. And second, to determine what type of business you or anyone else has, you only have to know how much client trust is being leveraged. That's it!

Trust not only tells you what type of businessperson you are, it determines what type of person you are as well—follower or leader. How does it do that? The more client trust you are willing to leverage in your business, the more responsibility you assume, naturally making you fulfill a leadership role. When you take on the challenge to build a powerful referral business, you accept the responsibility to first think like and then become a leader. It's a complete contrast to the followership dynamics occurring in a transactional business.

In the end, the most professional (and successful) way to conduct business is based on fully leveraging client trust. Such a way of business makes you feel worthy, while clients and business partners see you as being worthy of repeat business and referrals. You are competing at the highest level in a highly competitively world.

Who should be your business partners? Of course the answer resides with clients. Their *likely needs* guide the development of these partnerships. Ask yourself what other professions are associated with yours that clients will likely need the services of one day. It is those professions that will constitute your business partners. In all actuality, they are just a natural extension of your service, providing an excellent opportunity to link them to your clients and you to their clients.

But more than just a natural extension, your business partners are a *valuable extension of your service.* They will professionally serve your clients likely needs and then make a difference to them through service, just like you. That's what allows your words about them—written or spoken—to come out with passion. You feel as strongly about their business as you feel about yours. Reaching this personal threshold means you'll naturally insert their business into your business, thereby *actively* trying to generate referrals for them.

And the way you naturally insert them is by taking advantage of the flexibility feature of service. Your service can either be provided for the exclusive benefit of your business, or it can be *flexed* to insert your business partners into it. When you flex it, you bring substance to the phrase, *valuable extension of your service.* You'll see shortly a way to flex your service through a type of process that allows you to easily and professionally insert your business partners into your business.

So why is it you can hire business partners in your business? Simply stated, you followed the nexus of a powerful referral business. By doing so, you met the most basic rule of hiring—you have something people want. And what's the thing you have in your business that business partners want—referrals. By first building a level of service that connects clients to your business, you can then hire like-minded business partners to serve their likely needs. In a powerful referral business, partnerships go through clients, not through you, as it does in a transactional business.

To make certain you're hiring the right business partners, you need to conduct a face-to-face interview. You don't just have a partnership with them; you have a partnership with them and their business. You need to know them personally (at least on a casual level) and their business professionally. This is a very selective moment in your business. When you set time aside to interview prospective business partners, you're not only selecting the partners who will serve your clients likely needs, you're engaged in *the second leadership moment involving the people in your business.* As such, you may have to conduct quite a few interviews to find the right business partners. Just keep in mind, through a quantity of interviews emerge a group of quality business partners.

The business partner interview process is a two-step approach. The first step is to research the prospective business partner. You'll find such research (learning about her and her business through whatever means available) will be of great benefit to you, for it will limit your interviews to viable candidates. If she makes it through this filtering process, the next step is the interview itself.

During the interview, ask a variety of questions that help you gather personal and professional knowledge. This will help you understand what's important to her (her needs) and the framework of her business. After all of the inquiries and with the information you gather, just two questions will help you make your hiring decision. They are *core profile questions* because they reveal the type of business partner you desire as part of your business. The first question is, *"What is your level of client service before and after the business transaction?"* The second is, *"How is your business setup so that you can refer business?"* Why are these two questions so important in making your final determination?

The first question shows you what her intent is with a client—to close the transaction and hurriedly move on to the next transaction or to close the transaction and then continue serving the client to generate repeat business and referrals. If her business is transactional, she'll struggle with this question; and if she does provide an answer, it'll probably be limited to her service before the transaction is completed.

The second question is telling you she understands that referral language is the result of her service, and therefore, she should be able to detail for you when and how she is asking for business. Her answer will show you the depth of her commitment to try to generate referrals for herself and her business partners.

A quick analysis of both questions reveals that they are linked to each other through the word *value*. In the first question, you are looking to determine what she values—the transaction or the client. She has to first value her clients before you will make her a valuable extension of your service. In the second question, you are looking for the value she will bring to your business. Her value here is not based on professionally conducting transactions you send her (that is expected) but, rather, on her business generating referrals for your business through the clients she values.

A further analysis of the questions reveals that they are also linked to the concept of *leverage*. They not only expose the leverage the business partner is going to create in her business, but the leverage she is going to create for your business. Therefore, during the interview, you should offer to answer these two questions for your business as well. By doing so, there's no hypocrisy in you. You expect no more of a business partner than you expect of yourself.

Both questions combined not only unveil a level of character and commitment, they also indicate if there's a legitimate chance for a real partnership—is the business partner's business transactional or referral-based? It is a must thing to determine when considering developing a partnership. And just for a moment, consider the impact of these two questions from this perspective. *It is through these two questions that a business is nourished and business partnerships are nurtured.*

When you set out to build a powerful referral business, you not only look forward to asking the two questions, you are confident in answering them. The root reason for being able to self-assuredly ask and answer them is you simply chose the business psychology of clients over business partners (or advertising or anything else).

The business partner interview is a telling moment for yet another reason. To know if your business is transactional or referral-based, just ask yourself these two simple questions: "Are you an interviewer or an interviewee?" and "Are you the one doing the hiring or are you the one trying to be hired?" I know over the years Rose was an interviewee trying to be hired. She had no choice; her business was transactional.

So what's the ideal business partner interview? You want both people trying to hire each other. They both value their clients. And when neither one is hiring...oh brother!

When you choose to make the business partner interview the portal your business partners must pass through to enter your business, you are making the choice to assemble a group of *quality* business partners over a *quantity* of business partners. The significance of the difference is things of quality have a lasting value, while things of quantity are routinely replaced.

Make no mistake about it; *interviewing and then hiring the right business partners is the second greatest challenge you'll face in your business.* Much later on in this book, you'll see why. With that said, don't shy away from the interview process. Astute prospective business partners will embrace this time together because an interview clearly communicates to them you have something they want. Here shortly, you'll see the greatest challenge you face.

What type of business partners should you try to hire through the interview process? The obvious choice is the ones with a *mature business*—they had specific answers to the two interview questions. The referral support to your business will be immediate. With that said, also give strong consideration to those prospective business partners with a *maturing business*—their answers to the two questions reflected a work in progress. With these types of business partners it helps to remember the journey is more important than the destination. And a journey can only be shared if you're both heading in the same direction—which you are. The difference between the two of you is you're just a little bit ahead of them.

There's yet another pair of interview questions that could be asked. These two questions specifically address the unique business bond that occurs between mortgage loan officers and agents. Where the first question appeals to mortgage loan officers, the second one appeals to agents. The first question is: *"What is your service effort to attract new clients to your business?"* The second is: *"Are you receptive to conducting joint marketing?"* Why are these two questions so relevant to this type of partnership, albeit for different reasons?

Mortgage loan officers understand the home buying pattern of prospective clients. If clients are not first referred to them, they will start the buying process by searching for an agent through a variety of convincing service activities such as open houses, different advertisement mediums, Internet searches, and even an agent sign in a front yard. It is this buying pattern that causes mortgage loan officers to care so much about the first question. They know this ingrained client thinking serves as a driver for agents to refer clients, and they want to see the service effort to capitalize on this way of thinking. Agents also recognize this long-established home buying pattern of prospective clients, and that is why they are so focused on the second question. They want to determine upfront if mortgage loan officers will share some of the financial burden by supporting selective marketing opportunities, in a legally compliant way.

Here's the bottom line. The joint effort required to close a home loan, along with the overall way prospective clients tend to view the home buying process, makes these two questions *core profile ques-*

tions. In the end, they are really just an acknowledgment of the obvious—they directly speak to a very unique and deep-seated aspect of a mortgage loan officer and agent partnership.

It is important to mention that these two questions are in addition to the "just two questions" previously discussed. If mortgage loan officers and agents only focus on these two questions alone, you basically have two transactional business people trying to form a partnership—both of them are working hard and spending money.

This brings us to an obvious but essential acknowledgment. Out of all the partnership combinations occurring across the five professions (previously mentioned), just one will have a glaring inequality when it comes to referring business—the mortgage loan officer and agent partnership. It is this partnership that will most test the following rule: a successful partnership in a powerful referral business is based on business flowing back and forth, not one-for-one.

Once you successfully hire business partners, you need to take the next step—successfully execute your partnerships. This may seem like a just do it moment, but it's not. Keep in mind newly formed partnerships are nothing more than a handshake. There's nothing written or signed between the parties involved. Instead, there is only a personal commitment made between people. It is this nonbinding pledge that necessitates taking five diverse actions. If these actions are overlooked, you jeopardize a good faith handshake that is well-intentioned.

First, have your business partners provide you a profile of their ideal client(s). You have positioned your business through service to refer clients to business partners. To ensure you place the right clients with the right business partners, you need to have these profiles on record. The profiles should be simple enough to where they communicate the focus of the business. For example, some of your agent business partners may target first-time homebuyers, while some of your financial adviser business partners may prefer to only work with clients who have a specific dollar amount they can invest. An example of a profiled client for Rose would be military members. Learning this type of information upfront shows concern for your clients and respect for your business partners' businesses. You are recognizing the individuality of both of them, and thus, you only refer clients to partners who are suited to serve their likely needs.

Next, you have already taken the second action if during the business partner interview you asked the question: "What is your level of client service before and after the business transaction?" You specifically know how your business partners generate business; i.e., what sets them apart from their competitors. By knowing this information, you are prepared to distinguish their impressive and impacting service. You can tell a short, compelling story that conveys the advantages their business offers to your clients. It's the professional way to refer business, and the only way to successfully convince clients who are on the fence. It should go without saying that if some of your business partners have a maturing business, as mentioned earlier, your effort to refer them business will temporarily be limited to their technical and personal attributes.

Third, take your business partners through your required technical service. With this knowledge in hand, they can then show you the opportune times to refer them in the course of conducting your business. They can even tell you what to listen for. Taking this action adds value to their business because you can offer more service to your clients, which, in turn, brings more value to their business.

Fourth, you need to make your business partners a part of your client service experience while routinely providing them a level of business-building service. Here shortly, you will see both of these business activities thoroughly discussed and the benefit of them.

And last, to get new partnerships off to a solid start, introduce just hired business partners with a letter from you to that portion of your client base they are a good fit for. In the letter, endorse and personalize them and convey the distinct advantages their business has to offer. By doing so, you professionally follow-through on your intent to entrust business partners with your clients, and you bring *extended service value* directly to your clients.

The accumulative results of these five actions strongly position you to support your business partners with referrals. Here's how. You know the ideal client(s) they would like you to refer them; you can convincingly refer your clients to them; you situated yourself to refer business to them while conducting your business; you keep them in front of your clients throughout the year with your service, and you help them improve as business owners; and you introduce them to your clients with a personal letter. *Such acts reflect the most unselfish moments in business.*

It should go without saying that your business partners should reciprocate these five actions. When you and your business partners are willing to take these steps together, a nonbinding handshake turns into a firm grip.

The overall point of the business partner interview process is to build a business partner network you can entrust with your clients. When you build such a network, don't limit yourself to just one professional in each profession. To do so is to treat your clients with a monolithic mentality. Their individualism and diverse needs should guide the development of a business partner network that is compatible for them. Thus, the purpose for more than one professional in a profession is to partner with different entities that, when combined, serve the spectrum of your clients professional needs.

If one of your business partner professions is a primary source of your typical transaction and/or you need it to help you complete the transaction, then it is safe to assume your greatest number of partners will probably reside with that profession. Such a direct link not only leads to the most natural extension of your service, it should naturally produce the most referral opportunities. An ideal example of this is mortgage loan officers and agents.

Regardless of whether or not your profession has this type of unique and direct link with another profession, your business partner network will tend to qualitatively grow (ever so slowly) in proportion to your number of clients. The more clients you have, the more partners you will require to serve them. No matter how many business partners you have, remember that they expect you to refer them business—so don't overextend yourself. If you fail to meet this threshold, you'll always be looking for new business partners.

So what's the business dynamic that eventually makes your business partner network a sustainable success? It's the previously discussed mini-business concept. In fact, through the utilization of this concept you will leverage client trust on two different levels. That's what happens in a powerful referral business. You first leverage client trust for the benefit of the business partner you are in the mini-business with by trying to generate referrals between the two businesses. And second, because you serve your clients likely needs, you further leverage their trust by referring them into your other business partner mini-businesses. It is through the use of the mini-business concept that *your business of clients* can safely move among *your business of business partners*. When that occurs, a very interesting dynamic is created—both businesses are now serving each other's primary need. Where your clients serve your business partners referral needs, your business partners serve your clients professional needs.

Can you see the psychology of *clients over business partners* reverberating in your business? It is now showing you the internal working dynamics it creates between clients and all of your business partners. It's all happening because you put the client first in your business.

A business partner brings more than one thing to your business. In fact, just like a client, a business partner can do five things. There is yet another pentagon effect occurring in a powerful referral business to discuss. As you build your business partner network, you need to pay close attention to the *five business partner tenets.* By doing so, you'll fully integrate a business partner into your business just like you integrated a client.

The first thing a business partner does is *serve one of the likely needs of your clients you can't personally serve.* By allowing you to expand your service in this way, you fully leverage the trust your clients have in you, and you make stronger the business partnership between the two of you.

Next, a business partner will *refer both her new and established clients to you,* which accounts for two tenets. It may just sound like semantics, but it's not. If she can only bring you new clients, she has a transactional business. When she brings you new and established clients, her business is referral-based.

The activities mentioned above speak to three points of the pentagon. When you align yourself with this caliber of business partner, each business is professionally serving the other's clients and, therefore, growing through each other's business.

A business partner can also *help you improve your service.* She does it through two means. First, by sharing the feedback she received from her clients you served. It's her way of helping you stay on your journey of always trying to become better. And second, by giving you feedback on the business-building service you provided her to help her improve as a businesswoman and business owner.

Finally, *a business partner can help you acquire new business partners.* You'll see later why it's to her distinct advantage to do so.

For now just realize, when she becomes a business partner, she becomes a partner of your business with a vested interest to protect.

The telling insight of *The Business Partner Pentagon Effect* illustration below is it reflects what you expect from a business partner and what the partner can expect of you. *It's the business partner standards of your business.* You're requiring the partner to do exactly what you're ready to do yourself. That's what makes it a partnership—and it's why you have to work with like-minded business partners.

The shape of the pentagon shows the wide-ranging activities expected of a business partner. Just like the client pentagon, the top reflects the one tenet that must be present to achieve the other four. The activity of professionally serving the likely needs of your clients reflects the *cornerstone* of The Business Partner Pentagon Effect. It's what makes everything else possible. You are referring business to a business partner—creating a partnership. In essence, both of you are professional business servants in waiting for each other's referrals.

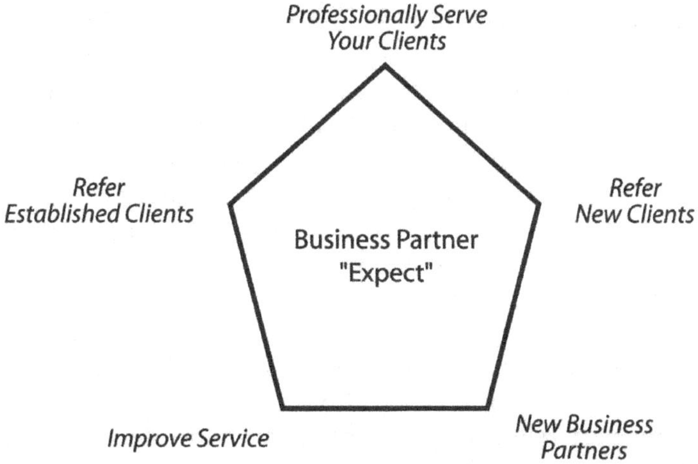

THE BUSINESS PARTNER
PENTAGON EFFECT

Just as it does with clients, the pentagon captures the significance of business partners; they're at every corner of your business. With business partners, you can serve all of the likely needs of your clients, receive referrals, provide better service, and acquire new business partners. The distinguishing difference between the two pentagons is with clients you *hope* to get the five tenets while with business partners you *expect* them.

And just like clients, business partners interact with the nexus of a powerful referral business—service, clients, and business partners. It's the underlying reason for them being business partners and not just referral partners or some other made-up name. *Business partners help you across your entire business.*

As a transactional businesswoman, Rose had an opposing view of business partners that greatly limited their impact on her business. Specifically, the purpose of business partners was to bring her business instead of helping her across her business. It's just another example of an either-or choice and how the gulf is made wider between transactional and referral-based businesses.

One of the underlying concepts at work behind a powerful referral business is *positioning.* By positioning your business, and that's the key, to first meet the needs of business partners, you increase the chances of them serving your needs. Conducting business in this manner separates a powerful referral business from other types of businesses; it truly is a business of firsts. Putting business partners first, positions you first in their minds. The psychological-effect created in a powerful referral business is one of helping. You don't feel like you're taking from business partners; you feel like you're taking care of them. It should go without saying that the concept of positioning applies to clients as well.

It is important to emphasis that just because you've positioned your business to take care of business partners doesn't mean you will always send the first referral. Worrying about or focusing on who sends the first referral is not only short-term silly thinking, it shows a total lack of respect for the interview process.

Your business partners really are a partner in your success. Not only do they address one of the three fundamental revenue streams of a powerful referral business, they work with the most important people in your business—clients. You are *entrusting* them with the power source of your business. This trust factor must be present between you and them because you can only build a powerful referral business when you entrust them to help you serve your clients likely needs.

When you convince business partners to join your business of clients, it defines the moment your business becomes a business. You have successfully hired the finest professional people you know to serve your clients likely needs you cannot personally serve. Combining the two of them (clients and business partners) gives you the best chance to overcome the soft underbelly of the service industry—seasonal business.

Ultimately, you know you have the right business partners to serve your clients likely needs when, barring special client requests or business partner niche limitations, you can confidently refer your best client to any of them. Freely putting such an important person in contact with business partners is the greatest indication of your true feelings. It's a powerful referral business that causes a natural sorting of like-minded business people working together to occur in the business world. Some things really do make sense.

Here's the bottom line on clients and business partners. Just as it was ill-advised to conduct a client transaction and then hurriedly move on, the same can be said for partnering with other business people who don't have clients they can refer to you. To take these two actions in business is to pick the business path of *struggle* over *progress*. You are choosing to only leverage yourself instead of your business. By doing so, there is no burden shift; there's only burden. It is business thinking that is destined to have you work hard your entire career.

The underlying principle that allows your partnerships to work is *you and your business partners' businesses are built on the same universal framework*. Consider the many similarities. Each business is based on the same business psychology while sharing the same three major components of traits, service, and execution strategies. With that said, you each individually apply your traits, service, and execution strategies, but the end business results are exactly the same—you have clients; you serve the clients to connect them to your business; you hope to achieve the same things from them; and you expect the same things from each other. Like business frameworks create likely business partnerships.

It is through the concept of framework—thinking below the idea level—that common core business principles of various professions are revealed, which then naturally groups them all together into a *common industry*. In this case, the common core business principles of the business people in the various professions are: they all have a choice regarding the level of service they provide; they each work with clients and business partners; and they are dependent on repeat business and referrals for business success. The significance of defining business people by the industry they work in is you remove the parochialism associated with their profession. You'll see shortly the industry that you and all of your business partners are proud members of. It's an industry based on mutual respect and referrals.

The preceding paragraph exposes the one major weakness associated with ideas. For as important as ideas are to a business, and they are fundamentally important, they unsuspectingly *fragment* what should be a common industry composed of a community of professions. The consequence of this fragmentation is a stovepipe-effect. Instead of ideas naturally funneling together business people from various professions to more closely work together and better support each other, they needlessly keep them in separate channels that hinder such synergy from occurring. In contrast, framework has just the opposite effect. Not only does it represent the most basic structure of a business, it's what binds together various professions as one. It just to goes to show you again, in yet another and more extensive way, that framework really does come first.

The Scientific Proof

Just thinking...
No argument here...there it is.

THIS IS THE MAD SCIENTIST idea moment of this book. Even the business world cannot escape the pull of the scientific world. Being a part of it means there is a truthful answer for every question. The natural bond between the two worlds is they both have fundamental questions that are answered through data. The challenge is uncovering the precise data within the mass of data that will answer the specific question being asked. Where the scientific world does it by going back in time through various means, the business world does it by looking deep inside a business.

Buried deep inside of your business is *performance data* ready to answer your most fundamental question. The question is quite simple but still very important, in that you just want to know, "Is your business a transactional, referral, or powerful referral business?" It will be one of the three. Before you answer that question, there are two points to keep foremost in mind. First, a referral business is predicated on clients sending you referrals, not business partners. And second, a powerful referral business simply extends the referral trust clients have in you to your business partners.

It's the one question in business that needs to be answered with actual data. If it's not, it tends to produce an answer based on perceived perception (everybody has a referral business). If the answer is fudged in such a way, it turns out to be both a good and bad answer. It makes you feel good personally, while it hurts you professionally. Such an answer can easily lead to being content, thereby wasting time in business before eventually failing in business.

It's not enough to assume that just because you work with clients and business partners you have a powerful referral business. The activity of working with them could only mean that you have a transactional business. I know that was the case for Rose. To determine your type of business, you must look beyond their presence and see what's specifically going on with them. You'll have the answer when you look at the *DNA of your business.*

To see your business DNA, you will require the aid of circles and lines. A circle represents a person, while a line illustrates an action. Together, they show the activity of people in your business. The two most basic things you can draw represent the molecular structure of your business. By visually revealing what's happening with the people in your business, you reveal its true identity. It's the signature moment of your business, written with circles and lines.

When clients and business partners first enter your business, they figuratively begin with a circle around them. The circle marks the beginning of their history with you. As they take action to refer or work together, you add a line emanating from their original circle and draw a circle around the people they referred or worked with and so on. The more they and the people they referred support your business, the more lines and circles are created. The end result is a visual picture that shows the lineage of your business.

If your business was transactional and you were to think of it in these terms, then it would be, for the most part, a business of circles with minimal lineage. Here is a description of the likely dynamics. The DNA of your business would be limited to some business partners supporting it with clients who are not particularly active after the transaction is completed. You may even have a business partner or two without any business activity at all (neither of you are referring clients to each other). Your business may have a client or two referring people, but it's not on a scale that makes a measurable difference. Maybe you found some clients on your own or through advertising and helped them, but they've since moved on. If these are all too common occurrences in your business, then your business DNA would look like the illustration below.

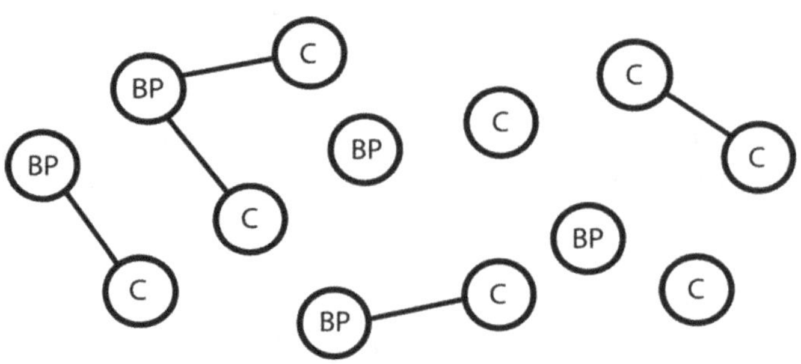

TRANSACTIONAL BUSINESS DNA

What the illustration on the previous page really shows is a scientific-like glimpse of Rose's business. When I thought of her business in these terms, I was able to clearly visualize for the first time its underlying weakness, thereby understanding its struggle. *Rose wasn't focused on the clients in her business but, rather, on conducting business (transactions) with whatever clients she could.* It's not only typical transactional business thinking, it's thinking that had her unintentionally following a business vision that would only lead to her working hard, no matter how long she was in business. You will shortly see the business vision she needed to create.

On the contrary, if your business is powerful referral-based, it is quickly adding lineage from multiple sources. Activity is occurring throughout your business. Clients are referring other clients and perhaps new business partners as well, while business partners are doing the exact same thing. And clients are working with your various business partners. Look at the business potential over a period of time with just a single client and a business partner with a great line of lineage emanating from them, one that continues with the new people they referred. It's quite revealing.

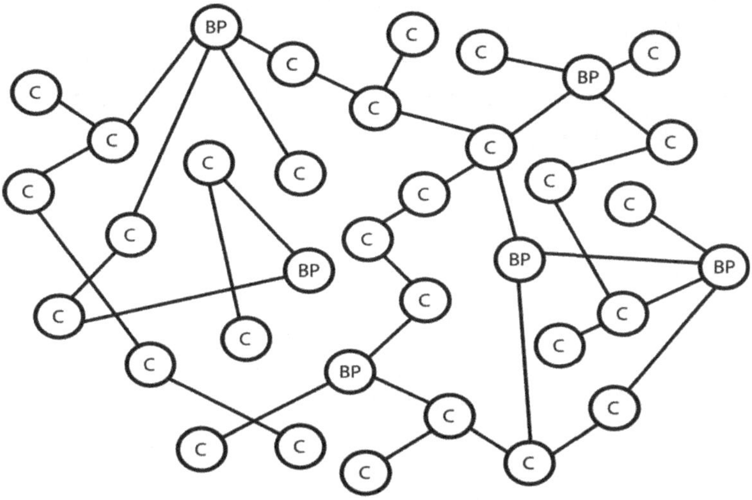

LINEAGE WEB

When you view the above illustration, it looks like just a jumbled mess of circles and lines, but it's not. What you're seeing is the

Lineage Web of a powerful referral business. By creating it, clients and business partners are sticking with your business, and they're helping you attract other people to it by referring them. And they are even working with each other. So how are you doing it? Not by luck! *You're creating a performance history with clients and business partners through service that makes a difference.* The Lineage Web gives strong credence to the hypothesis, service leads to sales.

When you become thoroughly familiar with your business DNA, you have a full grasp of your business makeup. You know its origins, current sources, and dead ends. You unequivocally know the center of gravity of your business. Your time is wisely spent only on those clients and business partners who have already shown a willingness to support your business. You know precisely who to pinpoint, those who have been attentive to your business. You never need to worry about being content and, therefore, wasting your time in business because you're not fudging what type of business you have—you have the performance data to prove it. Much later on in this book, you'll see the business activity Rose is now using to examine the DNA of her business.

The underlying importance of this type of information is it represents one half of what *business efficiency* is based on—people. Here shortly, you will start seeing the other half of business efficiency defined—the business itself. The reason business efficiency is based on people and business actions is you will spend time on both of them to produce results.

It's More Than Just Geometry

Just thinking...
What good is a story without a little bit of mystery.
Even a business book can have a suspenseful moment!

PAUSE FOR JUST A MOMENT to consider the two pentagon effects in your business and what they demonstrate to you. You may not be able to see it yet, but the pentagons are ready to reveal something much more than just geometry, along with the five things you hope to realize from clients and expect of business partners. A *subliminal message* is associated with the pentagons. When you see it, you'll see your business future. IT'S EYE-OPENING!

There's no doubt that clients and business partners are the two great forces at work supporting your business. Separately they create an energy; together they produce a synergy that literally brings your business to life. This synergy is achieved through an amalgamation of common work, shared work, and different work.

If you were to quickly compare the pentagons side-by-side, you would notice two similarities, a shared need, and two differences. The similarities are clients and business partners will help you improve your service and acquire new business partners. The shared need is realized when clients receive likely needed service from business partners. The differences are revenues come from totally different sources. It is these combined client and business partner activities that establish the criteria for what the two pentagons create, thereby revealing the subliminal message.

The only way to see the subliminal message is to capture the essence of the two pentagons at work in your business. But how do you do it? You do it by taking into account the three themes that are occurring between the pentagons. To stay true to the themes, the pentagons need to be the *same* shape, *work together,* yet be *different.* Before putting the pentagons together visually, it's important to recall the distinguishing feature clients and business partners bring to your business.

Clients allow you to build a referral business, while business partners allow you to build a transactional business. Together, they allow you to build a powerful referral business. It is only natural to show them together because they are both helping you work toward a common goal. There's just one way to merge the pentagons so they accurately illustrate the multi-dimensional characteristics both clients and business partners bring to your business. You do it by simply turning one pentagon upside down and placing it on top of the other. By doing so, they are the same shape, working together, and are different. What you've done geometrically is create a decagram. In your business, you have manifested the all important *Business Star* as illustrated below.

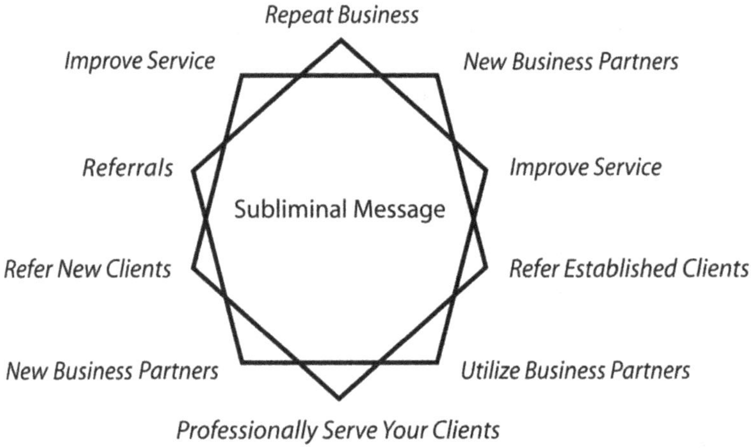

BUSINESS STAR

Look at the illustration again. It's hard to discern which pentagon is which and what activity is being done by whom, but it's all important work that blends together. Together it reflects clients and business partners performing multiple actions on your behalf. *Your business is working hard for you*, which means you are on the right side of the dichotomy of a business.

When you create a Business Star, you reach a level of success that is only possible when clients and business partners are fully integrated into your business. It's impossible to do it with just one of them, no matter how much they support your business. A Business Star visually captures the ideal clients and business partners you desire as part of your business. That's the challenge you accept when you try to build a powerful referral business.

If you haven't quite yet figured out the subliminal message, look beyond the ten activities for the answer. Together they are showing you something. A Business Star shows you what you hope for from clients and expect of business partners. Everything you do in your business must be geared toward making it a reality. When you look at a Business Star, you are looking at *the vision of your business.* It is the subliminal message of the two pentagon effects. Not only that, you are also looking at a visual interpretation of the right side of the dichotomy of a business.

On a personal level, the Business Star was *my biggest aha moment.* The reason being is it brought clarity to the following: I knew how to work hard (like everybody else), but I didn't know how to make a business work hard. The Business Star showed me how to do it while focusing and guiding my thinking going forward.

The subtlety of the vision is it doesn't tell you what you want to do in your business; it tells you what you want to achieve as a result of your business. And because Rose's vision was based on business (transactions) and not on the clients and business partners who interfaced with her business, she missed out on the six interrelated themes imbedded in a Business Star.

The value theme is based on applying a standard of value to clients and business partners in your business. You hope and expect, as appropriate, they add value to what you value the most: service, clients, and business partners. Just like everything else in your business has a purpose behind it, the same can be said for your clients and business partners.

The trust theme is based on the nexus of a powerful referral business. The trust you've created with clients and business partners through service has positioned you to ask them to help you across your business. You're utilizing the dependability of trust for their benefit and yours. By doing so, everyone is being better served and in multiple ways. Trust only flows one way in your business—both ways.

The revenue theme is based on generating revenue from others. Where transactional business people see revenue through themselves (they are working hard), you see it through your business of clients and business partners (your business is working hard for you). Where one business ends, the other begins. It's the difference between being in business or building a business.

The leadership theme is a CEO mindset. Just like a CEO, you understand that a successful business is about people. Where a CEO will always attribute the success of the company to the people within the company, you attribute the success of your business to the clients and business partners who interface with it. By focusing on them, you know over time they'll make your business great.

The emotional theme is based on helping others. Everybody's needs are being met. You meet the needs of clients and business partners by positioning your business to first take care of them, and together, they more than meet your needs. It never fails, when you take care of your people, they will take even greater care of you. That's the steadfast dynamic created when you help others.

The leverage theme is The Business Code of Leverage. Leverage is occurring throughout your business with everybody who is connected to it, and it all started with service. Why is leverage so important? With leverage on your side, things are naturally easier. It is a simple physics concept that when applied in the business world produces highly successful people. Highly successful business people don't work hard at creating business; instead, they work hard at creating leverage. Business people who work hard at creating business are destined to always work hard, while business people who work hard at creating leverage eventually shift the burden of working hard from themselves to their business.

When you achieve all six themes in your business, you are a leader who has created mutual caring throughout your business. Why? You completely understand every facet of your business.

It is through the vision of your business that you can clearly see what type of businessperson you are. The reason being is it'll clearly show the leverage you are trying to create with both clients and business partners. Said another way, a Business Star represents your "big what" in the sky. It reflects what you are trying to achieve with the clients and business partners in your business. Keep your eye on the Business Star, for it'll show you the way to a powerful referral business. Let's get started!

Talent

You're Not Alone Anymore

Just thinking...
You can never do alone what you can do with help.
It is the difference between giving your best and being your best.

EVERYDAY LIFE IS CHOCK-FULL of activities. Some of the activities are a one-person job, while others require someone else's help. You know which is which, and when it's time to do a job that needs assistance, you reach out to someone. By doing so, the job will be easier and you won't have to work as hard. The real advantage is you can finish the work at hand quicker, allowing you to do something else—a work ethic reflective of a motivated person.

Motivated people don't want to just work hard; they want to do more, which inclines them to get the help, keeping them motivated. As a motivated businessperson, the time has come to start building a leverage business model around you that will provide that necessary help and eventually allow you to achieve business success commensurate with your talent. Now what does that really mean? It means you are going to emplace a business framework around your talent that will allow your business to *bud out*. Over time, it will get bigger and bigger—with the right people.

Take a moment and think about the approach you are taking to your business through framework. You are choosing to take a *strategic approach* over a tactical one. Instead of your business being based on a series of random tactics (ideas) that leads to either delayed success or career struggle, it will be based on a well-defined strategy supported by tactics that achieves intended success. This brings to light the initial problem Rose and I encountered when I joined her. We were thinking backward in the sense that we were more interested in latching onto the next great idea instead of latching such ideas onto a predetermined strategy. Our thoughts were based on what could make us successful as opposed to what success was based on. Without even knowing it, we were getting ahead of ourselves in our business thinking. As a former military member, I should have immediately known better. Even I was successfully seduced by long-established profession thinking. What a big mistake! There's no justifiable explanation or defense for this blunder on my part. Here's the important takeaway—thinking strategically first, then tactically, is a basic leadership quality.

Now that you are familiar with the four weather phenomena and their correlation with a business model, the hidden complexities of a strong market, the three guiding principles, the nexus of a business, the multifaceted significance of clients and business partners, and a Business Star and its themes, let's take the first step and start constructing the framework of a powerful referral business.

As in the real world, a business framework needs to be attached to something that'll steady it. Said another way, you and you alone are the foundation upon which your framework will be built. Therefore, first and foremost, your business starts with your *talent*—you. You're the center of attention, and everything you create will evolve around you. Why are you so important? There are two diametrical reasons: one must come out of you, while the other must be inside of you.

First, you're the leader of your business and the *decision-maker*. It's a responsibility not to be shared. You have to step forward with authority if you want your business to move forward. And how do you do that? You do it by having a clear understanding of how a business works and why you do things—what this book is all about. As a leader, you don't have to know every detail, but you do need to have a working knowledge of how and why. When you do, you'll know what to do—and that's what leadership is about at its core, knowing what to do. Such knowledge empowers you as a businessperson, enabling you to start making decisions across a business that will eventually lead to building a business.

Second, even though a powerful referral business is based on service, it all originates from your *caring spirit*. It is this concern for others that makes everything possible in your business. This caring characteristic must be present in you before you start the journey of building a powerful referral business. It's what will bring truth to your business and eventually see you through the tough work that is ahead of you.

Even with the abovementioned knowledge and personal characteristic staunchly on your side, everybody still queues up at the same starting line when they enter the service industry. Regardless of talent level, everybody still starts at the same starting line. But this is the only time the playing field is dead even. From this moment on the race begins and every action taken creates a consequence. It all sounds easy enough, just run a race and finish. Did I mention it's mostly uphill?

Unfortunately, because the service industry is pretty much open to willing people, resulting in a high turnover rate, comprehensive *business-building education* is not always available or a top priority. As a result, from the moment you enter it, the service industry becomes the business of hard knocks with a survival of the fittest mentality. Such a dilemma produces a natural instinct—to create business right now. What could be more natural—show immediate success by creating business. DON'T DO IT!

At this beginning moment in business you have to resist this natural instinct. Why? It's the reason for the uphill race. *Instead of working to generate business through your business, you are working to create business through yourself.* By rushing to get busy creating business, you fail to create the one thing that is important, a leverage business model around your talent. That is precisely what Rose did when she first entered the mortgage profession as a loan officer. Looking back, and knowing what I now know, this business approach was by far *the biggest mistake* she made in business.

Maybe without even knowing it, your natural instinct has led you astray. It has placed you on the business path of just create business, which more times than not leads to busy work with negligible results. No matter how hard you work, and you'll work hard, your progress is slow because you are on the path of most resistance. A path so fraught with frustration it can easily lead to asking the question a leader never wants to ask: "What do I do?" *Don't Ask That Question.*

Don't get me wrong here, hard work is important, but it must be expressly directed at the framework building activities of a leverage business model. If it's not, all of your effort might simply create a business model no higher than tropical depression, where business people tend to be long on hard work and short on reaching their full business potential, like Rose for so many years. Can you see the importance of understanding how a business works and why you do things? Such intellectual knowledge is what puts hard work to good use, thereby eliminating wasted effort.

Here's the natural instinct bottom line—*don't focus on timely success, focus on timeless success.* With that said, don't have any illusions about where you are figuratively standing at this moment in your business-building journey. You are perilously standing near the edge of the wrong side of the dichotomy of a business. The personal challenges associated with a *young business* are broad and immense. At this embryonic business moment the world of success will be its most intimidating. It will seem as if everything is against you. To successfully overcome this most trying time, you not only have to work hard (on the right things), you need to believe in yourself, come out of your comfort zone, and overcome adversity. Doing so will allow you to confidently step beyond family and friends and into the world of success. You have, in essence, figuratively started stepping toward the right side of the dichotomy of a business. No other time in your business career will require more personal courage or more clearly reveal your true character.

O

Before you set out to build a powerful referral business, there is a personal quality you have to bring to your effort. It's so paramount that if you don't do it, your business will struggle and perhaps even fail. So what is it? It has nothing to do with your business but everything to do with you. Bottom line—you have to be *likeable.* It's kind of silly to talk about because it's the most duh common sense thing I will mention. However, it's so important to achieving business success that it merits mention—people associate with people they like. This simple concept of likeability not only applies personally but professionally as well.

Let me talk about the importance of likeability by focusing on prospective and new clients. When they come in contact with your business, they need to like you on some level before they'll like your business. If they don't like you, they will not like your business, no matter how good it is. Your likeability is what initially puts them at ease with you while giving you the benefit of the doubt with them. The business importance of that is they'll then be inclined to trust you, which will allow you to professionally perform your job—advise them. Likeability is what makes prospective and new clients receptive to you and the rest of your business. It's *the first sign of success* to look for when interfacing with them. The same can be said when meeting with prospective business partners you're trying to hire.

Pay attention to this vital human dynamic, but don't go overboard. People only have to like you, not be your friend. I know Rose achieves this likeability-quality when I hear her laughing and story-telling and when smiles are shared between her and somebody else. Let me put likeability in its proper perspective by briefly mentioning character and charisma. Character will always matter more than charisma. You don't have to be charismatic, but you do need to be a likeable person with character.

Before going any deeper into a powerful referral business, it's important to quickly talk about the one downhill aspect of the race you are running. For as harsh as the service industry can appear to be, it does provide a huge break that anyone can take advantage of. The break is somebody new to the service industry can immediately compete and win early. The reason being is time in the service industry merely gives you time in the service industry. Time becomes an advantage when it is associated with a leverage business model. The framework of a powerful referral business puts you on such an advantageous pathway, which makes it the shortcut to long-term success.

The First of Two Essentials

Just thinking...
You have no choice.

SOME THINGS ARE MORE IMPORTANT than other things, and then there are essential things. If people don't have the essentials when trying to do something, they might as well not bother trying. That's obviously true in the baking world and, surprisingly, true in the business world as well. For now, let me discuss the importance of essential things by talking about a recipe. Whenever people bake something, they begin with the essential ingredients. They are what make it possible to create something delicious that others will enjoy. But their overall importance goes much further than that. Not only do essential ingredients allow people to bake what they set out to make, they can make just about anything with them. That's what gives them their distinctive quality. Essential ingredients don't limit people; they inspire people.

Just like a recipe, a powerful referral business has essential ingredients you start with and then work with to create whatever you want. There are only two of them, but they're the essentials of your business model. Not unexpectedly, the first one affects you, while the second one affects the people who interface with your business. The two essential ingredients of a powerful referral business—*traits* and *service processes*—touch everybody who is important to achieving business success. If you recall, they are the first two of the three major components of a leverage business model.

Traits are critical because they are the distinguishing character features that define what you believe in and how you personally conduct yourself in your business. In essence, they are what make you...you. Service processes are just as important because they are a reflection of the service commitment you make to the people who interface with your business.

By enthusiastically embracing both of them, you meet the personal demands and the professional needs of the people who interface with your business. Traits and service processes are the core of your business model. *Once you adopt traits and build service processes, everything else you build and do will be in direct support of them.* That's the underlying simplicity at work behind the enormity of a business.

O

Let's focus our attention by talking about the first essential ingredient of a powerful referral business—*traits.* The reason traits are the first element to be discussed outside of your talent is you have to be willing to conduct business in a certain way to join the team of referral-based service professionals. This fraternity of professionals requires and demands a distinct type of businessperson. Surprisingly enough, the standards are not established by the people working in the industry but, rather, by the people who interface with the industry. You must meet their standards. This feature alone gives the industry its credibility and provides its lofty status.

At the end of each business day, it's not enough to just work hard; you have to work hard at the six traits of a powerful referral business. They are traits that will impact your clients and business partners in varying and different ways, but in the end, they'll make a difference to both of them. They're rather obvious, which makes them blah and yeah common sense, but oh so tough to master each day. What are they? We have arrived at my third framework question: *What are the individual demands?* The essence of each trait is briefly discussed below.

Integrity

Integrity is a must have for any type of business success and even more essential for a referral-based business. Integrity means two things—telling the truth and doing the right thing, especially when nobody is watching. More importantly, it ensures you do the right thing, for the right person, for the right reason. Integrity makes you a righteous person. From a purely business standpoint, it means you always advise clients; you never sell them.

If you don't have integrity, don't bother to read another word of this book. It is that critical. Outside of your personal being, it's the most important quality you possess to help bring you business success. Clients will only entrust their professional needs to you if they trust you. PERIOD! And business partners will only refer their clients to you if have integrity.

The unique personal feature of integrity is the only person who can take it away from you...is you. Once people lose trust and confidence in you, your business effectiveness is crippled, in part because bad news tends to travel faster than good news. Not only that, it can lead to people attaching a negative label to you and your business. Even if you do change for the better, the label can linger. Avoid any type of negative label at all costs because perceptions are powerful, whether they are true or not. Business is hard enough by itself without having to also overcome a negative perception.

Never compromise your integrity, no matter the circumstances or situation. It's not worth the price you'll pay. NEVER! If you don't have integrity, you will eventually die by way of the slow business death—people talk about you, they stop talking to you, you become lonely, you quit, and nobody cares. It's a justifiable business death for a dishonest person.

Service

Where your integrity allows clients to trust you, *providing service to them allows you to make a difference, thereby encouraging them to always remember you.* Providing service shows your caring spirit. Clients love great service because it touches so many emotions, and when they receive it, they can't wait to tell other people about it. If you don't read another word of this book, remember the sentence you just read. Let me share a personal story about great service.

Many years ago Rose and I took our three boys to Disney World, where we stayed in a cabin at the Fort Wilderness resort. We had a 6:00 a.m. wakeup call so we could get to the Magic Kingdom when it opened and ride the rides before the park filled with other vacationers. Well, the phone rang right at 6, and I heard Mickey Mouse's voice on the phone (very nice touch). Unbeknownst to me, I partially hung up the phone. I immediately woke up and started to get ready, when a few minutes later, somebody knocked on the door. It was still dark outside. Surprised, I walked over to the door and opened it. A Disney employee had driven to our cabin to ensure we were up so we wouldn't miss our day with Mickey Mouse. WOW!

I talked about that level of service for the whole day and still do to this day, as you can see. I couldn't believe that a big resort like Disney would take the time to personally care about the Kelly family vacation. Needless to say, we went back to Disney World over the years. So with that said, you must serve the clients who interface with your business. Your level of service to them, whatever it is, must make a difference. Never lose sight of the fact it's about them, not about you. By doing so, you wholeheartedly endorse the powerful referral business premise of service leads to sales. And don't overlook your business partners in this aspect of your business. In short order you'll see how providing them service can help them improve as business owners.

Communicate

A referral-based business needs to personally communicate on a regular basis with the clients who interface with it. Everyone knows it, but so few do it. *It is the greatest challenge you will face in your business.* No matter how difficult or uncomfortable it may seem to communicate with clients, it's your responsibility, not theirs. Therefore, avoid at all costs the following risky notion: if they need my services, they know how to get a hold of me. They won't need you if you don't need them first. And it should go without saying that you should communicate on a routine basis with your business partners as well. But as you'll see much later on, your communications with them will have a totally different focus.

The causal reason communicating is the most difficult thing to do in your business is you personally insert yourself into the lives of clients and business partners. Nothing else you do in your business is more intrusive or demands more of a reason than communicating. You must have a relevant reason you feel strong enough about to make such a call. And that reason is your service.

Service and communicating are inherently linked because each one provides the reason for the other. Here's how. The *easiest* thing to do in your business is to provide service from a distance by sending something in the mail or by email, while the *toughest* thing to do is to pick up a telephone and call someone. (Henceforth, telephone refers to a desk or cell phone, as appropriate.) It is these opposing factors that make them highly magnetic to each other. If it's important enough to take the time to send or email something, then it should be important enough to pick up the telephone and quickly discuss it. To do one without the other—just send/email something or just call someone—is to put forth an effort without much purpose, resulting in unfulfilled promise. With that said, there will be many times when a complementary phone call isn't necessary and shouldn't be made. Not only are service and communicating naturally dependent opposites that attract, together they characterize referral communication. They reflect the *crude elements* that must be present to receive referrals on a recurring basis.

Regardless of how hard communicating is for you, you must do it. If you don't, everything else in your business is relatively meaningless. It's that important. For something that is so difficult to do, the reason for doing it is simple. You communicate so you can *ask for business* (for yourself and your business partners) from the clients connected to your business. Your integrity and service is what makes them receptive to your request. And why not ask your business partners for business as well? You have already determined they will do that for you through an interview process. By not asking them for business, you respect the professionalism of the partnership and confirm the validity of the interview process.

Timeliness

On the surface, timeliness may seem inconsequential because the failure to do it only causes inconvenience. Everybody has experienced inconvenience at one time or another. In truth, timeliness is a way to formally recognize the importance of people to you, no matter the occasion. When you're timely, you shift the waiting or action burden from the people who interface with your business to you, and you reaffirm their important status. The diverse activities that timeliness affects in your business clearly illustrate its importance. It touches and affects every method of interaction—*responding, sending, meeting,* and *serving.* Here's an example of each.

People want to feel important and believe that you care about them. A powerful way to meet that expectation is by being timely in your *response* to them. This simple rule applies to anyone who is or could make a difference to your business. For example, you don't want these types of neglected thoughts creeping into their minds: When is he going to call back? Doesn't he care about me? I guess I'm not important to him. I'll call someone else and so on. Creating the feeling of being ignored is one of the quickest ways to lose business, from clients and/or business partners and from prospective ones as well. It can create a frustration unlike any other.

The key to responding in a timely manner is not standing by the phone and catching it on the first ring or immediately returning an email. Instead, it is setting expectations. For example, some business professionals may like to return calls within fifteen minutes, while others block certain times during the business day to return calls. Both situations are acceptable as long as expectations are established and communicated. People will be patient if they know when to expect the call. The same basic principle can apply to email responses as well.

Timeliness also means promptly *sending* items. The sent items discussed here are outside the purview of your established service. It could be anything from a note, letter, package, etc. being mailed to people connected to your business or people you just met. Being timely with such an item shows thoughtfulness on your part and conveys to them their importance to you. If the sent item is going out to new people you just met, it's probably the most powerful follow-on step you can take because you immediately start building an expectation about your business in their minds.

It sounds trivial, but showing up or being ready on time is a big deal and an enormous opportunity to impress, especially if people are *meeting* with you. The old rule of treat others as you would like to be treated holds true here. Conversely, when you choose to delay scheduled meetings or appointments, it doesn't show you're important; it tells people they're unimportant.

So what should your standard be? Simply put, treat people like you would the boss. If the boss came in for a scheduled meeting, you wouldn't expect him to wait to see you. Therefore, treat people who interface with your business like they're the boss—which they are because you're serving them. If they show up unannounced or early, which they will, give them the next best thing. Finish up what you're doing and then turn your attention to them.

Lastly, timeliness is extremely important when providing your *service*. If you want clients to depend on you for all of their likely needs, you have to first show them you're dependable. The best way to do it is to deliver your service on time, over an extended period of time, showing them you realize what they have come to expect. Not only does that reinforce your commitment to them, but it can lead to the conditioning-effect of them committing to you. Not to be overlooked here are your business partners. When you are dependable with your service to them, you meet a basic business owner need of always trying to improve while reaffirming you're in the people business first. It's the business you have to be in to support their business with referrals.

Altogether, timeliness allows you to show respect to people, no matter the occasion. It represents the servant moments in business.

Discipline

Just the word itself suggests you are a professional. The only way to effectively deliver on every aspect of your business is by having discipline. It brings everything to bear. The greatest attribute discipline brings to your business is it will ensure you *follow-through* on what you promised to do. That includes what you told people and what you told yourself. It sounds easy enough, but follow-through isn't all that easy to do every day.

As you embark on the exciting journey of building a powerful referral business, there will be many more demands placed upon you. These demands will come from various sources and will appear at varying time intervals: daily, weekly, monthly, quarterly, semiannually, and annually. It will be an unrelenting challenge you face every day. It never goes away or takes a break. If you lack discipline, you either get behind or fail to do it.

Further complicating your follow-through efforts will be distractions, which will routinely pull you away from what you set out to do. Only your self-discipline will bring you back quickly. You will develop many tools along the way to help you effectively and efficiently execute your business, but the trait that'll get you through each business day successfully will be your self-discipline. With it, you'll meet your daily commitment to clients and business partners and to prospective contacts as well, and you'll become a person of your word—to yourself and others. The unique feature of discipline to recognize is it works on a sliding scale—the more successful you become, the more disciplined you must be.

Tenacity

Tenacity is like the ocean surf, relentlessly pounding away day after day. When you have it, it will do three diverse things for you in your business: it'll allow you to see the business world for its opportunities, to capitalize on the opportunities your service presents, and to confidently conduct every activity in your business.

First, when you are tenacious, you view the business world differently. *You look to create your own opportunities* (big and small), either through your own initiative and/or with the help of your service. By doing so, you willingly go after or capture business opportunities other business people never realized were there or failed to act upon. You ardently seek out such opportunities and try to convert them when they become available, no matter how obscure or uncommon. With tenacity on your side, you bring an initiative that adds a vigor to your business and a unique quality of doing things that often, others won't do or don't know to do. In the final analysis, more people will know you and your business when you are tenacious, naturally bringing more opportunities to the forefront.

Second, over time, your excellent service will place multiple new business opportunities within easy reach. Only *your tenacity will allow you to grab every one of them,* either with the aid of a service activity and/or through your personal initiative. When you do grab them, you seize opportunities instead of letting them slip through your fingers like so many others do. You don't allow your service to go to waste, and therefore, you get everything out of it you should.

Lastly, if you want tenacity in a clear skies or tropical depression business, you had better have been born with it because your business won't encourage it. However, as you begin to build your business above the tropical depression level, *you naturally embrace a tenacious energy that empowers you to take on the crucial service-related deeds others are hesitant to do.* As your business grows so too does your confidence. A powerful referral business removes any hesitancy factor altogether by virtue of the service you are able and ready to deliver. You have reached the point where the convenient excuses of yesterday are now a thing of the past. Later in this book, you will see the most crucial service-related deed that a tenacious energy helps you accomplish.

If you don't have tenacity, you need to get it; your business can't flourish without it. So how do you know if you have it? Tenacity allows the door-to-door salesman mentality in you to come out. There will be no question in your mind if you have it or not. It's interesting to note that out of the six traits, the trait of tenacity most aligns with a transactional business because, through it, you are trying to create new business opportunities.

There are other traits that could be a part of your business model. The most obvious ones are motivational traits, which will be discussed much later on. With that said, if the core of your business includes the aforesaid, you strongly position yourself for success. Even though the six traits were only briefly talked about, don't be misled by thinking they are easy to achieve. A tremendous amount of work and detail needs to go into them to fully maximize their impact to your business. If you consider all six of them together, they touch and consume almost every moment of your business day.

With them, you're a businessperson with integrity who provides a high level of service that makes a difference—clients trust you and remember you, and business partners entrust their clients to you and improve as business owners. You communicate regularly with the clients who interface with your business, and thus, you routinely ask them for business for you and your business partners. You are timely regardless of the situation, and therefore, you always make clients, business partners, and prospective ones feel they are important. Everything combined means you are following through on every aspect of your business model, making you a disciplined professional. On top of all that, you are tenacious, which ensures you conduct every activity in your business while supplying yourself with a steady stream of opportunity to routinely apply the above-mentioned five traits.

Summing it all up, traits are what establish both your personal and professional reputation. If you're not fully capable of embracing these six traits, your chance of building a powerful referral business is greatly diminished. On the other hand, if you enthusiastically embrace them, the next essential component to have in your business is service processes.

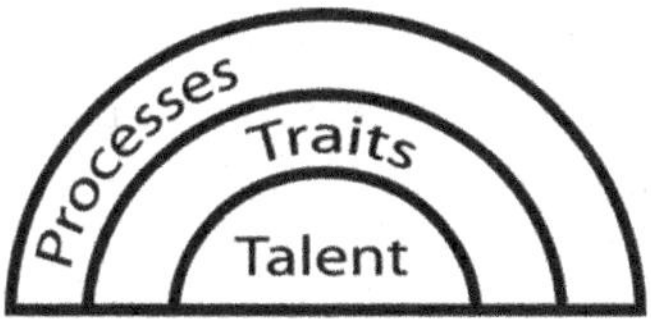

And the Last Essential

Just thinking...
You still have no choice.

JUST AS THE TRAITS in a powerful referral business work together in a comprehensive way so too does service. They are equals in importance and sophistication. Service also has a level of interlocking and interdependent complexity that includes a large amount of behind-the-scenes laborious work, different objectives and goals, a natural progression, and multiple insights requiring your close attention. It is important to be intimately familiar with all the aspects of service for the obvious reason that service is the premise of a powerful referral business. The not-so-obvious reason is when you have a complete understanding of service you have the unwritten formula to create leverage in your business. And just like that, we have arrived at my fourth framework question: *What are the aspects of service?*

When you first start talking about service, you have to begin with the element that makes service possible. Without this element in place, you only have ideas, service cannot materialize. So how do you turn an idea into service—by processing it. The service you provide in your business is nothing more than processed ideas.

To process an idea means to create a certain service action that can be easily repeated over and over again while achieving the same qualitative result every time—an exacting process. When you take this action, you are starting to systematize your business with processes. *This is the first level of systemization in your business.*

Not only do processes allow you to effectively serve others, but your efficiency and productivity as a businessperson is drastically enhanced because processes are how you bring operating speed to your business. You can do more because your business is at the *take action ready point.* Processes are not a choice; you must have them if you ever want to build a hurricane business. Unfortunately, processes were not a mainstay in Rose's business when I joined her, and therefore, her hard work only masked the level of inefficiency in her business.

To poise your business at such a forward leaning ready point, you will utilize two diverse courses of action to develop your processes. Where one course of action is based on building something, the other is based on directing someone. Whether a process uses both, or just one, depends on the specific process at hand. Either way, the objective is the same—you or someone else can accurately and quickly provide value.

The first course of action is to pre-build and then pre-position process materials (letters, notes, emails, questionnaires, surveys, packages, presentations, flyers, etc.) for immediate implementation. Taking the time to conduct such preparatory work is what prevents you from constantly having to prep over and over again—for the same things. *Nothing is more insane and inefficient in business than thinking about and working on the same things again and again.*

The second course of action to take is to make a checklist, form, or tracking sheet, as appropriate, the foundation of your processes when you can. The point being, you need to have some standardized way of *directing and documenting* the work being performed in your business. They are typically written at the *"what level,"* which means the person utilizing them already knows how to do something; she just needs to know what to do. First, let me talk about a checklist and its aspects.

A checklist is nothing more than the sequential written instructions required to accomplish a service action in an orderly manner. This is something I am quite familiar with, and equally appreciative of, considering I spent the first seven years of my Air Force career as a missile combat crewmember on the Titan II and Minuteman II intercontinental ballistic missile weapon systems. Both weapon systems were so dependent on checklists that every important action I ever took on a missile site was done at the direction of a checklist.

The most basic of checklists are composed of just three simple components. With these fundamental components in place, you can add other components, as required, but the end result achieved will still be the same—demand and response.

The first component is a title accompanied by a short narrative at the beginning of the checklist that states the purpose (entering argument) for using the checklist. The importance of the entering argument is every step in the checklist supports meeting its succinctly stated objective. The next component is the checklist step. In front of each step's narrative is a short line where you can make one of three marks: a checkmark signifying the step has been completed, a circle meaning that the step is being held in abeyance, or a slash indicating the step is not applicable for the situation at hand. Within each step's narrative is a clearly stated action representing your voice in written form. The last component, if required, is notes, which are a stand alone comment under the word *"Note."* A Note in a checklist can amplify following checklist steps or even direct accomplishing another checklist before proceeding.

The aforementioned three components combined allow a person who is unfamiliar with your business checklists to choose the correct checklist, to clearly know what's required of her, to show her work, and to know of any special instructions by reading the Notes. The point being, you don't have to be there to supervise her. The importance of properly written checklists is they empower you and the person running the checklist—you both can do what you have to do on your own.

Another way to direct and document the work being performed in your business is through the use of a form. A form is a less formal document than a checklist (there's no entering argument). Just like a checklist, it is primarily based on three components. It'll typically consist of a title, places to write down information, and steps to execute specific actions. The steps can mirror those of a checklist and/or be a menu list of directives. No matter how you do it, just like a checklist, the end result is demand and response.

The final common way to direct and document work is through the use of a tracking sheet. A tracking sheet provides a visual look at an elongated process. It will show current status, progress made, and work remaining. An obvious alternative to a tracking sheet is a visual board, which can achieve the same objectives.

Collectively, a checklist, form, and tracking sheet are three mutually exclusive tools that provide a wide-range of means to direct and document the work being performed in your business. No matter which one(s) you use in your business, the litmus test for each is to clearly communicate beyond the *figure it out* point.

And a tool that helps you *just direct work* is procedures. Their primary purpose is to account for those miscellaneous activities that are in *direct support* of your service. They are typically written at the *"how level,"* which is a step-by-step approach of how to do a specific activity. Some examples are: overnight mailing instructions, database maintenance activities, sending a fax, operating a postage machine, and other general business activities, to name a few.

When you combine checklists, forms, and tracking sheets with procedures, you can both deliver and support your service. Altogether, they will help you effectively achieve the first level of business systemization.

It's important to keep in mind when you build checklists, forms, tracking sheets, or procedures, they are *living documents*—they will evolve over time. They will be imperfect when you first build and implement them in your business, but they become perfect as you use them, discover their imperfections, and revise them. Buying into the simple concept of *imperfect leads to perfect* permits you to quickly insert them into your business with the understanding you will improve them over time. The business significance of this is a systematized business of processes sooner rather than later.

The development of processes (discussed above) formulates the behind-the-scenes look of service. The people who receive your service never see the passionate and laborious work involved; they see the result of that work—your service in action. So with that said, let's move out front and talk about the first type of service you should have in your business, and that is your *service processes*—the second essential component of your business model.

Service processes reflect the service commitment you make to the people connected to your business. This is the leap of faith moment in your business because you're going to provide service over an extended period of time, not knowing when or if you will receive repeat business and referrals in return. Your only chance to receive them is to deliver a level of service that encourages people (clients and business partners) to support your business with sales.

It's important to realize that the service processes you build and provide in your business will be highly personal to you. Why? They reflect your imagination at work and, therefore, what you believe will make a difference to the people who interface with your business. They are as unique as a person is individual.

Buried within your service processes are *business partner service processes.* What are they? They are the service processes that have a *dual purpose*—serving your clients and allowing you to easily and professionally insert your business partners into your business, either verbally or in writing. They are the processes that allow you to flex your service, giving you the greatest opportunity to generate referrals for your business partners and are, therefore, central to successful partnerships. They bring truth to your decision to fully leverage the trust your clients have in you.

You have already seen one business partner service process—professionally manage the transaction. When you conduct this activity with your clients, it's easy to ask them if the business people who are currently serving their other likely needs are conducting this vital service activity with them. If they're not, you have business partners in those professions who do, that you can refer. If you remember, this is the service activity that speaks to the *continuing professional need* clients have of business people.

To have successful partnerships across your entire business, you need to incorporate business partner service processes into your overall service. When you flex your service in such a way, you provide it for your benefit and the benefit of your business partners. You've formally recognized *a successful partnership is based on forethought with a conscious effort.* As you continue to read this book, you'll see other examples of business partner service processes.

The unique aspect of service processes is they cover the *service lifecycle* for clients and business partners. For as long as they're a part of your business, you will serve them with your service processes. Such a lengthy period of time involves many details that demand your attention when providing your service.

There are two distinctive timeframes of service you provide with your service processes. This is a very basic but extremely important concept. The reason to break down your service in such a way is because of *The Need Shift* that occurs during the course of providing service. Let me explain The Need Shift by talking about clients. When clients first come to you, *they need you* to conduct a business transaction. However, as soon as the transaction is completed, the need immediately shifts. They don't need you anymore; *you need them.* It is this simple fundamental shift in need that requires service to be broken down, bringing a level of sophistication to it.

This brings me to another pause moment. It is important to acknowledge that The Need Shift was an aha moment for me (maybe it was for you, too). Even though it is a simple and obvious thought, it was still an aha moment. Let me take a minute here and delve a little bit deeper on the importance of aha moments (I've already had a few) and the profound impact they have had and will continue to have on my journey of thinking. They function in a stimulating way that is quite thought-provoking. Here's how. Aha moments are not so much important for the initial insight they provide but, rather, for the many supporting insights they will provide. They unleash an effort of concentrated directional thinking that, in all probability, would not otherwise occur. They are, essentially, the underpinning of substantial development—they produce both direct and indirect discoveries. As such, discovering the framework of a powerful referral business greatly depends on aha moments. That sounds much more difficult than it actually is, for such moments are sometimes wide-ranging, other times narrow; sometimes obscure, other times obvious; sometimes complex, other times simple; but always tremendously relevant. Aha moments are the gatekeepers of discovery. They don't make it easy, but they don't make it impossible either. Here's the bottom line. If I am to successfully continue on my journey of discovering a powerful referral business framework, I'll need to discover more damn aha moments!

Let's get back to discussing the sophistication of service. It is your formal recognition of The Need Shift that leads to connecting clients to your business. Let me say that one more time: *it is your formal recognition of The Need Shift that leads to connecting clients to your business.* If you don't recognize this shift in need, your business is transactional; and in time, you will agonizingly confront the question: "What did you build?" When you have to face it, and answer it, the end is near, for it is the question that adorns the entry gate of the graveyard of failed transactional businesses. Thankfully, Rose never reached such a low point in her career where she had to face this question.

Where the question, "What did you build?" is the most agonizing question for business people *in business* to answer; it is an achievement question for business people *building a business.* When their time comes to face it, it will not signal the end is near. Instead, it'll function as a positive progress check on the never-ending pathway of achieving business growth.

Regardless of whether business people are in business or building a business, the question of "What did you build?" is inherent to either way of business. Whatever the answer is, it'll unambiguously reflect on them professionally by objectively holding them accountable for their business actions. Can you see the *leadership responsibility* within the dichotomy of a business at work?

Let's start examining the sophistication of service by discussing in-depth the two timeframes of service. Within each timeframe there are different objectives you are trying to achieve. As you'll see, there is a simple sequence to follow that reflects the natural progression of service. For now, let me talk about the first timeframe of service to clients and its objectives.

The first timeframe of service is from initial contact until you have completed the business transaction into which clients have entered with you. Your objective during this timeframe of service is to simply *help* clients with a transaction and *impress* them with your service. Even though it's a rather short timeframe of service, it's still an incredibly powerful business opportunity for two reasons.

First, consider your clients state of mind. Their business transaction with you is foremost in their minds, and *they need you.* During this short-lived time period, even when you're not talking to them or reminding them, they are thinking about it. Make the most of this occasion by providing a level of service that impresses them, reminds them you run your business by referral, and are ready to provide your service to people they know. Don't wait until after you have completed the transaction. If you do, you miss out on and fail to recognize a referral opportunity.

And second, clients will make a long-term judgment about you based on this short time with you. It's almost unfair for such a burden to arrive in such a short period of time, but it does. However, if your service impresses them, they will generally be receptive to the next timeframe of service, which is where the real referral wealth resides. The first timeframe of service clearly leads to the second. As you will see, it leads right to the front door of your business.

The second timeframe of service entails the service provided over a typical year and every subsequent year. Your objective during this timeframe of service is to *impact* clients with your service, thereby *connecting* them to your business. During this time, if clients have you on their minds, it's only because you have reminded them. The need has shifted—they don't need you anymore, *you need them.*

Therefore, provide a level of service that impacts them by making a difference, by keeping your name in front of them, and causing them to recall you run your business by referral. Just like in the first timeframe of service, the aim is to keep you foremost in their minds. You can only achieve that now by the service you provide. And remember, it's during this timeframe of service you accomplish three activities: professionally manage the transaction, provide a level of service that makes a difference, and ask for business. It is also during this timeframe of service that you become a leader—you are now impacting lives, which is what a leader does.

Each timeframe above serves a different need, in that they complement one another and deliver a powerful one, two punch. Where one makes an impression, the other delivers impact.

There is a critical moment within each timeframe of service. It comes at the very beginning of each one, so you have to be totally prepared to act as soon as you enter them. Failure to do so causes an unnecessary delay to what your business is all about—referrals.

During the first timeframe of service, you need to be prepared to immediately do two things, apart from providing your required technical service—preferably in the initial meeting you have with clients. First, explain the level of service they can expect to receive in this timeframe of service, above and beyond the required technical service. In other words, what makes your service uniquely impressive. Second, let them know you run your business by referral and continue to do so as you provide your service during this timeframe. By doing these two items, in this order, you're following the premise of a powerful referral business, and you have rightfully placed a *dual stamp* of importance on the activity at hand—the business transaction and your business.

During the second timeframe of service, the same concept applies. As soon as you can, after the business transaction is completed, meet with clients and explain the level of service they can expect to receive from you every year. Doing so avoids a lapse in service by you and a lapse in judgment by them.

It's critical to explain your service at the beginning of each timeframe because it starts their *referral clock* and puts into motion the result of your service for each timeframe. Don't overlook the fact that when you start their referral clock, they start their *trust clock* of you. And how do you keep your trust clock running—deliver what you promised. That's the burden of providing service. TICK-TOCK, TICK-TOCK!

I need to be crystal clear about this. Taking the time to *explain your service* serves as the *clarion call* of your business for both you and the clients who interface with it. So much comes out of this one simple step. Where your clients now know what to expect, you have an expectation to meet. Where they know what you want them to do, you know what you have to do. Explaining your service creates a co-existence of understanding and mutual respect between you and clients that makes a powerful referral business possible.

It all sounds easy enough to do—providing two timeframes of client service—but it's not. In fact, it was a steep challenge for Rose when she first started. She was so accustomed to only focusing on the transaction that to now slow down and explain her service within each timeframe was uncomfortable. Why? She had never done it before, and she knew when she explained her service she had to not only deliver it, she also had to ask for business. However, by doing so, Rose was changing the core dynamic of her business—she was transitioning from transactional business to referral business.

Here's the not-so-obvious core dynamic that was occurring—Rose was changing what she valued. *When she was a transactional businesswoman, meaning her service stopped in the first timeframe, she valued the transaction. When she started providing the second timeframe of service, she valued the client.*

Service is the truth serum in your business. It will unambiguously reveal what you value. Your intentions will be clear, regardless of what you say or how loud you say it.

When Rose made the decision to start providing the second timeframe of client service, she immediately created a business dilemma. All of our so-called clients had only received the first timeframe of service, along with some marketing material afterwards. Now we had to determine which ones to make true clients by providing them the second timeframe of service. We could have gone in many different directions to resolve this matter, but in the end, we decided to send out a *Starting Anew* letter announcing our new personalized service and asking our so-called past clients to contact us if they wanted to receive it. In the letter, we did not apologize for the way we had conducted business (we were doing what we thought was right) but instead focused on the excitement of starting anew. Our approach was to simply start serving the so-called past clients who wanted to be a part of our new business and serve new clients from that day forward. Our interest was not in regret but, rather, in a fresh start. Those clients who did respond to our letter were contacted by Rose so she could explain our service to them. We had made a clean break from the past.

Not only had we finally made a clean break from our past, but the service commitment Rose was making to the second timeframe of client service would at long last bring *predictability* to our business. Sending out this letter was important for yet another reason. It represented both a significant personal and business moment for us. Through it we were making a commitment to be a different type of businessperson while trying to build a different type of business. We had taken the first formal step of our new professional future by publicly announcing our intentions—there was no turning back.

For all of its sophistication, the essence of client service is captured in just one word—*experience*. Service creates an experience, good or bad. Clients will talk about both of them. Your goal is to create a service experience they will want others to experience.

In the course of creating your unique client service experience, you should be ever mindful of two important words—*educate* and *advise*. You should educate clients in the first timeframe of service and advise them in both timeframes. Let's take a quick look at both words as they relate to service.

An aspect of your impressive first timeframe of service should be to educate (in layman terms). It makes perfect sense—you're a professional in a profession providing a professional service. You have something of value you can teach, albeit briefly. By taking the time to educate your clients during this timeframe of service, you empower them to make an informed decision about their money. Just as empowerment is important to you when it comes to your business, it's equally important to them when it comes to their money. Education that empowers fulfills a basic need.

The attribute that makes your profession unique is it provides you the opportunity to advise clients. Consider yourself fortunate to have such a revered word associated with your profession. Not all service-oriented business people have such a *trust building moment.* The word "advise" has complementary meaning for you and clients. Where it identifies you as a professional businessperson, it unmistakably communicates to clients their best interests will be served. It is an integrity word for you and a comforting word for them. Advise is the word that trust is built upon, for it constrains you to only do what's right for clients, which sometimes means you'll tell them "No." Ironically, it is the one word in business that most captures the essence of being a PARENT!

It's imperative to embrace education and advisement in your client service experience. When you do, you recognize the significance of your profession, and you professionally serve the clients who enter it. And here is a quick side note about the word "advise." It is such an important word in and of itself that a profession rooted in it is *a profession of integrity.*

Just as it's important to serve your clients, the same holds true for your business partners. Even though they won't typically receive the first timeframe of service, they should receive the second one. That said, the occasion may present itself when business partners receive the first timeframe of service on a limited basis. For example, our agent business partners receive this timeframe of service because of their direct involvement with clients during the business transaction phase. Of course we don't ask them for a referral, but we do *proactively* keep them up to date regarding the major milestones in the closing of the home loan. By doing so, they can focus on generating new business (for themselves and us) instead of worrying about the business currently being conducted.

When you provide the second timeframe of service to business partners, your goal at a minimum should be to add value to their business by providing *business-building information* every month. The value you provide can range from helping them grow new business to creating new business from within their existing business. By doing both, you're helping them get the most out of their business today and tomorrow. So why should you expend time and energy to do this when they have already decided to partner with you and your business?

By doing so, you reinforce your obligation to them; you make a difference; and you have a built-in reason to stay in touch. You also position yourself to purposefully remain close to them, even when business is slow between the two of you. Yet, the most important reason for doing this is to help them improve their business, which, in turn, allows them to better serve yours. Without them realizing it, *it's the most selfish activity you do in business.* On a more positive note, never lose sight of the fact by serving them first, you're usually first in their minds.

And just like client service, explain your business partner service before you deliver it. But keep in mind, your focus and intentions will be different. Your goal here is to provide your partners a level of service that helps them improve as both a businessperson and owner. By making this service investment in their professional lives, you can eventually help make their personal lives better.

There you have it—the aspects of service processes and how you deliver them through the two timeframes of service. By knowing and paying attention to the continuum of service, you will always bring a meaningful purpose to your service, no matter who is receiving it or where you are in its delivery.

Let me wrap up by once again talking about traits and service processes in tandem. Traits and service processes are at bedrock-level and form the core of your business. You have to wholeheartedly embrace both of them if you ever want to build a powerful referral business. Yes, they're difficult to do every day, but when you couple them, you create an undeniably powerful mixture that will separate you from your competitors.

So just how difficult is it to master the six traits and build the client service processes? I would suggest it's much harder than you might imagine. As talented as Rose is, she only had sporadic success with them. Why? Her focus was on business transactions instead of on the clients who were in those transactions. She needed to be focused on both. Let's take another quick look at Rose but this time through the perspective of a trait and service lens.

First and foremost, Rose was technically disciplined through the closing of the home loan: She easily handled every facet of the loan process. She met all of the deadlines. And her integrity was beyond reproach. These factors were primarily responsible for her success and tropical depression level—she was very good at providing required technical service and conducting transactions.

Her written and personal communication skills were wonderful, but because she had a weak level of service, outside of the technical requirements of her business, they were hardly ever showcased. Her meager service prevented her from seeking and receiving referrals.

Rose was committed to being timely across her business. She was quick to send out required technical items, and her timeliness with meetings and appointments was strong. If her branch manager responsibilities got in the way of making timely transaction-related phone calls (which it often did), she would do the next best thing by staying late into the evening to make the calls before heading home.

Rose is an incredibly disciplined person, but her daily business activities only tapped into her technical, not her service discipline. As such, she couldn't make a difference through service.

Her tenacity was on display every time loans with rare or very challenging circumstances came her way. And more times than not, she found a way to get them done because she never quit trying until she exhausted all avenues. Even with this intensive effort, she never once crossed over the line from advising to selling. In fact, there were more than a few times when I saw her morally say, "No" when she could have technically said, "Yes." Putting clients first was always more important than making the sale.

I have to admit that was especially impressive to me in light of her being a transactional businesswoman, where selling tends to be the norm. It was this singular action by her that made me the most proud while at the same time reminding me of military professionalism. Advising a client, in any type of business, is the purest and the most impressive display of integrity a businessperson can show. At this still early moment of our journey together there wasn't much we agreed on business-wise, but this we did.

What the above review reveals about Rose is she was great at every trait and she cared about people. The fundamentals for referral success were there. To achieve it, she needed to apply herself to the service side of her business. Until then, Rose's business and personal being would remain out of sync. Only when her business reflected who she was inside could she reach her full potential.

So in the end, why is it important to take the time and make the effort to provide service to clients and business partners? Service is like a bonding compound; it strengthens the commitment between people and figuratively keeps them connected to one another. Its real value is it keeps your *established business* intact, which then allows you the opportunity to grow new business through another means. And that's done by providing another type of service that should be a part of your business. Therefore, let's now turn our attention to the other type of business opportunity you can capture—*prospective business.*

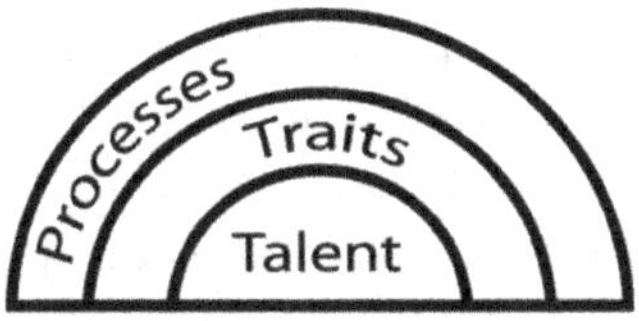

Gotcha!

Just thinking…
I know what to do; I've done this before.

STAY IN BUSINESS FOR a long enough time and you'll start to see the same things happen over and over again. They have a propensity to repeat themselves every so often. See them enough times and you'll know exactly what to do, for the answers and the actions are the same. You can continue to use them over and over again—and they work. Knowing that a specific activity is going to happen in your business is as close to a glimpse of the future as you'll get in your business. No other time will afford you the chance to be as ready as when you know something is going to happen. You know what to do—you're just waiting—ready to pounce!

To have a legitimate chance to capture the business spectrum around you, people inside and outside of your business, you have to both serve and pounce. You can do so by having the second type of process that needs to be a part of your business. It serves a completely different need than the timeframes of client and business partner service already discussed, and by having it, you strongly position yourself to expand your business in another way.

Your business is constantly interfacing with people who are already connected and committed to it. It is these people who bring vibrancy and success to your business today. However, there will be many times, and in many different ways, when you try to reach out to convince people who are not yet connected to your business. It is these new people who will expand your success tomorrow. For one reason or another, they're just not committed to working with you. It could be for a variety of valid reasons, to include they're shopping around, don't know you're interested, don't know you, or they're not convinced yet.

Instances like these require a totally different service approach so you can eventually begin serving them. You can unflinchingly go after these people by adding *pounce processes* to your business. What are they? A pounce process is just what it suggests; *it permits you to convincingly strike quickly and professionally when common business opportunities present themselves.* The challenge associated with employing them is to identify recurring business opportunities unique to your business and then pre-build a level of service that'll give you the best chance for conversion.

With that said, there's an exception to the above rule. The reason being is there's a onetime convincing business opportunity that every new businessperson should strongly consider conducting. It's what could be considered *the first pounce process in business.* When business people first enter their career, it is important for them to reach out to the network of people they know and do two things. Specifically, inform the people of their new professional status and try to convince them to either utilize their professional services or to refer somebody they know. This announcement/request type business activity can be achieved in a variety of ways, to include face-to-face conversations, telephone contact, and even some type of mailing. The end point of this activity is to get the word out to as many people as soon as possible. In all probability, this business activity will account for early success while serving as the first of many opportunities to leverage trust.

Pounce processes will fall into one of two categories, *impersonal* and *personal.* The impersonal focus will reach a larger audience, but the conversion rate can be low relative to the number of people who come in contact with it. These types of processes would primarily be directed at establishing name recognition and attracting new clients. You can work on them alone or with business partners. If you work on them with partners, you're conducting joint marketing. The same can be said if you do them with business associates. The most obvious impersonal pounce process is advertising. A couple of other examples are: utilizing social networking sites to create an online presence and mailing a postcard campaign to a neighborhood. Additionally, impersonal pounce processes can just as easily be applied to affinity groups. Some examples here are: sponsoring an annual event, a presentation in front of a group, or a mailing/flyer promotion to an apartment complex, to name just a few.

The other type of pounce process is personal and tends to be directed toward attracting just a single person. The person can either be a prospective client or business partner. On average, this way is much less expensive, but just as effective, if not more so, for it provides the opportunity to be specifically aimed with a personal touch. Some examples here are: an informative flyer to convince a prospective client to utilize your services, staying in touch with a prospective client for an extended period of time through email or other means, and a pre-built strategy to hire a business partner.

Our most effective pounce process, which happened to be a personal one, was attending an annual military relocation fair for Army officers relocating to Colorado Springs. This pounce process was a joint marketing effort with an agent business partner who was also retired military. As a retired military couple, this two-day fair was a natural fit for Rose and me and a big driver for our spring and summer business. During the event, Rose would meet one-on-one with officers to discuss their financial situation (pre-qualify them), while the agent would explain an executive-level relocation binder. In the binder was a welcome letter that introduced us and the agent and the many benefits of working with our teams. Also in the binder were several tabs to include school district information and a variety of suitably priced homes for sale with corresponding finance options. After the fair ended, we would stay in contact with the officers through email and the telephone until they and their families arrived in town, typically months later.

The above paragraph captures both the simplicity and the focus of Rose's transactional business. If some type of pounce process wasn't bringing her business, then an agent was. The end business result was Rose occasionally spent money and always worked hard.

And a type of pounce process that uses both a personal and impersonal approach is a *business alliance*. The reason it utilizes both approaches is you have to successfully target an individual (typically a Human Resources (HR) person) before you can target the sales force itself. If you choose to pursue this type of business opportunity, your business is properly positioned to capitalize on it. Why? You and the business you want to build an alliance with both share the same core value—you both care about your people. You show you care through two timeframes of service. It's this shared bond that enhances the chances of you successfully convincing the

HR person. If you can, it means prospecting access on a level that affords you an advantage not enjoyed by your competitors and a built-in market of people to serve. A business alliance pounce process is the one time when your business will impress another business that's not a business partner or business associate.

Whether impersonal or personal, pounce processes allow you to go after new business in a multitude of ways. They are the type of activities you can build once and continue to use over and over again—common occurrences. Pounce processes are the hodgepodge part of your business, for there is usually no link between them. They are typically based on stand alone opportunities, and they can be for any length of time to anyone. It is through the development of pounce processes that you can develop niche marketing.

An essential aspect of a pounce process is an *after action review*. Such a review is a mental retracing (recognizing the strengths and weaknesses) of the just completed process. Such a review will produce lessons learned that can then be applied to better execute the process the next time around. Not only will an after action review increase your efficiency, it'll enhance the future performance of the process. With that said, some pounce processes (in particular simple ones) will not require such a review.

The subtle flexibility feature of pounce processes is *they're the processes that are market sensitive.* Let me explain. It's inevitably that market conditions will routinely change, for better or worse. Different types of markets will invariably provide different common occurrence business opportunities. Two examples here are: Declining home values can create a wave of first-time homebuyers. A strong jobs economy can cause both a steep rise in personal financial investing and an influx of every type of homebuyer—new, move-up, and second-home. You can effectively and quickly react to these *emerging opportunities*, if you so choose, through the development of pounce processes. By doing so, you respond to changing market conditions while uninterruptedly serving your established business through service processes. This shows a crucial flexibility feature of framework—it's responsive to any type of market.

This also shows, yet once again, another contrasting dynamic of transactional and referral-based businesses. Where transactional businesses change their focus to respond to changing markets, referral-based businesses merely change their pounce processes. This sharp distinction between the two businesses makes perfect sense; transactional businesses primarily depend on prospective business, while referral-based businesses chiefly depend on established business. Where one business is destined to always chase business, the other routinely contacts its business year after year.

Pounce processes force you to look outside of your established business for recurring business opportunities and encourage you to build a level of service that will convince people of something. The advantage of this type process is you position yourself to automatically and/or quickly respond and capture new business by replacing thought with action. Put another way, when routine business opportunities present themselves and you have to ask yourself what you should do—you're broke. By having them in place, you don't have to think about what to do and/or what to build—you just do it or it happens on its own.

A pounce process can best be summed up by saying if you are trying to convince people to join your business by doing a pre-built activity, you're pouncing. It's like having a portion of your business on the shelf, ready to go at any moment.

The relative importance of pounce processes in your business is directly related to the maturity of it. The younger your business is, the more you'll depend on them for success, for they can help a new business get off the ground. As your business begins to mature by adding clients and business partners, you'll become less dependent on them. They will always have a role in your business, just not as prominent a role.

The above paragraph brings to light the *early challenge* associated with building a business. Your professional career will typically start out with an emphasis on pounce processes over service processes, which means when you start building your business you will face far more failure and rejection than success. If there is such a thing as a *weeding out process*, this is it. You must prove early on you have what it takes to build a business before you can actually build it. By virtue of this service sequence, you're firmly tested first. You successfully pass this test when you eventually shift your emphasis from prospecting for new business to contacting your established business.

It is important to take a moment here and briefly discuss two more words in business: *prospecting* and *established.* One word is obviously used more often than the other, but they equally tell an insightful business story when you look beyond the words themselves and instead focus on the far-reaching impact of them. Just as the two words customer and client had underlying meaning, the same can be said for prospecting and established. So much is associated with each one of them. Here is a small sampling. When business people only prospect for business, they are always *looking* for business; they are transactional business people; they will always work hard in their business; and they are a follower. And when business people contact their established business, they are always *seeing* their business; they are referral-based business people; their business is working hard for them; and they are a leader. I could go on and on with the contrasting business dynamics if I wanted too. Here's the key takeaway. Hopefully through this short analysis of these two words you can see both the actual business significance of The Look or See Concept and the downright importance of positioning yourself to see your business.

The one thing to always remember about pounce processes is they are a part of your business, not your entire business. The key is to use them to become more successful, not successful. If you depend on pounce processes for success (for example, buying advertising or leads), you're primarily a money spending transactional businessperson—one step above where Rose was at tropical depression level. She didn't spend money in such a dependent manner. In time, you will eventually face the question always lurking for transactional business people: "What did you build?"

With pounce processes as a part of your business, you now have an important symmetry to your overall service. Through the development of service and pounce processes you have brought operating speed to both your established and prospective business. Where the two timeframes of service represent you *service plan*, your pounce processes represent your *marketing plan.*

It is through your service and marketing plans that you'll generate either *immediate* or *future* business. One is real; the other is potential. That's the direct output of your total service effort. Together, they represent your today and tomorrow business.

For the immediate client business generated, you'll initiate the first timeframe of service. And for the immediate business partner business, you'll start the second timeframe of service. In each case, you're right away applying the premise of a powerful referral business by providing a level of service that'll lead to sales. And if the immediate client business generated is repeat business, you'll again provide the client the first timeframe of service before returning him back to the second timeframe of service.

For the potential future business (you're still in the process of convincing prospective clients or business partners), you'll need to position it in a way that allows you to effectively work it. Probably the best way to do it is to first separate it by group (clients or business partners) and then categorize each group with enough detailed information (on a spreadsheet or other means) that allows you to proactively work it in a timely manner. Just like processes, the aim is to quickly and accurately work through this potential business at the opportune time. In certain cases, the proactive working of this business could be through a pounce process, while other times it could just be a scheduled follow-up action. No matter the method employed, the end point is to simply convert potential business into real business. When you're able to successfully do it, you're realizing every possible sale from your service. Can you see the trait of tenacity at work in your business?

Think about the dynamics that are now occurring in your business. Every day you'll be providing two timeframes of service and on certain days a pounce process. The output of all of this is you'll be generating both immediate and future business. When you put it all together, providing service creates a self-sustaining loop of business. And as you'll see much later on, both transactional and referral-based businesses have a business loop in them, albeit opposing.

Now that service and pounce processes have been discussed, it's important to shift the focus to some contrasting process analysis. With service playing such a leading role in a powerful referral business, it's crucial to be able to delineate the difference between the two processes and recognize the subtleties between them.

The distinctive difference between service and pounce processes is captured in just two words—*providing* and *convincing*. They are the difference between serving people or marketing to people. For example, Rose and I don't market to our clients or business partners—we *provide* them service through our service processes. Our goal is to provide something of value that will make a difference and hopefully or expectantly, as appropriate, encourage them to support our business with sales. Conversely, when we market to people, we are trying to *convince* them of something through our pounce processes, so we can eventually provide our service to them.

The best way to illustrate the marked difference between pounce and service processes is by applying them to a situation that directly affects you. So here's the situation. You are casually flipping through a magazine and you come across marketing for a beautiful resort in an exotic location. The resort's marketing does its intended job—it *convinces* you to pick up the phone and make a reservation. At the moment you arrive, what do you want the resort to do—continue marketing to you or transition to *providing* you a great service experience? Here's the bottom line—market to the people outside of your business, provide service to the ones in it.

Since there is a distinct difference between service and pounce processes, they naturally produce different things. *Service processes will generate referrals, while pounce processes will create leads.* Once again, two words in business—referral and lead—that tend to be used interchangeably, even though the methodology to create them is significantly different. Let's look at them through the eyes of clients. Where service processes make a difference to clients in your business, thereby encouraging them to personally endorse and recommend you to people they know; pounce processes try to convince prospective clients outside of your business of something you said (verbally or written). Where one is based on trust between two people who know each other, the other is based exclusively on your spoken or written words. They are obviously not one in the same, and the conversion rate is not the same either. Referrals and leads are both important, and you should, therefore, have both of them in your business, with an unambiguous focus toward one. To determine if your business is transactional or referral-based, just ask yourself which one is your business focused on producing.

There is yet another subtlety to processes. Processes are designated as pounce or service processes based solely on their intent at a particular moment. Their designation is derived from the words *convince* or *provide*. For example, if prospective clients are surfing the Internet and they happen upon your website, and are convinced to contact you, your website is serving as a pounce process. Conversely, if you have clients and you provide them valuable information by directing them to your website, now your website is serving as a service process. The bottom line on processes is they're flexible. To determine the characterization of a process at a particular moment just ask yourself the following question: "What need is being met—convincing or providing?"

Here's another insight to be keenly aware of. It is important to recognize the similarity between the two timeframes of service and pounce/service processes. They share a natural progression and transition. The progressive transition for the two timeframes of service is from help/impress to connect/impact, while for pounce and service processes it is from marketing to serving. In both cases, the end result is a higher level of service with a personal touch, and the clients who receive both, know it.

And one more distinctive difference to recognize when it comes to service and marketing. When you provide service, you first explain it and then you deliver it. When you market, you just deliver it. Where service keeps you in touch with the clients you know, marketing tries to put you in touch with prospective clients you don't know. With that said, don't underestimate the value of marketing to your business. It fulfills a very important role, for it serves as the bridge prospective clients cross over to enter your business (two timeframes of service).

Let me close out this contrasting process analysis discussion by talking about them in combination. Through the three type of processes in a business—pounce, service, and business partner—you can see the evolution of business people. For example, when business people limit their service to only pounce processes, they have a transactional business. If their service consists of pounce processes to attract clients to their business, along with service processes to connect them, they have a referral business. And if their client service includes business partner service processes that allow them to easily and professionally insert business partners into their business, they have a powerful referral business. Yet once again, service acts like a truth serum. But this time, instead of revealing value, it reveals type of business people.

The catchphrase that best captures the difference between transactional and referral-based businesses is *"marketing and sales"* versus *"service and sales."* Each one is a respectable way of business with one focused on creating transactions, the other on serving people. Where the forte of marketing is product driven (transactions), the forte of service is taking care of people. The significance of the difference is one is based on an individual event, the other on an individual. When a profession provides the option to do either one, the greater success will reside with serving the individual.

Let's move forward and start on the critical task of taking apart the service portion of your current business model. By doing so, you can build it into something much more meaningful to the people who interface with your business and to those who might consider doing so.

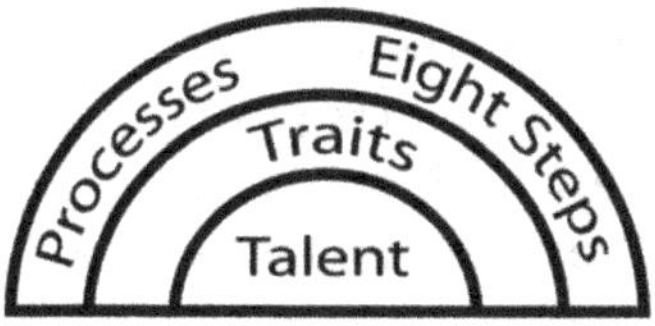

Where the Rubber Meets the Road

Just thinking...
Get a grip; you'll need every bit of it.

ANY BUSINESS CAN STAY in business as long as people come to it. Your goal initially is similar but also significantly different, for you want the same people to come to your business over and over again. Making such a thing happen foretells of future success to come. Therefore, when building your business, you need to build it so it literally grabs people and keeps them connected to you. You can only do it through service, which figuratively keeps your business moving forward because the rubber does meet the road. And the best way to achieve such traction in your business is to first connect clients, which then attracts business partners. If you don't build a level of service that keeps people connected to your business in such a way, you're spinning your business wheels, never really going anywhere in business, no matter how hard or long you try.

To avoid this predicament, it's time to start building service and pounce processes that'll serve your current and prospective clients and business partners while creating referrals and leads for you. To do it, you'll utilize the systematic approach of the *Eight Step Process*. As you accomplish this process, both service and pounce ideas and processes will be referred to as ideas and processes only, unless otherwise stated.

Don't lose sight of the focus of your effort here. You will build both types of processes, with an unmistakable focus toward service processes. Why service processes over pounce processes? By choosing service over marketing, you're positioning yourself to *contact* your established business instead of *prospecting* for new business. Both ways can bring you business, but only one way allows you to build a business of clients. It's another either-or choice.

Furthermore, choosing service processes over pounce processes is the corresponding decision of the psychology of clients over business partners. It only makes sense; service and clients are the first two components of the nexus of a powerful referral business. If you were thinking like a transactional businessperson, you would have chosen business partners (or advertising or something else) over clients, and marketing over service. That's exactly what Rose did when she first entered the mortgage profession—she selected business partners over clients while narrowly focusing her service effort on marketing through the utilization of pounce processes.

When you're building processes, you're working on your business, not providing or convincing. That may seem a little unsettling at first, but don't shy away from this pausing activity. A pause like this is good because it permits work that will eventually fast forward your business. Now what does that really mean? It means that service, and service alone (not marketing), officially starts the transition from creating business to creating leverage in your business. Therefore, it's essential to exercise due diligence and patience here. By doing so, you position yourself to realize the essence of a powerful referral business, which is quite hard to accomplish.

Think about the task at hand; you are trying to build a level of service that completely serves three different needs—your clients, your business partners, and yours. Think about it some more: *service is a subjective opinion with an objective answer*. Therein is the difficult challenge of a powerful referral business and why you must take enough time to apply serious thinking so you can give yourself the best chance to meet this high, almost unfair, standard.

Before you get started on the Eight Step Process, it's important to note it's both daunting and mundane. There's no getting around that fact. The only thing that makes this slow and methodical work bearable is it will take a patchwork of ideas, partial and/or fully developed processes and produce a level of service that's well thought out and effective. Have you detected the acronym "ESP?" It ironically captures the difficulty of the task at hand. And don't forget, the Eight Step Process brings the nexus of a powerful referral business to life. It just goes to show you how fragile the nexus is and the importance of the work ahead.

The Eight Step Process utilizes a progressive approach, in that each step builds upon the previous step. It starts with the ideas and service you have in your business today. Along the way it creates a level of effective service that addresses the two timeframes of service and pounce processes. It ends with assembling it in a way that positions you and your business to be efficient. Altogether, the Eight Step Process covers the simple *evolution of service*. It takes a raw idea and processes it through a systematic approach, thereby creating a service action that can be properly and quickly repeated over and over again.

Unfortunately, Rose never went through this type of service development effort because the focus of her business was hard work leads to sales, not service leads to sales. She saw business success through herself instead of through her business. In doing so, she failed to include the *referral generating element of a business*.

In all actuality, the procedure is common sense; and over time, you won't even have to refer to it. At first the steps can be challenging only because of the work associated with them. However, if you accomplish them, you'll be on your way to elevating your business toward hurricane level by being able to answer my fifth framework question: *How do we build valuable service*? Get ready to go deep inside your current and new service with the help of the Eight Step Process.

As you do, I can't overstate the importance of the work at hand. This is the early hard work of a powerful referral business. It is this body of work that will eventually allow you to shift the burden of working hard from yourself to your business. How? You'll leverage this service experience over and over again to generate sales.

1. Your ideal service

Let's get started by tearing down the service piece of your business model. The first thing you need to do is write down *"Your ideal service."* This list should first reflect all of the ideas and/or processes (partial and fully developed) you have in your business today to serve clients and business partners or to one day serve them. Next, include all of those great ideas you read about in magazines, books, heard about in seminars, or listened to over conference calls that interest you. Add them in because you now have context to measure against. As you do, keep in mind the two distinctive timeframes of service you provide clients, what it means to have clients, your service to business partners, pounce processes, business partner service processes, and the two pentagon effects. Also, keep technology in mind. Your clients and business partners are aware of the technology around them and will be impressed to see it in some aspect of your service. By including it in some way, it allows your service to change with the times and stay modern. The inclusion of technology is even more important for agents. Why? They are highly dependent on it in the first timeframe of service. Not only that, they have an added requirement placed upon them in the first timeframe of service, in that they have to build two distinct levels of service—one for buyers and the other for sellers.

It's not important at this time to distinguish between ideas and processes. At this point it's nothing more than a brainstorming session. This is your chance to write down your ideal level of service. And what exactly is the realm of ideal service? You should consider the gamut of service—from personal to value. For example, personal service could be a birthday card, a thoughtful handwritten note, some type of gift, a couple of movie passes, a handy mailing, etc.; while value service items could be a profession-oriented newsletter, a profession update mailing, or technical service above and beyond that required of your profession (annual transaction review).

There will be time later to break down what's an idea and what's a process. Don't assume you will think of everything at one sitting. Always have a pen and paper nearby, for ideas and processes may pop into your head at various times throughout the day and in the places you least expect. Once you have taken this first easy step, it's time to refine the list by breaking it down.

2. Identify each item as an idea or a process

Break down "Your ideal service" list by identifying each item as either an idea or a process. An idea is just that—an idea that hasn't been developed in any way. It may be something you have wanted to do for a while but just never took any action on, or it could be something you heard about in a seminar, or read about in a magazine or a book. A process is an idea that has been partially or fully developed. Once you've done this, you'll have two lists: ideas and processes.

Next, you need to identify your fully developed processes and set them aside in their own list. A fully developed process is something that's being done now, on a routine basis, because everything is pre-built and pre-positioned. The litmus test of a fully developed process is it allows you, or even a new person you hire, to accomplish the action with ease and without guidance. We will address these processes later in step 4 because it's assumed they add value to your business, and no further action is required at this time. If you're unsure of their value, then don't separate them.

Don't be disappointed if your idea list is quite a bit longer than your process list; that's normal and to be expected.

3. Review each idea and process for value

Now it's time to individually review each idea and process regarding their value to your business. It is important to do this now, so when you get into the later steps, you're only working on the ones you have determined are of real value to current and future clients and business partners. Give special consideration to those ideas and/or processes that possess a unique quality. They could be the gems in your business that separate you from your competitors. Also, give special consideration to the ones that touch you emotionally. You'll see the importance of this later.

For each service idea or process ask, "If implemented, would it make a difference to the clients and/or business partners who interface with my business?" If the answer is no, remove it from your list. However, if the answer is yes, ask, "Is the time, effort, and/or money needed to fully develop it worth the value it will bring to my business?" Once again, if the answer is no, scratch it from your list.

For each pounce idea or process ask, "Is this a common occurrence in my business?" If the answer is no, remove it from your list. However, if the answer is yes, then ask, "Is the time, effort, and/or money needed to fully develop it worth the value it will bring to my business?" Once again, if the answer is no, scratch it from your list.

For just a brief moment, consider the thought process at work behind the simple two-question scenario above. The first question merely asks your opinion, while the second one makes you consider the consequences of it. Together, they give you *the best chance* to build a level of sensible service for your current and prospective clients and business partners.

And that exposes the vulnerability of this step. There is no right or wrong answer; there's only your opinion. Strong ESP would be helpful here. With that said, can you see the uninhibited creativity of framework? You are creating a level of service that reflects your individualism by picking and choosing from anything in the marketplace or by creating everything from scratch. The other added flexibility feature of framework is you can tailor portions of your service to address specific people demographics you desire in your business. It is through the development of pounce and service processes that you can attract and connect, as appropriate, predetermined profiled clients and business partners.

You've now sanitized your idea and process lists for value and are ready to start assigning them to the various groups of people you serve.

4. Assign each idea or process to a group(s)

You have identified every idea and process you feel is important to providing a high level of service to the clients and business partners who interface with your business and to those who may. Now it's time to appoint each idea and process to a specific group or groups, depending on its appeal. Identify your groups and write them down. Your primary groups would be clients and business partners. Your business, like ours, should include different groups of professional business partners who serve your clients likely needs. For this exercise, Rose and I would break down our business partner groups into agents, financial planners, CPA's, and insurance agents. Our goal is to provide a level of service to each group. Some of our processes will impact them all, while some will be specifically targeted to only one. As you can imagine, some are easier to serve than others.

Begin this step by writing down your various group headings. Then under each one of them write down the three subheadings of "first timeframe" (as applicable), "second timeframe," and "pounce." Next, assign each idea or process to a group(s) under the appropriate subheading, and don't forget to do the same for the fully developed processes if you set any of them aside in step 2.

Before going any further, it's time to reflect. Take a moment and look at what's in each group, under each subheading. Focus your attention on the ideas and/or processes that depicted your business before you started this process. That was your level of service for each group you served. It's a personal moment that's quite revealing. Maybe you were making a difference with your service or maybe you weren't. What focus was revealed—generating referrals or creating leads? What did you value—clients or transactions? And what type of business was revealed?

After you complete the above actions, you will see for the first time whether you're providing (fully developed processes), working to provide (partial processes), or thinking about providing (ideas) a robust level of service for each identified group. You'll see where you are strong and where you are weak.

Look at the groups again and at the items you have associated with them. As you look at the level of service, focus on each subheading individually. Because the first timeframe of service is so short, think about each item in context to one another. For the second timeframe of service, you need to think about each item from the standpoint of: am I doing this daily, weekly, monthly, quarterly, semiannually, or annually?

Looking at each timeframe from these perspectives will tell you if your service is balanced. It's important to do because you want your service and your name to be in front of people throughout each timeframe of service. There's nothing worse than doing multiple things and having them all jumbled together on top of each other in a very short time period.

And don't forget, buried within your client service are business partner service processes. Make sure that you have included them in your service (primarily in the second timeframe) to where your business is positioned to actively try to generate referrals for all of your business partners. And just like service processes, make sure they're balanced to where they professionally keep your business partners in front of your clients throughout the year.

If you have weakness under a certain subheading, go back to step 1 and refocus your energy to come up with new ideas you can turn into processes. Then complete the remainder of the steps. On the other hand, if your level of service is too strong under a certain subheading, consider removing some ideas or processes to bring it in line with what you feel is the appropriate level of service. As you will see, you can use step 5 to assist you in retaining the most valuable items.

Now take the time to look at your pounce processes. You should have at least one for each group so you have a predetermined plan-of-attack to add people from the group to your business. Doing so means you're just as thoughtful and respectful of prospective business as you are about established business. Because of their diversity, pounce processes can be executed at any time, for any length of time. There's no rule about them other than to have them so you can readily expand your business into the group when common opportunities unique to your business present themselves.

You must make certain of a couple important things before proceeding on to the next step. First, each group should have a level of service that includes service processes and pounce process(es). By doing so, you're serving current clients and business partners while being equally prepared to convert prospective ones as well. Second, the level of service you identify here will carry an inordinate amount of weight in eventually helping you build a powerful referral business. Make sure your service has a touch of uniqueness and provides real value. It definitely needs to slant more toward value than personal touch. Personal is nice, but value makes more of a difference and will help drive business in the door.

By choosing value over personal touch, you start creating the all important business persona. You present yourself as a professional businessperson with a level of service that'll genuinely make a difference. You must select this path if you want people to respect you and take your business seriously. If your service is weak in any area, you need to return to step 1 and rerun the process to correct the deficiency.

For future reference, maintain a computer file that identifies all of your groups with their fully developed processes. You'll see the importance of doing this later.

5. **Prioritize the ideas and processes for each subheading**

When prioritizing each subheading list, consider putting at the top those value items that are easiest to do. Focusing first on value will bring credibility to your business. As a secondary consideration, prioritize each subheading based on speed and cost factors. What can you do quickly and inexpensively that will cause immediate, positive impact to clients and business partners? It's important to take some time here because this is where your initial effort will occur, and it will define your level of service until all of your processes are put in place. When you're done, you should have prioritized subheadings from most to least important for each group. If your service is too strong within a subheading, cut from the bottom up.

Let's look at what you have created up to this point. You have identified all of your ideas and processes, reviewed them for value, and prioritized them by subheading within each group. You know what you need to work on first. Slowly but surely, you are starting to get your arms around the service portion of your business model. Don't expect the picture to be pretty at this time. You're in the early stages of building a hurricane business.

6. What I need to do

Now the hard work begins, determining the administrative portion of your service. Don't be misled by the tedious word, "administrative." The administrative portion of your business functions just like the oil in your car. Without it, your business will operate poorly before eventually breaking down altogether.

For each idea and partial process, under each subheading, write down *"What I need to do"* and get ready to make your longest, most in-depth list. This is going to take some time and serious thinking. For each one, ask yourself what you need to do to bring it to full maturation. What you're doing is identifying the specific actions you must accomplish to build each idea and partial process into a fully developed process. Remember the goal of a fully developed process, it allows you, or even a new person you hire, to carry out the action with ease and without guidance.

As you conduct this step, keep in mind that with such a broad range of processes, there is a corresponding range of generic elements that might be conducive to helping you create a fully developed process. This is definitely question and answer time.

The myriad of questions you face will be on multiple levels. The first level will be what can you pre-build and then pre-position. Some of the more obvious questions you might ask yourself here are: What can I pre-write (like letters, notes, emails, or scripts)? Do I create something (like a package to be mailed, a presentation to be given, a flyer to be handed out/emailed, or a questionnaire/survey to be filled out)? The second level will be along the lines of what can you build to direct and document the work being performed. Some of the more common questions you might ask yourself here are: Should I create a form? Do I need a tracking sheet? Should I build a visual board? Should I write a checklist and so forth. And a third level of questions might be along the lines of what can you or someone else develop (website, social networking accounts, various types of videos, etc.).

And here is a sampling of some other questions that could be asked to further drill down on all levels: Do I have to mail or email something? Do I need to print or copy something? Should I make a telephone call and if so, when or how often, and what do I say? Do I need to make a database entry and if so, when and what? How frequently should I do it? Should I schedule a day and time for this to be done? Do I need a meeting? Can I do it myself, or should I have someone else do it? Do I need to order something? Do I need to deliver something? Who will do the technical development work? Who will maintain and/or update it? Do I need to purchase some type of supplies? Do I require some level of training to conduct the activity? The questions can go on and on.

The critical importance of asking the questions above, and others that you can think of, will determine how systematized your business will be through processes. The excellence is always in the small details. By paying attention to them, you'll ensure a level of standardized excellence throughout your service.

And remember, checklists or forms are powerful business tools and a wonderful thing to have as part of a process because they allow you or somebody else to do sequence work. They also have a flexibility feature, in that you can bundle multiple processes within one checklist or form to tie together related service. But more than that, you can seamlessly intertwine unique and required technical service together.

Rose and I have done exactly that in our business. We bundled together on one checklist our unique and required technical service from the time we meet clients until the closing of their home loan. Within that checklist we account for the first timeframe of service and our required technical service by specifying database entries, mailing loan forms, making service-related telephone calls, sending letters, writing notes, locking an interest rate, ordering an appraisal and so on. If you prefer, a tracking sheet or board is just as efficient and can accomplish the identical thing by producing a visual picture. In our business, we use a checklist and a visual board.

When you've completed this step, you should have a list of specific actions for each idea and partial process under each subheading. Organize each list in sequential order so your work flows in an orderly method. By doing so, you will develop your ideas and partial processes in an efficient manner and may be able to make them a part of your business even though they're not yet fully developed.

The amount of work remaining for each idea and partial process should now be clear. More than likely it's quite a bit, but don't get discouraged in the slightest way from the amount of work you now face. Take some comfort in knowing that at least you're aware of the early hard work remaining to shift the burden of working hard from yourself to your business. You could just work hard with no chance of shifting the burden. A hurricane business takes time to build just like a real hurricane takes time to strengthen to full force.

7. Start on the work associated with each idea/partial process

It's time to get started on the work associated with each idea and partial process. The work you accomplish here will be long, but it'll eventually produce a high level of service that makes a difference to the people who interface with your business and to those who may. Remember to stay focused on the value items. You're in direct competition with your competitors, and you can only win with value. It's important to be genial; it's even more important to provide value.

It's paramount to make time available each and every day and slowly start nipping away at your specific action item lists. This will involve some long hours, maybe even lots and lots of hours. Trust me when I tell you that at this point you'll need to summon all of your inner strength and willpower to get you through this tedious, mentally challenging work. It's definitely roll up your sleeves time. This is the heavy lifting portion of your effort. This is where the rubber meets the road.

This is also a defining and pivotal moment for you and your business, for you are standing at the crossroads of either conducting transactional business or building a referral-based business. You are at the *determining business premise moment.* Will you press on and build a level of service that leads to sales, or will you decide not to go on and settle for your hard work creating sales? To ascertain what you'll do, just ask yourself this one simple question: "Is it worth it to you?" Before you answer that question, let me put a different perspective on the situation at hand.

On the day you joined the service industry, it provided nuggets of opportunity through the database of people you knew. In all likelihood that database has since grown. Deep within that group of people and the people yet to come are referral riches beyond your wildest dreams. It's potentially better than the greatest gold mine ever discovered, for it can be an inexhaustible source of income. The perplexing question is, "What needs to be done to continuously tap into it?" You may find a referral or two here and there, but the real referral wealth is buried deep inside of the people. The only way to successfully mine it is through the valuable service you provide. There is no other way. That's the gravity of the situation facing you and why you're doing the Eight Step Process.

Now, is it worth it to you? Before answering, remember, *adversity introduces you to yourself.* For that extra spark and determination you'll need, tap into your discipline by following through and don't stop until you have developed every idea and partial process into a fully developed process. When you do, not only do your traits serve the people who interface with your business, they serve you as well. They really do make a difference in your business and on multiple levels.

8. Build a continuity binder

Now that you have processes in place, it's time to assemble them in a *continuity binder.* Processes are not considered fully developed until they're in your continuity binder. Such a binder is a vital business tool because it does just what it suggests, it brings continuity to your business. This continuity is even more important if you decide to form a team around you. In reality, it's nothing more than a reflection of the service you have built in your business. People who read it will have a clear understanding of your service and be able to step in and immediately be a contributing member.

At a minimum, your continuity binder should contain all of your processes, which are hopefully based in either a checklist, form, or tracking sheet, when possible. For those processes that are not, a short informative narrative should accompany them. The narrative should discuss the purpose of the process, just like a checklist's entering argument does. And lastly, for each applicable process, you can either attach all of the pre-built supporting documentation (letters, notes, emails, scripts, surveys, questionnaires, packages, presentations, flyers, etc.), or you can identify their electronic or physical location. Whichever way creates the most efficiency and convenience for you is correct.

For simplicity sake, organize the continuity binder in a manner that mirrors your business. For example, if you have five different groups of people you're serving, have a section for each group in your binder. If certain business groups are receiving the same service, then group them together under one section. Organize the information by service processes (first and second timeframe) and then by pounce process(es). By doing so, you'll recognize the natural order of your business—serve the people connected to it while being ready to convince new people.

Three other items should be a part of your continuity binder. The first item is your procedures that are in *direct support* of your service. The point being, your continuity binder needs to be comprehensive enough to where you can deliver and support your service without having to look elsewhere. The second item is both your preparatory and execution goals. They will be defined and discussed later. And the last item (if you have a team) is your policies. Policies are written guidelines that ensure rational team decision-making. They will empower each team member with the breadth of authority you deem appropriate. They'll be discussed in-depth much later on.

Building a continuity binder adds standardization and a high level of organization to your business. You'll always know what you should be doing now and what you need to do next. The same rule applies to the people you turn your business over to when you're out of the office for an extended period of time.

Its true worth will be realized if you decide to build a team or if you have a team and its makeup changes, and the last thing you have time for is extensive training, questions, and confusion from a new member. You can't stop your business to deal with this inefficiency, but your business will stop if you're inefficient.

This step is important for one other reason. If you do decide to build a team around you, it drastically reduces your business oversight responsibilities, allowing you to choose between generating more business or freedom for other activities that can bring balance and joy to your life. Much later on in this book, the team concept and its development will be discussed in-depth.

With a continuity binder, your business is as close to auto pilot as it can get. Probably its most important aspect is it positions your business to grow without growing pains. Your business is now situated to achieve scale—the first two major components are in place.

The importance of taking the time to complete the Eight Step Process is you create the *unique magnetic point* of a powerful referral business. And no, it's not your service. Instead, it's the end result of your service. The unique magnetic point of a powerful referral business is YOU HAVE CLIENTS! It's the number one thing your business partners want you to send them. Nothing else is a stronger attractor. And nothing else will give you a greater sense of dignity.

The Eight Step Process is probably not as daunting an undertaking as it seems. The chances of you building service and pounce processes from scratch are minimal because of all the pre-processed ones in the marketplace today. No matter which way you do it—new ideas with no development, partial processes with little or significant development, or fully developed processes—the procedure is flexible enough to handle any situation. In each case, the end product will be fully developed service or pounce processes that are completely integrated into your personalized service. The procedure has merit, regardless of the ideas or maturity of the processes.

With that said, it's prudent to take advantage of pre-built service and pounce ideas when you can. Why? The most cumbersome activity you will do in your business is building your total service effort. It's such a burdensome assignment that for some business people it can actually cause them to turn away from building a referral-based business.

Yet another challenge associated with service is the fact that so much of it today is based on a technology backbone—the development of websites, blogs, virtual videos, personal videos, web casts, webinars, interactive software applications, the utilization of social networking sites, etc. It's leading edge service application that both marvels and provides unparallel convenience for the people (established and prospective business) who interface with it. The overall impact is technology is both reinventing some old ways of service and introducing new applications. Unfortunately, some of its development is far beyond common sense thinking and more like rocket science. This technological barrier will in all likelihood require you to depend on outside professionals to help you effectively integrate it into your business. If you take this path, you'll probably require some level of complementary training as well.

This situation brings to light that certain aspects of your business will be beyond your intellectual capability. By quickly recognizing and then willingly accepting your personal limitations in these various areas, you can prevent yourself from unnecessarily getting bogged down in trying to develop and/or learn things that are better left in the hands of experienced professionals. The business significance of taking this action (depending on others) is twofold: where technology makes you efficient, it makes your business effective. As you'll see shortly, there are two other times in your business when you will most likely need to reach out and briefly depend on an outside expert to help you with a technology challenge.

Let's move on from discussing the many aspects of service and how to develop it by shifting our focus to yet another part of a powerful referral business framework that's just as important.

Why Isn't Your Hurricane Rotating?

Just thinking...
To be on the verge is exciting, to be there is rewarding. To know how to get there is the joy of it all.

YOU HAVE DONE EVERYTHING YOU were supposed to do. You adopted the six traits of a powerful referral business, and you completed the Eight Step Process and now have fully developed service processes and business partner service processes ready to make a difference to clients and business partners. You even know what you hope and expect of clients and business partners. So why isn't your hurricane rotating? What you have done is significant, but there's much more to be done. All of your hard work up to this point has simply *poised* your business for success. The two essentials are in place, and now it's time to add the final ingredients. For extra good measure, you even have pounce processes at the ready to convince prospective clients and business partners.

A real hurricane is a very complex weather phenomenon. Only on the rarest occasion, and under the ideal situation, will it develop. There are many things that go into making a hurricane, and it must have all of them to become one. Remove something and it weakens. It's a powerful yet so vulnerable force. The same is true for a powerful referral business.

Do you remember what I said earlier about a cloud formation? It represents your traits, fully developed service processes, and the strategies employed to execute your business. What you have done up to this point is assemble an imposing mass of clouds reflective of your traits and fully developed service processes that's starting to look like a hurricane. It's not a hurricane yet, because the strategies employed to execute your business, the third and final major component of a leverage business model, are missing. Without them you have a cloudy day, but with them you have the perfect business storm. We are ready to answer my sixth framework question: *How do we best execute what we have built?*

The answers to that question are in the next ten *turning point chapters.* Within each chapter are simple but powerful why-you-must-do-it thoughts. The focus is on the why, for it provides the influential answers necessary to fully embrace the activity. When you accomplish all of the activities, you naturally embrace the six traits you adopted and the service you built. That's the dynamic created when you execute your business—traits, service, and turning points all come together and work in harmony as one. The framework is now starting to interlock and become interdependent.

Most of the turning points will be quite familiar to you, just like the six traits were. You may already be executing some of them. The challenge you face will be executing them all well, on a routine basis. *And when you execute them well, you have systematized your business once again.* Where the first time it was with processes, this time it's with execution.

The turning points are an extensive assortment of fundamental business practices that are intended to achieve a single purpose—to ensure an uninterrupted continuation of your business journey. The ten turning points are to business model development what favorable weather conditions are to helping a storm grow into a hurricane. Just as favorable weather conditions allow a storm to reach its full force, turning points allow you to reach your full potential as a businessperson. They truly are the final ingredients to achieving business success commensurate with your talent.

Don't get the wrong impression about turning points. They are not based on a slow winding turn; they are a stop and a hard right-way turn. As you begin to incorporate them into your business, but before you finish, you will reach the *tipping point.* The criticality of the tipping point is once you reach it you don't want to turn back because of what it offers. In short, you're on the other side. It's like getting the secret handshake as you are welcomed into the referral club. I can't tell you exactly when it'll occur because it's a personal moment that is unique to the individual. I can tell you that when you reach it, you'll know it.

All of a sudden, what you're doing will make perfect sense; you will believe in it and commit to it, knowing it is the only way to do business. You will have transitioned from a reactive to a proactive businessperson. You're no longer depending on surges for success. At this moment, it will be as if you have been swept up into your storm as it begins to slowly circulate for the first time. You are no longer building it alone—it's building around you. You have created a *synergy* between your talent and leverage business model, and for the first time, your business is starting to work for you. It's a powerful moment when you reach it and realize it. It's a very exciting time in your business, for you have finally figured *it* out. There's no doubt in your mind; you're now on your way. At last, the seminal moment is behind you.

Just because you have reached and passed your personal tipping point doesn't mean you have finished with the turning points or that your business has become a hurricane. There's still work to be done with them, and every one is important in varying degrees. Failure to do one means you may miss the opportunity to create the *by-product* of a powerful referral business that will finally give your hurricane its rotation and subsequent powerful strength—making it roar ahead. *Don't look ahead; the by-product is the second suspenseful moment in the book!*

As you incorporate the ten turning points and build your business, there will be many struggles along the way. Don't be surprised if they get to the point where they seem almost impossible to overcome. If they do, it is comparable to facing the *eye wall* of a hurricane. From a hurricane standpoint, that is where the winds are the strongest. What that means for you and your business is a very difficult and challenging period of business model development.

For example, you may come to the conclusion it was easier to build the service processes than to pull it all together and execute it smoothly. That's what happened to Rose and me in our business model development. I was building service processes faster than we could properly execute them and faster than Rose could change as a businesswoman. It didn't take long for us to realize that transitioning from a transactional to a powerful referral business was a bigger adjustment than we anticipated. We had to not only physically change our business, but we had to change our minds as well. We had hit the eye wall in our business.

It may appear at first that this formidable eye wall phenomenon is impossible to penetrate. IT'S NOT! Now, you have to figuratively lean into your business and keep your head down to come through it. It's almost as if a teetering-effect has entered your business, and you're literally struggling for a successful transition from a transactional to a powerful referral business. Whatever you do, don't quit. A fighting spirit with a can do attitude will eventually win the day. Therefore, when you come up against the frustration of struggling to implement what you have built within a normal business day and/or change your mindset, just realize it's a natural occurrence, and most importantly, a positive sign of progress.

You might feel overwhelmed at the thought of executing a powerful referral business. Don't let that thought or the potential oncoming eye wall phenomenon deter you. You are more prepared for the work ahead than you realize, for the execution of a powerful referral business has its roots in youth. Each turning point has a youthful quality that provides a direct linkage back to a happy or important time in your past. You have probably already experienced each one in some way. In all likelihood, some were certainly more enjoyable than others, but you made it through all of them. The reason that's important is the execution of a powerful referral business is in many ways just a continuum of what was once familiar or pleasurable many years ago. It's almost as though activities of yesteryear reconnecting with the adult world of today, in that you are re-experiencing a past experience. What that actually means is anyone can do it if they really want too.

Along with that, here's the underlying dynamic at work that will eventually allow you to build a powerful referral business. The one word answer is *"repetition."* The execution of a business is a set of *predetermined repetitive actions* meant to produce specific results. The phrase, business execution, is just a metaphor for the word—practice. You will do the same activities over and over again, and in due time, you will become highly skilled at each and every one of them. You will move from doing something new and uncomfortable to doing something natural and comfortable. With that said, don't overlook the fact that this also explains why it can be so difficult to change as a businessperson, especially if you have been conducting business in a certain way for a long time. That is exactly what happened to Rose; the legacy of being a transactional businesswoman for several years functioned as the resistance to her business transition effort. Even though she truly wanted to change, it was still a long, hard struggle for her.

Let's move on to the ten turning point chapters of which one will be your personal tipping point and will come to pass before you create the by-product of a powerful referral business. It is through the turning points you will see the body of *execution work* required to build a powerful referral business. As you read them, you'll continue to see Rose's transactional business tendencies, along with the positive changes she has recently made in her business.

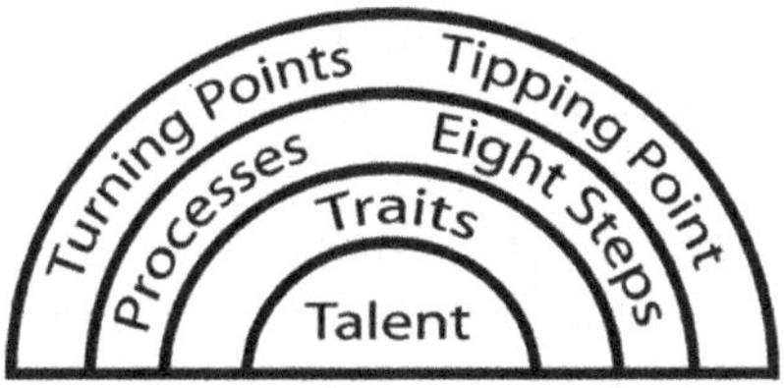

The Passion Moment

A time past...
Did you ever have something special you shared with people and when you did, they were appreciative toward you?

BEFORE YOU BEGIN TO EXECUTE your business, you have to first give some thought to what successful execution is based on. The apparent answer is the tangible answer—your actions. It seems like the right answer just by the amount of work you will perform. But this is one time when volume of work by itself will not carry the day. Such volume of work must be complemented by an intangible, which brings us to the not-so-obvious answer, and the correct answer. It is an intangible that allows your actions to generate business. And the intangible has nothing to do with you and everything to do with your clients and business partners. Therein is the underlying reason why successfully executing your business is so hard.

The intangible you have to create is the distinguishing characteristic between a transactional and referral-based business. Where a transactional business is predominately conducted with actions, a referral-based business is conducted with actions that create *emotion*. The significance of the difference is one business is always hurriedly moving on to *look* for the next person, while the other is *seeing* the same people over and over again. And how do actions create emotion—by delivering valuable service. Once again, another simple equation of success, but this time the equation is *actions that deliver valuable service leads to creating emotion.*

And that's what a powerful referral business is—an emotional way of business. Why emotion? There's no greater force that genuinely moves people more than emotion. When people feel something for you, they will do something for you. It's the in-kind way of doing business.

On the contrary, when you're at the clear skies or tropical depression level, you really have nothing of much value, outside of the technical requirements of your profession and your personal attributes, to offer people who are interfacing with your business. Sadly, that was Rose's business for so many years.

With that said, it's important to acknowledge that Rose created emotion in clients. She received several heartfelt client thank you cards over the years. One of those cards was from a church janitor who had saved his money for years so he could buy a home for his children in a well-respected school district. Inside of his card was a gracious note along with a $50 gift. I have never seen Rose more touched. She told him that she couldn't possibly accept the gift, but he insisted. As a compromise, she donated it to his church, along with a matching $50 gift. He was so full of emotion (ready to support her), but like so many others before him, he was quickly gone. Why did it occur? Rose's business wasn't built to capitalize on this type of client emotion; i.e., she didn't have a continuing service experience (second timeframe of service) that could build upon this initial showing of emotion. Sad to say, clients were willing; her business wasn't. Ouch! The negative business outcome was this highly hoped-for emotional client reaction in the first timeframe of service fizzled into a fireworks moment...a *burst* of emotion and then poof! That's not the type of client emotion occurring in a powerful referral business. Such a business creates an *ongoing* emotional feeling, resulting in repeat business and client referrals.

Rose's business actions had her deeply mired in a transactional business—a business of actions (with periodic episodes of inconsequential client emotion). In the end, she was just one more victim of the transactional business glass-ceiling of *"I'm just too busy."*

The problem with always being busy is it perpetuates *you* always being busy. It keeps you in an unending business loop of just creating business you can't break free of, for you're always busy. You'll see shortly the business loop you do need to create in your business. When you're busy, and not your business, you have a poorly developed business model around your talent. The reason being is you haven't shifted the burden of working hard from yourself to your business. You have only leveraged yourself, not your business. You're on the wrong side of the dichotomy of a business.

The only certainty in your business is the uncertainty that is created. You have replaced the pleasure of serving your clients and their likely needs, and their referrals over and over again, with the high anxiety of wondering when business partners (or advertising or something else besides clients) is going to bring you the next transaction. You are, in essence, alone in your business, just waiting for something to happen through yourself or other means outside of your control. I watched Rose face this type of lonely business situation many times in her transactional business.

Here's another bottom line thought—don't create business, create emotion. When you create business, you're working hard. And when you create emotion, your business is working hard.

Take an even closer look at a poorly developed business model and you'll notice it predisposes the conversations of a business in a way that causes loss of control. There's yet another struggle going on in business. Where the first struggle was between clients and business partners, this one is between you and clients. The struggle this time is, *"Who will control the conversation?"* When you sit down with clients to help them, each of you has your own best interest at heart. The clients' best interest is their money, while your best interest is also their money (you do need to be paid for your professional services). Both of you value the same thing. So how do you successfully defuse such a natural confrontation and get them to gladly hand over their money to you? You have to keep control of the conversation by replacing their value with your value. You right away provide your valuable service. You'll see later how Rose has taken control of the conversation in her business.

If you don't recognize and meet this replacement need immediately, the control of the conversation reverts to clients, and they will naturally see what any person would see—cost. And when they see cost, you will see close scrutiny—something transactional business people are quite familiar with. Business people who routinely fall victim to this scenario may have fallen victim to the following.

Why do so many people struggle in the service industry? There are many different ways to answer that question, but I believe the telling answer is at the moment they decided to join. For example, when people make the decision to become mortgage loan officers or agents, their first thought might be to say, "I'm in the mortgage lending or real estate industry." NO THEY'RE NOT! That statement couldn't be further from the truth. The truth is they're loan officers or agents in the *Referral-Based Service Industry*.

I think that's why many individuals struggle and don't make it. They fail to see that subtle but distinctive point, and therefore, their mindset is dead wrong from day one. Failure to recognize the industry one has joined can only lead to misguided effort. Without even knowing it, from day one, their small thinking limited them to small results. OUCH! So how do you know for certain which industry to claim as your own? Ask yourself this one question: "Do you work harder before or after the business transaction is completed?" Simple question, telling answer. It's almost a silly question to ask because it's only natural to think one would work hardest where the rewards are the greatest.

So what's your industry? You're in the Referral-Based Service Industry. It's important to make that affirmation to yourself. Why? Once you acknowledge it as your industry, it's only natural for you to then build your business to be successful in it. And just like you, your business partners need to make the same statement to themselves. Successful partnerships are based on both partners being in the Referral-Based Service Industry. Both of you have chosen the psychology of clients over business partners (or advertising or anything else).

There's an interesting insight to be familiar with when discussing the Referral-Based Service Industry. It is an industry that requires both referral-based and transactional business people. Let me put it in plain words. Where referral-based business people help clients with a transaction and then connect them to their business through service, transactional business people conduct customer transactions and then quickly move on. This contrasting business dynamic gives rise to a question all business people face: "Will they be a member of the Referral-Based Service Industry, or will they be an enabler of the industry?" Where referral-based business people bring value to the clients in their business, transactional business people bring value to a whole industry. In other words, never look down on transactional business people, for it is they who make the Referral-Based Service Industry possible.

I know over her career Rose has been on both sides of the Referral-Based Service Industry. For many years she was an enabler and most recently a proud member. As a past enabler of the industry, she enriched many other loan officers who subsequently helped her past customers. Those days are long gone. Nowadays, she is in the business of enriching herself by connecting clients to her business through service that makes a difference. In fact, Rose now tells people she is a businesswoman in the Referral-Based Service Industry who just happens to professionally advise clients about mortgages. Every time I hear her say that I see an empowered businesswoman. Rose doesn't know it, but this is my *proud husband moment.* I know all that it took to be able to say those words with conviction.

Somewhere along the way you made a career decision to enter the Referral-Based Service Industry. Many people shy away from it because they don't like the thought of bearing so much responsibility for their own business success. NOT YOU! Just the fact you're in it says a great deal about you as a person. Why did you join? Maybe because there's only one thing that could hold you back, or it might have been the allure of having total control of your journey. You could be an excellent test-taker and know all too well there's not a tougher business test to pass than making it in the Referral-Based Service Industry. Then again, maybe you're the type of person who enjoys walking on a tightrope high above the ground with no safety net underneath. Or just maybe, you don't like ceilings.

No matter the reason, you're here and you now base your livelihood on that industry. You owe it to yourself and the profession you entered to take the time and make the effort to embody the traits, build the service processes, and employ the execution strategies necessary that will help you realize your full potential and achieve sustained business success. When you do, you not only start creating emotion, you start valuing your business.

To value your business means to make it the best it can be for both you and the people who interface with it. The *Value Your Business Concept* is not one-dimensional but, rather, multi-dimensional. The concept crisscrosses your business by affecting *you, how you do things, your business partners, and your service.* Here's how.

Become a good listener

You must be a good listener. Unfortunately, listening is a skill that tends to get overlooked or underutilized, even though it can reveal personal insights that provide the opportunity to add tremendous value. The information you may glean is invaluable, and it will help you professionally and personally serve people who interface with your business—an unbeatable combination.

As a good listener, you have a written or mental list of questions ready to ask, and you meticulously record the information for immediate or later use. By being a good listener, you send an early signal to clients, business partners, and prospective contacts that you respect them, value their needs, and are interested in them. The real advantage of doing business like this is you can tailor your comments to what they said, not what you want to say. You're not pitching; you're responding. The time spent together is focused on them, not you.

Conducting business in this fashion confirms you follow this simple rule: *don't impress with your knowledge, impress with your knowledge of them.* It's a subtle but powerful distinction that allows you to connect on a personal level with people. Something that's not possible with business people who are inclined to do all the talking. You respect the elementary rule of look, listen, and learn. A timeless rule, for it has great relevance to both children and adults.

And here's the somewhat veiled value of being a good listener. You may well pick up on casual client comments that'll allow you to easily and professionally insert your business partners into the conversation in a meaningful and helpful way. When you're able to effectively do it, on a routine basis, *your listening skill is serving as a business partner service process.*

Being a good listener not only helps you better serve your clients, it can also help you better serve the referral needs of all your business partners.

The nuance factor

Another way to add value to your business is to keep a sharp eye out for the *nuance factor* in it. When you do, it will surely affect *how you do things.* Savvy business people pay attention to, pick up on, and deftly act on nuances. They clearly understand that the shades of gray world is where little changes to something said or done can have significant business impact. Sometimes so significant they can make-or-break a business.

For now, here's an example of a nuance that can impact your business. If a business partner has somebody they want to refer to you, which way do you think is the most reliable? Hand that person your business card and tell him to call you, or take his name and number and have you call him? Only one way guarantees a contact. It's a nuance that can have a dramatic impact over time.

By their nature, nuances appear to be small things that don't really matter, but that couldn't be further from the truth. Pay attention to the nuance factor in your business. It's everywhere, and it's impacting you and your business. The great thing about recognizing it is you can easily control it and turn it to your advantage. You will see other examples of nuances and how Rose is adeptly using them to help her in her business.

Hand-off and hand-back

It's important for you to personally value your business. When you do, you will expect *your business partners* to do the same for their business. It's only natural you would expect the same from them as you would from yourself. This is an important concept to embrace because your business partners are an extension of you.

This will make sense every time one of your clients asks you to refer them to a business partner to serve a likely need with which you can't personally help them. When this happens, and it will, you need to have complete confidence the business partner will provide the same level of service (two timeframes) that you do. If you overlook this important detail, you risk jeopardizing your good standing with clients when and if they receive poor service or a level of service that's not compatible with yours.

When you hand-off a client to a business partner, you should track the status of the service through a minimum of three contacts. The first contact should be from you to the partner informing him of the referral. This is by far the best call you'll make to a business partner, so don't miss even one. Remember, this is the cornerstone of The Business Partner Pentagon Effect. By calling, you take ownership of the referral and have the opportunity to share information that will help facilitate a successful transaction.

The second contact should be from the partner to you, summarizing how the transaction went with your client. This telephone call is nothing more than a professional courtesy. You *handed-off* a portion of your business to him, and now he's *handing-it-back* to you with feedback.

The third contact should be from you to your client, following up to ensure her needs were promptly and professionally served. It shows genuine interest in her well-being on your part and keeps the door wide open for her to utilize your other business partners in the future. Regardless of the feedback she provides (positive or negative), share it with the business partner. When you do, you're complying with another tenet of The Business Partner Pentagon Effect. What the client says will determine if you have any follow-on action. And what are the words you expect her to say, "Thank you for referring me to...!" Such a simple comment unquestionably confirms you have the right business partner.

When you choose to conduct business like this with your partners, you recognize the valuable service you provide to clients is not wholly due to you but, rather, by you and other professionals that you carefully selected. So step up and value your business first and then demand that every business partner who works with you do the same. Can you see the value of a business partner interview?

Value your service

There's an underlying reason why the Value Your Business Concept is in the first turning point chapter. It has a unique feature, in that it can turn you back around to fix something before you go ahead. What's the thing you can fix—*your service.*

Before going any further, you truly do have to value your service—it's not enough to just say it. In fact, it's not even enough to try to convince yourself of it. You truly do have to believe it. This is an honest moment, a personal moment, an emotional moment, and an incredibly important concept. If you don't value your service, it will always lack substance, and you will lack passion.

To really understand and appreciate the impact of that last sentence, a little bit of analysis is in order. If you were to read between the lines of the powerful referral business premise phrase, service leads to sales, here's what you would read: *your sense of valuable service leads to your passion of asking for business.*

Can you see the subjectivity of service at work? Where you may have to touch your clients 24 times a year through various means (personal and value) to feel you're providing a level of valuable service, another businessperson might only have to do it 18 times a year. Each level of service is correct as long as the personal threshold of being able to ask for business is met. *A sense of valuable service recognizes a person's individuality.*

There's a simple test to pass to determine if you value your service. It's not quantitatively-based but qualitatively-based. The test is: *when you value your service, you become selective.* This is where you give the first thought to which clients should receive your service. By doing so, you're not only facing *the third leadership moment involving people in your business*, you're taking a significant step to molding your business into something special. You are choosing to serve those clients you believe you can achieve The Pentagon Effect with—you deem they can help you across your business.

If you have to ask yourself if you value your service, trust me—you don't. It's kind of like love; if you have to ask yourself if you're in love, you're not. You value your service when you are willing to choose the clients you will serve. Just like in your personal life, you should only professionally share something of value with those whom you value. That's what gives it value and makes it special to those who receive it.

The clients you should provide your valuable service is revealed in the first timeframe of client service. It is there you will look for four positive client signs. Specifically, was there a personal connection; were they low-maintenance; did they trust your advice; and were they receptive to you leveraging your service experience to generate referrals. It's these four criteria that will give you the best indication if your time will be well spent serving them in the second timeframe. In other words, was there an emotional connection, and did they have trust and confidence in you? Both are essential to them supporting your business going forward. By quickly stepping through this simple assessment, you can enter the second timeframe of client service *hopeful* instead of wishful. If this threshold is not met, politely thank clients for the opportunity to help them with a transaction and professionally move on.

With that said, much later on in this book, you'll see how you can take a *probationary* type of action, if you so choose, with those clients who didn't quite meet the criteria it takes to enter the second timeframe of service. This shows yet another crucial flexibility feature of framework. Where the first time it was responsive to any type of market with the help of pounce processes, this time it is responsive to those clients who didn't initially measure up by providing them a second chance.

Why is it you're only selective with your service to clients and not with business partners? Business partners are selected through an interview process. With that said, it doesn't lessen their service standard. By making a difference to them through service, they can improve their business, which allows them to better serve yours. No matter which way you select someone—through service or an interview—the point of being selective is everybody brings value to your business.

Not only does your valuable service make you selective with the clients you serve, it might very well make you selective with your words when you talk about it with them. For instance, instead of reminding clients you run your business by referral, you just might positively make the following statement: "I love to provide my service." When you do, you have made the emotional connection with your service. You have also shifted the focus of your business from conducting transactions to providing service. In your mind, *you've made the decision to generate business through your service instead of through yourself.*

Selectively sharing something of value and providing it over a sustained period of time should produce the responses you hope for and expect. First, clients should respond in a positive way by allowing you to continue serving them through yourself and your business partners, and by referring you business. And second, business partners should be equally enthusiastic because your service to them is helping them either grow their business or generate new business from within their existing business.

O

It is imperative to acknowledge the important role passion plays when it comes to your pounce processes. It's different from the passion mentioned above. Where your sense of valuable service leads to your passion of asking for business, pounce processes you believe in leads to your passion of prospecting for business. The critical significance of this is when you start out in business you will primarily depend on them for beginning success (the most vulnerable time of your career). Irrespective of what type of business opportunity (established or prospective business) is at hand, passion is incredibly important, albeit for different reasons.

So if you are not there yet, especially with your client service, turn back around and add some more gripping value to your service so the rubber does meet the road. I mean it. Don't go forward. You'll be wasting your time and everybody else's time as well. Why? The primary purpose of executing your business is to simply create a client service experience that leads to repeat business and referrals for you and your business partners.

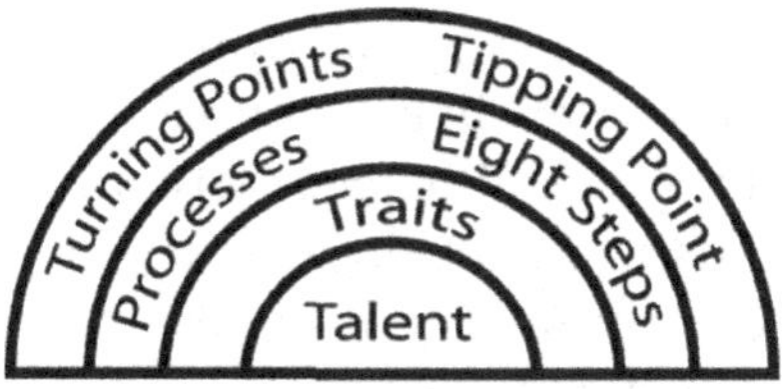

Making a Difference Begins

A time past...
The things that meant the most didn't
cost the most. It was the thought that mattered.

CONSIDER YOURSELF INCREDIBLY LUCKY IF you are in possession of something scarce. Why? Other people want it, which immediately makes it valuable. There are many things in this world that are scarce, but there is only one thing that people want the most, because it can do the most. It's so desirable it is universally recognized just by its color. When you hold it in the palm of your hand, you see power in its rawest form, meaning that it must be converted into something else before it can do some good. In the hands of the wrong people, it is eventually wasted and lost; while in the hands of the right people, it grows exponentially.

If you were to look at two common possibilities with it in a business, you would quickly realize people can either invest it or spend it. Who would have more over time? Of course the people who invest it. But why? They are investing in themselves through other people. They understand if they leverage it to help others, it will help them even more. Providing value for others first will subsequently generate more value for them. When you possess a scarce resource and then share it with others in another form, you're as close to a guarantee of success as you'll have in your business.

It's time to talk about what is probably the most sensitive issue in your business and in your life—MONEY! Money is an interesting business asset because it can either make you a transactional or a referral-based businessperson. By itself it guarantees nothing other than the fact you have it. The business determining factor is how you allocate it. Money in a business can either be *spent* or *invested.* If you spend it, you get an immediate return; and when you invest it, you get a long-term return. Just as money is an either-or choice so too is the type of businessperson you are. Interestingly enough, they are inherently linked to each other. Here's how.

If you look within a typical office, there are business people who spend money and those who invest it. The people who spend money in their business are transactional, while the people who invest it are referral-based. You know who's who. It's so noticeable it's glaring. It's kind of like a woman being pregnant, she either is or she isn't—there is no in-between.

Can spending transactional business people have success in the service industry? Sure they can, and you probably know people who are successful. This can be a tempting path to take, for the rewards can be immediate; and at first, it's easier. However, by doing so, you ignore the underlying principle of the service profession and take the short-sided view, which in time you'll probably come to regret. The easy way is not always the best way—it's true in this situation.

I remember when I was a college student I asked my professor why I should sit in class after class when I could go out and make $10 per hour driving a truck. That was a lot of money in 1980. Back in those days, I was far more interested in the now than in the future. He explained the virtues of an education and how it would serve me the rest of my life. Fortunately, I stayed in school, and in my case, he was absolutely right. I believe the same thing will happen to you when you choose the money path of investing in your business instead of spending in it.

Through the allocation of money you will figuratively choose the transactional or referral-based fork in the road. It's the most important fork in the road you'll face because it'll determine your professional future. You're really deciding if you're going into business by spending money or building a business by investing money. It is through the use of money that you'll either prospect for new business or contact your established business; i.e., market to the people outside of your business or serve the people in it. They are worlds apart within the business world. Think about the consequences of your choice—one leads to career changes, while the other leads to a long career.

Your only chance of having your business serve you the rest of your business career is to build it based on serving others. If you choose transactional business and you're successful, it's only because you're working hard—never is your business working hard. Not surprisingly then, there's glory associated with a transactional business; you get all the credit because you did it with no help from your business.

Until recently, Rose had been on this path as evidenced by her long hours with lower than expected production level. Interestingly enough, if transactional business people started to provide service, their business would only improve. Think about it—service always makes them better. Why wouldn't they do it? Think about it some more. What's easier, to serve clients already connected to a business or to constantly find new customers through various marketing means to conduct transactions? Cynical business people might conclude only one of the ways requires strong ethics. Successful business people would say, "Service cost less and pays more."

So is it worth investing money in your business? In all actuality, you can't afford not to invest in it. Here's why. Your business and your retirement are linked to the same business principle. Just as it is important to invest money on a regular basis for your retirement years, it is equally important to invest in your business. Over time the money invested for retirement will grow considerably, and the payoff will be sizeable. You will get significantly more out of it than you ever put in. It's a great concept, and it really works. Invest a little every month and let it start working for you. As time goes on, it works harder and harder so you can work less and less. The same great concept is true for your business.

You can't build a level of service that you, clients, and business partners will value without investing some money. It's going to cost money to create a level of valuable service. You should be willing to invest 10% of your earnings back into your business. By doing so, you're not buying business. Instead, you're providing a level of service that makes a difference.

Don't look at investing in your business as spending money. If you do, you may well view it as lost money. Instead, think about making money. That's what investing is about, and that's exactly what you're doing. Remember the old adage here; it takes money to make money. It didn't take very long to see why it's so important to value your service.

Just like when asking yourself where to invest money for your retirement, you need to ask the same question regarding your business. You have a finite amount of money and need to make allocation decisions that will offer you the greatest returns. So how do you best put your money to work? You put it to work in a progressive way that supports the premise of service leads to sales.

O

Clearly, all of your money should not go to just one area of your business; it needs to be spread out. Diversity matters, even when it comes to business investment. Therefore, first focus investment dollars on the people who already interface with your business. When you do, you're investing in the second timeframe of service, which is the one place you must invest to build a powerful referral business. The impact will be immediate—they know you, and you have previously determined you want to serve them by the fact you selected them.

The savvy financial reason for investing in the people connected to your business is *it's the safest investment with the greatest return.* It flips conventional investment strategy on its head. It's the perfect investment. Without a doubt, the best return on your money is with the people connected to your business. They have brought you success in the past, and they will continue to do so if you continue investing in them.

Don't be misled into thinking that investing in your business is solely based on money. Rose made that assumption and invested in her business by sending a quarterly newsletter and an anniversary card, but she didn't call her clients. She had incorrectly assumed that investing in material things was the same as investing in people. It wasn't. Money is not an answer by itself. That's why there are ten turning points instead of one. If Rose would have added more service to the abovementioned, along with investing herself in the other nine turning points, her business wouldn't have stagnated so long as it did at tropical depression level. At the end of the day, her good intentions to financially invest in her business turned into spent money. That's what tends to happen with money when you're a wannabe referral-based businessperson.

O

If investing in people connected to your business is the safest investment with the greatest return, then investing in people not yet connected to your business comes with some obvious risk. However, it is a risk worth taking only because you're doing the aforementioned. Just as your business is based on a multi-dimensional approach, your investment strategy should follow the same type of principle. Therefore, the second place to put investment dollars to work is in your pounce processes. The fact that they reflect common occurrences unique to your business and can be reused multiple times further mitigates the risk of investing in them.

When you make use of pounce processes, you either go after people you know or people you don't know. Your effort may be directed at a single person or at multiple persons at once. The bottom line on pounce processes is there's no hard-and-fast set of rules on them, and they can, therefore, greatly challenge the creative spirit. How you use them in your business really does come down to personal preference.

The importance of pounce processes as a part of your business investment is they allow you to put in place a stand alone marketing plan outside of your existing business. Any new business opportunities realized from such a plan is immediately added to your established business. It's like having a secondary business supporting your primary business. That's the only reason pounce processes are considered an investment—they are in support of your established business. If you were only doing pounce processes in your business, you would be spending money, not investing money.

The obvious other place to put investment dollars to work is in the first timeframe of client service. For most professions this is a short timeframe of service, and therefore, the opportunity to invest dollars is very limited. The exception to this rule is the real estate profession because of the nature of the process required to sell or buy a home. As a result, its view of this timeframe of service will probably have just as high or higher priority than pounce processes. Regardless of which situation applies to you, an important aspect of this timeframe of service is to impress clients by being proactive.

Your financial obligation to invest money in your business must be complemented by a commitment to follow the money. Money has a long string attached to it. You have to receive something in return. More specifically, the financial cost of your total service effort has to be far less than the realized financial gains of your sales. There has to be a clear-cut positive return on investment. Therefore, when investing money in your business, you have to be thoroughly familiar with three obvious things: what phase of service (first timeframe, second timeframe, pounce) you are investing in, exactly how much you are investing in each, and the actual return on each area of investment. By doing so, you know two very important things. First, you know the focus of your business; and second, you know what works and what doesn't and you make better money-related business decisions. The importance of this is money is the driving factor behind your service, which is the driving factor for your sales. By paying close attention to the business results of three distinctly different pots of money, you ensure a scarce resource is only put to good use: it's *impressing, impacting,* or *convincing.* Hopefully by now you can see the full spectrum of service in those three words. If you can, you're already starting to think in Framework Language.

To help you out with this sensitive aspect of your business, you should give strong consideration to a software program. Whenever you can integrate any type of technology into your business (at a fitting price) to help you better run it, you should do it. Not only will it make you more productive, it'll keep your business modern, which is vital to do in a rapidly changing technology period (like which we live). Just as the development of processes brought efficiency and speed to your business, the same is true for technology. This type of software utilization, helping you maintain "the books," is even more important because it directly aids the decision-making of the lifeblood asset of your business.

This is possibly the second technology barrier you will face in your business and, therefore, require the brief services of an experienced professional to properly exploit the software and provide you a tutorial session. The mere fact that your service has been broken out into three markedly different phases, with a distinctive meaning assigned to each of them, should allow a software setup that best organizes and accurately measures service results.

And don't forget to account for the ancillary costs that are in direct support of your service. You cannot deliver your service without these behind-the-scenes costs. Some examples here are: a sundry of supplies, printing and mailing costs, fuel costs, and maybe even equipment rental costs. As such, both your service effort and your direct support costs have to be comfortably within your means for an indefinite period of time.

The obvious side benefit of utilizing a software program to track and organize your various business expenses is you ensure both accurate recordkeeping and maximization of tax deductions.

Another technological way to help you manage your investment dollars, but with personal involvement, is to include an "opt out" feature on that part of your service delivered through email. It's an efficient, immediate, and instantly recognizable approach that gives control to both you and the people who are opting out. Where they can be in charge of what they receive, you can better manage who you serve. If the opt out option is chosen by long-established clients and/or business partners, then a follow-up telephone call from you to them would be a sensible measure to take. And when you talk to them, take to heart what they say because there's mutual respect, trust, and support between the two of you. For those clients who don't meet this high threshold but still choose to opt out...you need to just move on and realize they have done you a service by refining the people you serve.

Much later on in this book, you will see a different way you can further aid your investment decision-making ability.

It's very important to recognize that money is the *limiting factor* in your business; you will never have enough of it. It doesn't mean you can't accomplish what you set out to do; it just means you will accomplish it through prudent fiscal responsibility. You will be constrained only to the point of having to make difficult choices that produce the best results. The burden of having to deal with limited dollars forces a leadership moment out of you. That by itself makes it a worthy exercise to go through. It encourages weighted decision-making on your part while helping to season you for the many other hard choices you have to make in your business. It's all just part of being a leader and the many diverse responsibilities that come with the job of serving others.

If you haven't done so already, start investing in your business today. Begin distributing your investment dollars among the people currently connected to your business and among entities not yet in place. Both are important in varying degrees to building a powerful referral business. No matter the money you put into your business, *never cross the buy your business line.* Standing firm on this principle reaffirms your respect for yourself, for the business you built, and for the industry you entered: the Referral-Based Service Industry. It's confirmation you're a proud member of a prestigious industry. If you compromise this principle, you devalue yourself and your business, and you just might end up working for nothing.

When you value your service, you'll invest in it, thereby making your business more valuable. Conversely, how can you with a clear conscience put money into service you don't believe in and, therefore, don't value? To confidently invest money in your business you have to believe you'll get it all back, and then some. If you've built your business based on *service you believe in*, then investing money in it should be seen as nothing more than making a deposit on a sound investment that will give you a steady return.

In the end, the heartbeat of a powerful referral business is service. It's what brings enthusiasm to the people connected to it and life to your endeavors. For as good as you think you may be, you only have a powerful referral business because of the people who support you. Once again, it's not about you—it's about them, and that's a theme you must never lose sight of. In no way do you ever want to try to become bigger than your business. A great way to remind yourself of that important fact is by investing a little bit of money every month on the people who make a difference in your life because you're making a difference in theirs.

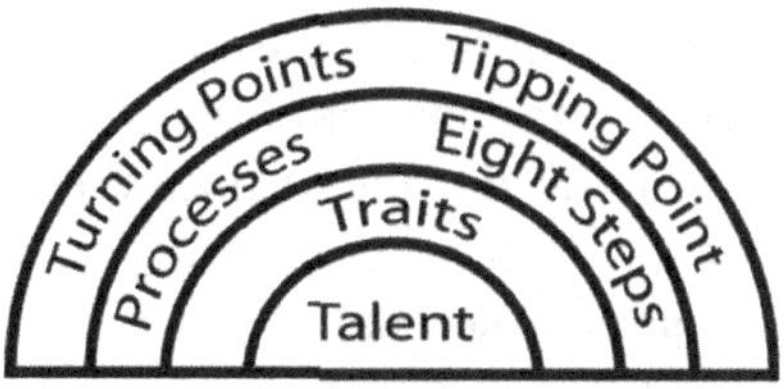

Become a Manipulator

A time past...
When something made your life easier, you wouldn't readily admit it. Instead, you would keep it to yourself and reap the benefits.

IT CONJURES UP A NEGATIVE first impression doesn't it—people who do whatever they want, whenever they want, and eventually getting what they want. It's all about the want! They have total control, and it's all for their advantage. Such actions reflect exploitation at the highest level. How could honest business people do such a devious thing? If we were talking about people, they couldn't. But we're not talking about people; we're talking about a business. Business people want to manipulate their business, for the consequence of idly standing by is they and their business become slow, forgetful, and blind. The ramifications are that widespread and that dire.

To become a manipulator and gain total control of your business you need to first have a clear understanding of success. Talk to a mixture of people who have achieved success in life and every one of them will almost certainly tell you a story of humble beginnings. Such beginnings form the foundation upon which success is built. That's the all too common starting point for success stories—humble beginnings. Such is the moment at hand in your business. It's time to back up, back way up, and recognize the humble beginnings of your powerful referral business. Just as in life, if you are to achieve success in business, you must understand where success starts at. So what exactly are the humble beginnings of your business success? Of course it's *the most menial work in your business.*

It's only fitting that simple and tedious work is a significant part of your success. Too often it's the type of work that gets overlooked or doesn't get its just due—but no more. Success is not achieved from the top down but, rather, from the bottom up. It's what allows magical moments to eventually occur. Such is the opportunity at hand in your business if you do the menial work of loading a variety of information into your database management system.

It was the advent of the database management system that allowed menial work to create the opportunity to leap from a transactional to a referral-based business. *It was a revolutionary moment for those who embraced it and a demarcation moment for those who did not.*

A database management system, henceforth referred to as database in this chapter, is the magic wand in your business because of what it materializes with the stroke of a key or the click of a mouse. Its magic-like quality further astounds by easily merging together two personal behaviors that would ordinarily clash with each other. It effortlessly combines a caring personality and a manipulative behavior and turns them into an advantageous spirit that leads to the care and feeding of the most people with the least amount of effort. Its astonishing efficiency will assist in presenting the impression you're better than you seem. With a database at your side, you can perform at a level that wouldn't otherwise be possible, and its impact is visible in three diverse areas. When you become a manipulator, you're not manipulating people; instead, you're technologically manipulating the *service, personal information,* and *data* within your business.

O

Business people at tropical depression level may have a database at their disposal, but more than likely it's ineffective, for they haven't built a robust level of service that can be manipulated. Rose was at this level, and it hindered her ability to provide an effective second timeframe of service. Sad to say, her business wasn't built to function in that timeframe. She failed to embrace the revolutionary moment in business, and therefore, she paid the steep price of missing out on the client revenue streams of repeat and referral business.

Just like anyone else, Rose had the opportunity to leap into the Referral-Based Service Industry, but her business wasn't designed to allow her to enter it. Even in the first timeframe of service, if she needed to contact clients or send them something, she would utilize contact information from their loan application—a part of her required technical service. By not having a level of service that could be technologically manipulated, she couldn't capitalize on technology meant to advance her business. Without even realizing it, she allowed rapidly improving technology to push her business further and further behind the times. Her business was not cutting-edge competitive in a relatively new competitive world.

When you take the time to build a level of service that can be manipulated, a database allows you to provide it with timing. I'm sure you've heard the phrase, timing is everything. It's true in delivering service. When your service has it, it's the best it can be because you are capturing moments with something you say or do. Your service is in sync, being delivered at the precise time you determined will make it the most *impressive* with the greatest *impact.* A database perfectly tees up referral language because providing service is the prerequisite requirement for asking for business.

It should go without saying that loading the correct information in your database is key to referral success. The information typed in will be used over and over again and in far too many ways to count. When it's correctly loaded, your service gets delivered. And when it's not, it keeps on coming back to you, no matter how many times you try to deliver it. Therefore, take the time to quickly verify the information input. Such a momentary act will keep you in touch with the people in your business instead of putting you out of touch with them. It's the most important *momentary pause* in business.

I know this is a simple and obvious rule. In fact, it's a blah common sense rule in a sea full of blah, yeah, hmm, and aha common sense. Prior to us implementing it in our business, there were more than a few occasions when an incorrect home address, telephone number, email account, name, loan information, etc. caused us to waste valuable time to track down the correct information. We had let a fat finger develop into an unnecessary friction to our business-building effort. There were already enough *friction moments* in our business without us adding an unnecessary one to the mix. Jeez! The obvious reason to avoid these types of situations in your business is they are a drag on business efficiency. They either delay or take you away from necessary work, which then adds undue stress.

The distinct power of a database is it can easily handle all of the diverse activities required to deliver every aspect of your service. It can even play a role with people not yet connected to your business, for it can deliver and keep track of current pounce processes. Indiscriminately, it helps you serve everybody.

At the end of the day, manipulating service is the most important thing a database does because it provides the perfect delivery of the premise of a powerful referral business. Business people at the tropical storm or hurricane level know this all too well; it's one of the secrets of their success. They realized a long time ago that a database is the complementary tool service has been waiting for—they were made for each other.

Just as it's important to serve the people who interface with your business, it's also important to communicate with them in a meaningful way. The not-so-obvious attribute of a database is it allows you to record personal information, which then gives you a long memory. When you take the time to document information learned from conversations, no matter how forgetful you are, you can't forget. A database allows you to have total recall of small bits of personal information picked up in earlier conversations, regardless of how long it's been since you last talked to the person.

Having this type of personal information at your fingertips naturally brings a one-on-one feeling when talking to a client or a person you recently met who is not yet connected to your business. It enables you to easily mesh together personal and business comments. By doing so, you can immediately disarm the person on the other end of the line and turn a sales call into a conversation. When you adopt this type of people-first philosophy, you position yourself to treat people as people instead of just as a business resource. You have recognized and met a basic human quality—people like to talk to other people (and they like to talk about themselves).

A database keeps your memory sharp, thereby allowing your caring spirit for clients to genuinely come through and be felt. The end result is *you can get closer to your clients because you know them better.* Not only can you ask for business, but you can also ask the emotional questions as well. The meaningful conversations you share with them has allowed you to move your business beyond just business. Positive proof that you have achieved such a level in your business is they openly share milestones that occur in their lives when they are in a conversation with you. Even better yet, they call you about them. An equally convincing sign is when they send you family pictures celebrating an important occasion or even refer you to their family blog.

Don't overlook your business partners here. You will also want to store and recall their personal information as well. However, your talks with them will be conversational and business-building-based. There's no need to ask them to refer you business since that was a requirement for them becoming business partners.

There is an interesting way to look at what's happening at this point in your business. If you don't naturally have the *gift-of-gab,* your database can artificially give it to you—when you store and recall personal information.

There's yet one more way for you to give yourself the gift-of-gab. You can search for your clients on social media websites. There's a wealth of personal and professional knowledge on these sites, and you can effectively use it to better serve and deepen the conversation between you and them. Such information will allow you to talk to them about various subject matters (family, friends, work, hobbies, music, etc.) in a conversational way. You might even be able to talk to them about an important event that just occurred in their lives. It should go without saying that you can obviously do the exact same thing for prospective clients and business partners and even for your established business partners.

And here's the extended value to recognize when it comes to the abovementioned types of calls. If during a conversation (with a client, business partner, or prospective one) you pick up a follow-on action, assign yourself a future task date to do it. And when the day arrives, you once more, in another way, demonstrate your memory is sharp and long. But this time, instead of storing and recalling information to help personalize a call, you're now serving a previously identified personal or professional need. Once again, a database indiscriminately helps you caringly serve everybody.

Not only does a database allow you to provide timely service and get closer to the people who interface with your business and to those who may, it is also ready to store and recall almost limitless bits of crucial data. Through data you have complete control of how much your database can take you behind the curtain to look inside your business at any time. It objectively answers your questions by revealing the data.

Out of all the data you can possibly look at, what should be the most important to you—*performance data.* You need to examine the data that reveals the business performance of you and the people connected to your business. You will find such data within the first two dominos of your business—focus and effectiveness. Did the focus of your business (service) create effectiveness (sales)?

To determine the answer to that question, you will need to examine two things—your personal effort during the two timeframes of service and the repeat business and referrals you generated from the clients and business partners connected to your business. By looking at this scope of data, you answer the question at the heart of a powerful referral business: "Is your service generating sales?"

If you need to expand your performance data collection effort beyond your database's capabilities, consider developing a custom-made spreadsheet. We've done exactly that in our business, thereby expanding our data manipulation efforts to specifically examine the performance data we feel is most important to our long-term success. Through the use of a spreadsheet we look at the nexus of our business. On a weekly basis, we examine our effort to deliver two timeframes of service and the repeat business and referral performance of both our clients and business partners. By doing so, we are *proactively* working our business in a steady way instead of *reactively* having to surge for business at some point because of our own inaction. Also on the spreadsheet is a space on the right-hand side to write down diary notes (positive or negative). These bullet-type notes provide a supporting written history of the performance data being reviewed.

The spreadsheet is based on a thirteen-week period. The reason being, at the end of each quarter, we examine the worksheet in total to once again identify business weaknesses, strengths, and trends. But this time, instead of getting a *snapshot* assessment, we have moved to a *patterned* assessment. We are now getting a *stable* look at both our work ethic and the performance of our business over a considerable period of time. At the end of the year, we look at all four quarterly spreadsheets in combination. By doing so, we visually recreate a year's worth of performance data and written history that we have deemed important to our long-term success.

No matter the way you accomplish it in your business—a database, spreadsheet, combination of both, or other means—the end result is to simply store and then review data that reveals business-building answers. The point being, you are using technology to manipulate data.

Once you make the commitment to first store and then recall data, you automatically make a commitment to have goals in your business. Data and goals have a natural link and a co-dependency, in that they are both symbolically important, but their importance is only realized when they directly support each other. One without the other diminishes them to no more than nice-to-know information. Where goals make data relevant, data makes goals motivating.

When you make goals a part of your business, you bring a motivational factor to it. You're now working toward things that are just out of reach, and they, therefore, constantly beckon you to reach for them. When you do reach them, you adjust them higher, thereby keeping you on your journey. Achieving goals in your business is what allows you to keep building upon success, year after year.

A goal is composed of two linked things. First, the goal itself is a measurable, specific statement relevant to your business success. Second, you'll achieve each goal through *stated objectives.* A stated objective is a short action bullet that represents a specific activity you have to accomplish to eventually achieve the goal. There's no limit on the number of stated objectives per goal. Just as each goal is unique so too are the number of stated objectives to support it. It is stated objectives that make goals tangible.

With the introduction of goals into your business, you introduce a personal responsibility that is on-going throughout the year. You accept personal responsibility for the following four crucial actions: *determining* goals (to include the stated objectives for each), *tracking* each goal's performance, *measuring* each goal's outcome, and if required, *establishing* new goals. Let's briefly take a look at each one.

The *determined* goals in your business are as unique as your service. You can have as many or as few as you want. However, to stay true to what you're building, your goals should aid in measuring you, your service, and the value of every client and business partner interfacing with your business. All of them are essential to building a powerful referral business. Whatever your goals are in these various areas, they should provide useful feedback and insight that push you and your business to become better. They hold everybody and everything important accountable.

Once you have goals as a part of your business, you need some type of systematic approach to give you the best chance to achieve them. The best way to do it is to *track* the data within your business that directly supports the stated objectives. When you do, you prove you're serious about reaching your goals. You keep them (goals and objectives) squarely in front of you throughout the year and facilitate business practice changes from the inside out—you're looking inside of your business to make changes to the outside of it. The finely-tuned adjustments bring near real-time fixes to your business and keep you working proactively toward goals throughout the year. You, in essence, never lose your focus on what you have predetermined long-term success is based on.

Where tracking primarily allows for fine-tuning, *measuring* goals shows results and can lead to changes in you, your service, and the clients and business partners connected to your business. Measuring goals is the moment of truth in your business, and it marks when you enter the brief but emotionally charged period of your business. It's where some feelings are likely to get hurt because of the decisions that must be made, for you have to be true to all of the goals, even the ones that measure your personal performance. No other time in your business will include more important decisions or be more difficult. It's the most comprehensive test of leadership you will face. Adding to your leadership challenge is the fact that some of the judgments will require a subjective opinion, truly requiring a leadership decision. If you fail to follow-through on what you discover, your business will surely slow before eventually losing its sense of forward direction. Measuring goals is not the time to blink but, rather, the time to prove you're a leader. You'll see later the specific business activity utilized to measure your goals.

The life-cycle of tracking and measuring is when it comes time to measure goals, tracking is momentarily suspended. After goals are measured, tracking resumes again in earnest support of either the reaffirmed or the *established* new goals, until it's time to remeasure them yet again—typically one year later. The importance of establishing new goals in your business is, in all likelihood, it has changed in some way, for better or worse. Establishing new goals formally recognizes these changes, ensuring your business maintains its motivational factor of always reaching for things that are just out of reach. And remember, newly established goals requires newly stated objectives.

To help Rose and me adequately address the diverse responsibilities associated with goals, we have chosen what we believe is an equally diverse business tool—the previously talked about spreadsheet. It provides us the best chance to efficiently and effectively achieve our goals because it directly supports the various responsibilities associated with goals. Here's how. The spreadsheet not only reflects stated objectives, it helps us to first track and then measure performance. And when we establish a new goal, to include stated objectives, we'll accordingly modify our spreadsheet as well. When you consider the sum of these activities together, the spreadsheet serves as the *action document* for our goals. It not only shows us the actions that are occurring across our business, it causes us to take actions, during and at the end of the year, based on what it visually reveals to us.

So how do you know for sure you have the right goals in place? When you achieve all of them, you achieve the vision of your business (the Business Star). Every goal in your business must directly support your vision in some way.

Here's one last key thought on the significance of having goals in your business. They identify the moment you take command of your business. By choosing to make decisions based on unbiased information, you have brought objectivity to your business. At last, performance matters in your business.

O

The goals discussed above are execution type goals. Altogether, they measure the overall performance of your business. There's yet another type of goal (also with stated objectives) you should develop—*preparatory goals*. They are the goals that address the precursory work of successful business execution. Motivation and accountability are just as important for "get ready success" as they are for success itself. Some obvious preparatory goals are: developing your overall service, creating a pounce process as a result of a changing market, or building your continuity binder, to name just a few. The distinguishing difference between preparatory goals and execution goals is a shelf-life. Preparatory goals have a timeline to accomplish actions. Once all of the laborious work is completed, the goal goes away. In contrast, execution type goals stay with you throughout your career—business execution is a constant.

O

Just when you think a database can do no wrong, it rears its *humanistic-like qualities*. When you first start working with it, it seems perfect, but as you get to know it better, you start to see its flaws. It doesn't mean you think any less of it or stop using it; it just means you accept it for what it is. The point being, you focus on the good—it's what allows you to keep it as part of your business. Somewhat like dating and marriage all rolled into one! Thank goodness Rose has looked beyond my flaws over the years. Here are a couple of obvious flaws to avoid.

Database systems are so powerful today they can literally overwhelm the senses. It's easy to become enamored with them. That's why it's so important to have a level of service to manipulate when you start using them. The boundaries of what you have built should focus and limit your database activities—it's your best chance to resist the temptation of doing activities for the sake of doing them. You can further tailor your database activities by only performing those activities that directly support your business model and its corresponding definition and premise (the three guiding principles).

On the other hand, if you choose to focus on system capabilities, you can quickly become slave to something meant to work for you. One of the fundamental challenges associated with a database is awareness of the imaginary line that divides efficiency from inefficiency. If you cross it, you're always catching up. As you build your business, you will probably struggle with this line, but knowing it is there should keep you focused on making sure you never work for your database.

To help you effectively integrate a database into your business, you may have to one more time reach out to an experienced professional. This is the third technology area of your business that can easily be far beyond your capability. I know it was for Rose and me. The fact that you have a specifically defined business model, with a vision, should allow the person helping you to effectively setup your database and then tightly tailor a corresponding training program.

Another thing to watch out for is don't allow your service to lose its personal touch. This can quickly come about if you produce and send out an excessive amount of service-related material. If you abandon a personal touch, your business loses it uniqueness, and you lose your identity. All that you have done is create junk mail, and we all know where that ends up. Your objective should be to have your clients and business partners always feel you're personally involved. Some easy ways to do this is addressing typed letters and notes with their first name and signing it, writing handwritten notes, or adding a sentence or two (about you or them) to personalize an email, note, or letter. They're little things, but they keep your service personal. In other words, a nuance. By taking these small steps with your service, you are managing your database of people with quality in mind, not quantity.

When you make a database a part of your business, there are some basic things it needs to do for you. You need an individual record of every person who interfaces with your business. Within that record, you must have contact information (to include email account and maybe even social media accounts), the ability to build a business and personal history, and track the level of business support. You must be able to produce letters, notes, or emails that are linked to the database and create a corresponding historical note within each individual record.

Because your business serves different groups, you need to be able to organize people by specific groups (clients, business partners, business associates, and prospective clients and business partners). One of the advantages of this grouping action is you can better provide your service. Here's one example of how. If you contact your clients quarterly, you can build quarterly groups. The first group would be Jan, Apr, Jul, and Oct; the second group would be Feb, May, Aug, and Nov and so on. Once you create these groups, you then populate them with the appropriate clients, and when the month arrives, you make your client telephone calls. You can take a similar type grouping action to help you more easily professionally manage the transactions of your clients. Rose and I conduct both of these grouping actions in our business.

You can further organize the people in your business by breaking down the aforementioned five groups into smaller groups, combining various groups as one, or joining portions of different groups into a single group. The service value of this *advanced grouping* is you pre-position yourself to efficiently and effectively serve the various needs (personal and/or professional) that are unique to your business. Some examples of advanced grouping might be: people who share a personal interest of yours, monthly birthday card mailings, small business owners, military members, big investors, and multiple property owners, to name just a few. It is through the activity of advanced grouping that your individualism, business focus, and the demographics/individualism of the people in your business are further revealed. You'll see shortly the specific business activity you conduct to take advantage of this pre-grouping work.

The importance of creating groups cannot be overstated. They allow you to partition your database of people in untold ways that allows you to both effectively manage them and deliver your service to them. Without the aid of groups, it's hard to imagine how any businessperson could effectively serve more than a handful of clients and business partners. And if one of them could somehow pull it off, it would certainly be an exercise in inefficiency.

Additionally, you must be able to build and schedule an *activity series* for an individual or a group. This is a key capability because it allows you to *digitize your checklists.* We have done exactly that in our business. By us taking this action, our database precisely manages the execution of our checklists by populating on a single page the checklist activities scheduled for that day. We work through the open checklist steps from most to least important by visually prioritizing outstanding work. Not only has this database capability significantly improved the efficiency of our checklists, it has helped us increase our personal efficiency as well. All of our pre-planned work is waiting for us every morning.

And finally, a schedule and email activity must be an integral part of the database system. They are both essential tools that help you deliver your service, albeit in different ways.

By having a system with these industry standard capabilities, you can store pertinent information concerning every single person in your database. The business significance of that is you now have the ability to stay in touch on a regular basis, provide timely service, record business history and personal conversations, personalize letters, notes, emails, conversations, and send individual and group mailings. You'll know who's supporting your business and to what degree. It's simple information with powerful application. No matter how large your business grows, a database allows it to maintain an individual characteristic. Succinctly stated, a database allows you to provide personal service to everybody.

For Rose and me, the introduction and then utilization of a database has fundamentally changed the core dynamics of our business. Its importance is captured in the fact it brings an individual characteristic to the three areas of service, information, and data.

Consider the people in our business: We know the service we provide them. We can talk to them on a personal level. And we know how much they're supporting our business with sales. Our database management activities have permitted us to make a difference in their lives and determine if they're making one in ours. A database brings to life the premise of service leads to sales—it first delivers the service and then it measures the sales performance.

A database also brings new meaning to the phrase, brain trust. It has the capability to store and recall unlimited information just like a *brain* does, and it leverages client *trust* for the benefit of you and your business partners through the delivery of service. There's an old saying that states, "Two brains are better than one"—it's absolutely true in your business.

The presence of a database in your business practically allows you to see your business. It puts it at your fingertips and makes you look brilliant in so many ways. It truly is a marvelous tool that adds the engineering-effect to your business. Through its sophistication you can serve the most people while providing service with a personal touch. It's a business multiplier that has its roots in menial work.

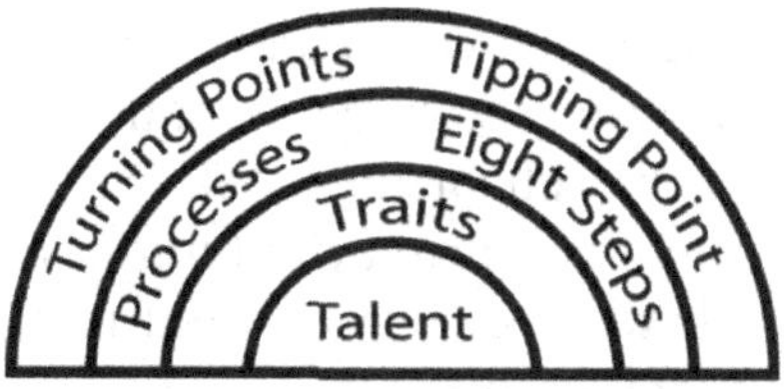

Do What You're Told

A time past...
Throughout your youth a school schedule was very important to your future success. Even today, a schedule has great significance to you.

NOBODY LIKES TO BE TOLD what to do. When it occurs, it's a clear sign you're not in charge. But that's not always the case. Such a narrow way of thinking is reflective of what a follower would say. Remember, you're a leader. Therefore, if you haven't already done so, you need to quickly abandon the attitude of "I can do it all by myself." This isn't the time for a strong opinion of yourself. On the contrary, it's time to think less of yourself so you can do more for yourself. The *nag moment* in business is upon you because you're going to place something in front of you every day reminding you of what to do and when to do it. No matter how good you get, it never, ever goes away. You need to be nagged to become a successful businessperson. In fact, the better you get, the more you'll need to be nagged. Not everything in the world makes perfect sense.

You have accomplished a large amount of work in preparing you and your business for constant success. A fair amount of the necessary ingredients are in place—traits, processes, business value, investment dollars, and database management. The challenge you now face is how to keep it all congruent and working efficiently.

The only way to effectively accomplish it is with a schedule. A schedule puts the traits you adopted and the processes you built to work. It allows you to confidently juggle every aspect of your business and impressively showcase it. Scheduling your day gets you out of the "I'm sorry" or "I forgot" syndrome. I promise, if you're not on a schedule, all of your hard work will go by the wayside. You have created way too much in your new-found business to commit it all to memory. It's crucial to get on a schedule right now. Just the fact you can interface it with your database management activities should be enough to convince you to get on an electronic schedule.

Until recently, Rose used to have a small day planner book that sat on a bookcase to the left of her desk. She used it to schedule her business day, which was primarily limited to business and personal appointments. It was your traditional transactional businessperson thinking and scheduling. It was all about business, never about her business. She had more darn sticky and scribble notes in that thing. One day I built her an electronic version. When I showed her what I built, she was actually comparing it page-by-page to her day planner. She stopped me more than a couple of times to verify I didn't miss anything, in particular her hair and nail appointments. I didn't say a word. She held on to the planner for a few more days for security and old-time sake before moving exclusively to an electronic schedule. It was the horse-and-buggy moment in our business journey. Needless to say, she can't live without the electronic schedule now. All of the new structure we've added demands it.

As you might suspect, Rose's business day has recently undergone a dramatic change. Wherein the past it was primarily conducted with generality in mind, it's now based on planned activity. Her business day of today looks nothing like that of yesterday, for she has turned her day inside out. She doesn't work and wait for business; she works to bring business in.

Such an important shift in work philosophy represents the second great shift in business—*The Work Ethic Shift*. How did it occur in Rose? Naturally over a period time by virtue of the service she built. It was an expected yet powerful shift that had to take place if she was to get on the powerful referral business pathway. That's the power of service, it causes a shift to occur in you, while it tectonically shifts your business from conducting transactions with whomever you can to generating repeat and referral business from clients you selected and business partners you hired.

Scheduling your business day moves you from a *let it happen* to a *make it happen* work ethic. Only one word is different, but it is a one hundred and eighty degree change of direction. The personal outcome is you are no longer *reactive* in business; you are *proactive.*

Putting yourself on a schedule means you are willing to be led. By doing so, it speaks more about your leadership skills than lack of them. It's not a sign of weakness; it's a sign of strength and a reflection of the confidence you have in yourself. Successful people are not afraid to be led. In fact, they like when it occurs because it confirms people depend on them, and it's a strong indication things are going well.

When you put yourself on a schedule, you readily understand you can't do it all by yourself, and you need help to make it through the day. That's not always an easy thing to do or accept because you may feel like you're giving up control. In reality, though, just the opposite is occurring. You're gaining control not only of your business day but of your personal life as well because a schedule allows you to get the most done in the least amount of time. It leads you from one important activity to the next, bringing a level of supervised responsibility throughout the day. When you fully embrace a schedule, you introduce *activities* and *time-management* into your business day, which will make you a highly productive person. A scheduled day is the closest thing you have in your business to a personal coach because it holds you accountable every day by guiding your business day.

The reason why you must eventually put your day on a schedule is *specificity.* Specificity in your day ensures you are either *impressing* or *impacting* the people who interface with your business or *convincing* those who may. There are those three words again! A scheduled business day is formal recognition your work is essential and confirmation you view each day as important. What are the actions that should fill your daily schedule?

The answers are found in the traits you adopted and the service and pounce processes you built. Remember what the six traits combined requires of you, and look at all of the service you have created and are now ready to provide. Within all of that are expectations and easily identifiable work you must conduct and deliver daily. Build your schedule around these activities. By doing so, you connect with and stay true to what you have adopted and built. More importantly, you'll make a difference to people.

A schedule not only lets you efficiently conduct planned activities, it allows you to easily react to unexpected happenings. The basis of a business day is various types of appointments, working on transactions, phone calls, emails (and possibly text-messages), loading a variety of information into your database management system, and delivering service—with the understanding there will be interruptions. Seldom will a business day go as planned, especially if your business has vibrancy to it. A schedule is the only way to bring a sense of order to what could easily become an un-orderly day.

It's a given there will be many times when important and not so important things come up that get you off-track. Because a schedule guides your daily activities, not direct them, it's a flexible document that can and should be adjusted as needed. By doing so, you meet the challenge of conducting business and delivering service while at the same time *successfully integrating interruptions.* When you're pulled away from your schedule, for whatever reason, always commit to getting back on it as soon as you can. Adhering to this simple rule confirms you respect everything you built in your business and the work you put into developing the day's planned activities. More importantly, you keep specificity in your day.

There are two particular interruptions that require quick discussion. They are the interruptions most destructive to a productive day because they usually come throughout the day—incoming telephone calls and emails. Some business people could easily add a third interruption—text-messages. Altogether, they put the greatest pressure on a business day because they can frequently pull you away from planned activities meant to create success. It is ironic that such important business communication tools can harm your business so much. Therefore, the key is not to ignore them but, rather, to integrate them into your business day so they don't interrupt it. If you don't take control of them through the concept of *timeliness* (previously discussed), they will take control of your day. In essence, you have remained a reactive businessperson instead of a proactive one. In some regards, your business success will simply come down to how you handle incoming telephone calls and emails (and text-messages) during the day. Will you keep an organized day that creates success, or will you let your day become unorganized through near constant interruptions that impede success? How you answer this one simple question will determine your commitment to a scheduled day and so much more.

Rose has effectively taken control of incoming telephone and emails by blocking time on her schedule and by utilizing the concept of *categorization.* Much later on, you'll see how she specifically categorizes and handles various types of calls, to include incoming telephone calls. As for emails, she categorizes them through the use of folders. For example, she builds an individual folder for each client who is in the first timeframe of service. Such a folder contains both technical and service-related items, and it remains active until the transaction is completed. She has other folders, as required, that address both the technical and service sides of her business. It is through the utilization of categorization that she can store, retrieve, and act upon an enormous amount of diverse information in an efficient manner. As for text-messaging, she's not big on it...yet.

Here's the bottom line on a schedule: it formally recognizes the *duality* of your job—technical and service. There will be time allotted in the day for technical work (conduct business) and time allotted to deliver your service (generate business). It is imperative that you equally respect both sides of your business during a business day. A strong indication you're doing it is you treat the planned service activities with the same reverence you do a business appointment—not interrupting them unless absolutely necessary.

To know if you are a *disciplined* businessperson, look no further than a schedule. It is the business activity to look at to determine if you have truly adopted this trait. Following a schedule brings the trait of discipline to life. Just as service revealed what you value (the client or the transaction), a schedule will reveal if you're disciplined. They both act as a truth serum in their own respective way.

I don't want to make it sound or appear that a schedule is just about work, because it's not. On the contrary, a schedule is the one tool in your business that addresses the *whole person concept.* Not only does it ably schedule both sides of your business, it can selectively schedule your during and after business hours personal activities as well. By doing so, you place an equal importance on that aspect of your day and your life and you prevent untimely or unwanted interruptions.

The true worth of a schedule is it allows every business day to be a successful one. Not a single day is wasted. So how do you do it and achieve specificity in every business day, including the slow ones? You do it by having a *boilerplate schedule.* Such a schedule reflects the necessary activities you need to accomplish every day to ensure you are either impressing or impacting clients and business partners. A boilerplate schedule is the predetermined starting point for your business day, and you build it up from there. In short, pre-planned activities are a part of every business day. There's a litmus test to determine if you have an effective boilerplate schedule. The test is if you have no interruptions, return phone calls, emails, text-messages, or appointments in your day, it would still be considered successful. It's amazing how delivering service alone can make for a worthy day. *An effective boilerplate schedule keeps you close to your established business.*

The most productive way to get your scheduled day started off right, so you maintain your focus throughout the day, is to have a morning *business look*. Such a quick business look is meant to address the all important three-P's that should make up every business day: review your *planned* obligations, ensure your work has a meaningful *purpose*, and deliver what you *promised*. If you have built a team around you, a business look will synchronize your team's effort by briefly detailing the major activities, what everybody's working on, and the service being delivered to current and prospective clients and business partners. It will both coordinate and bring cohesion to your team's daily effort. Whether you have a team around you or not, near the end of the day quickly review and determine if anything in particular needs to be accomplished before the end of the day. Carry forward any items not done to the next day.

The importance of the morning business look and the end of day review is they establish personal responsibility and reinforce your daily commitment to the people you serve. With them as an integral part of your business day, you'll always know what to do during the day, what you need to do before you go home, and how you start the next business day.

Clearly, a hurricane is a very powerful and efficient storm, and to build your business into one, you must have your day thoroughly planned. From the moment you arrive in the office, until the time you leave, you should have a schedule in place that supports your total business effort (conduct and generate business). There's nothing worse than having traits and processes ready for daily execution and no schedule to hold you accountable. To take control of your business, you have to control your day, thereby eliminating wasted energy. Therefore, get your business day on a schedule and follow it. It's the one time when being a good follower will attest to your leadership qualities.

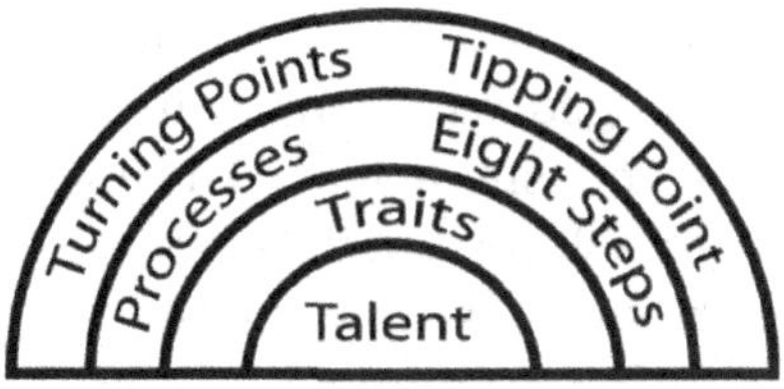

You Better Say It

A time past...
If you remember your teen years, you know the artistry of presenting a forgotten thought. Referral language is your chance to act.

WOULDN'T IT BE NICE to be able to build a powerful referral business without having to do something that's uncomfortable? It would be, but unfortunately, it's not possible. You need to get used to asking for something. The sooner you accept this fact, the sooner you'll see referrals. We have arrived at the *camel straw moment* of your business, because it's time to decide what goes on top of your two timeframes of client service. You either put referral language or straw on top of it. It's make-or-break time in your business.

If you are at either the clear skies or tropical depression level, you haven't done near enough to ask for or even hope for referrals (on a regular basis). In all likelihood, your customers weren't overly impressed with your service experience and have already moved on and forgotten your name. That was Rose, she was personally impressive but her service wasn't, and therefore, her customers very quickly moved on and forgot her name. There was no chance for her to build the Lineage Web. But if you are at the tropical storm or hurricane level, you've worked hard to develop a level of noteworthy service and have more than earned the right to ask for referrals. In fact, referrals are already an inherent part of your business because you know clients will only give them to you for one reason—they trust you. It can only be earned by your integrity and the service you provide.

Even if you have built your business based on integrity and service, it can still be hard to ask for referrals when you first start doing it. A guilt complex may be present, or you may just feel uneasy about it—all natural feelings, but you must overcome them. That's exactly what happened to Rose when she first started providing both timeframes of client service. It was an expected response because she not only changed what she valued, she changed the industry she worked in—no small feat. The mere fact that she had now earned the right to ask for business through service still wasn't enough by itself to overcome the initial uneasiness of doing it.

Let me try to put referral language in context to what you do in your business by talking about *The Something Concept.* I wrote this at about 2:00 a.m., so you might have to read it twice! The concept goes something like this. Referral language isn't about begging for something. Begging is asking for something without knowing you'll receive something in return. What you're doing is providing something with the hope of receiving something in return. It's something completely different. And if you don't receive that something, you still provide something, hoping one day to get that first something. You never quite reach the point of asking for something and expecting something in return. But if you get that first something, you'll then know the something you provide has the potential to generate a whole lot more somethings. And that's definitely something you want to achieve in your business. What it all means in the end is your somethings add up to the fact you don't have to apologize or be embarrassed for asking for something. HUH? Plainly said, the client service you provide has more than earned you the right to ask for, and hopefully receive, referrals.

Referral language truly does have to be everywhere in your business and in every form. It must be both spoken and written. If you don't have it in your business, you do a disservice to your service. Why? *Referral language is the why of your service.* It's why you labored day after day for a while to develop a high level of client service (first and second timeframe) and why you provide it. As such, referral language isn't the result of business people conducting a transaction in their profession. Instead, it and the subsequently generated client referrals are the result of business people professionally conducting a transaction that is complemented by a continuing service experience. As more and more clients come to embrace this point of view, the business world will become even more professional. The primary reason being is business people love referrals, and they will do what is necessary to generate them. If I had one more "hope" for clients (outside of The Pentagon Effect), this would be it.

This brings to light a notable observation about Rose. Through the concept of referral language she was unknowingly displaying her integrity as a businesswoman in yet another way. Rose did it by simply being true to her transactional business, in that she didn't call clients and ask for business. She intuitively knew she hadn't earned the right to ask (she was only professionally conducting a transaction). Without her even realizing it, she was subconsciously respecting the fact that referral language is the result of a service experience. Instinctively, she knew the difference between right and wrong through her uneasiness. Her righteous conscious was intact and serving her well.

Referral language is not something you employ only once. Its importance is, in fact, realized when you employ it more than once. This principle is best illustrated by a simple interaction between the boss and an employee as told to me by my Superintendent, Senior Master Sergeant Al Recke, when I was a captain in the Air Force. The boss walked by and saw the employee dumping the unopened day's mail in the wastebasket. The boss loudly said, "Hey, you can't do that; we need to open that mail!" to which the employee calmly replied, "If it's important, they'll send it again." The point is you can only demonstrate that your clients' referrals are important by saying it again and again.

The most powerful ways to seek referrals are over the telephone and during face-to-face conversations. In these situations ask for the referral *at the end of the conversation* so it appears as an afterthought instead of it being your primary objective for spending time with them. This is your chance to *act* because you're just waiting for the right moment to say your line. STOP! This is a profound moment, but not for the reason you might think. When you do speak up and say your line, it's confirmation of multiple dynamics finally coming together. The coalescing dynamics are: You truly value your service. You are putting the result of your service to work through your voice. The right psychology is in place because you have chosen clients over business partners (or advertising or anything else). And tenacity has at last worked its way into your business because you are capitalizing on an opportunity many business people allow to pass or don't even realize is there. To muster up referral language in your voice is to know several things are right with you and your business.

Another way to make referral language a part of your business is by putting it in your letters, notes, and emails. We like to remind people in *a tag line at the bottom of such correspondence* that our business is built on referrals, and we are ready to provide our high level of service to referred clients. We never say it in a directive way, and we never sound desperate. Instead, we come across as offering a service—which we most certainly are doing. That said, don't limit yourself to just repeating the same old tag line over and over. Stay true to the message (your business is about referrals), but every now and then consider complementing the statement with a specific fact, unique feature of your business, an emerging business opportunity in a changing market, breaking news in your profession, etc. This subtlety will always keep your tag line fresh and keep people reading it. This is yet another business nuance.

Consider the placement of referral language in your business. It doesn't matter if you're talking or writing, referral language has a designated spot in business. It truly is the result of service. That is, when you create emotion in clients through service, you can then ask them to perform an emotional act for you by referring people they know and care about. When they do, you realize the simple essence of service and referrals—transferring emotional acts back and forth between people who mutually care about each other.

Because referral language is the result of service, it naturally needs to be a part of your service from the first moment clients start to interface with your business (initial client appointment). The importance of that is your referral business starts when clients enters your business, not when the transaction is completed. If you recall, clients will receive two distinctive timeframes of service.

During the first timeframe, they have you and your business in mind because of the transaction they're involved in. Be ready to tap into this human emotion by having referral reminders in the level of service you provide them. The reminders can be both verbal and written. Regardless of how you do it, never ask for a referral until clients know the level of service they will receive. Explain that at the beginning so you can provide required technical and unique personal service, coupled with referral reminders.

An excellent goal to have during this first timeframe of service is to generate one referral for you or your business partners. This shows you're paying close attention to the human dynamics of your business and confirms you don't let opportunity pass you by.

As important as the first timeframe of service is, the second one is even more important. It is during this time you try to engender repeat business and multiple referrals—for you and your business partners. During this timeframe you must co-mingle explained service and referral language together because if a bond develops between you and clients, you want it done on the terms you set. The terms are verbal and written referral language.

It's important to take a moment here and become visually familiar with the internal business dynamics occurring between both timeframes of client service. They actually do work together, in that one leads to the other, which then leads back to the other and on and on. When you provide both timeframes of service, you create *The Business Loop* diagramed below. Start with the 1st Timeframe and work your way clockwise around the loop.

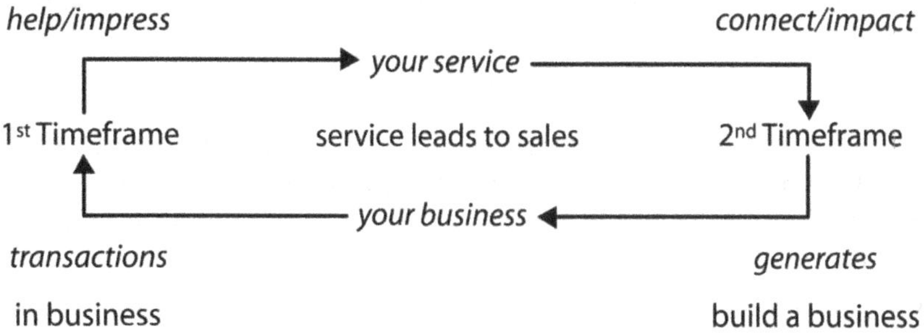

THE BUSINESS LOOP

Here are the takeaway insights from this diagram. The striking differences between each timeframe of client service (*help/impress* versus *connect/impact*) cause *your service* and *your business* to flow in opposite directions. The importance of that occurring is the timeframes naturally connect to one another, creating a business loop based on the premise of *service leads to sales.* That is, your total service process effort *generates* your business *transactions* of repeat client business and client referrals. If you don't take the time to build a business model that creates this loop, you're only *in busi-*

ness, never *building a business.* What made it all possible is your formal recognition of The Need Shift. Nowadays, this is the business loop Rose depends on for her success.

When you don't formally recognize The Need Shift, there is yet another type of business loop created. This loop is based on the premise of *hard work and pounce processes leads to the first time-frame of service.* As soon as you complete the transaction at hand, you immediately loop back around to once again depend on yourself and pounce processes for the next transaction. This type of business loop always has you busy and spending money. There's no chance to shift the burden from yourself to your business. That was the exact type of business loop Rose depended on for her success when she was a transactional businesswoman. She not only worked hard for her agents, she spent money on pounce processes.

Here's the bottom line. Both a transactional and referral-based business has a business loop in it. The main difference between the loops can be summed up in just two words: *hard work.* In a transactional business you work hard, while in a referral-based business your business works hard. It only makes sense; sales have to come from somewhere. It's just another example of an either-or choice.

Providing a high level of service obviously encourages you to ask for referrals from clients, but it also provides another less-obvious side benefit to you and your business. It allows you to confidently speak in a direct way to the clients you have become close with. In all likelihood, these are your best clients because they have moved their trust of you beyond just business. They represent the *ideal client,* given that they have made the personal and professional connection with you and your business. It's what you hope for from all of your clients.

Such a dual emotional connection should confidently allow you to use *direct referral language* when speaking to them. For instance, instead of saying, *"If you know,"* say *"Who do you know?"* On the surface that may seem to be a subtle difference, but in all actuality, it's a nuance of significant dimensions. Why? You have asked them a question that requires an answer instead of just reminding them of something. And if they don't have an immediate answer, they just might be willing to try to get you one. If that's the case, it would be more than appropriate and prudent to ask them if you can schedule a follow-on call to check back with them. This is yet another opportunity to utilize your database management system.

Direct referral language is a powerful business tool that can deliver impressive results. With that said, it should be used thoughtfully and with supporting conversation that softens the directness yet clearly conveys the message. In the end, it's the firmest hopeful message you can deliver to your closest, most supportive clients.

The use of direct referral language in your business recognizes the *hierarchy* within your client base. And that is, not all clients are the same, and not all clients should hear direct referral language. You have recognized an important client base subtlety and, thus, started the process of categorizing your clients in a way that sharpens and enhances your referral generating effort.

The best way to formally categorize this particular type of client is to create an advanced grouping of *ideal clients*. When you do, you have completely flipped the purpose of a group. Instead of creating a group to serve a need, you'll now turn to this loyal group of clients to help serve your referral needs. It's like your "ace in the hole" referral group. They will be there for you in the worst of times and the best of times. In a perfect business world, these would be the only type of clients in a powerful referral business.

The all too obvious direct output of referral language is client referrals, which brings us to a nuance opportunity. When a client refers somebody, they will typically tell the person to contact you. It's the natural way to refer business. You can nuance this client action, if you so choose, by politely suggesting to your clients that when they take action to refer somebody to ask the person if it would be okay if you contacted them instead. Such a nuance has multiple positive effects: It makes the client place a call to you to personally relay the referral. It provides you the opportunity to quickly reconnect with the client and personally thank him. It gives you the opportunity to briefly talk to the client beforehand to learn any type of information that might help you better serve the referred client. And it guarantees a contact will be made. When you take this type of action, you are as thoughtful about handling client referrals as you are about handling referrals between business partners (the earlier discussed hand-off, hand-back approach).

At the beginning of the year, we talk about referrals in a direct way to all of our clients with our Happy New Year letter. Through this mailed letter we *reset* our level of service by clearly communicating what they can *expect* from us during the year and what we *hope* from them in return. There are those two words again. As it should be, we carry the greater burden. We wish them a happy and prosperous New Year and send them a yearly refrigerator calendar magnet with our picture and pertinent business information. We also let them know we are looking forward to providing another year of personalized service, professionally serving their likely needs through our business partners, and maintaining our association with them, wherever that might be. We close the letter with referral language that states we run our business by referral, and that we are always ready to help people they know and care about.

The importance of sending the letter is twofold. First and foremost, *we formally enter the second timeframe of service every year with our clients.* Second, the letter functions as a *business partner service process*—we've easily and professionally inserted our business partners into our business.

When using referral language in your business, you should also use a corresponding strategy to thank clients for supporting your business. It's vitally important to say thank you. Just as you hope for something in return for your service to clients, they should expect something in return for their referrals to you. It's this expectation that makes a powerful referral business unique—mutual respect for one another. A referral is earned, never bought.

Every time you receive a referral, say thank you immediately in two ways—by telephone contact and by sending a thank-you note. Each form of contact brings with it a different message. The telephone call is about the client, and the note is about your business.

The telephone call is to personally thank the client and reassure her you will treat the client she referred with the utmost respect and professionalism. In doing so, you're making her feel good about her actions by letting her know she has just helped somebody she cares about. By taking this action, you formally and personally recognize she put her credibility on the line for you. In the handwritten note, you need to touch on two things. First, thank her for thinking of your business and for having continued trust and confidence in you. And last, once again remind her you run your business by referral, and you always look forward to the next opportunity to provide your service to others of her acquaintance.

The above telephone call and note has no bearing on whether you complete the transaction or not. Just the fact you have been personally recommended warrants some form of thanks.

If you complete the business transaction, follow-up with another telephone call and note because not only are you the benefactor of financial gain, you can now develop another referral source. In this telephone call and note, focus on the referred client. In particular, how it was your pleasure to help the person and how you look forward to again helping someone else she cares about. Taking this action puts a finishing personal touch on the completed transaction and sets in place the condition for the next one.

By placing two telephone calls and sending two notes, you have clearly communicated the importance of a referral—from beginning to end. The added value of a telephone call as part of your referral thank you strategy is it's as close to a hug as you can get.

It is important to quickly reemphasize that the abovementioned referral thank you strategy is only applicable to clients. The referral strategy between business partners is handled through the previously discussed hand-off and hand-back approach. With that said, it doesn't mean you are any less thankful; it just means you recognize the difference between the two, and you respect the professional commitment of a business partnership.

Referral language can be conveyed to your clients in a variety of ways. No matter the method employed, always remember no other time will bring more personal scrutiny from your clients then when you ask them for a referral. Therefore, before asking them to make a difference to your business, make sure you have met the prerequisite requirement for asking—providing service. *Asking for a referral is the moment of conviction in your service.*

A final remark on referrals, and that is they briefly reintroduce the teacher-student dynamic back into your business. The difference is this time you're the student and the client is the teacher. The reason this dynamic occurs is because of the report card you will receive after the referred business transaction is completed. Remember, a client puts her credibility on the line to somebody she knows and cares about when she refers you business. That fact is very important for you to acknowledge and respect throughout the business transaction because she will eventually talk to the client she referred, and it will definitely matter what's said between them. You don't know the grade earned, but you can't wait to hear it. At the moment you hear it, it'll bring out the student in you as you attentively listen to what the teacher has to say.

Everybody Needs to Get Mad

Just thinking…

If only everybody were mad, everybody would be happy.

YOU'RE HALFWAY THROUGH THE turning point chapters, so now is the ideal time to take a break from them and reflect. Somewhat like halftime at a football game. The first five should have solidly positioned you to reach your tipping point. Passing through it is important for the reason previously mentioned. But it is equally important for another reason as well. Your tipping point signifies you are well on your way to building a powerful referral business while unsuspectingly signifying bringing madness to your business. It sounds mad, but you must achieve it if you are to build a powerful referral business. It's time for another mad scientist-like idea!

Your business at the human interaction level is simply about people who interface with one another and the subsequent dependent dynamics that are created. Therefore, to truly determine the effectiveness of your business, you need to consider three criteria: what you're doing, how they feel, and what they're doing. From a purely business standpoint, you're measuring the *effectiveness* of the *focus* of your business; while on a personal level, you're assessing the success of the interaction between you and them.

Think about the dynamics occurring in your business of clients and business partners. It's quite a convoluted gathering. You are trying to weave together a group of diverse people who don't know each other, have different needs, and are from various professions. Think about it some more: some of them get paid, others only pay; some always help, others always need help. And to top it all off, you want the people who are paying to brag about the people getting paid. Seriously! Maybe without even realizing it, your business is just as mad as the real world, given that both are constantly trying to convert diversity into unity. Where the real world measures success in an untold multitude of ways, you'll do it by determining the level of madness in your business. Once again, don't be skeptical.

To truly join the Referral-Based Service Industry, you must provide *MAD, M.A.D. Service*. I know, hard to believe but true! There's no way around it. It may sound confusing at first, even unbelievable, but MAD, M.A.D. Service is a fairly simple and straightforward concept that will clearly indicate where your business is based on a rather unorthodox rating scale. The key to understanding the concept is knowing the definitions of "MAD" and "M.A.D."

The word "MAD" means two things that can inspire different emotions ranging from anger to enthusiasm. For example, someone can be *mad at you* or *mad about you*. The definition of the acronym "M.A.D." means *make a difference*. It's what you are trying to accomplish with the clients and business partners who interface with your business and what you hope and expect, as appropriate, they do for your business.

On the surface, the MAD, M.A.D. Service concept may appear to only be a fun and whimsical notion. But in all actuality, it's a serious look at the premise of service leads to sales. When you provide MAD, M.A.D. Service, you're not only selecting the clients and business partners you will make a difference to through service, you are trying to create MAD, M.A.D. Clients and Business Partners in your business. They are making a difference to your business through sales. That's both the input and the output of MAD, M.A.D. Service.

With this basic knowledge of the three definitions of "MAD" and "M.A.D." in hand and the brief explanation of the concept itself, it's now time to talk about MAD, M.A.D. Service to clients.

The life-cycle of client service is based on two timeframes of service because of The Need Shift. The first timeframe is meant to impress, while the second one provides impact. In the first timeframe, you meet clients and complete the business transaction at hand. Depending on how you served them will determine the madness created. In the second timeframe, the transaction is completed, and now the attention turns exclusively to your business. The type of madness your business creates here will ultimately determine your level of success.

Let's look at a client through the lens of the MAD, M.A.D. Client Service rating scale on the following page. Start at the bottom, move from left to right, and then work your way up by focusing on the corresponding symbols in each column.

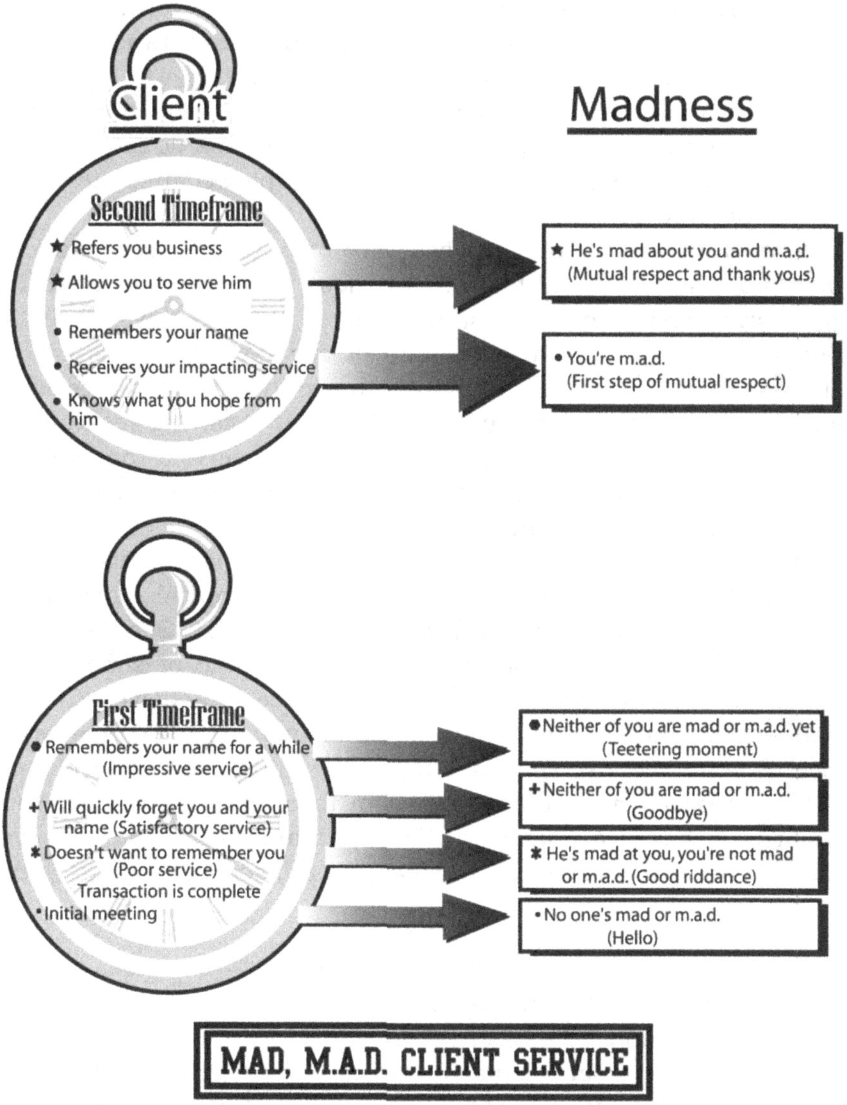

Here are some general observations about the MAD, M.A.D. Client Service rating scale above, along with some business impact thoughts. Within the first timeframe of service are four levels of madness. If you provide impressive service, you can easily transition to the second timeframe of service, which is the Referral-Based Service Industry. However, if you are a transactional businessperson, you stay within the first timeframe of service, and your business is primarily limited to saying hello and goodbye, for you are very quickly moving on to look for the next business transaction. At best, you are at the tropical depression level; clients will eventually forget you and your name because you haven't made a long-term service commitment to them. Sad to say it, but thank goodness for hello and goodbye transactional business people because they allow the rest of us to say hello.

Something else to be equally aware of is prematurely thinking your business is referral-based. How does it happen? You provide impressive service in the first timeframe, but you never formally transition to the second timeframe of service, yet you say your business is referral-based. At best, you are in the pseudo Referral-Based Service Industry because you are only receiving residual referrals from your first timeframe of impressive service that eventually fades with time. That was Rose in a nutshell—briefly impressive but not long-term impacting.

It's during the second timeframe of service that clients become connected to your business. You first attain tropical storm level, then hurricane level when you reach MAD, M.A.D. Service. When you take the time to build the second timeframe of service, you clearly understand that MAD, M.A.D. Service is achieved first by what you do and then by what clients know and subsequently do. They respond because you have taken the initial step of developing mutual respect between you and them through your service. Your business is based on saying hello and thank you, over and over again. *Even in a MAD, M.A.D. Business World, service leads to sales.*

The dynamics are different for business partners, but your success with them can still be measured on a MAD, M.A.D. Service rating scale. Where client service starts with the first timeframe of service, business partners usually start in the world of success. It takes a different strategy to convince them to enter the second timeframe of service with you. If they do, the results are the same with them as it is for clients; they connect to your business and together you support each other's business with referrals.

Let's look at a business partner through the lens of the MAD, M.A.D. Business Partner Service rating scale on the next page. Start at the bottom, move from left to right, and then work your way up by focusing on the corresponding symbols in each column.

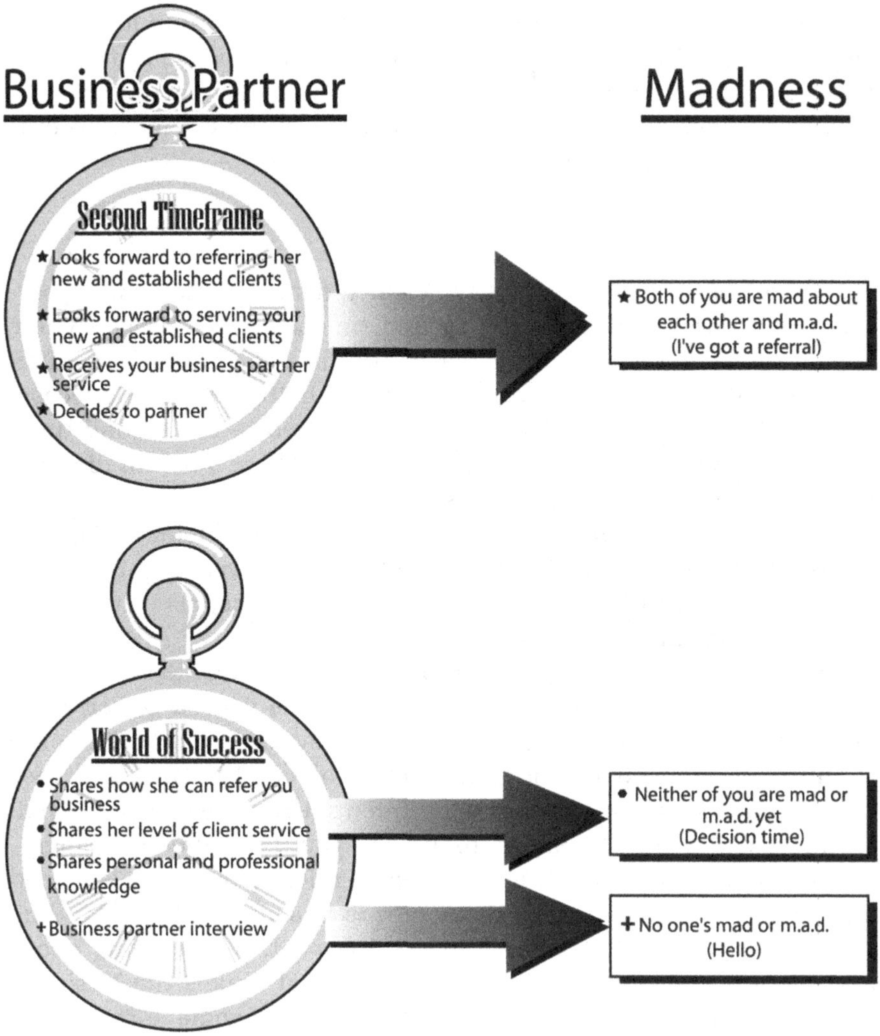
Business Partner
Madness
Second Timeframe
★ Looks forward to referring her new and established clients
★ Looks forward to serving your new and established clients
★ Receives your business partner service
★ Decides to partner
★ Both of you are mad about each other and m.a.d.
(I've got a referral)
World of Success
• Shares how she can refer you business
• Shares her level of client service
• Shares personal and professional knowledge
+ Business partner interview
• Neither of you are mad or m.a.d. yet
(Decision time)
+ No one's mad or m.a.d.
(Hello)

MAD, M.A.D. BUSINESS PARTNER SERVICE

Here are some brief observations about the MAD, M.A.D. Business Partner Service rating scale above. A business partner will not typically receive the first timeframe of service. To add a business partner to your business, you have to start with a pounce process, which is an interview consisting of *just two questions,* among other things. And don't forget about the other two interview questions if you are in a mortgage loan officer and agent partnership (discussed earlier). Only if you see benefit for your clients will you enter into the second timeframe of service. It is at this point a partnership begins in earnest, for each one of you exposes your business to outside forces you have carefully selected.

Hopefully, both illustrations have clearly demonstrated the importance of doing business in the second timeframe of service. Where client transactions are conducted in the first timeframe and business partners are usually acquired through the world of success, business success with both of them is achieved in the second timeframe. It is only in this timeframe of service where you will discover the Holy Grail of referrals. It is also in this timeframe where you can achieve the *trifecta business day.* In just a single business day you generate business from the three fundamental revenues streams of a powerful referral business: repeat client business, client referrals, and business partner referrals.

The reason to pay close attention to MAD, M.A.D. Service is it is the emotional barometer of your business. It is what a powerful referral business is all about. When you do make a difference to the clients and business partners connected to your business and they to you, you become a lasting, consequential business professional. Each person in your business, to include you, is a *difference maker.*

When all is said and done, a powerful referral business is a tried and proven way of business because it is based on a long-standing venerable concept that has a universal appeal. Where going above and beyond makes the world a better place, it makes the business world more professional. In both cases, there is some sort of commitment made to others. Making a difference is a win-win personal concept because, regardless of the situation or the setting, it brings out the best in the people who give and in the people who receive.

If I hadn't yet shown you that I have a touch of madness in me, I probably just did with this chapter. The reason being is a powerful referral business is a sane way of business with a bit of madness in it. Let's get back to the last five turning points and the eventual by-product they create.

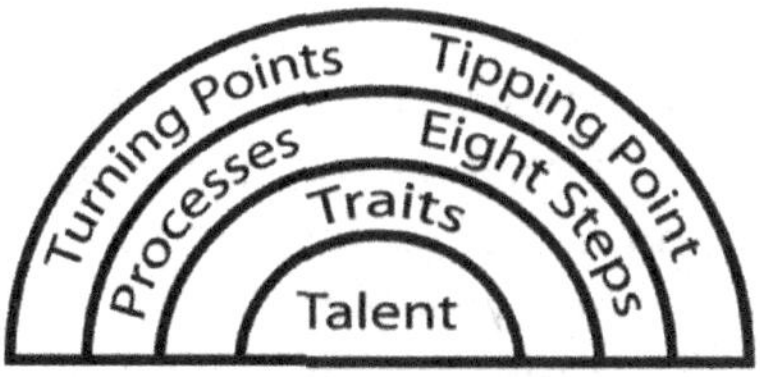

Get the Branding Iron

A time past...
Whether you were writing on your skin or buying a specific name of clothes or shoes, branding's been important to you.

IN THE COURSE OF LIVING your life, you will acquire all kinds of, and way too many possessions to possibly count. Most of them will be matter of fact, some will be valuable, some will be emotionally invaluable, and if you're lucky, a select few will be personally meaningful. While you will own all of them, it's the personally meaningful possessions you will take ownership of. In some way, you've personally put your touch on them, and now you're ready to share them with others. They're yours and you want people to know that. When they see them, they'll recognize them as yours because they reflect upon you in some way.

Just as it's important to take ownership of certain possessions in your personal life, the same holds true for your professional life as well. It's time to take ownership of your business by rightfully placing a defining thought on all of your hard work. When you do, you'll realize you can't be everything to everybody. If you try to be, it's kind of like being a business weather vane. You don't believe in anything—you believe in everything. My point is it's time to put an indelible branding mark on the service experience you created and value.

And when you do, you need to keep this one thought in mind. Even though you provide service to both clients and business partners, your brand should reflect your client service. It is they you serve first, which then allows you to hire business partners to serve their likely needs. Whenever business partners see your brand, they should be getting an *essence glimpse* of how you'll generate referrals for their business and how you'll serve their referred clients.

Branding may be an afterthought to you and, as such, not seem very important. But that's exactly why it is important, it attaches an afterthought to your name. Therefore, stop and think about all of the client service processes you have meticulously built up to this point. They should be a reflection of what's important to you while hopefully making a difference to the clients who interface with your business. Somewhere in all of that early hard work is your brand. Your service now has a distinct personality. It's making some type of statement. What is it? It's looking for a certain type of client. Who is it? Your brand may not be right in front of you, but it's nearby, embedded in your service.

Branding entails the deep thinking period of your business. You are figuratively looking inside of you and your client service to try to find the essence of both. It can be quite a revealing time because your brand isn't something that you create. Instead, it's a reflection of you and what you have created in your business. Therefore, don't put yourself through the exhaustive, painstaking exercise of building great client service and then not take the time to put a face to it. It's a natural progression of the work you have done, so do it.

Branding can easily be overlooked in a business because it may seem like bragging. As a general rule, people don't like to heap self-praise on themselves. Branding isn't bragging, though. Instead, it captures what you and your business are all about. It's *the moment of brevity,* in that it's your opportunity to succinctly portray your business through a message and/or an image. The obvious ways are by writing a short catchy phrase or by developing a logo. You can have one or both as part of your brand. Whichever way you do it, the end game is to try to create something that will lodge in the consciousness of your clients and business partners and prospective ones as well.

By establishing a business brand, you produce another influential communication tool for your business. Not only are you speaking for your business, but your brand is as well. Take full advantage of this unique opportunity by putting it on your letters, emails, business cards, and anything else associated with your business. If you don't take the time to establish a brand, look at the powerful but inexpensive opportunities you are missing out on to positively present you and your business.

Just for a moment, think about branding from this perspective. If your brand is on your business card and you or your business partners hand it to someone before engaging in a conversation, your brand becomes the very first words of your business, creating the very first impression the person gets of you and your business. Everybody knows a first impression matters and is enduring, so make your brand count.

Whatever your brand is, make sure you can back up what you publicize with integrity and service. People who interface with your business should see your brand at work. Don't say it unless you can show it to them. That's what branding is, your business in action. That is so important to keep in mind because a brand is not something you just throw out there on its own. It's a well conceived thought that is highly defendable by you and your service—not so much by what you say but, rather, by what you provide. Therefore, heed this warning on branding: you have to stay within the natural boundaries of common sense. In the end, it has to be supportive and believable; otherwise, you risk not being taken seriously.

Rose and I didn't have a brand until we started the process of looking at the client service we had built around her talent. It was then we realized we hadn't put any thought to the message or image we wanted to portray to the clients who interface with our business today or who might one day. We were like most everybody else, a name and a phone number. We were safely with the crowd—there was no standard for us to meet or for clients to expect. We cared about our business and our clients, but since we hadn't taken action to distinguish ourselves through a brand, we may have come across as not caring enough about either one.

When we started the process of developing our brand, we kept in mind that it must reflect on the clients who interface with our business. Our service is about them, and we felt our brand should follow the same principle. When they read our brand, whatever it is, we want them to know what they can *expect* from us. There's that word again!

So what was the mental process we went through to develop our brand? We simply took a step back from our business and took a concentrated look at four things: the client service we had built, our core belief, our leading personal strength, and who we are inside as people. Altogether, it would lead us to what we wanted to be known for. In short, we were searching for the truth that would seamlessly merge our business and us as one.

After considerable discussion that went back and forth, we drew the following conclusions. We were committed to providing a level of service that helped our clients professionally and personally. Integrity was an unbending principle when I was in the military and still is today for both of us. We loved serving while I was on active duty, and it naturally carried over into the business world. And finally, we believe in taking the time to get to know our clients and their families. What it all boils down to is we wanted to be known for our service, trust, and long-term personal commitment to our clients.

We came up with a phrase that we use throughout our business today—*Trustworthy Service for Life.* We felt completely comfortable with this brand, in part because of our commitment to the second timeframe of client service. By branding ourselves in such a way, we have tried to capture the true essence of us and our business. Now that we have taken the time to develop our branding message, we're spreading the word through various means that includes business cards, letters, emails, business merchandise, and conversations.

It is important to mention that we could have easily taken our brand in another direction by making it about the clients' aspirations, which would have been fine under a different business circumstance (referral business). But when we took into account the four core business dynamics occurring in a powerful referral business (serving clients, clients referring other clients, clients working with business partners, and business partners referring clients), it made more sense and was a better fit to take the path we did—to try to develop a brand that would have a specific meaning for both clients and business partners. It would communicate something important to each of them, albeit different messages. First, our clients would know their best interests and the interests of the clients they refer would always be our top priority. And second, business partners would know our business is not only positioned to serve their referral needs through the clients we serve but how we would serve the clients they refer to us. Even though the two messages are different from one another, both of them still share the same core theme—they are meant to encourage clients and business partners to first come to our business and then to support it.

It is equally important to mention that if we would have been interested in only building a transactional business there would have been yet another direction to take our brand (price). In such a business, a client becomes a customer and a mortgage becomes a product. The focus of the business is on an individual event rather than on the individual, hence the focus on price.

As you can clearly surmise from the above scenarios, a brand is a concisely written expression that directly reflects the type of business being built. It sounds like an easy enough task to accomplish, but I would suggest to you there's no greater effort of thinking occurring in business for so few a number of words.

When you take the time to brand your business, it's like throwing down the gauntlet and guaranteeing something. It comes with a heavy burden of *responsibility*, given that it puts your *credibility* on the line and makes you *accountable*. Can you see the subliminal leadership qualities associated with a brand? Accordingly, a brand isn't something to be taken lightly. On the contrary, it needs to be taken very seriously. If you don't meet the standard you established through your brand, your business becomes hollow, and you fail as a leader. You haven't measured up professionally and personally, which means you failed at your *public leadership challenge*. Where the premise of a business is the most basic thought of a business, a brand is the most public thought of a business. When you think about your brand in this highly personal way...you'll deliver it.

And when you deliver your brand, you provide both your clients and business partners a progressive and persuasive way to refer you business. Here's how. The subtle feature of a brand is it can be effectively used as a *transition* between your name and your service. For example, clients could say, "My mortgage advisers are Rose and Michael Kelly. They provide trustworthy service for life. They send me..., they call me..., they conduct..., if I need..." and so on. When clients take this type of action on your behalf, they are not only true believers in you and your business, they are mentioning your brand in a way that brings your business to life. Such an endorsement is highly convincing because they are optimistically talking about you, your brand, and your business. Business partners can perform this action as well. Even you can utilize this simple (pounce) process. When you meet someone new, start with a personal introduction, identify your brand, and then briefly expand on your client service that supports your brand. It's interesting to note this is a pounce process you, clients, and business partners can all use.

Branding allows you to attach a carefully crafted thought with your name. People see your name and then associate with it in a way that generates an emotional feeling about you. It can stir a positive image of you in the minds of the people who interface with your business and to those who may. That's just one of the many reasons why a brand is a natural fit for a powerful referral business—it can create emotion.

Branding is one of the freebies in business that shouldn't be free, considering what it can do for both your name and your business. You hit the mark on branding when your brand becomes synonymous with your name. You also hit the mark when you want people to ask you about it so you can eagerly defend it.

A well-positioned brand will communicate two things. First, it'll show your clients what they can expect of you while showing your business partners how you hope to generate referrals for them. And second, it'll communicate something about you and your business.

If you don't take the time to establish a brand, you are unintentionally reinforcing the perception your business is made up of just you in a profession. Through your own inaction you are unexpectedly doing transactional business branding. You are explicitly communicating what type of businessperson you are. People who look at your business card will only know *three things* about you: your name, your contact information, and your profession; i.e., call me and I can do a transaction for you.

If you haven't already done so, start taking advantage of branding in your business. It can go a long way in creating and establishing your business identity and helping you build a reputation in the crowded marketplace. If for no other reason, it is important for people to know *four things* about you: your name, your contact information, your profession, and the essence of you and your business.

At the end of the day, a brand is a multifaceted essence statement—it can peak one's interest, serve as an influential communication tool, make a first impression, create an emotional feeling, act as a transition, lead to a conversation, and even motivate you. It is for all of these reasons why you need to brand your business.

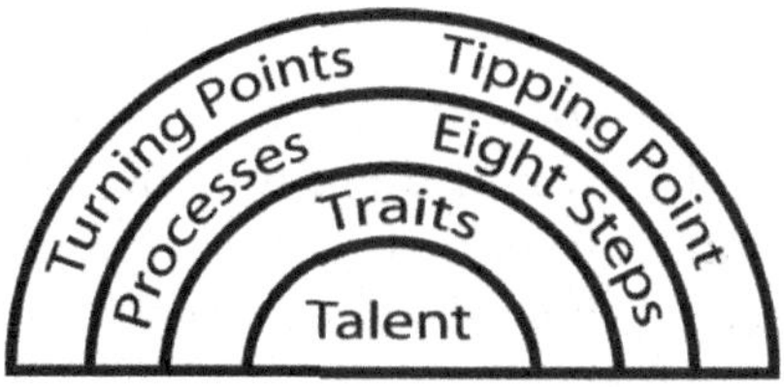

Prepare For the Moment

A time past...
The teen years are the most difficult and awkward years of youth. Even the business world has teen years in it.

IF YOU WERE TO STEP onto a stage right now to give a presentation, the audience members would cordially clap, slyly glance down at their watches, and then stare straight back at you. You suddenly realize the last thing to think about when building a presentation is the first thing to say when you speak. You have less than five minutes to convince them it's to their benefit to stay awake through the one-hour presentation you worked so hard on. Every word matters during this opening moment, for it will serve as the gateway to the rest of the presentation. The pressure is on to deliver a *precise message with an intended purpose.*

It almost doesn't seem fair the opening moment would warrant such a great deal of attention and carry so much weight. The audience members wouldn't think that way, though. They are looking to be grabbed in a way that makes them lean forward and listen. They know a lot is riding on this early moment, for it will help them decide whether they are going to be receptive to the rest of the presentation or not.

This situation brings to light the current state of your business. No matter how hard you have worked on it or how much you have done, it's still not enough. It's going to need a little bit more help. Your business at this stage of development faces the identical challenge as that of the presentation described above. The majority of the work has been accomplished, and now the attention-grabbing opening moment remains. But where a presentation only has one such opening moment to successfully traverse through, your business has multiple type moments you must smoothly and effectively navigate through.

What is an opening moment in a business? It is a scripted moment. When you combine all of them together, they reveal the array of *business opportunities* intended to accomplish a specific purpose. They will unequivocally show the scope of the business, thereby revealing the type of business.

Where a successful presentation rests on immediately connecting with the audience members and then moving them in some way, the same is true for you when you talk to the clients and business partners in your business and prospective ones as well. It is through the articulation of prepared words you can move them in a precise way that allows you to achieve the desired end result of the moment at hand.

The amount of work and hours you have put in up to this point is staggering. So much so, you may want to try to wing it through this phase of your business. And why not, we are just talking about talking. Finally the easy part has arrived—now you just have to do it. What could be easier?

Think about the gravity of what you have done up to this point. You didn't just make a minor adjustment or midcourse correction; you fundamentally changed the dynamics of your business, from the new service you provide, to the things you do in support of that service. You've created numerous new entry points into your business that are intended to achieve a specific purpose. To ensure that you properly enter each one of them, you have to articulate just the right message. Therefore, the very next thing you have to fundamentally change in your business are the words you speak. Just as your service dramatically changed so too will your voice. You need to start speaking in a precise way that directly supports the various new entry points of opportunity in your business.

Unfortunately, old vocal habits are hard to kick and that could be truer here than you might imagine. In all likelihood, you are trying to break free of old vocal habits, possibly learned over several years. I know that was the case for Rose. Why? Business conversations are not conducted in a vacuum; they are conducted in regard to how business is done. She was a transactional businesswoman, and therefore, she spoke the conversations of a transactional business. She was just being true to her business of many years. Can you see why it's so important at this point to believe in the service you built? If you don't, excuses will show up everywhere encouraging you to slip back into what's comfortable to say.

At this juncture you're validating all of the work you have done. If you weren't true to yourself in the service processes you developed, it will all come crashing down right here. If you do believe in what you developed, then you stand a fighting chance of breaking old vocal habits and creating new ones. To help you successfully navigate this challenging stage of your business, you will need the two tools of slowing down and scripts.

The first tool to help you through this business model development phase is to *slow down and think before you speak*. You are now doing things in your business that demand you speak in a fresh and exciting way. Accepting the fact you are learning a new way of business should give you the self-control and strength of mind to slow down. So for now, it's much more important to get your messages across than trying to deliver them effortlessly. Focusing on trying to being effortless at this point is self-defeating because you will surely stumble. Such a high standard so early on will lead to frustration, which can easily keep you stuck in what's comfortable, on outdated vocal habits. Don't do it!

The second tool is *scripting*, an unbelievably powerful, necessary business activity. Few things are more important in your business than scripting. You could have done absolutely everything right up to this point, but by going forward with your new business unscripted, you risk having a disconnect between you and what you've built. If this happens, you can miss out on business opportunities or even worse, create uncertainty with the people who interface with your business, resulting in hesitation on their part to support it. This actually happened to Rose with a past client, and it resulted in one of the more eye-opening comments of her professional career.

The client had assumed Rose was too busy to help her with an investment property purchase and told her so. The client wasn't being mean-spirited in any way; it was just what she thought because she knew Rose was the branch manager, along with being a loan officer. It's amazing how this one brief comment opened Rose's eyes up to scripting. She finally realized that without scripting she was playing the dangerous assumption game of *"they know,"* which more times than not leads to missed business opportunities. Rose subsequently helped the client, and now she knows Rose is never to busy to serve her professional needs. In fact, since then, she has conducted repeat business and sent Rose referrals. Through this one client experience Rose realized the real meaning of scripting. Scripting is the bridge between you and what you have built, in that it connects the two great forces at work—you and your business.

Scripting is nothing more than writing down on paper what you would like to say in a conversation. The things you can write down range from questions to narratives. The complexity associated with scripting is identifying the moments in business that need to be scripted. You don't need to script everything. To do so would create the impression everything you say is important. Not true. Scripting opportunities need to be limited to the point where they are used to formally recognize the *generator moments* in your business.

Generator moments are primarily one-on-one interactions that not only make a difference, they *produce* long-term impact. They are the business generating conversations of your business—for you and your business partners. They can happen in any of the three phases of your service, from your first and second timeframe of service to your pounce processes. Several examples are: initial client meeting, explaining the first timeframe of service to a client, client interactions during the first timeframe of service (to include both required technical and unique service interactions), contacting a prospective business partner for an interview appointment, interviewing a prospective business partner, explaining the second timeframe of service to a client or business partner, contacting a client who sent you a referral, a client telephone call during the second timeframe of service, professionally managing the transaction, sharing business-building information with a business partner, referring a client to a business partner during the first or second timeframe of service, contacting a prospective client who is referred to you, asking a client or business partner for a prospective business partner referral, introducing a new service, asking for service feedback from a client or business partner, advising a client, explaining your required technical service to a client, and even explaining your experience to a new client or prospective business partner.

It is in these types of encounters where you need to be at your precise best because they serve as the strength points within your framework. They bear the greatest burden in keeping the framework strong, which will eventually determine the level of business success you achieve. They are the bread-and-butter scripted business moments of a powerful referral business. The words spoken during these moments not only serve as the gateway to achieving the intended result at hand, they address the tenets of a Business Star (the vision of a powerful referral business).

Not to be overlooked within your numerous generator moments are the common occurrence comments you might face. A generator moment is a shared interaction between you and either a client, a business partner, or a prospective one. It's not only an opportunity for you to be at your best but for them as well by responding constructively to what you say and by asking pointed questions. Their commentary can vary from frequently asked questions, normal concerns, and/or objections to counter arguments. Preparing for these common occurrences within a generator moment may seem secondary to you, but that couldn't be further from the truth. They're just as important, if not more so, for *they are how you show your total command of your profession.* You can't be any more convincing then when you know both what to say and how to respond. When you can do both, no situation is too big or too difficult for you.

Out of all the bread-and-butter scripting opportunities in a powerful referral business, just one of them will stand out above all the rest when it comes to common occurrence comments (objections). In fact, it's a scripting opportunity that's indigenous to every type of business—required transaction activities. It only makes sense that this activity would present the greatest challenge; it deals with what is most important to clients—their money. Such a response is to be expected, so you need to be fully prepared. To ignore the obvious is to show poor judgment, something a leader never wants to do.

A far less seldom used type of generator moment, but still very important, is speaking in front of a group of people. These types of moments can either be in the form of a service or a pounce process. The most common ways to carry them out are through the use of a workshop, seminar, meet-and-greet, etc. During such events, you can either provide valuable information to people already connected to your business, or you can try to convince people (typically prospective clients) of something. Just like one-on-one generator moments, you have to be prepared to both deliver your message and respond to a variety of commentary. These types of scripted moments can be the most challenging and nerve-racking in your business for two very different reasons. First, you have to stand up and speak in front of a group of people for a lengthy period of time. And second, you may well have to literally think on your feet, sometimes in front of several people you don't know.

When you script generator moments and the associated common occurrences within them, you connect yourself to your business, prepare for every important situation, and become *a strong closer* of the business opportunity at hand. Not only will your conversion rate rise, you may well pick up follow-on business because you are saying the right things at the right time in the right way. When you take the time to script such moments in your business, you understand the awesome power of words and how a carefully crafted message can literally move people to do what you need them to do. Scripting a situation gives you the confidence to face it because you have prepared for the moment. No matter if the moment is sitting across the table from one person or standing in front of a large group of people you may or may not know.

Another type of scripting opportunity to pay attention to in your business is the *impression moment*. What can you script that will make an impression on the people who come in contact with you and your business? The point of this type of scripting is to create positive interest or a feeling about your business that is both inviting and professional. Just like generator moments, these scripting opportunities can occur in any of the three phases of your service. Some examples are: the telephone etiquette people encounter when they call your business, the greeting clients receive when they come to your office for their appointment, and what you articulate when you first come in contact with somebody you might want to make a part of your business. The inclusion of these types of scripting opportunities further confirms you have to first impress people before you can impact them.

Scripting presents an even greater challenge for agents for two very different reasons. First, they have the responsibility to *negotiate* on behalf of their clients. To effectively conduct this unique and quite fluid scripting activity, they need to first identify the influential dynamics (no matter who they favor). It is only then that agents can find the appropriate words and the right approach that gives them the best chance to reach an agreement that creates a win-win situation for their clients. Even better yet is a win-Win outcome. In such a situation, the client and the other party involved benefit from the negotiation—both of them have a win, with the client having the bigger Win! And second, because they provide a distinct first timeframe of service to both sellers and buyers, they have to develop a distinct set of scripts for each one.

o

The unique feature of scripting is it brings *forward-thinking* to your business. It has you verbally planning ahead for what will eventually materialize and matter most. In other words, thoughtful conversations through forethought. With that said, don't get the wrong impression on scripting. Scripting is not about speaking prepared words but about believing in those prepared words when you speak. It is an authentic means of highly effective communication. When you make scripting an integral part of your business, you bring a professional aura to you and your business. That's the underlying character feature associated with scripting—it's not meant to apply pressure to a generator moment; it's meant to apply persuasive professionalism to it.

You know you have mastered the art of scripting when you can turn a contentious interaction (individual or group setting) into a trust building moment. Why? There's no other time in business that requires more thoughtful words.

o

Over time, and through plenty of repetition, you will eventually get comfortable with every generator moment in your business and the scripted material will slowly be put away. Until then, regularly practice reading it aloud so when you're in a conversation with an individual or a group of people, it sounds natural, not scripted. When they listen to you speak, they feel the words are coming from your caring spirit, not from your many hours of memorization.

To help you quickly learn all of your scripts and acquire an ease about them, consider trying the following technique. Instead of focusing on each word when practicing, focus on the theme points to be made. In other words, don't tie yourself to the words, tie yourself to the points you are trying to make. It is a much faster and easier way to learn, and it will give you the flexibility you need to come across as natural. When you learn scripts in this way, you subconsciously recognize that a scripted moment is a precise message, not precise words.

And here's one more technique to help you with this aspect of your business. To remain sharp with all of your messages, no matter how long it has been since you last used them, consider reviewing and quickly practicing seldom used generator moments before delivering them. This act will remove an expected layer of rust while keeping you confident and your messages intentional.

Don't think you will identify every scripting opportunity. Scripting can involve some hard knocks because you'll eventually have to build a script for a situation (beyond the bread-and-butter scripts previously identified) you weren't prepared for. When that occurs, and it most certainly will, don't fret about one lost opportunity. Instead, focus on scripting a message that allows you to convert future opportunities into positive outcomes.

And don't think for a minute you won't require the two tools of slowing down and scripting to help you through this business period. I watched Rose struggle mightily on many different occasions. For as smooth and talented as she is, it was still very difficult and quite awkward to go cold turkey and start sharing a slew of new business messages. It is not easy to move from the conversations of a transactional business to the conversations of a powerful referral business—comparable to learning an unfamiliar language...as an adult! We wrote scripts and in the process I reminded her many times to slow down, to her great chagrin. Even though she has now mastered most of the generator moments in her business, it's still an ongoing process and will probably be for some time to come. In time, scripts will become just another part of her planned day and turn into comfortable conversation.

When you take the time to build and then learn scripts, you formally recognize that each type of business (in this case, a powerful referral business) has a *corresponding language* associated with it. It only makes sense; they (transactional, referral, and powerful referral) all have a different business objective. Out of the three businesses, a powerful referral business will require the most scripting because it has the most entry points of business opportunities to pass through.

This brings to light the broad-based subtlety of your scripts. A fair amount of them will always stay the same because they reflect the predetermined business opportunities that will occur over and over again. It's this aspect of scripting that allows you to eventually master *the language of your business*. The scripts that'll be in flux and, thus, pose a recurring challenge, will be the ones that support pounce processes developed as a result of a new common occurrence or a changing market. It is these types of business opportunities that will not only require you to develop and learn new scripts, they will be the primary source for the continuing challenge associated with scripts.

And one more quick point to make. There's an interesting link between service and scripts to recognize. They both rely on a *belief threshold* to achieve their intended purpose. Where belief in your service leads to your passion of asking for business or prospecting for it, belief in your scripts leads to you being authentic. No other business activities will reflect your individualism more and your need for framework.

Here's a cautionary caveat when it comes to scripting. Initial scripting efforts can tend to gravitate toward the *conduct* (transaction) side of your business instead of the *generate* (repeat business and referral) side. It is an expected and natural response because business success is progressive, in that it begins with conducting transactions and then builds upon that success by generating repeat business and referrals. To ensure you effectively address this *progression of success*, make sure your scripts address the duality of your business, just like a schedule does.

As a transactional businesswoman, Rose never formally recognized this progression of success in her business. Her scripting efforts were limited to the conduct side of her business. And she was very good at it. She professionally advised clients in a manner that showed her caring spirit while at the same time displaying complete confidence in herself. She easily handled the *leading conversation* of a transactional business—leveraging client trust to close the transaction. This brings to light yet another interesting contrast between a transactional and referral-based business. A transactional business is primarily a single event business—look at its name. While on the other hand, a referral-based business encompasses a set of important events. As such, there are a host of leading conversations that bear weight. Altogether, they make the business possible.

It's quite evident that scripting is primarily viewed as a highly effective means of verbal communication. But in all actuality, you communicate in your business through two means—verbal and written. It is essential then to quickly mention the importance of written scripts as well. Just like verbal scripts, written scripts (pre-written and pre-positioned letters, notes, emails, seminar slides, questionnaires, surveys, etc.) can occur in any of the three phases of service. And just like verbal scripts, they are intended to move people in some particular way and cause long-term impact across your business. Therefore, give equal consideration to your written words as well. When you do, you are thoughtful in your thoughts, whether they are spoken or written.

Scripting can easily be the least appreciated activity of a powerful referral business because it deals with the most youthful activity—learning how to speak. What could be more of a waste of time? Don't underestimate the importance of it to your business for this one simple reason: scripting brings an eloquent voice to your business. It takes what might otherwise appear to be an obscure, unimpressive pile of service and turns it into a captivating piece of work that connects clients and attracts business partners while fully leveraging them. Scripting is the business-building voice of your business. At the end of the day, your service can only stand out among the crowd when you place it on the shoulders of scripting.

Here's the bottom line on scripting. For all of its dynamics and importance to your business, scripting at its core is simply *intended conversations with intentions.* Such purposeful conversations will be comprised of bread-and-butter scripts, scripts beyond bread-and-butter, pounce process scripts, and scripts for unanticipated situations. Altogether, they strongly position you to speak with an influential voice during any type of meaningful business opportunity.

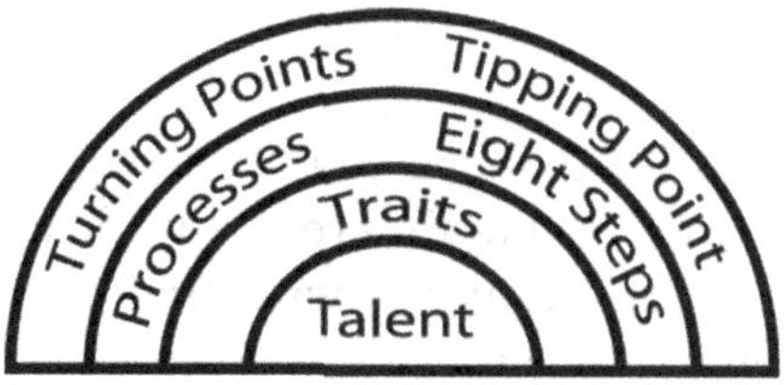

Just Thinking About You

A time past...
Did somebody ever tell you something
that was just too good to keep to yourself?

YOU ARE ALWAYS AT YOUR personal best when you are *unexpectedly thoughtful* to other people. Such moments are never about you but always about them. At no other time is your caring spirit felt more or on greater display. Each and every time you focus your actions in such a helpful way, the people on the receiving end are appreciative, which makes these interactions *moments of reciprocating kindness*. Predictably, the framework of a powerful referral business provides the opportunity to be unexpectedly thoughtful. In fact, you can be unexpectedly thoughtful in a variety of ways.

The powerful referral business you are building has never been about you but, rather, about the people who interface with it. That simple theory is about to be tested because the business you have built now embodies much more than just you. It touches and impacts clients and business partners who depend on you in various ways. To serve all of them, with a personal touch, you must start thinking on multiple levels. When you do, you add another dimension to your explained service experience. Not only are you *providing*, you're also *thinking* and *caring*. This is the excitable moment in your business because you know something you just can't wait to share. No other time in business is as sure a moment as this.

Very rarely will a business day pass by without receiving and/or learning some type of information. On the surface, it may appear to be a nuisance, of little value, even worthless. That's probably true for most of it, but not all of it. One thing is for certain, information is only information until you do something with it. *Sharing information that can make a difference renders it service.*

During the course of a business year you will likely be bombarded with information from various different sources: print and talk media, Internet, email, conversations with friends, contact from other business professionals, all manner of sources. The information will cover every subject imaginable and will usually fall into one of two categories, *business-related* or *other matter.* Regardless of how you receive it, the natural inclination is to filter out the other matter information and determine the value of the business-related information on your business. If you tend to assimilate new information in this narrow manner, you're thinking about yourself instead of the people who interface with your business. This is a precarious view, for it weakens your service by keeping it in a single-dimension.

Single-dimension service is where you stay in front of clients and business partners with a predetermined level of service—and that usually costs you money. For instance, this may entail sending some type of monthly mailing, quarterly newsletter, burned business-building CD, or Happy New Year letter with a business calendar magnet, to name just a few. They are all important to success in varying degrees, but there's another dimension of service you can add to your business, which doesn't cost money.

Given that information is everywhere, its value can tend to be diminished and, therefore, easily overlooked because the common perception is things of value cost money. Surprisingly enough, information that costs nothing can provide the greatest value to your service, meeting both professional and personal needs, when you're a businessperson who thinks and cares on multiple levels.

Learning about new *business-related* information should always have you determining how it impacts your business and the people who interface with it. Natural instinct will have you first assess and determine the impact to your business. You'll do this without even thinking about it. It's instantaneous. Once you're done with this self-assessment, you then need to immediately turn your attention to how it impacts the people who interface with your business. Remember, you're serving different groups of people (clients and various business professionals) with dissimilar needs so you need to think on multiple levels.

If the business-related information affects one of your advanced groupings (previously discussed), you can quickly and efficiently serve this predetermined need. We've done exactly that in our business. Here's how. We advanced grouped our military clients (which also included some of our business partners), and when an aspect of the Veterans Administration (VA) home loan program changed, we right away sent out this new information to all of them via a *pre-built email group*. Not only did we keep them proactively informed on information relevant to them, we generated business from it.

It's important to take a moment here and quickly expand on the significant role of pre-built email groups. They are the complementary delivery system for your advanced groupings. When you build an advanced group, you're acknowledging upfront there's a group of people within your database who have a common professional or personal need that will eventually be served. When this need finally surfaces, it's your pre-built email grouping that'll allow expeditious delivery of the information to them. When you combine advanced groupings and pre-built email groups in this manner, they symbolically represent one more step of many you're taking on your steady march toward business efficiency.

And where some business people would altogether filter out the *other matter* information because it doesn't impact their business, you realize it may impact someone who interfaces with your business. This type of information contains the real nuggets because it's obscure and not easily revealed. It is also this type of information that reveals yet another important reason for being a good listener, storing personal client/business partner information in your database management system, and having advanced groupings unique to your business. By embracing all three activities, you can capture personal service-related opportunities that others routinely miss, whether to an individual or a group. There is no better way to demonstrate just thinking about you.

You can also apply the concept of just thinking about you to people who are outside of your business. It can just as effectively be utilized with prospective business opportunities as well. Here is an example of how Rose and I are doing exactly that. As a retired military couple, we routinely interact with military families—some of whom are still on active duty and some retired. When we are in a conversation with them, we willingly share a piece of obscure but long-standing information concerning the VA home loan program. If they are classified as a disabled veteran, the VA funding fee for a home loan is waived. This information impacts them in decidedly different ways. For retired disabled veterans, this can provide an immediate opportunity to upgrade to a larger home with minimal cost. For members still on active duty, it can alert them to have all of their medical conditions fully documented and instead of buying a home just before they retire, wait and have the VA first determine if they are a disabled veteran. This can amount to thousands of dollars in savings when purchasing a home. Our well-timed sharing of this relevant information has resulted in some of these people coming to us for their home financing needs. We obviously share this information accordingly with our active duty and retired military clients.

Being a good listener and having advanced groupings is the best way to fully tap the value of information. They are what allow you to successfully channel it to the appropriate people (group or individual) at the opportune time. You can't be any more caring or proactive in your business than sharing information that meets a need without being asked—it's a real head-turner. It evokes the best responses you'll get from the people connected to your business because *it's the most personal service you can provide.*

Once you have this type of information in hand, you must then communicate it in a timely manner. The most powerful and effective manner is to telephone the people involved and tell them about it. If the information needs to be shared with an advanced group in a short period of time, then a pre-built email group format may be the preferred method. In either case, don't forget to ask for a referral if the information is being shared with clients. And why not ask business partners for a referral if the information is being shared with them? They don't need to be asked. They are already making a *conscious effort* to generate referrals for you, just as you are for them.

When you think and care in your business, you add another dimension to your service, and you allow your personal side to come out. Where pre-planned service creates a conditioning-effect over time by keeping your name front and center, sharing real-time service information says you're watching out for your clients' and business partners' best interests every day. Thinking and caring on multiple levels turns the second timeframe of service on its head because you've completely flipped the dynamics. Now, clients and business partners feel they're in your forethoughts. As a result, you have passed the most basic test of a powerful referral business; you turned theory into reality—it really is about them.

As versatile as just thinking about you has already proven to be to your service, it still has more versatility to offer. It can also be used to *extend your business* in four distinct ways (the first two ways are business partner service processes). Just like the previously talked about scenarios, limit the utilization of this concept to the people it affects. By doing so, you strongly position yourself to make a difference instead of wasting your time and the time of others. This is yet one more occasion to possibly serve an advanced group. Let's take a look at an example of each.

First, just thinking about you is a unique service opportunity for your business partners. Because they are an extension of your service, when *business-related* information occurs in their profession that benefits their clients, it will more than likely benefit your clients as well. Sharing this type of information with your clients is a genuine way to not only *extend your service* but also to possibly generate referrals for your business partners. It's a natural and professional insertion of them into your business because the insertion isn't driven by you or them, but by their profession. When you and your business partners share valuable thinking and caring information with your clients that isn't being shared by the business people currently serving that likely need, competitive service conditions are at work. *It's the high-road way of competing against rival business partners.* There's no more professional way to win against rival business partners than doing it with service.

It is equally important to take a look at the above scenario from the other viewpoint by completely flipping the dynamic. It reveals an interesting insight. For example, when the home mortgage interest rates fell rather sharply, we informed our clients, and we informed our business partners who then shared the information with their clients. Our business was now working for us on two levels—we were refinancing clients in our business and our business partners' clients as well, who we then turned into mutual-clients because we chose the psychology of clients over business partners. Instead of extending our service through business partners like mentioned above, we were now *extending the reach* of our business through them. Can you see how important it is to identify your clients' likely needs and then partner with like-minded business people in those professions?

The causal reason why just thinking about you is such an important business partner service process is it primarily deals with what's most important to clients—their money. You are proactively delivering money-saving or money-making opportunities to them across various professions. You have, in essence, expanded on the concept at work behind *the decisive service activity* (professionally manage the transaction) by applying it to your business partners.

Another service opportunity associated with the just thinking about you concept is to utilize clients in a *liaison role.* When business-related information occurs in your profession that doesn't personally affect your clients but it could affect someone they know, share it with them. Make sure to clearly communicate upfront you know it doesn't impact them, but it might impact people they care about and you would hope they could tell them on your behalf. When they do, you have now extended the reach of your business through your clients. You have, in essence, temporarily transferred your caring spirit to them. Rose utilized this type of service opportunity when the federal government implemented the $8K tax credit program for first-time homebuyers. She asked her clients to act as a liaison for her and share this information with the people they know and care about who could possibly benefit from this program (which they did). Through their efforts, on her behalf, she generated new business. This unique type of service activity (utilizing clients in a liaison role to pass on an important message from you) is a perfect opportunity to reach out to your advanced grouping of ideal clients.

This situation brings to light the importance of social media as it relates to your clients. The widespread acceptance and utilization of it (in various formats) has made it easy for them to quickly reach out to their network of friends in multiple ways to disseminate this type of information on your behalf. In all actuality, they can reach out at any time. Your hope is they only do it in a positive way (sharing an aspect of your first and/or second timeframe of service) or at your request like discussed above. Where you can utilize social media in your business to make a difference, it will help your clients brag about you and your business and/or share messages from you in a far-reaching way. The use of social media is a powerful way for clients to try to refer people they know. The others ways, which are also powerful, are the long-established standbys—email, telephone conversation, and face-to-face conversation. When all is said and done, clients can reach out to people they know through electronic, emotional, and personal settings.

And finally, just thinking about you is an opportunity to pounce as well. For example, if you are working with prospective clients or trying to attract new business partners and something happens in your profession that could impact them, immediately share it with them. The specific information shared may not be a common occurrence, but the occasion to share new information that can make a difference is a common occurrence, one that reoccurs over and over again in business. Hence, a pounce process opportunity. To expedite the delivery of this type of just thinking about you information, you can pre-build an email with a canned introduction/closing and then insert the new information in-between as it becomes available.

Just thinking about you is *the most fluid* service, business partner, and pounce process you have in your business because you never know when or how often it will occur. That in itself makes it a *critical process* to have as a part of your service—it's genuine positioning with genuine information throughout the entire year. You're not pushing (selling) somebody or something. Instead, you're real-need and real-time informing, which makes it the most thoughtful type of service in your business. At the end of the day, just thinking about you is *targeted service within your service* that provides an excellent opportunity for a deep engagement.

When explaining your service (especially the second timeframe), make it a point to briefly discuss your effort to deliver just thinking about you service. Doing so will illustrate the full dimension of your service while vividly displaying your caring spirit. Later on you will see how Rose and I make just thinking about you a part of our explained client service experience.

Yet another application of just thinking about you involves knowingly sending out service items that are outside of your explained service experience. This type of service is not a spontaneous effort like that just mentioned, but it will still come across as spontaneous to the people who receive it. The reason being is you don't mention it when explaining your service. These items will usually be sent out in the second timeframe of service, and they can be to both clients and business partners. Some examples here might be: a holiday card, a birthday card, a personal note or card acknowledging an important event or achievement, or a daylight savings reminder letter along with some seasonal home tips, to name just a few. Yet another aspect of this type of service in the second timeframe might be to host market-driven educational seminars for clients or business partners. Not to be overlooked, this type of service can even be applied in the first timeframe. Here's one example of how. Buying a home is a stressful activity. Mortgage lending and real estate business people can try to lessen the stress by sending out a small gift card with a note meant to relax clients.

Because all of the above service is unexpected, it naturally creates a different personal reaction than what explained service does. Where explained service creates a conditioning-effect, unexpected service creates an appreciative feeling. In the end, this type of service adds a nice (topping-off) touch to your explained service. One way that Rose and I utilize this type of service in our business is by sending our clients and business partners a birthday card. Regardless of how you use it or how much, it's this particular kind of service that most allows you to *over deliver.*

When you start habitually thinking and caring on multiple levels, you bring more value to your service and capitalize on opportunities narrower thinking business people fail to see. It sounds easy, but it tends to get overlooked. It's human nature to think about oneself, but in the end, that tends to restrict one into thinking small. Come out of that box and expand your thought process to the people who are bringing you business success and to those who may. New information, no matter if it's business-related or other matter, should always have you subconsciously asking this one question: "How does this impact me and the people who interface or may interface with my business?" By doing so, you are capitalizing on a very important aspect of a powerful referral business—providing the most value touches.

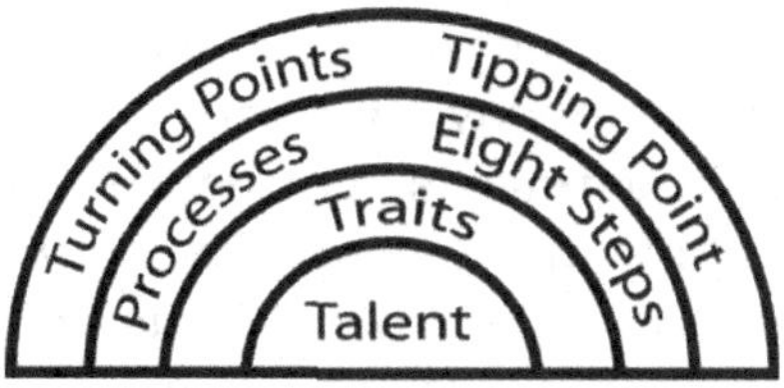

Get Some Fresh Air

A time past...
The best thing about childhood was playing outside. Early on you knew it was special because you had to ask to do it. Now, you don't have too.

ALL OF YOUR HARD WORK has finally brought you to the moment you have been waiting for, the shiny car moment. Spend most of a day washing, cleaning, and polishing a car—and now it's time to take it out for a spin. It wouldn't make much sense to do all that work and then keep it garaged. Such is the moment at hand in your business. It's time to take your service out for a ride and show it off. Welcome to the world of success and the land of pounce.

You knew this book would eventually strike your comfort zone, and it has. It's time to get up out of your chair, get some fresh air, and leverage what you built. It may sound a little frightening, even intimidating at first, but networking isn't nearly as difficult as it seems. It really is a low-threat environment. You don't have to walk door-to-door or cold-call. That's old-school thinking, and it's not even your industry.

You're in the Referral-Based Service Industry and in possession of the biggest leverage stick in business—*service*—which completely changes the dynamics of networking. Where some people see networking as a chance to hand out a business card and mention they have a business, you see it as an integral part of your business that helps you accomplish multiple purposes. When you network, your focus is on how to leverage your service.

The task of networking is important because it's what gives your service its *dual purpose*. Your service is ready to do two things for you in your business, but only if you network. The obvious thing it does is serve the people connected to your business. That's what brings you your success today. But your service is ready to do so much more for you; it just needs your networking voice to be heard. In a powerful referral business, *networking is the intermediary activity between your service and the people who need it.* It's not a stand alone activity but, rather, a supporting one for your service. When you actively network, you bring to fruition the second thing service can do for you: *attract new people to your business.* By doing so, you fully leverage your service experience, and you avoid keeping a secret that shouldn't be kept.

The other telling reason networking is so important is *it's the fourth fundamental revenue stream of your business.* Where the first three streams of repeat client business, client referrals, and business partners tell what's happening in your business, this one tells what's happening with you. It deals with your personal effort to look outside of established business to bring in new business. In no uncertain terms, it'll reveal what you really think about your service.

When you confidently act upon the broad spectrum of opportunities networking presents to you, everyone important in your business—you, clients, and business partners—is now working together for a common goal, a powerful referral business. The service you provide has created the expected dynamic of four revenue streams at work in your business. Why is that significant? It's the definition to the phrase, *you and your business.*

Look even closer, and the phrase reveals yet another interesting insight. There's a reason why you're first in that phrase. Not only does everything start with you, but *your networking effort serves as the feeder revenue stream of your business.* When you network, you literally feed your business revenue streams by attracting new clients and business partners to them. You can somewhat control the speed of growth in your business by your extent of networking, for it serves as the accelerator of your business. The more clients and business partners you add, the more people you connect to your business, the more repeat business you have, and the more referrals you give and receive. Networking, along with a strong market, is what enables you to bring explosive growth to your business.

Don't lose sight of the primary role of networking. It is nothing more than trying to add clients and business partners to your established business you're already providing the second timeframe of service. Keeping this simple concept in mind puts networking in its proper perspective and keeps you true to the philosophy of service leads to sales.

And don't overlook the side benefit of networking. You will in all likelihood expand your *business associate network* during this activity. This expansion will occur through the various interactions of meeting, introducing, and recommending. You will personally meet new associates, people you just met will introduce them, or somebody you already trust will recommend them. Regardless of how it happens, this residual-effect of networking enhances your ability to serve the diverse *might needs* of your clients.

O

The comfort associated with networking is that there are always people who need your service. And that's the key—they need your service. Just as your service is important to them, it is to you as well because it will determine your conversations and eventual effectiveness with them. By having service on your side, you can have convincing conversations with the spectrum of people around you: *casual acquaintances, someone new, friends, business associates, clients,* and *business partners*. Here's an example of each.

Casual acquaintances

No other way brings you in contact with as many people as when you are involved in your community through various organizations. That in itself makes this an awfully important networking activity. It gives you the most exposure and introduces you to the most people while allowing you to make a difference on two levels—your community and to new people. It's a landscape of *casual acquaintances*, accompanied by the opportunity for casual conversations. Why? The bringing together of people isn't caused by you but, rather, by a common interest. It's what removes the initial communication barrier and makes conversation a natural occurrence. It allows you to easily engage in stress-free conversations and, in the course of doing so, nonchalantly transition to what you do professionally and even more importantly, how you do it.

During these types of one-on-one conversations, pay close attention for bits of information that may allow you to serve the person or someone he knows. The information he shares with you may even be about a prospective business partner. No matter the type of business opportunity presented, always be ready with a short and direct script. Don't underestimate or under prepare for this common networking opportunity. This is probably the simplest pounce process you will develop. Be ready to pounce with another one if the opportunity at hand lends itself to a more comprehensive process.

And even if you don't have a business opportunity presented to you, you still have a chance to *passively generate business*. How? Just the fact that you are active in your community means your name is well-known in many circles, which means more people will naturally have the opportunity to mention you and your business at some point. This is the one and only time when a powerful referral business embraces the numbers game. Also of note is this aspect of networking most aligns with a transactional business.

Someone new

Because you provide a high level of service, you have a powerful tool at your disposal. Leverage it to your full advantage. Don't be short-sighted and think the only time you can offer your service is after you've provided your required professional service. Wrong! The nice thing about your service is there's no hard rule about when you can start providing it. Therefore, when you meet *someone new* (prospective client) and personally connect with him, consider adding him to your service (second timeframe) in the hope he will not only utilize your professional services one day but refer someone to you in the meantime. Taking on such a service commitment without an obligation speaks to the confidence you have in your business and shows the commitment you have made to the clients already connected to it. It's a powerful discriminator—one that people rarely experience. Catching people off guard with such an unexpectedly kind gesture can create a surprised reaction based in a special moment that may lead to a personal bond and new business.

Friends

Friends can be a great way to help you build your business. First and foremost, don't be pushy or come across as being entitled, but make sure they know what you do and how you do it. Don't assume they do. You could even introduce them to your service to further gain their trust and confidence. Taking this action means you are treating them the same way you treat people from the world of success—you want to earn their business, not have them give it to you. If they are receptive, spend some quality face-to-face time with them to determine if there's a way they can help you.

That is, can they provide you warm introductions to business partner candidates and/or refer their friends, colleagues, and family? In other words, you want them to be both a friend and a client. Still, there is one cautionary note about friends you must keep in mind. Never exploit friendships for business purposes. Friendships are always more important than any business benefits you may receive. Being highly respectful of this tenet just might further convince friends of your above-reproach character and in a subliminal way encourage them to take on the dual role of friend and client.

Business associates

Business associates afford you an even better occasion than friends to help you with your business. Where the bond with friends is first personal, with business associates it's business first. There is no need to pass through the personal barrier; you go straight to business opportunity. Even though you're not technically building a partnership with business associates, they do trust you, and that's what opens the door for them to occasionally refer people to you, new clients and/or business partner candidates. When they do, it's your service that allows you to connect or hire, as appropriate, the referred people to your business, making these business associations highly worthy.

Your business associates can be people you know as an individual business owner, somebody who works for a company, and/or as a member of a group you are connected with. No matter how you are associated with them, it is important to recognize the core similarity they share with business partners. You can *expect* business associates to ask the same of you. Just as you'll leverage their trust of you for your benefit, expect them to do the same for their business as well. The point is, you assume a level of risk when referring your clients and business partners to business associates. It should go without saying then, make sure you know and trust each other. Even better yet is if you have personally experienced their service or someone you know and trust has.

When you do refer a client to a business associate, you should consider, as appropriate, utilizing the hand-off and hand-back procedure that was previously discussed. You can just as easily lose a client from a business associate providing poor service as you can from a business partner providing poor service. In the end, both of them can enhance or compromise the trust clients have in you. And not to be overlooked, you should also consider taking the same type of action when you refer a business partner to a business associate.

Clients

One of the tenets of The Pentagon Effect is acquiring new business partners. Therefore, when you want to add a business partner to your business, consider turning to the people you expect to turn to you when they need professional service—your *clients*. Think about how your service to them has made this an easy course of action to pursue. For example, you could call a client and say, "Mitchell, I'm looking to add a financial adviser as a business partner. Do you know one who does business like me?" Simple and powerful! You can repeat this same action with other clients as well to ensure you have a couple of viable business partner candidates to interview. Your clients trust in you and your proven service commitment to them should confidently allow them to provide a warm introduction, along with a strong recommendation. Just as it was easy for you to ask them the above question, it'll be easy for them when calling on your behalf.

Business partners

Even *business partners* provide a business networking opportunity; it's a tenet of their pentagon effect. You might not want to ask them to recommend business people in their own profession; however, it is more than fair to ask them to recommend people from other professions. Because they have a vested interest in your business, it really is to their benefit to refer like-minded business professionals akin to both of you. Here's why.

Business partners in a powerful referral business are a *consortium*. Even if they don't know each other, they are still helping each other. Here's how. When one of them professionally serves one of your client's likely needs, that client will not only be inclined to come back to you for other business partner referrals, he will tell other people about you because you were the referral source. That same type of support repeated over and over again with other clients eventually leads to you referring business to all of your business partners. Without your partners knowing it, they are helping you strengthen your other partnerships while revalidating the trust your clients have in you. This is just one of the many reasons why it is so important to be selective with your business partners and why they shouldn't be shy about referring a future business partner of yours and theirs.

When somebody does refer you a prospective business partner, just think about the persuasive pitch you can make with service and clients on your side. It is profoundly different from what a transactional businessperson would utter. For example, a transactional businessperson is primarily limited to the required technical aspects of his business and his personal attributes: I can close the transactions you refer to me. I can do it on time, without any problems. I will work hard. I'm available at your convenience and so on. All he's really doing is making a big deal about his job and how hard *he* works. In other words—blah, blah, blah! Conversely, as a powerful referral businessperson, you can also talk about your job and your personal attributes, but what you're really interested in talking about is how the prospective business partner can *leverage your business* to grow her business. You have clients she can professionally serve; you provide business-building information to help her improve as a businessperson and grow her business; and you build a mini-business with a business partner. That's the attracting aspect of a leverage business model, it not only creates leverage for you, it does it as well for a business partner. Now, you have her really thinking—does she go *in business* with a transactional businessperson or does she *build a mini-business* with a powerful referral business partner...hmm. Here's the bottom line decision in this situation—if she's truly focused on building a business that works hard for her, there is only one choice.

No matter the occasion, with service on your side, networking becomes the occasion to make the impressive sell instead of the hard sell. Why? You truly believe what you have to offer prospective clients and business partners will make more of a difference to them than it will to you. You have positioned your business to take care of them. Such deep-rooted belief is what makes the networking ride enjoyable and leads to new business opportunities and new friendships. By taking the time to attract people to your business, you constantly revitalize it, keep a fresh feel to it, and keep the feeling of being on a journey because you're always meeting new people. *Networking is all about the nexus of a powerful referral business—service, clients, and business partners.*

Rose's networking activities consisted of a much narrower approach and took on a completely different tone. It was all about her profession instead of about her service. Once again, in yet another way, she was leveraging herself instead of her business. It was your typical transactional business networking effort—I am in a profession, and I can close a transaction on time without any problems. When you network in this fashion, *you* better be good because you have nothing else to offer outside of yourself. It's just one more example of a transactional businessperson being lonely in business.

Regardless of the type of business you have, the task of networking still represents the *front line* of the world of success, and it comes with risk. The risk is the uncertainty of the response you will receive from people. No doubt there will be many times when people choose not to work with you; it's the price you pay to work in and eventually achieve success in the world of success. When it happens, and it will, never take it personally. If you do, you show your total disregard for the prerequisite rule of the Referral-Based Service Industry: *only thick-skinned people need to apply.* Simply and swiftly move on to the countless other prospective clients and business partners looking for somebody of your caliber to make a difference to them through service.

Let me take a minute here and shine a glaring light on Rose and me to show you how revealing framework is and how easy it is to see your whole business in the pieces that form it. I can tell you unequivocally that our business partner network really needs work. Through no fault of anyone but ourselves, we haven't built the robust business partner network across all the professions our clients will likely need one day. We know how to do it and have the service and clients to leverage; we just have to do it. This is by far the most pressing challenge we face in our business today. Now that I told you what ours is, do you know what yours is?

Before we started to think of our business in terms of framework, we couldn't readily see this deficiency. Our antiquated way of thinking, of seeing things in totality, left us with nothing more than jumbled thoughts in our head with no real way to un-jumble them. Framework has allowed us to clearly organize our business model thoughts, to be completely cognizant of our deficiencies, and to specifically focus our energy to correct them. Instead of just working harder like we did in the past, we now work harder on the things that will make our business better. Because of framework, we now know we must build a stronger business partner network before we can create a Business Star in our business.

When you are able to confidently do the abovementioned type analysis, you have established a *command presence* over your business. You can very quickly get to the bottom of any issue negatively affecting your business, and you know exactly what to do to resolve it. This is yet another important facet of being an effective leader.

I want to share with you upfront that your effort to build a Business Star will be more difficult than you imagine. The reason being is business people don't tend to think about a business in the way I have discussed in this book (*fully leveraging* client trust). Instead, their focus tends to be oriented toward creating business for themselves (a natural instinct). I observed this narrower business thinking firsthand over an extended period of time. For a year, I taught Rose's loan officers the many concepts of a powerful referral business, and we looked across their business every week with the aid of the previously discussed spreadsheet. At the very bottom of the spreadsheet was a section for business partner performance (each loan officer had business partners from the various professions that have been highlighted in this book). Week after week, month after month, the spreadsheet revealed the exact same thing—solid business support from agents and very little support from the other professions. It was apparent to me and everybody else that there was *limited leveraging* of client trust occurring across the various professions. It was another example of systemic thinking, this time occurring across multiple professions. What that means for you is a strong headwind as you attempt to build a Business Star. The end result is you'll have to conduct a quantity of business partner interviews before you can hire a group of quality business partners. Now you can see why I believe hiring quality business partners is the second greatest challenge in business. Finding leaders who serve others is no easy task.

The task of networking steadies you as a businessperson by bringing a sense of balance to your work. Not only do you work your business from inside the office, you work it from the outside as well. You are vigorously working the diametrically opposed business opportunities—established and prospective business. By having both of them as a part of your business, you keep you and your business busy. It's another example of how two halves equal a whole.

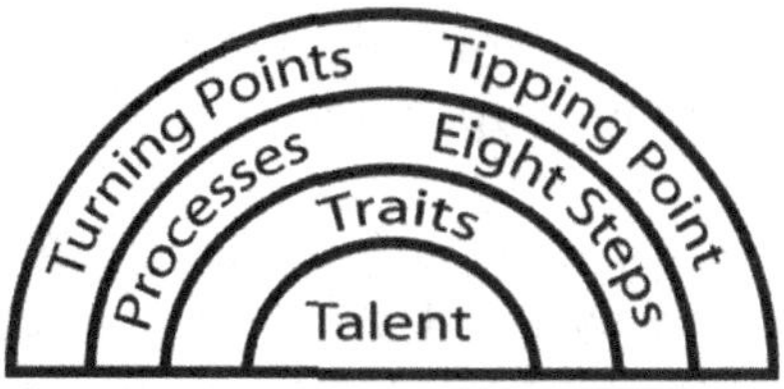

The One Thing You Must Do

A time past...
You loved it in your teen years. You valued it so much you may have occasionally yelled at somebody about it. My, how times have changed!

IN YOUR PERSONAL LIFE it helps to have a long list of atta-boys. You know, good deeds you have willingly done to help somebody in need. If nothing else, it makes a positive statement about you as a person. You have shown through your actions you are an individual who is there for others instead of just being here for yourself. Atta-boys are very important because they have a dual purpose. Not only do they make you feel good about yourself, they are very helpful when you get into trouble. They can either help you avoid it altogether or at least lessen the penalty. I know this all too well from personal experience. I have been married to Rose for over 28 years.

You would think you could accumulate enough atta-boys to get you through or overcome just about anything. You can, unless you come up against an aw-shit—the one thing that can make all of your atta-boys irrelevant. It almost seems unfair for one thing to carry so much weight, but it does. When you fall victim to an aw-shit, it means your atta-boys only add up to a moral victory. There are several good things to talk about, and you might even be upbeat for a brief time. In very short order, though, reality kicks in, and the moral victory becomes hollow because you know you have lost. No matter how many atta-boys you have, they don't trump an aw-shit. Not surprisingly, the business world mirrors everyday life. It's time to talk about the aw-shit in your business.

If you thought networking was the tall order of your business, it's not...this is. The good thing is you are almost finished. You have finally reached the last of the ten turning points, and therefore, you know almost everything required to build a hurricane business. You are at last on the threshold of achieving business success commensurate with your talent. As you might have guessed, I saved what I believe is by far the most important and difficult turning point for last. Here's why.

This turning point by itself can render ineffective absolutely everything you have done so far. I am quite certain it has led to the demise of many well-intentioned referral-based businesses in the service industry. It's so important that if you don't do it, there is a weather phenomenon that can rip apart everything you have painstakingly assembled and built thus far. That weather phenomenon is called *wind shear.*

Wind shear can prevent further development of a tropical storm and rip the top off a hurricane. A storm doesn't want to encounter wind shear and neither do you in your business model execution. So what's the one thing you must do to avoid it? Of course, it is probably what you dread the most. That's why it can either be all powerful or totally destructive. YOU GET TO DECIDE!

Such an important thing represents the third great shift in your business. Where the first two shifts, The Need Shift and The Work Ethic Shift, clearly separated a transactional business from a referral-based business and put you on the pathway of a powerful referral business, this one does both things. So what's this shift?

It's *The Behavior Shift,* and it represents the greatest personal challenge of your business. What's the one behavior that'll determine if your business is transactional or referral-based and if you'll build a powerful referral business? You carry one around all day and another one sits on your desk every day ready to personally link you to your business world. You know what it is: the telephone. *You have to use the telephone.*

If you can tell stressful stories about the telephone all day long, it's probably because you see it primarily as a means to *solicit.* An attitude reflective of a transactional businessperson, and the exact way Rose thought about the telephone in her business. She would not use it to ask for business from clients. Such a pessimistic view of something so vitally important to your business success is destructive and detrimental to its growth. Maybe at the clear skies or the tropical depression level that's the way you looked at your telephone, but times have changed.

You and your business are on the brink of becoming a hurricane, and you have built a level of service that's making a difference to people. Somewhere along the way, during your charted journey of change, you became a trusted professional to clients and a valued business partner as well. People now look forward to receiving your service, count on you for advice and referrals, and give you referrals. Your business is now properly positioned to have telephone *conversations*. It's what made all of the *early hard work* and the *execution work* worth it.

So why is the telephone so important to your business success? The business answer is it's the linchpin between everything you have built and the clients who interface with your business. The touchy-feely answer is it allows you to tap into the emotion your business has created. Once again, like a broken record, can you see the value of service? Both answers reveal why it should be easy to use—it puts the finishing touch on a tremendous amount of hard work.

It is only through personal conversations that clients will realize the true value of your service and for you to reap the highly-desired rewards of it. What that really means is service that makes a difference is based on a layered approach. It's not one-dimensional but multi-dimensional. That's what makes it so appealing and hard to resist.

Service to clients requires the following three elements to maximize its effect. The elements don't have to all be done at the same time, every time, but they do need to be done on a routine basis so an undeniable pattern is clearly established. The elements are: providing something of value, personal contact by telephone, and a scripted message that includes referral language. By routinely doing these three diverse activities together, you successfully interweave things you provide with things you say, and your business becomes a part of the conversation.

It's through the use of the telephone that service can achieve its two primary value objectives. First, clients will always understand what's valuable about your service because you personally tell them in a (short) conversation; and second, you will realize the value of your service because you can ask them for business.

Another interesting aspect of the telephone is it adds the *real-person factor* to your service by giving it a distinctive personality through the sound of your voice. The telephone turns service into personal service by putting you as close to your clients as you can possibly be without actually being there with them. It can't put you there physically, but it does place you there *emotionally*—which is what a powerful referral business is all about.

Not to be overlooked, the telephone is also vital when it comes to your business partners. The difference being, your conversations with them will be focused on sharing/discussing business-building information that makes a difference. So why the difference? Where business from your clients comes from asking them for business, business from your business partners comes from them building their business. You keenly recognize this subtle difference between the two of them, and therefore, you are right-focused when talking to them.

The telephone is the final crucial piece of the framework that at last positions your service to become personally valuable for you, clients, and business partners. It's the final joint to building a level of service that completely serves three different needs and is, therefore, the last and most important turning point.

The traits and service processes you've worked so hard to develop, and that now guide your business, should give you the strength and confidence to pick up the telephone to call clients. It's essential you do this. The absolute worst thing you could do, after building everything you have built, is to not pick up the telephone and call. Service processes are not near enough by themselves; they must be complemented with the telephone and meaningful conversation.

The personal conversations you have by making calls are what provide the *connecting strength* to your service processes. Without telephone contact, they are weakened; and over time, they lose their effectiveness. If you allow it to happen, your service processes turn into marketing material. They have been rightfully reduced to a *convincing* service activity. And you personally start turning back into a transactional businessperson. Such a transgression represents *the retro moment* in business.

You have to routinely connect on a personal level with the clients who interface with your business. If telephone calls are not a routine practice during the day, your effort to build a powerful referral business will come up short. Put another way, *your telephone is like a cash register; if you want the money, you're going to have to touch it, and not just when it rings!*

On the downside, why don't business people like to make telephone calls to clients? More than likely it's due to *call-reluctance,* and I would suggest one telling reason for it is they know they're not providing a level of service that makes a difference. Once again, you can see the value of valuing service. As stated earlier, these types of business people could be at the clear skies or, at best, the tropical depression level. If your business is at one of these two levels, you should have call-reluctance—you're not in the Referral-Based Service Industry. There's nothing more unprofessional and uncomfortable than asking for business when you haven't earned the right to ask. It's just plain wrong.

On the contrary, just because you provide a high level of service is no guarantee you won't have call-reluctance. You may still need some help in overcoming the anxiety of placing a service call. Rose faced this exact challenge with her clients and dealt with it by taking the following action.

When explaining her second timeframe of service to clients, she makes it a point to say she loves to stay in touch and will call them quarterly. Just by stating that simple fact upfront, she tore down all of the barriers. This was a make-or-break business nuance. Simply put, she told them what her service standards were, and they accepted what she had to say. Now when she calls, she looks forward to it, and the clients first comments aren't, "Who's this again;" "Why are you calling;" or "Is something wrong." Instead, their first comments are more along these lines, "Hi Rose;" "How are you doing;" or "So good to talk to you again." Try it. I'm confident it will work for you as it has for her.

Before she calls, Rose is given a copy of all the service items she has provided since she last talked to the person she's about to call. She reviews the material (picking out one or two discussion items) before making the call so the emphasis is on service first, then on sales. Even during a telephone call, the exact same business principle applies—service leads to sales.

The reason the telephone was your last turning point is you had to have every opportunity to build something more important than it. So what's the one thing you built that is now more powerful than the telephone? It wasn't your business because your business can't pick up a telephone. It was your self-confidence.

How's that possible if all you did was build your business? Your business is you, and you are your business. There's no distinction between the two. As long as you were willing to do one, you were doing the other. You've slowly but surely transformed yourself right along with your business. You and your business have both grown substantially through steady, positive change.

Think about it: you don't perform business the same way, and you're not the same businessperson you were. Really think about it: six traits, Eight Step Process, and ten turning points. It may seem hard to believe, but out of everything you now do, the telephone will give you your greatest joy. It'll allow you to positively and personally connect with clients you value and business partners you selected.

When you provide a level of service that makes a difference, you want a telephone nearby. You understand the key to a good client telephone call is to not make it entirely about business but, rather, about the person, your service, and a friendly business reminder at the end. In other words, *the art of the call*—and another nuance. When you do this, not only will you look forward to calling clients, they'll look forward to talking to you. The reason being is you're using the telephone to leverage your service experience; you're not using it to create business. Those two words—*leverage* and *create*—are what differentiate a referral-based business from a transactional business. Where one business is working hard, the other business has you working hard.

The other key ingredient to a good client telephone call is to not overstay your visit. You should always plan for a short call and extend it only if the client is driving the conversation. No matter the duration of the telephone call, make sure you emotionally connect, share something about your service, and mention your business.

It wasn't easy to arrive at this point in business, but now that you're here, embrace the telephone and make it a part of your business day. Expect great conversations, new friendships, repeat business, and referrals.

It is important to quickly acknowledge the obvious outside pressure the telephone faces—social media. As more and more people electronically connect, they are personally disconnecting. This realization doesn't negate this crucial activity. Instead, it shows the underlying importance of being likeable, providing impressive service, and emotionally connecting in the first timeframe of service. It is these three things in this short timeframe of service that prepositions you to overcome this outside pressure and routinely *personally connect with clients* in the second timeframe of service.

O

With all of the good a telephone can do for a business, you would surely think it is a natural fit for every type of profession building a powerful referral business. Unfortunately, it's not true. The one profession that comes to mind is CPAs. Their view of the telephone can easily be seen through the lens of providing consultative work that requires financial compensation. How? During client telephone calls the conversation shifts from leveraging an explained service experience to addressing tax-related questions. I don't believe this potential shift necessitates eliminating client telephone calls altogether. However, I do believe that some upfront creative thinking is in order to effectively prevent this awkward situation from occurring. A possible solution for CPAs might be to address this issue when explaining the second timeframe of service, and make clear that they gladly provide free advice when the answer is straightforward and doesn't require any research. Any other type of advice is considered a consultative service that requires financial compensation. It should go without saying that if CPAs are going to charge a fee for advice, they need to communicate that upfront and give clients the choice. This simply courtesy goes for any businessperson in any profession.

This unique situation serves as a reminder that for all of the commonality occurring between the professions building a powerful referral business (and there's quite a bit of it), there still exist peculiarities between them. These peculiarities don't mean the discussed framework is illogical and should, therefore, be dismissed in total. They do, however, mean that when these types of situations arise, action should be taken to resolve the issue at hand in a manner that ensures the viability of the framework. When you embrace such a thoughtful approach, you'll view a peculiarity to the framework of a powerful referral business as a leadership challenge—the answer will typically require some resourceful thinking, with a bit of pragmatism sprinkled in.

Now that I have discussed why the telephone is the most important and difficult turning point, let me flip the dynamic and talk about the importance of it being the most difficult. The telephone provides an answer to the perplexing question: *"Why is service so important?"* It's the last thing to know before revealing the by-product of a powerful referral business. For the answer, you'll need to mentally turn back the pages for a minute and think about a Business Star once again. It has one more important message to divulge, with the help of the telephone.

As you already know, when you view the Business Star image, it shows your business at the highest level. But if you think about it, it will reveal why service is so important. Look at the Business Star below. The outside shows the vision of your business, while the inside reflects a cross-section of business activities—traits, service, and execution strategies. Altogether, it characterizes what it took to build a powerful referral business and what that looks like visually.

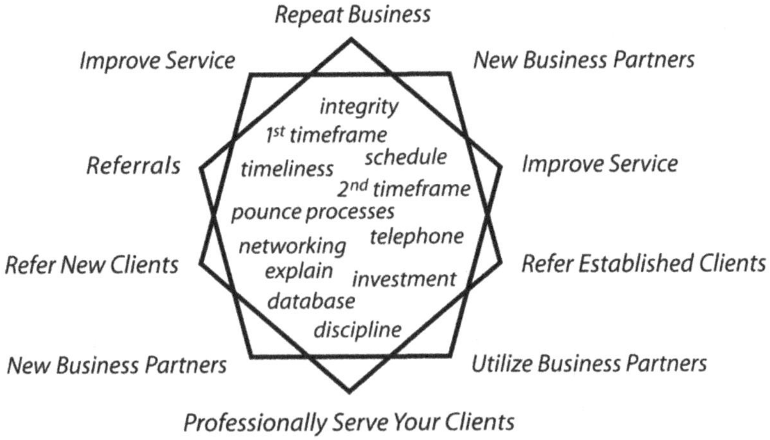

BUSINESS STAR

Look at the Business Star image again, focus on the inside, and think about your entire business and every activity associated with it. What you'll see and realize is some activities are easy, some are difficult, but just one is *the most difficult*—using the telephone. Fittingly, it delivers the greatest impact to your business. It's the accomplishment of this activity that ultimately draws the line between a transactional and referral-based business and, as such, is a great way to reveal why service is so important.

The obvious thing service does is it allows you to serve the people who interface with your business. The not-so-obvious thing it does is provide the impetus that energizes and empowers you to accomplish the most difficult activity of your business. *Service creates your energy!* Let me say that one more time—service creates your energy. It's a tenacious energy at that.

That is precisely what happened to Rose as she improved the business model around her talent. Providing two timeframes of client service that *she believed in* not only changed the dynamics of her business, it changed her as a businesswoman as well. Wherein the past the telephone would cause her great anxiety, even though she knew how important it was to referral success, she now freely uses it with clients to ask for business. This deep-seated change in Rose made me realize that service is the *transformative element* in business—personally and business-wise.

Service is the *perfect activity* because it helps everybody in your business, to include you. Once again, why wouldn't everybody want to provide it? Service is the premise of a powerful referral business because it leads to sales, and it's the only reason you're standing at the doorstep of the by-product.

There's no greater force in your business working in so many different ways than service. Can you see the significant worth of the pause you take with the Eight Step Process to build your service? And remember, it's the Eight Step Process that represents the early hard work of a powerful referral business.

Let me share one final thought concerning the telephone before revealing the by-product. It's inevitable the business world will continue to evolve and change in many different ways. No matter how much it changes, one thing is for certain, the telephone will always remain the linchpin of a referral-based business. There's no getting around that fact because *a telephone is as timeless as a referral is wanted.* I know that is a rather bold statement to make about the telephone in the face of the revolutionary changes it has and will continue to experience. But I firmly believe that regardless of how much smarter it gets, it will always remain a telephone at its core, which means it will continue to be *the most convenient way* to have a conversation, whether the conversation is by ear or video. That's what makes it timeless.

It might be hard to believe, but you are finally done—six traits to guide your personal behavior, eight steps to build your valuable service, and ten turning points to execute your business. WHEW! It all adds up to twenty-four, but that doesn't mean you work twenty-four hours a day. Quite the contrary. You've successfully assembled the entire framework for your hurricane business, and as a result, you have created the *by-product* found in a powerful referral business. Do you know what it is? I'll give you a hint; I haven't used the two words yet. Together, they are the ultimate secret of a powerful referral business.

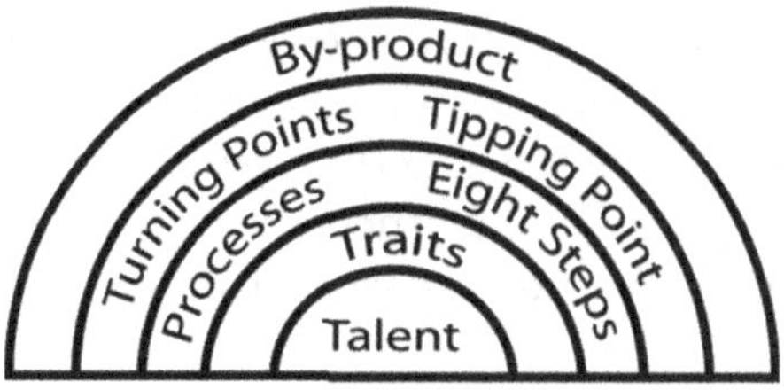

The By-product

A time past…

It was your best day because everybody was proud, especially you.

YOU HAVE FINALLY MADE IT. YOU ARE A ROARING HURRICANE! You probably already figured out the answer, but if you haven't yet, *consistency* and *relationships* are the by-product of everything you have done up to this point. No other two words in your business require more to be done to achieve them. They are the *culmination words* of a powerful referral business, and thus, there's no diluting of them through casual or premature use. They're the cornerstones of a powerful referral business because they stabilize your business and bring vibrant life to it. They give your hurricane its rotation and subsequent strength. Your hurricane is now roaring ahead, not a wobble to be seen—it's the perfect storm.

The whole point of this book was to bring you to this apex moment. As much as business people would like to, they can't choose to have consistency and relationships *throughout their business.* These two qualities have to be earned by doing several things right every day. There are no shortcuts to achieving them. You would expect something of prime importance to a business model to be difficult to obtain, and it is. Your achievement of them is positive proof you have taken a strategic approach instead of a tactical approach to your business.

The painstaking patience you have shown in building your business has brought you *consistency throughout your business.* It's confirmation and corroboration your work is complete, and you are conducting business at the highest level every day. How did you do it?

You meticulously constructed an interlocking, interdependent business framework comprised of traits, service, and execution strategies. They seamlessly fasten together and jointly interact with one another, each one making the other stronger. The end business result of this is your ideas now fit perfectly over the strongest framework in business.

By virtue of its natural output attribute, consistency is creating the hoped-for and expected responses from the clients and business partners who interface with your business. They are fiercely loyal, bringing you a sustained book of business, even in a slow market. You're now in possession of that rare form of advertisement highly coveted by everybody in the service industry—word-of-mouth. You have met *The My Threshold* with clients and business partners. And just like you, they have also made the emotional connection to your business.

Just as impressive are your relationships. Relationships at this top level are entrenched, or if new, they're on their way to lasting a very long time. You know they are the lifelines of a business, but yours are secure—ensuring you will always be the storm, never facing the storm. *You have highly productive relationships at every level of your business, and you continue to acquire new ones.* Your business is quite animated. You learned a long time ago not to fall into the trap of trying to have a relationship with everybody you meet. You aren't afraid to pick and choose your relationships. You know it's okay to say no and sometimes you do.

And you're realizing the value of your valuable service. By being selective with your clients and hiring the right business partners, you have produced the expected results—repeat business and referrals. You know all too well that satisfactory service leads to transactional business, while valuable service leads to repeat and referral business. You've made the hard choices with clients and business partners and it's paying huge personal and professional dividends. *You measure success in the number of relationships you have in your business.* You realized a very long time ago you could never work as hard as they do.

Something else very unique and special happens at this level. Your relationships are so unshakable they work for you on a scale not imagined by the tropical depression or even the tropical storm business levels. Where they have natural barriers, you have none. Your business is not only powerfully conducted in the local community in which you reside, it now has a national presence as well. Long distance relationships are of no concern to your clients. Therefore, whenever or wherever they move, they want you to continue serving their needs, and, in turn, they continue to refer you business. Their referrals may encompass both new clients and business partners. The outcome of everything you have built has you gaining footholds in distant new markets courtesy of loyal clients. Where technology is shrinking the distant business world, your clients are expanding your business world. The end result is you have achieved an even greater presence in the world of success.

And your business is positioned to go generational if it hasn't already done so. Clients now confidently refer their children to you. The fact that they are willing to trust you with the people who mean the most to them in life indicates you have achieved the *gold standard of trust* in your business. It's this highly personal action that best shows the depth of trust associated with an ideal client.

The truly wonderful thing about your relationships is they raise your margin of error, for you have created a higher tolerance level among clients and business partners through your sustained excellent service. Your effort to build the perfect business has been rewarded by relieving you of the pressure to be perfect. After all, the strong only get stronger. And your relationships closely resemble a friendship because you personally stay in touch. That's what makes them so endearing and enduring. You abide by the most elementary rule of a relationship: People have a relationship with other people. They don't have a relationship with mailed items.

A hurricane business is such a rewarding way of business it naturally creates a by-product of the by-product. To see this second by-product, think about you, your clients, and your business partners. A *triangulation-effect* is occurring among all of you, and you made it possible. For as important as clients and business partners are to your business success, you are the most important because everything goes through you. Consider the people dynamics occurring in your business. Clients trust you; you trust business partners and then entrust them to serve the likely needs of your clients, which they do; your clients continue to trust you; you continue to trust and entrust business partners and on and on. What does it all mean? When you build trust throughout your business, you create *The Eternal Triangle* as simply illustrated below.

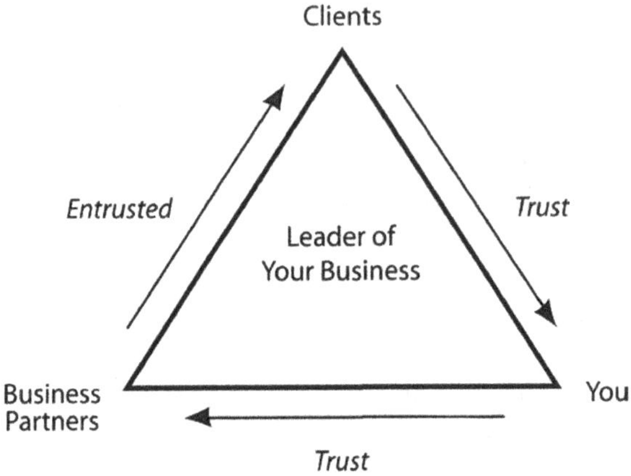

THE ETERNAL TRIANGLE

Look at the triangle again and think back to the two pentagon effects occurring in your business. It doesn't matter if you're looking at a pentagon or a triangle, clients are always at the top. Your business truly is about them. No matter how you draw it, they always come out on top.

By achieving The Eternal Triangle in your business, you are personally serving clients while being equally prepared to serve all of their likely needs through your business partners. You are now the leader of your business. Here's why. You are the most important person; you are trustworthy; your clients trust you; you serve them; you surround yourself with business partners you trust; you delegate by entrusting them to serve your clients likely needs you can't personally serve, which they do; and you build a powerful referral business. It's The Eternal Triangle that captures the confluence of the word *Referral.*

You see a business every day that others can only dream about. Everything now fits perfectly together. For the first time, you and your business are one. People will wonder how it was possible for you to build something so big and powerful while somehow increasing your personal work capacity to support it. Conventional wisdom would have you think it's impossible, but it's not. The fact of the matter is, *when your business is truly working hard for you, you can do less, which, in turn, increases your capacity to do more.* Simply and succinctly stated—you shifted the burden of working hard from yourself to your business. Therein is the essence of a powerful referral business and why you were able to grow your work capacity right along with your business.

Your business now performs with a perpetual motion powered by an explained service experience. The internal dynamics this creates within your business pulls everything you've deemed important toward you, naturally making business easier. Just as impressive is you. Your personal productivity is off the charts because business efficiencies are everywhere. You never need to be concerned about busy work because you always have *make a difference work* to do.

Not to be overlooked is the subtlety of efficiency. You've rightly recognized that your efficiency as a businessperson was achieved through both your business and your people. Where systematizing your business on two levels created business efficiency, choosing to only serve those clients and business partners you could create leverage with brought efficiency to the time you spent serving others. You know all too well that your time is valuable; achieving business efficiency is what makes your time valuable.

The willingness on your part to construct the proper framework has allowed you to finally achieve business success commensurate with your talent. Can you see *Success* at work? You have achieved the desired end result, and you're a better businessperson for it.

It truly is incredible what happens at hurricane level. There's nothing like it or even close. It has taken a tremendous amount of time and effort to build, but it's very special because you've built a business that works for everybody. Take a minute and really think about that; everybody's needs are being served. You professionally serve your clients needs through various means; you refer business to your business partners; and in-kind your clients and business partners refer business to you. PERFECT!

Your competitors will rack their brains out trying to deduce why they can't effectively compete. They'll probably never figure out that you're performing in a way they're not familiar with, and clients and business partners feel it's a privilege to work with you.

A hurricane business really is the perfect business. Not only are you blowing away your competition, but your clients and business partners are blown away by you, too. That's the beauty of it all.

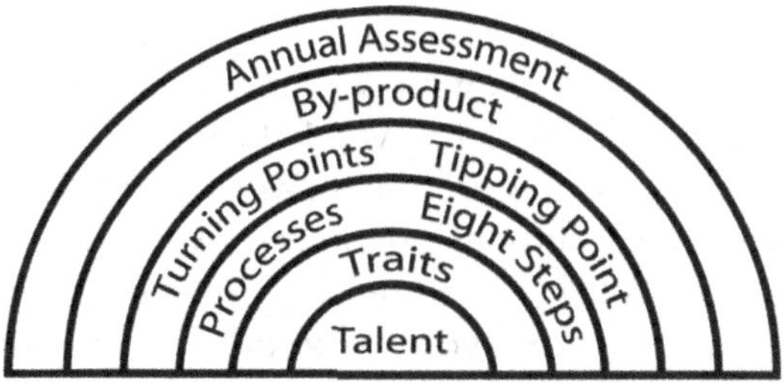

It's a Journey, Not a Destination

A time past...

When you graduated, you may have thought you were done. Thank goodness you weren't because it's what allowed you to grow and get better.

DON'T POP OPEN THE CHAMPAGNE YET! Just when you assume the game is finally over and won—another twist. The moment you think you reached your destination is the moment your hurricane starts to weaken. That's true in the weather world and the business world as well. Never lose sight of the fact that you're on a journey, never to reach your destination. It's what keeps you diligently pursuing it. The closest you should ever get to your destination is to see it on the distant horizon. No matter how hard you try, you must never reach it, for it's the *island of content.* Sad to say it, but I was definitely hanging out there my first year in corporate America.

A powerful referral business really is a lifework. It's not something you build in a hurry and then move on. Along the way it turns into a wonderful career because of the lifetime relationships that are put into place. That's the alluring dynamic of a powerful referral business—*the money doesn't come from creating business; it comes from having relationships.* If you ever do reach your destination, it's probably because you have chosen to end your career. When you reach that moment, you won't reflect on the destination but, rather, on the journey you traveled. You will probably laugh and cry about special and not-so-special moments that occurred along the way. I guess that's why the journey is always more important than the destination, it's where the great memories are created.

Still, that's down the road. So for now, how do you stay on your journey? You stay on it by answering my seventh and final framework question: *How do we continually improve our business*?

To keep your powerful referral business vibrant, it must continue to improve and change with the times. The only way to do it is through an *annual assessment*, which formally recognizes the failings and the successes of your business over the last year. Assessment is the reality moment in business, given that it equally deals with the truth, whether it's good or bad. No other work you perform in your business will cause you to *adapt and change* more, which makes an annual assessment a leadership activity in and of itself. Outside of learning the framework of a business, an annual assessment is the *greatest learning experience* in business.

Where a comprehensive business assessment should be accomplished once a year, your service will probably require a more periodic review. Here's why.

Almost every day, newly created service ideas are entering the marketplace. You can hear about them at a seminar, over a conference call, read about them in a book or a professional magazine, etc. Whichever way you find out about them, some will be good and some not so good. When you come across one that could possibly benefit your business and it can't wait until you conduct your annual service review, assess it by referring to the applicable portions of steps 3 thru 8 of the Eight Step Process. Remember, whenever you consider adding a service activity to your business, you must first measure it against the context of the service you're providing today. That's why I earlier asked you to save a copy of your groups with their associated service.

Every year you should conduct a comprehensive annual assessment of your business. Assessment lets you see your business for what it is, not what you think it is. Instead of looking the other way, you're looking right at it. Initially you may not like some of what you see (which is to be expected), but you will when you make the changes that improve you and your business. That's why assessment is important and change is good. You have to look back on the year before you can look forward to the New Year.

The interesting and key insight to be aware of when it comes to an annual assessment is referral-based business people are keenly focused on it, while transactional business people are not. Why the divide? Referral-based business people generate business through their business, while transactional business people create business through themselves. Where the marked improvement of a transactional business comes from the person working harder, the marked improvement of a referral-based business comes from the business working harder, which is what an annual business assessment is all about. Once again, the dichotomy of a business rears its head but this time during an annual assessment. And because Rose was initially on the wrong side of the dichotomy of a business (she was working hard, not her business), an annual assessment was not a ritual she conducted before entering the New Year.

Just as an annual assessment clearly shows a glaring difference between transactional and referral-based business people, the same can be said for when times are tough (business is slow). Such a trying time brings out a completely different response in them. Where one looks outward, the other looks inward. Transactional business people tend to place blame beyond themselves and their business. They are far more interested in making a point than doing something productive. For example, their commentary will tend to fall along these lines: Our interest rates are too high. I can't compete with our programs. I don't have enough support. The market is too slow and on and on. Such commentary is not about them or their business but about something else or some other person. On the other hand, referral-based business people look to accept responsibility by examining their personal effort and their business. Their commentary will tend to fall along these lines: How can I improve on my client telephone calls. What should I focus more attention on? Am I capitalizing on just thinking about you opportunities? Can I improve my service? Their commentary is all about making themselves and/or their business better in some way.

Here's the important takeaway. An annual assessment, tough times, networking, and a strong market all share the same common core quality—they cause a further widening of the already existing gulf between transactional and referral-based businesses.

So what do you assess? You assess *the four pillars* of your business: you, service, clients, and business partners. Each one of these business pillars bears a distinct responsibility essential to achieving business success. Altogether, they give credence to why a powerful referral business is so stable and strong, and why you must give equal attention to each one.

When you assess the four pillars of your business, you should be measuring them against the backdrop of established goals. Your goals, whatever they are, should measure your expectation for success for each pillar mentioned above. And what should your expectations be? You should be examining your effort to build a business and be a member of the Referral-Based Service Industry. By achieving both, you're meeting the vision of a powerful referral business.

Since you now provide a high level of service, expecting and demanding more of yourself and your business will produce results. Failure to meet a goal will require some type of action that can result in a change to you, others, or service. Let's take a closer look at each pillar from a general standpoint. It will give you some insight into what you should be measuring. Let's start by looking at you.

You

When you assess your business, you should always start with yourself. Just as you served as the foundation upon which your framework was built, the same basic principle applies during your annual assessment. The primary reason to begin with you is you, and you alone, are at the origin of your business. More times than not, the greatest deficiencies will reside with you. What should you assess? Meticulously examine your ability to daily perform the six traits of a powerful referral business and the integration of the ten turning points into your planned day. Self-assessment is always difficult to do, but if you go into it knowing full well there is real opportunity for improvement (which there is), you will find areas where you can become better. The key is to turn a constructive but critical eye on your daily performance. This is an uncompromising personal leadership moment. In short, this is the time to reflect.

To help you accurately reflect, review the personal performance history you documented through your database management system or other means, as applicable. It's the only way to truly bring honesty to this phase of your assessment. To help Rose and me effectively and candidly get through this personally reflective work, we utilize our spreadsheet that was previously discussed.

By documenting and reviewing actual job performance, you will get a true reflection of yourself. If you fail to do this and the problem(s) rest with you but you change something else, you only end up treating symptoms, not causes. This simply lets the problem(s) linger and fester. By first looking to place culpability upon yourself, you readily accept *accountability* for your actions. You clearly realize that the greatest gains made in your business are from personal changes that cause a ripple-effect throughout your business. Nothing else in your business has such a far-reaching effect as you. Not even your best client or your strongest business partner.

Another dimension to you that needs assessing is your effort to insert your business partners into your business. They are a part of your business by being a natural extension of your service. Just as you will shortly review their performance of supporting your business with referrals, you must look at your effort to support their business as well. Are you making a *conscious effort* throughout the year, through various methods, to include them in your business? Remember, successful partnerships start with you.

Now turn your attention to the two aspects of your business premise—service and sales. You need to equally consider both of them during your annual assessment. Where you will assess your service to see if it's making a difference, you will assess your sales force of clients and business partners to see if they're making a difference. There's no other way to state it; this is the make a difference moment in your annual assessment. It's time to validate the definition of a powerful referral business.

Service

When you assess your service, you should jointly review all of your current service and pounce processes with the new ideas and processes you're considering adding. Such a joint review should be done with the aid of the Eight Step Process. What was cutting-edge service a year earlier might be ordinary or worse yet outdated. If you allow your service to degrade to such a point, your financial investment in it rightfully turns into spent money. Investing money on ineffective service is the most wasteful thing you can do in business.

By using the Eight Step Process, you can assess the latest and best service and pounce ideas/processes in the marketplace today by applying the same standard to them you used to establish your current service. By annually evaluating in this fashion, you render your service the best it can be every year. Remember the one limitation of the Eight Step Process—it's based on your opinion.

Not to be overlooked during your service assessment are your business partner service processes. Remember, you flexed your service to provide it for the benefit of you and your business partners.

By paying close attention to these processes, you every year apply *forethought* to the type of process that allows you to easily and professionally insert business partners into your business throughout the year. The reason this step is so important is business partner service processes are the primary means utilized by you to sustaining strong partnerships across your business.

If you want a second opinion on your service to determine if it's really on the mark, survey some of the people who receive it. It's one of the tenets of both pentagons. You will find the best answers are always at field level—the level encompassing clients and business partners. Your service is a reflection of you, but at the end of the day, it has to be meaningful to the people it serves by making a difference to them. There is only one way to know its impression and impact: ask. It's human nature for people to help, and they will, especially when you have worked so hard to serve them. They are the arbiters of your service. This is an opportunity to have your *ideal client group* help you with your business in yet another way.

You can ask for service feedback either informally or formally. An example of an informal survey would be to ask a question or two at the end of a client or business partner telephone call, while a formal survey would be in writing. No matter how you do it, don't be fearful of critical feedback. That's what you hope for and need to hear. Embrace it because it will help you grow your business by improving your service. At this moment, it helps to be a humble person and to remember that change is a constant and a necessity for continued success.

When you're willing to take this step, you are utilizing the second way to aid your investment decision-making ability. Where the first one was with a software program (analysis-based), this time it's with the people connected to your business (personal feedback). When you utilize both approaches to determine the effectiveness of a service and/or a pounce process and there's no clear-cut conclusion to be had, give more weight to the personal feedback approach. Why? It comes directly from the source of your success.

A great time to survey the clients and business partners who interface with your business is near the end of the year. That way, by the first of the year, you're ready to send a Happy New Year client letter and a business partner note reintroducing your service and perhaps introducing new service for the upcoming year. By taking such actions, you always explain your service before you deliver it—the first rule of providing service.

In the end, you know you have your service just right when it fulfills two diverse needs—it makes you passionate, while it makes a difference to clients, business partners, and prospective ones.

O

Let's now talk about assessing the people who interface with your business. As we do, it is important to recognize upfront that if you have grounds to cut a client or fire a business partner at anytime during the year—do it! You don't have to wait for your annual assessment. When you are willing to take this type of action with a client (even in the first timeframe of service), you respect and protect your service investment throughout the year; and when you immediately fire a business partner, you remove a known risk from your valuable client base. Even though these unexpected business moments are not favorably anticipated, they're the type of moments a leader never avoids. By dealing with these situations right away, you yet again, in another way, demonstrate you're in charge of your business every day of the year.

When you assess the people who interface with your business, you are involved in *the fourth leadership moment involving the people in your business.* From your clients to your business partners, take the time to determine the value of each one and decide if you want to continue the relationship. The critical importance of doing this is it's what allows your business to grow bigger with the right people instead of just growing bigger because of more people. It ensures you only surround yourself with people who will make a difference in your business. It's now time to recall the business DNA you stored in your database management system.

It is exactly for moments like this why you manage your business with a database management system—you can track repeat client business, client referrals, and business partner performance. Can you see the CEO mindset at work? You're determining the people who will be a part of your business next year. Let's start looking at the people in your business by first looking at your clients.

Clients

The primary criteria for determining if clients will remain a part of your business is twofold: will they allow you to continue serving their needs (the cornerstone of their pentagon), and are they supporting your business with referrals for you and/or your business partners? Where the first question might require a subjective answer, the second one is strictly objective. The potential oncoming subjective decision is just one of many reasons why it's so important to stay in touch (with the telephone) and not just with things you provide. By doing so, you can make the best subjective decisions when you have too—truly reflecting a leadership moment.

The underlying reason for the two questions above is you're determining if clients still have *trust and confidence* in you and your business. If the answer to either question is yes, maintain your service investment in them. If the answers are no, remove their level of service. The service you provide is a financial investment on your part, and you should see some return on it. This brings to light the most glaring inequality between the professions capable of building a powerful referral business. For certain ones, like insurance and financial, this can be a more complex and difficult decision because of the recurring annual income received from the transaction. There is only one thing to say—don't the rest of us wish we had their *peculiar* problem.

It's important to quickly acknowledge that this peculiar problem can have a far greater negative impact than the obvious positive impact. How? The residual recurring income can function as a crutch, propping up a business just enough to where being a transactional businessperson is acceptable (there's a diminished need for the second timeframe of service). This is a *limited temptation* in a powerful referral business, in that it only affects two professions. As a temptation, it'll both test and reveal the depth of the caring spirit of the people it does affect. In its own way, this situation is one more example of a truth be told moment in a powerful referral business.

For the first time in her business career, Rose is asking these two questions of her clients. And yes, she now cuts clients from her business every year. This is just one of many new firsts she has experienced in her transition from a transactional to a referral-based businesswoman. Through an *evolutionary approach* she's slowly but surely surrounding herself with clients who will make a difference to her business. She's in pursuit of MAD, M.A.D. Clients!

Business partners

The business partner assessment is far more complicated because it involves current and prospective partners. There's no doubt that some existing relationships will go by the wayside, while new ones will replace them. That's part of the natural evolution of a powerful referral business. A simple and important rule to remember when determining your business partner relationships is that it's business, not personal. Highly successful business people recognize this distinction and ardently comply with it. They clearly understand it's a necessity to keeping a business moving forward.

Start your business partner assessment by first assessing your current partners. When you do, conduct each assessment in a face-to-face setting. Just as you sat down with each partner to begin the process of working together, you will now sit down again to determine if you want to continue that work. A partnership is a *collaborative effort* between two professional business people that demands the respect of this set aside time. Just as you looked at two criteria for a client, you will do the same for a business partner.

The first thing to look at is the mini-business you have created together (cornerstone of the business partner pentagon). Reviewing it will not only show what you have jointly built, but it will reveal if the partnership is truly a partnership—who is referring to whom. The standard here isn't one-for-one but, rather, back and forth. The other thing to look at is the level of service—is the business partner still generating business through two timeframes of service? If she is, you know she values the client instead of the transaction and you can be assured your referred clients will be well served before and after the transaction. To help you better analyze this aspect of the assessment, you can review the feedback you received from the clients you referred to her. If you recall, this information is gleaned from the third call of the hand-off, hand-back approach.

If you see positive signs in both areas, continue the professional relationship and focus the rest of the assessment on how to grow the partnership. There's always an opportunity to improve on both sides, and that's where the discussion should turn. The scope of the discussion should range from what can be done individually or collectively (i.e., improved execution of business partner service processes, joint marketing, or hosting some type of function together) to better support each other with referrals in the upcoming year.

Some clear signals that a business partnership has soured and it's time to move on are: there is a loss of confidence in the partner for whatever reason, referrals are only flowing one way (from you), the partner doesn't conduct business like you anymore, it becomes far more work than business, or worse yet, no work and no business. It's never easy to cut a business tie, but there's no value in holding onto a sentimental partnership that doesn't work.

There is one time when you should *consider* ending a successful partnership. That time is when there is a breach of a mini-business. Specifically, the business partner refers a mutual-client or their referral to someone other than you. Ouch! A mini-business represents the *bond of trust* between partners. It must never be violated. If it is, it leads to a loss of confidence. Once that happens, there has to be overwhelming reasons to continue the partnership. You can easily prevent yourself from making this unfortunate and costly mistake by building advance groups for all of your mini-businesses and then checking them before you refer business out.

There's an important distinction to know when removing a client or a business partner from your business. That distinction is a client can be cut without any notification, while a business partner should be let go in-person with the why reason provided. Why the difference between the two? The standards are different—you hope from a client, but you expect of a business partner. Such a move by you not only speaks to your professionalism but your leadership qualities as well because you are willing to face the uncomfortable moments in business. And remember, whenever you cut or fire someone from your business, you need to remove that person from your database management system. This simple rule also applies to business associates and prospective clients and business partners. By doing this deletion measure, you proactively keep your database of people sanitized.

Now that you have assessed your current partnerships, determining who will stay and who will go, turn your attention to prospecting for new business partners. You should never enter into a New Year without first giving careful consideration to what you need in business partner relationships. Doing so would mean you're satisfied and eventually content—you reached your destination.

When considering new partnerships, it's very important to keep two main points in mind. Because you *value your clients* and your business partners are an *extension of your service* to them, your business partner standard has gone up. You now focus on quality, not quantity. In short, you're looking for like-minded partners. Surprisingly, in a roundabout way, you can use some of the Eight Step Process to help you here. For example, at step 1, *list* all of your remaining business partners; and at step 4, *assign* them to their professional group. At step 6, *identify* which group(s) you need to make stronger through prospecting. And finally, at Step 7, *start* prospecting for new partners. You can sharpen your prospecting effort by calling on both clients and business partners—it's a tenet of their pentagons.

Prospecting for new business partners is an opportunity to use your pounce processes. As you do, remember the business partner pentagon and the two interview questions that will help you decide if you partner. Keeping these things in mind will ensure you hire new business partners because you believe you can build a partnership with them, not because they're in a profession where you look for business partners. And if you're a mortgage loan officer and an agent, you need to keep in mind the other two questions (previously discussed) that directly speak to the unique business bond occurring between the two professions.

Let me talk about Rose again. Just like with her clients, Rose is becoming selective with her business partners. In the past, business partners pretty much consisted of business people (agents) who could send her their business. Business success was primarily achieved through a *quantity* of business partners, not through her own business. Now that Rose has a business of clients who are hers, she is moving toward *quality* business partners she can truly partner with—each business is growing through the other. Finally, she is supporting their business with referrals.

The fact that Rose is now becoming selective with the clients she serves and the business partners she makes an extension of her service is proof the DNA of her business finally matters to her.

Let me take a quick moment here and point out what I believe is the most striking and significant contrasting dynamic occurring between a transactional and powerful referral business—*people decisions*. When Rose was a transactional businesswoman, she never made people decisions in her business. She didn't select the clients she served; she didn't hire business partners through an interview process; and she didn't determine if she wanted to continue client and business partner relationships through an annual assessment. In a sense, she was alone in her business. It is through her choice to serve clients first that she now has these broad people responsibilities. It is also through these responsibilities that she has become a leader in her business, just as she naturally was outside of her business.

O

Goals

After you complete your annual assessment, it's time to review your execution type goals. Your business has in all probability changed in some way, for better or worse. If that's the case, your goals may need to be changed or adjusted accordingly. You may even delete some of the old goals and replace them with new ones that help you more effectively measure your business in the upcoming year. Remember, anytime you modify existing goals or add new ones, you need to reconsider or develop supporting stated objectives.

If goals become weak or outdated, they are no longer just out of reach, which removes a primary motivational factor from your business. Your opportunity to build on success year after year is tenuous at best because you're not reaching for anything. Not only that, you greatly jeopardize your chance of achieving the vision of a powerful referral business. For the sake of you and your business, and its vision, you need to remain a goal-oriented businessperson.

Don't overlook your preparatory goals. If you still have them as a part of your business, you need to review them to ensure they are up to date as you enter the New Year. Completing them in a timely manner will strengthen your business position in the marketplace and further push you along on your never-ending journey.

O

Assessment is not something that you would usually look forward to because it can show personal weaknesses, cause changes to your service, reduce the size of your client base, and end/initiate partnerships. However, by taking the time to do this essential work, you demonstrate your total understanding of a hurricane business and its natural cycle. Just as it was important to pause to build your processes, it is equally important to pause to assess you and your business. Where the first pause helped you *build* what you have today, a pause now helps you *maintain* it. It's interesting how the two pauses come at almost opposite ends of the spectrum of your business. It clearly demonstrates their significance and how they complement one another. They are a lot like framework and ideas; you need both of them to have a lasting powerful referral business.

Assessment is not only important for the physical changes it will bring to your business but also for the positive change of mind it will instill in you. The untold attribute of an annual assessment is it energizes you for the New Year. How? It marks the beginning of renewed energy that excites the senses and confidently allows you to go back out into the world of success and succeed.

By conducting an annual assessment, you demonstrate there's no room for *complacency* in your business. The mention of that may come across as an unheralded comment, but the results sure are not. *It is complacency that will eventually cause a successful businessperson to fail.* Don't allow complacency to creep into your business in any way.

This book has revealed business-building answers that were perhaps just out of reach for some undetermined reason. In the past, you may have felt like you were on the outside looking in. No more! You now know what it takes to be a member of the Referral-Based Service Industry. You have the knowledge it takes to tap into all the great ideas you need to build your business into a hurricane. They truly will make all the difference in your business—and now you have the framework with which to do it. *Ideas bring framework to life.*

Let me finish discussing a hurricane business by sharing some closing thoughts about framework and why it should be important to you. A sundry of insights can be drawn.

First, framework is reflective of what's necessary, which naturally prevents wasted energy and time. Purely from a business point of view, you've created a self-sustaining business economy through diametrically opposing dynamics. Where you *economized* yourself and your service through six traits, passionate service, and two levels of systemization, you *maximized* the participation of clients and business partners through two pentagon effects.

Next, framework doesn't determine your business but instead supports what you want it to be. Said with a little bit of slang, you can do your own thing. The reason being is framework isn't a system; it's how a business works and why you do things. *When you learn a system, you do it that way; when you learn framework, you do it your way* (you have creative control). That's an important distinction because you have to first believe in your business before others will. The best way to believe in it is to build it in a way that reflects your individualism.

Even though framework and a system are based on opposing business approaches, they do share a common bond. The bond is a system will usually comprise a portion of the framework discussed. It is a more focused effort to achieving business success rather than a comprehensive one. At the end of the day, both approaches can bring you success, just through different methods.

When you truly know the entire framework of your business, you know more than just framework. It tells its secrets in untold ways because you can figuratively look beyond what you see and discuss *how* it works and *why* you do things. It's simple yet sophisticated. But sophisticated in the logic of common sense, meaning that to learn it just takes time—it's accessible to everybody. That's the only reason I figured it out. In the end, framework doesn't make a business simpler; it makes it simple to understand.

Yet another key insight is from the framework of your business will emerge the service side of your business plan. Embedded in your business framework are: traits, two timeframes of service, service and marketing plans, client and business partner expectations, business activities, vision, execution and preparatory goals, annual assessment, etc. The framework of your business represents your business plan in action. It's what you'll depend on for success (generating business).

As you would expect, the framework of a powerful referral business captures the full measure of leadership. First, it provides you the many answers you need to make informed business-building decisions; and second, it demands difficult people decisions of you. And that's what leadership is—a combination of personal and professional responsibility. You're fully accountable.

And finally, the framework of a powerful referral business is not based on an oversimplification of a business, anecdotes, snippets of a business, motivational words, inspiring stories, a list of things to do, discussion of business buzzwords, enticing marketing phrases, etc. Instead, it's based on the beginning, middle, and end of a business. As such, it absorbs such hyperbole into its framework, puts it into perspective, and then converts it into common sense. And that really is all a business is from beginning to end—just a bunch of interlocking, interdependent common sense.

Early on in this book, I took on the challenge to do three things: provide you the volume of the answer, present it in a way that allows you to easily assemble it in your mind, and empower you to work with it. You know this threshold has been met when you can apply intellectual thought to whatever words you hear or read about a business. In all likelihood, you're not fully at this level right now (which is to be expected), but you will be when you learn the framework and then master its interconnectivity. When you join together those two things as one, your mind will hear and comprehend all at the same time, which means it can instantly retrieve both obvious and subtle answers from anywhere on the framework. Such astute thinking ability will mentally empower you like never before.

As I near the end of discussing the framework of a powerful referral business, it is important to take a moment here and share a personal insight. I have come to realize that there is a question that comes before the two headwater questions of: *How* does a business work? and *Why* do you do things? (If you remember, they were first mentioned in the "Introduction" of this book.) This one question is so significant it determines the many acumen answers that will flow from the headwater questions. Accordingly then, it's *the first question to ask in business*. And that question is: How much client trust do I want to leverage? The answer to this question (previously discussed) will determine what type of business is going to be built—transactional, referral, or powerful referral business. It's only after this question has been asked and then answered that the *appropriate* acumen answers can flow from the two headwater questions of "How" and "Why". What that means is these two questions are organic to discovering any type of business. Here's the bottom line. Trust has always been at the center of business success. And now it is at the center of understanding a business.

And if you think about the client leverage question mentioned above, you will notice a couple of other interesting insights. First, this question is at the heart of the psychology of a business. When business people determine the psychology of their business (the nexus), they are deciding how much client trust is going to be leveraged. And second, a quick analysis of The Third Question (How do I lead and serve others?) reveals that this question is fully leveraging client trust.

Suffice to say, so much originates from trust. Consequently, it is at the forefront when it comes to the following: the type of business being built, understanding a business, achieving business success, leveraging people, and becoming a leader. Trust is integral to each one of them in its own unique way. You can't discuss them without somehow mentioning trust.

There's one more personal insight to share with you. I have seen firsthand the difference between working with family and friends and working with people in the world of success. There is a sharp contrast occurring between them to recognize. Specifically, where some family members and friends will be hesitant to let you serve them (which we saw in our business), people you meet in the world of success will look forward to it. Why the difference between them? The mortgage profession, like the other four professions highlighted in this book, peers into the financial world of clients. Such a look reveals highly personal financial information and standing, which naturally makes family members and friends uncomfortable. People who know each other just don't talk about this subject. Conversely, this type of financial information is easily shared among people who don't know each other. The reason being is the business interaction starts out on a professional level, not on a personal level. With all of that said, it's important to recognize the common bond among family, friends, and people from the world of success. And that is, they will all refer you business. So what lessons did I learn? First, family and friends can put you on the road to success, but real success is achieved in the world of success. Next, if you want to win in business, you have to have a well thought out framework. And the most important thing I learned—bona fide success doesn't come from building upon the existing friendships you already have with family and friends but, rather, from developing new friendships with people you don't know.

Let me close this chapter by saying you now know what it takes to build and maintain a hurricane business because you know the *Purpose* behind every activity you accomplish in your business. At long last your *Curiosity* has been quenched. So take off your hard hat and toss it high into the air, because a comprehensive blueprint building plan for a powerful referral business has finally been unfurled and thoroughly revealed. What that means for you on a personal level is you have acquired a business-oriented clarity to the timeless, universal rule that affects both young and old alike: *every action has a consequence, so make good decisions.* NOW YOU CAN POP OPEN THE CHAMPAGNE!

The Bud Effect

Just thinking...
About her...she is my girl!

THE MANY CONCEPTS of a powerful referral business have at last been presented, and the case has been made for its functionality and sustainability. You are finally at the point just before you hear the proverbial question during a presentation that signals the end is near, "Are there any questions?" As you then know, it's time to summarize by compressing 200 plus pages into just a couple of pages. It's time for the executive summary version of the book.

The outcome of everything you've done up to this point is called *The Bud Effect* and is so named because it reflects that building a powerful referral business is done over a period of time. It reveals the *steps* you have taken and the framework you have put up. The Bud Effect shows a chronological sequence of the steps necessary to move from an individual with talent to an individual who has created a powerful referral business. The importance of this natural order can't be overstated. Pay close attention to it. By doing so, you will bring efficiency to what's already a daunting task. When you accomplish the steps and build the framework, you slowly expand your business and it, in essence, *buds* out.

Let me briefly recap the journey of this book and recount what exactly makes up The Bud Effect. The first step is you and your talent, the most basic requirement of any service-oriented business. Traits are vital because they are your distinguishing character features that make you...you. Service processes reflect the service you provide to make a difference, while pounce processes convince people to become a part of your business. Together, they cover the full spectrum of service. And don't forget about business partner service processes, a subset of service processes, which are hugely critical to building lasting partnerships.

The Eight Step Process is a systematic approach to build, add, and maintain all three types of processes. It can even be used in a roundabout way to assess the current state of your business partnerships and subsequently point you in the right direction to prospect for new ones.

The turning points are how you execute your business. They will eventually lead you to your tipping point, which creates a synergy between you and your business. For the first time, your business is starting to work for you. Consistency and relationships are the by-product of everything you've done, and they confirm you've built what you set out to build. And finally, assessing your business ensures you're never content; you're always looking to improve; and you're renewing your energy every year.

If you were to take a hurricane business and expose its elements, you would see the all too familiar diagram below, which illustrates The Bud Effect.

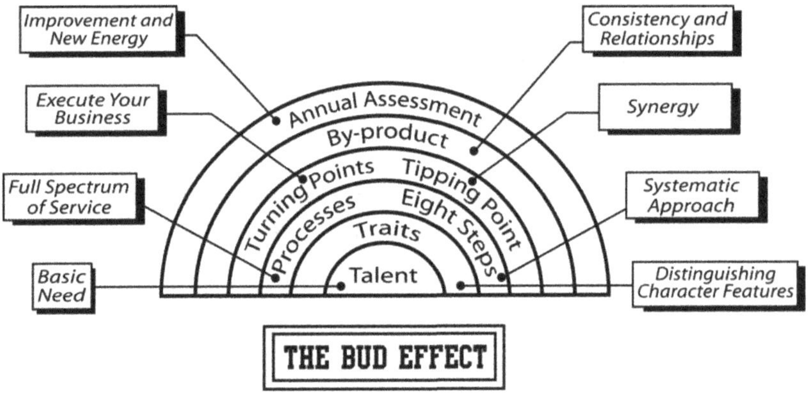

All of the above steps combined put you in command of your business and empower you. Instead of people telling you what they think you need, you can look at your business model and tell them what you do need. Put another way, I hope The Bud Effect does for you what it did for me, slow down the business world around me so I could catch up and walk in step with it. It took quite a while, but I finally know how to think about a business because I understand a business. In short, I'm immediately synthesizing what I hear or read into the framework of a powerful referral business. From a metaphoric standpoint, my brain now thinks at the speed of a hare!

Now I know with so many concepts comprising a powerful referral business it can seem almost impossible to build and execute. On the surface, it would certainly appear to be that way. Keep in mind, though, this book has meticulously taken apart the business, piece by piece. Each concept has been *independently* discussed. In all actuality, a business doesn't work that way. Instead, it works in an *interdependent* way, in that various concepts concurrently work together to perform a business action. For example, when you make a client telephone call, you are drawing on all six traits in some capacity; you are leveraging your systemized service experience; and you are utilizing more than a few turning points. It is this interlocking dependency of several concepts at a time, coupled with some concepts being knowledge-based and some being action-based, that makes the seemingly impossible possible, allowing you to build and execute a powerful referral business.

Regardless of whether you're *building a business* or *in business*, you are going to take countless steps during your career. And as much as you would like them to be, they are all not 30-inch strides forward. Instead, when you build a business, you simply take more steps forward than backward; and when you are in business, you repeatedly take steps in place. The significance of the difference is one way you build a career; the other way you are in a career field. For the first time in her career, Rose is truly taking steps forward in her business. She has figuratively stepped from being in business to building a business.

When you build a business, you will at some point face two inevitable lurking matters. One of them you know when it will most likely occur, and the other one is always present. They're *The Stress of Success* and *The Constant Challenge*. To truly stay on your journey of building a powerful referral business, you must effectively deal with both of them when they present themselves. Let me first talk about The Stress of Success.

There will come a time when production exceeds capacity (usually during a strong market). When it happens, your business will be under stress to keep up. Such stress will affect people and business in decidedly different ways. First, if you have a team around you, your people could become short with their comments and may say or do things they regret, or they may cut corners to try to keep up with the unusually high business volume. The same thing can happen to you if you are working alone. Finally, your processes will be stressed to the point where their well-hidden inefficiencies will be exposed. By recognizing The Stress of Success and properly reacting to it, you can keep your team or yourself from overreacting or improperly responding to a real but temporary situation, and you can improve your business to where it will better perform the next time it encounters stress.

A challenging business moment like The Stress of Success is a leadership opportunity for you. In all actuality, it's a crucial leadership opportunity for two different reasons. First, you can demonstrate your breadth of leadership ability by *calmly leading under pressure*—no easy feat. To best illustrate this type of scenario, the following situation comes to mind. In the face of difficult times (your business and/or your people are stressed beyond their limit), you're the calmest person in the room, which then leads to clear-minded thinking and precise directions.

I watched Rose deal with this exact situation in her business. It was brought on by a combination of exterior and interior business dynamics. The exterior business dynamic was a strong market driven by a significant drop in interest rates, while the interior dynamics were repeat business (refinances), client referrals, and business partner referrals flowing back and forth. She was fully reaping the benefits of conducting business in the second timeframe of service. Rose's business was generating multiple trifecta business days, but unfortunately, her team was being pushed to the limit of breaking. In the end, it was unsustainable. She calmly and confidently took control of the situation by taking the following actions. First, she explained The Stress of Success to her team, thereby showing them the big picture and putting things into the proper perspective. Next, she temporarily streamlined her business by suspending those activities that didn't compromise her two timeframes of service. These two steps brought a calming-effect to her team while still keeping her and her team true to the premise of her business. By thoughtfully reacting instead of emotionally overreacting to this (temporary) situation, she properly positioned both her business and her team to professionally handle The Stress of Success—which they did.

The second leadership opportunity associated with The Stress of Success is you can *direct fixes for things that are broken*. These directed fixes (both big and small) will make a real difference in your business and to your people as well. Where some business people might see this as a negative situation, you eagerly embrace this opportunity because you realize your business is showing you its inefficiencies without you having to look for them. How sweet is that? I know that may come across as an overly optimistic viewpoint, but if you think about it, how else can you look at this situation? I mean, who are you going to get angry at? Remember, you are the master craftsman of your business!

In both of the situations, you are the voice of calm and reason—a highly desirable leadership trait, one that the people on your team will greatly appreciate. And here's the subtle but key takeaway from the two situations above. If you want to know the type of leader you *truly* are, look no further than The Stress of Success. Where adversity introduces you to yourself, The Stress of Success will introduce you to the type of leader you are.

When you make a commitment to the premise of service leads to sales and the dual sophistication associated with it, you naturally embrace The Constant Challenge of trying to achieve efficiency. Any time you have well-established expectation standards to meet, you will invariably notice deficiencies that bring a friction to your business-building effort. If you recall, one of these types of deficiencies has already been discussed—our fat finger when loading information into our database management system. It is the early recognition and then subsequent tackling of these business and/or people issues through goal tracking, annual assessment, and just plain daily vigilance that validates your unwavering commitment to your business premise. Even with this diverse responsive effort in place and working, you never quite get there, but you always try, which is why the pursuit of efficiency is The Constant Challenge in business.

As if that's not already enough by itself, adding to The Constant Challenge will be the never-ending innovation of technology. For as long as you are in your career, it will always be advancing, and you will always need to consider it. This filtering challenge is made even more difficult by the fact not all technology will make you more effective and bring business efficiency, but technology will make you more effective and efficient. The utter importance of wading through it and then determining what's applicable to you and your business is technology functions in a demarcation role—it either keeps you in lock step with the times, or it places you behind the times. It's that consequential, which is why you have to consider it.

It is important to quickly note that the leadership challenge you face with The Constant Challenge is far different than The Stress of

Success, in that it's a daily occurrence. Together, though, they ensure you're always leading, regardless of whether it's under routine or difficult circumstances.

Here's the bottom line. Through your composed and thoughtful reaction to The Stress of Success and being ever mindful of The Constant Challenge you'll always be in a forward leaning business posture of trying to improve, no matter the situation.

The Sand Has Sifted

Just thinking...
Someone or something is going to work hard.

MY JOURNEY OF DISCOVERING a powerful referral business began with an hourglass. It was through the sifting of sand I would understand people and business and how they fit as one and work together. While you've been reading this book, the sand has slowly but surely been sifting through your hourglass as well. Every concept you have read and learned about along the way has let a little bit more sand drop into the bottom of the hourglass. At last, it has all sifted and settled into a powerful referral business.

The significance of that occurring is you have *created leverage on two levels*. First, you leveraged your business by organizing it in such a way that it *connects* clients and *attracts* business partners. Second, you leveraged your clients and business partners by *hoping* and *expecting* they make a difference across your business. It's a powerful referral business that brings together—people and business—and then fully leverages them both through service.

Not to be overlooked is the natural order occurring between people and business. One obviously influences the other. The way you think about the *people* in your business (the nexus) will determine the internal workings of your *business*. Really think about that for just a minute. Consider transactional and powerful referral business people and their decidedly different interpretation of the three major components of traits, service, and execution.

Both of them will have integrity, but only powerful referral business people will provide two timeframes of service and routinely ask for business from an established business of clients. Transactional business people will have pounce processes to convince people, while powerful referral business people will have both pounce and service processes to convince and connect people, and business partner service processes to easily and professionally insert business partners into their business. One business will have limited revenue streams, while the other will have multiple revenue streams that create a river of business. A database will at best be a seldom used tool in transactional businesses and a mainstay of powerful referral businesses. One type of business will spend money, while the other one will invest it. Transactional business people will focus their day on creating business through themselves, while powerful referral business people will schedule their day to dually focus on conducting transactions and generating business for themselves and their business partners through their business of clients. If I wanted too, I could go on and on.

Who am I really describing? It's just one person—Rose. Not so long ago, she was that transactional businessperson portrayed. She had integrity, but *she had only positioned her business to where she would work hard.* Now today, she's that powerful referral business-person depicted. She still has integrity, but through many personal and professional changes *she has finally positioned her business to where it's starting to work hard for her.*

Can you see the downright importance of the psychology of your business—it determines what you will do in your business. It truly marks the very beginning of your business journey. I have seen this firsthand through Rose. All of the changes in her business can easily be traced back to the new psychology of her business. Once she switched who was most important in her business (from agents to clients), she began traveling a *rewarding* business journey. She has supported this new business psychology decision just as much as she had supported her old business psychology decision of agents over clients. Never lose sight of the fact you are in the people business first. And in the people business, success goes through your people—starting with your clients.

o

Once you create leverage on two levels, you can then *leverage on a third level,* if you so choose, by building an admin team around you. When you do, you formally recognize that a business is basically an administrative effort that leads to successful people interactions. It is the behind-the-scenes administrative work that creates the *consistency* required to have *relationships* across your entire business. Putting such a team around you means you have hired people to create that consistency for you so you can then focus on personally developing and maintaining relationships.

The addition of an admin team to your business brings with it many new leadership responsibilities. The preeminent way to professionally handle all of them is with a *job description.* Such a document is multifaceted because it enables you to effectively do four diverse things: delineate job responsibilities (theirs and yours) by separating consistency and relationship business activities from each other, hire qualified people, annually evaluate their job performance, and, if needed, fire them for failing to meet the functional requirements of the job. By taking the time to write a job description (consisting of a job summary, a list of activities to perform, and specific qualifications), you extend the efficiency of your business to your team. You are as thoughtful about your team as you are about your business. And don't forget to write your job description (based on leadership/relationship activities)—you also have a role to fulfill.

There's yet a *fourth level of leverage* for you to consider in your business. Your business is now *properly positioned* to add a partner(s) to it. If you choose to do so, you will simply wrap your administratively supported leverage business model around their talent. It's all easy enough to do now, but it took a tremendous effort on your part to finally reach this moment in your business. And what exactly is the moment you are at? It's the *exponential scale moment* in business.

If you decide to add a partner(s) to your team, it's equally important to have a job description for them as well. By doing so, you can accomplish the same four diverse things as mentioned above. You have recognized their unique role while applying the same standard to them that you did for your admin team. The importance of taking this action is you steer clear of creating a double standard between admin people and partner(s), which is very, very important to do in a team setting. You have confidently taken command of your entire team in a *fair* way. The end personal result is *all of your people* will respect you. Mutual respect is just as important to a team as it is to a business. That's an essential element for you to have when leading a team. Not only that, you have avoided favoritism, which is one of the most corrosive forces to a team—it slowly destroys it from the inside out.

The importance of job descriptions for both your admin team and partner(s) is they ensure clear lines of individual responsibility have been drawn, and thus, there's no creeping of one job into the other. If a team is to work efficiently as a cohesive unit, partner(s) must understand and step up to their identified responsibilities (required technical and service) while knowing exactly where the admin team responsibilities end. The simple reason why this is so important is *relationships come from consistency, not the other way around.* It's this clear-cut sequence that beckons you to respect and protect the integrity of the work being performed by your admin team. If you make compromises on this body of work (having them regularly perform work outside of their purview), you compromise the relationships of your business.

The other important reason for job descriptions is they establish *expectations.* Where it was important to set expectation standards for clients and business partners through two pentagon effects, it is equally important to set the same type of standards for your admin people and partner(s) through job descriptions. And where do team member expectations originate from—the Business Star. Beyond its vision is an identifiable body of work (everything that has been discussed in this book) that makes the vision possible. Just as a Business Star guided the establishment of your goals, it will now guide the development of your job descriptions. Where a Business Star illustrates the vision of your business, job descriptions will reflect the body of work it takes to achieve that vision. And here's the other value of the Business Star to recognize. It allows you to clearly show your people the overarching goal of your business, thereby bringing both an understanding and long-term focus to your team.

The development of well-defined job expectations can't be overstated, for they are the precursory work of successful team execution. For example, when a team succeeds, its success can easily be traced back to this early work—everybody knew what was expected of them, and they stepped up and accomplished their individually identified job responsibilities. In contrast, when a team is unsuccessful, its failings can also be traced back—revealing that the early work wasn't done. Consequently, the people didn't know what was specifically expected of them, and they, therefore, struggled to properly perform the many aspects of their job, which reflects a complete failure of leadership.

To avert a failure of leadership on your part with your team, you need to accomplish three successive activities: develop well-defined job description expectations, clearly communicate them, and hold people accountable. As you do each one of these activities, keep this one thought in mind—people want to meet expectations. I would even go as far to suggest they want to meet high expectations. Just as you want to be a successful businessperson, people want to be on a successful team.

Here is yet one more bottom line thought for your consideration. Where providing explained service is the *jell agent* for your business team (you, clients, and business partners), job descriptions are the jell agent for your personal team (you, partner(s), and admin people). In both cases, it's the jell agent that unleashes potential.

When you leverage your business on all four levels, you have recognized the dichotomy of a business and systematically *shifted the burden* of working hard from yourself to your business. Basic physics are at work in your business.

That's the simple game at work inside a business, trying to shift the burden. There's always going to be hard work when it comes to your business. The only question is, "Who will be performing that hard work—you or your business?" Take a look at *The Burden Triangle* below. Start at the base of the triangle and work your way up. As you do, you'll be working your way through both the dichotomy of a business and the four leverage levels.

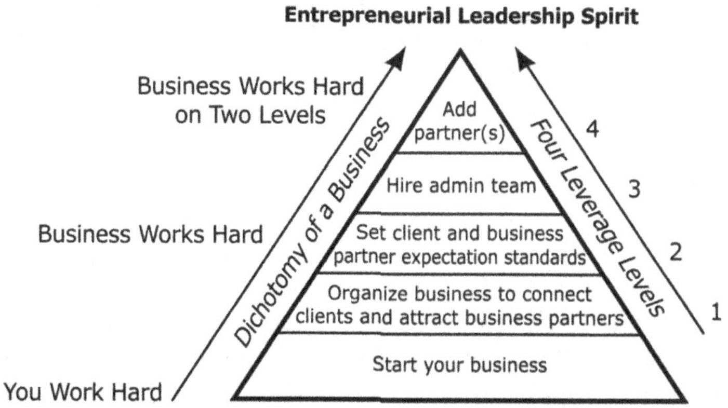

THE BURDEN TRIANGLE

Here are the takeaway insights from the illustration. When you first start your business, you will work hard. There's just no getting around that fact. However, with the right decisions and actions, you can in time shift the burden of working hard from yourself to your established business of clients and business partners. By doing so, you are traversing through the dichotomy of a business while stepping through the first two levels of leverage. You can continue your journey through the dichotomy of a business by leveraging on two more levels. First, by emplacing an admin team around you and, second, by adding a partner(s). When you do, you've leveraged your business on a whole different level by going outside of your established business. You have expanded your leadership responsibilities even more. It is through your decision to serve clients first that your *Entrepreneurial Leadership Spirit* is fully realized. It is also through this decision that the full potential of a business is realized.

When you choose to expand your leadership responsibilities by leveraging your business on four levels, you right away assume the additional responsibility of determining the division of team decision-making responsibilities. You can lead a team by yourself, but you cannot make all of the team decisions by yourself. Therefore, whenever you hire people, you have to be willing to trust and empower them. An effective leader shares decision-making responsibility. Just as you had to trust other people for your business success, you will now trust your team for team success. To effectively accomplish it, you will develop *team policies.* Such policies are your instructions on how you would like your team to handle the collective decisions that are expected to occur while you're leading them. As such, your team policies take into the account the various types of relationships occurring on your team. For example, between you and your team members, between the various types of team members, and team member interaction with clients, business partners, and the people outside of your team who have a direct impact on a transaction. In short, policies clearly communicate what your team members are authorized and not authorized to direct or decide. They delineate clear lines of decision-making responsibility, thereby keeping everybody in line. Policies not only make it easier for your team members to properly interact with each other, they make it easier for you to quickly intervene and fairly resolve team conflicts. They are the final layer of precursory work to successful team execution. And here's the added importance of team policies to be familiar with. They mesh together job descriptions by acting as the adhesive that creates optimal team cohesion. There's now a unity of effort being put forward by your team.

In the end, it is the development of both job descriptions and team policies that ensures each member of your team clearly knows his or her specific job responsibilities and the scope of his or her authority. Your team now has as much interlocking, interdependent structure as your business does. And you have the standards you need to praise your people in public and discipline them in private.

O

Now that the many concepts of a powerful referral business and a team have been thoroughly discussed, it is important to quickly acknowledge what they create when you meld them together as one. And that is, they create a *culture*—the third and final by-product moment in this book. A culture is nothing more than the sum of all the business actions. As such, it reflects a leader's broadest leadership responsibility while shining either a positive or negative light on him or her. It will do one or the other. Because you have chosen to base your culture on serving others while managing each member of your team in an equal and fair way, you don't have to worry about the negative aspects associated with a culture. Instead, you'll only realize the positive aspects of it when it comes to the following thought: *a culture is your business beliefs in action.*

O

For all of its sophistication and extensive inner workings, the simplistic truth about your business is you will never work harder then when you first start out, and your business will never work harder for you then when you *logically* leverage it through the four levels.

From a Revolving Door to a Front Door

Just thinking...
She's a businesswoman acting like a businesswoman.

IT IS A FOREGONE CERTAINTY the sun will set every night and rise each morning. Where the evening sunset marks the brilliant end of the day, the morning sunrise on the distant horizon starts the glorious beginning of a new day. Together, they dramatically change the sky from night to day. Not surprisingly, Rose figuratively had a sunset and a sunrise that had to occur in her business. She had to *end* the business days of a transactional businesswoman and *begin* the business days of a powerful referral businesswoman. Doing so would cause a night and day change to occur in her business.

I want to share with you the wonderful changes Rose has made in her business day. It's through these changes that our business is moving in a new direction, which is keeping our journey going.

Before doing that, though, let me for just a moment turn back the pages one last time and quickly reflect on a typical business day for Rose. In the past, she would come into the office and immediately start working on whatever work was in front of her. When the telephone rang, she would briefly interrupt what she was doing but then quickly get right back to it. Her day was intensely focused on doing two things, branch manager work and brilliantly serving new clients through the closing of their home loan.

Rose's no-nonsense work ethic not only allowed her to get the most done in a day, her desk was always clean at the end of the day. Where I was comfortable in clutter, she was always organized. The importance of the difference is twofold. First, opposites do attract! And second, Rose had the essence of business success in her DNA makeup—organization.

Unfortunately for Rose, though, she only brought her organizational prowess to the technical service side of her business, never the service side of her business. Her service was primarily limited to required technical work, and once she closed the home loan, for all intents and purposes, she was done. There were no in-depth service processes in place during the business transaction period or after the home loan closed to allow her to provide a high level of service and ask for referrals. Her poorly developed business model resulted in a short care timeline, and, in turn, she had *revolving door clients.* As quickly as they entered her business, they would depart.

Let me expand on the *Revolving Door Business Model* Rose had created. By embracing such a model, she was destined to work hard because her business was only based on the premise of getting clients to the revolving door. They were usually brought there by agent business partners (typical mortgage business thinking). Once they were there, and the transaction was completed, there was figuratively nowhere else for them to go but back out. Her business was only setup to operate in the first timeframe of service.

No matter how brilliant Rose was in this timeframe, and she was technically brilliant, there was absolutely no place for her clients to go but back out once their home loan closed. They couldn't stand in the revolving door. If they came back, and some of them did (as previously mentioned), it was because they did it on their own. Just as before, though, they had no choice but to quickly leave again because she hadn't allotted any time and effort in her business to build a relationship with them. She was always looking for and moving to the next person arriving at her revolving door. Rose had fallen into the trap of becoming a quintessential transactional businessperson by having a Revolving Door Business Model as simply illustrated below.

Those days are long gone. Now when clients come to the door of Rose's business, they don't face a revolving door. Instead, they face a front door. She selects who comes in and who doesn't. Sometimes she shows them where the door is! As more and more clients continue to come through the front door, her business grows. They are staying because she has allotted time and effort to serve them and build lasting relationships. It is the second timeframe of service that is allowing Rose to have a *Front Door Business Model*. Now she's in the business of building a powerful referral business as illustrated below.

How did she do it? How did Rose change the door on her business from a revolving door to a front door? She simply moved from conducting busy work to performing work in the second timeframe of service. A fair amount of Rose's business day is now committed to this timeframe of service. She knows that's where she'll find sustainable success, and she's focused on it. Here are some examples of her new daily work habits, which form the basis of her boilerplate schedule.

Rose's day now starts out with a quick look at her electronic schedule and a check of the bond market and the interest rates. She wants to not only get a feel for her business day but also a feel for the technical side of her business as well. She's now prepared to provide service and conduct business.

She chairs a morning business meeting that provides the team's focus for the day. In short, the meeting directly speaks to the three-P's that should make up every day (review your *planned* obligations, ensure your work has a meaningful *purpose*, and deliver what you *promised*). As the leader of our business, this quick and informative meeting allows her to take charge of the team and the day.

Because Rose has management responsibilities, she blocks time during the day to work exclusively on her established business. She understands that her work during this time creates the energy that holds the business together and keeps it moving forward. It has her highest priority. To prove it, she closes her office door so as to stay focused on the work at hand. That's not easy to do for a person like her who firmly believes in an open door policy. Her employees know if they need her help they can come in; otherwise, they wait until she reopens the door. The challenge during this blocked period of time is to keep her productive and focused so as to *not break stride.* The point being, she quickly moves from one important activity to the next.

During this time, she performs multiple activities that are in direct support of the service side of her business. She actively works the three revenue streams of her business by making various types of telephone calls to clients and business partners, sending and returning emails, meeting regularly with business partners, and signing prepared letters and notes, among other things.

To help facilitate this business-building work, systems are in place to bring information to her in a way that allows for a smooth flow of work. For example, various types of correspondence to be signed comes to her in appropriately labeled color folders; while her telephone calls are sorted by the categories of return calls, follow-up calls, client/business partner telephone calls, and client mortgage review calls. They are all located on a single page within her database management system. And they are detailed to the point where she has enough information to immediately engage the person she's calling in a helpful way.

The point of this preparatory work, and others like it, is to place Rose in an *executive position*—when work comes to her desk, it's ready for her immediate action. Additionally, our executive assistant knows she can walk into the office at any time (except during appointments) and drop off work. And when she does, no acknowledgments are shared between her and Rose. Instead, both of them continue their important work at hand uninterrupted.

Near the end of the day, a quick business review is conducted and anything that couldn't be completed is moved to the next day. This may include such things as various types of telephone calls and open digital checklist steps, among other things.

The new framework of Rose's business not only has her thinking and performing like a businesswoman during the day, it has her readying herself for the next day as well. Finally, she is working her established business every day, and therefore, she's focused on developing and maintaining *relationships.*

Helping Rose round out her boilerplate schedule is our executive assistant, who professionally conducts the important tasks of loading pertinent information into the database management system, accomplishing the digital checklists, controlling Rose's schedule with the aid of a color scheme, screening and handling incoming telephone calls, placing outgoing telephone calls, and providing the team's explained service experience, among numerous other things. Through the accomplishment of these administrative actions, and others like it, she's creating the *consistency* of our team.

It is important to take a moment here and briefly reflect on the collective business actions mentioned above. They reveal an interesting insight. Rose understood all too well that if her team was to achieve the by-product of a powerful referral business, she would have to divide the work they did along the exact same lines. She did precisely that by first identifying the numerous business activities they needed to accomplish and then assigning each activity as either consistency or relationship type work. The end business result of this tedious (but important) task management exercise is her and her team is both right-focused and right-tasked. It is the powerful referral business by-product of consistency and relationships that guides the development of team member responsibilities. This realization brings to light a notable observation about the by-product. And that is, both business and team success are based on it, albeit in their own unique way.

Furthermore, Rose will regularly pull the team together for fifteen minutes or so to review an existing process, discuss one in development, or evaluate a new idea. It's her way of staying connected to her business and always trying to improve it. It's also one of the ways she is addressing The Constant Challenge of a business.

What all of these changes in Rose's business day signify is she realized if she were to retool her business, she would have to retool her day—which she has done. That's what the many business concepts of any business, to include a powerful referral business, boils down to—just a typical day. That's the simple output of the underlying complexity of a business.

The above paragraph brings us to a full circle moment and right back to the business dominos of focus and effectiveness (discussed earlier). Where the first time they illustrated scale of business, this time they will be used to stress the importance of a business day. And that is, a successful business day has a *focus* bent on trying to accomplish a predetermined *effectiveness* with the people who interface with the business. This simplistic thought equally applies to a transactional, referral, or powerful referral business. In fact, they will all depend on focus and effectiveness to both achieve their intended business objective and reach their desired scale of business.

Let me get back to Rose. For the first time in her career, Rose's business has become an extension of her. What I mean by that is Rose has always been a caring person. The only difference now is the people who interface with her business know it because she has taken the time to build a level of valuable service that expresses her to them. It took a while for her to learn, and at times it was a hard lesson, but she finally realized it was important to connect her business to her emotions. And now that she's done it, she's doing what she wants to do, which is making her and her business one.

Our Client Service Today

Just thinking...

We're just trying to make a difference. We know what it'll mean if we do.

SINCE I FIRST JOINED ROSE in her business, we have both grown professionally. She is a much better businesswoman, and I am finally at the point where I have stopped observing and am now making real contributions to the team that bears our last name but is built on hers. I can now share with you the level of service we provide our clients. It's been a long road, but it was worth every bit of sweat, frustration, discussion, and disagreement we shared. We never thought of quitting, for we knew the road to building something of lasting value only knows one way. Somewhat like a marriage, we had our testy times, but we came through it together.

It's interesting to quickly note that out of all the disagreements we shared (and there were many over the years), there was one that was far more prevalent than others. I had to remind Rose on several early occasions not to defend the old way of business based solely on how she had done things in the past. Instead, I encouraged her to base disagreements only on a strong belief that something didn't make sense to her. This simple rule served to limit our disagreements while still reminding me that change is very difficult. The importance of this little rule can't be overstated. It helped Rose replace her resistance and fear (expected feelings) with acceptance and confidence. The end result was a potentially crippling barrier to a successful business transition had been overcome with a simple rule.

Before I share the service our clients now receive, it's important to quickly tell the untold story within the story. All of the changes Rose has made in her business (big and small) are not only an exciting story for me to share, I'm excited to be a part of them. However, the untold story is the one that made it all possible. Simply told, it was her ability to first be humble and then courageous that's the other story to know. Specifically, she was willing to listen, absorb a new way of business, and then have the personal courage to do it. It's what allowed her to grow as a businesswoman. What she did may sound fairly easy to do, but when you consider it against the backdrop of her 30 years of experience, and my inexperience, it truly was a leap of faith. In the end, *Rose didn't allow her vast experience to work against her.* As I look back, her greatest challenges were not in her business but, rather, in her personal makeup. She needed to be *humble* to be willing and to be *courageous* so she could make the right changes. These two traits were indispensable to her *journey of change*, because it was no easy feat what she did when you take into account that she went through both a dramatic business change and a traumatic personal experience at one fell swoop. She simultaneously moved from a transactional to a powerful referral businesswoman and from a follower to a leader.

And when I think about the gravity of what she did, it was an incredible gesture of trust in me on her part. It was as if she said, "OK" in the face of great odds. Her open-mindedness served as a reminder to me that there are a select few times in the course of a long marriage when one spouse shows the true depth of their love and respect for the other; this was one of those rare moments.

Wherein the past our annual client service entailed sending out two marketing items (a quarterly newsletter and anniversary card), our clients now receive personalized service. To more easily manage our new service, we've, as pointed out earlier, broken it down into two distinct timeframes. Let's look at the first timeframe, which is from initial client meeting until the closing of the home loan.

When our clients arrive at the office, they find their name on a welcome board. Our executive assistant or I come out and personally greet them with a short script and ask them to fill out a questionnaire. We want them to know from the first moment they enter our business it's going to be a mortgage lending experience that is much more than just about rate. More importantly, we want to immediately signal to them their needs are our top priority. We have taken control of the conversation by starting to provide our valuable service.

The mortgage questionnaire form takes about five minutes to complete and asks pertinent professional questions aimed at understanding their knowledge of the mortgage business, what's most important to them in purchasing the home, and what they expect from us. The information they provide allows Rose to both educate and advise them. She can tailor her comments to their knowledge level and structure a deal that's right for their family. Also, she can address what they expect from us. Collecting such information up-front positions Rose to provide a personalized experience. *That's the bottom line power of listening—individualized service.*

Not only is the questionnaire form important for the three reasons stated above, but it also has a symbolical importance as well. The form sets the tone for our business—it's about them. It's something we never lose sight of, and they never wonder about.

And here's the added flexibility feature of a questionnaire to recognize. If a portion of its questions includes your business partners' professional services, then the questionnaire is formally functioning as a business partner service process. You cannot insert your business partners into your business any sooner.

There's one more crucial insight to know concerning the questionnaire. It not only allows Rose to take control of the conversation, it positions her to immediately pivot away from a question that is inclined to put cost at the forefront of the transaction. And that question is, "How can I help you today?" It's a good-natured question that's well-intentioned. Unfortunately, though, it causes a double shift to occur—it shifts control of the conversation to the clients, which naturally shifts the focus of the conversation from service to money. It only makes sense for them to first talk about what they value the most, just like it only makes sense for Rose to talk about what she values the most—the premise of her business (service).

After the clients complete the one-page questionnaire, they meet with Rose in her office, everyone sitting around a table. She briefly tells them about herself and the company to put them at ease and to start earning their trust and confidence. She gets to know them personally (what they willingly share) and goes over the mortgage questionnaire form (taking notes as she goes) before getting into the number-crunching aspects of the meeting. If the opportunity to recommend a business partner presents itself through the information shared, she will do it in this meeting. The moment clients enter her business is also the moment her business partners enter it.

There are times when Rose doesn't personally meet with clients because they are located out of town, or they prefer to do business over the telephone or Internet. When that happens, she still stays true to what she built by saying and doing the same things. The only difference is, instead of the clients filling out the questionnaire, Rose gathers the information by asking the questions. Whether the initial loan consultation is in-person, over the telephone, or over the

Internet, it has no impact on the level of service she provides in this meeting or what the clients understands when it's over.

When this first meeting is over, the clients unequivocally know their interests are her interests. They also know the level of service they'll receive between now and the closing of their home loan, and that Rose runs her business by referral and always looks forward to the opportunity to help somebody they care about. Rose has rightfully placed a dual stamp of importance on the transaction at hand and her business. Any personal information learned in the meeting is added to their database record to personalize future contacts.

The underlying importance of this first meeting, regardless of whether it's conducted in-person, over the phone, or over the Internet, is to develop some level of bond with the clients. Rose tries to achieve it by learning and sharing personal information. The most natural sharing of personal information is with military clients. Regardless of the information shared, what she's really doing is introducing the human-element into her business. She subconsciously recognizes that she's in the people business first.

Even though Rose is only in the first moments of a hoped-for relationship, she is already thinking long-term. She has started the process of putting the connecting pieces into place—pleasure, service, and business—reflecting what she hopes the relationship will eventually be based upon. Did you notice her client relationships and the art of the call are based on the same concept?

It will typically be anywhere from to two to four weeks before we close the home loan. During this time period, clients know to expect five contacts from us. We'll immediately contact them (through various means) for credit approval, order and receipt of appraisal, full loan approval, and a pre-closing call. We chose this level of service for two reasons. First, all of these moments are milestones on the way to getting their loan closed; and second, they position us to ask for business throughout the timeframe. We have other letters and notes readily available, depending on the conditions with their loan. The clients don't know it, but no other time period in our business requires us to be as ready or work as much behind-the-scenes.

The point of our effort in this short timeframe of service is to *proactively* keep the clients informed and only show them the end product. We know what they expect—a difficult and stressful process. We do our best to give them what they don't expect—a smooth and pleasant home closing. By impressing them in this way, we confidently allow them to refer somebody if they have the opportunity. But the more important reason for impressing them is it allows us to easily transition to the second timeframe of service, consisting of the service provided over a typical year and every year thereafter.

When the home loan closes at the title company, Rose and I attend with a thank-you note in hand. The reason we only show up with a note, and not a closing gift, is we are positioning ourselves to *formally enter* the second timeframe of service: the Referral-Based Service Industry. This is the beginning moment of our long-term service effort to try to connect clients to our business. The thank-you note we give them after the transaction closes says:

> *Thank you for allowing Michael and me to serve your home financing needs. It was a real pleasure for us. We'll be contacting you soon to deliver your closing book and some gifts for your home. We'll also be introducing you to our personalized client service...we hope it makes a difference to you. Thanks again and enjoy your new home...we know wonderful memories await you!*

When we arrive back in the office, our executive assistant starts building their closing book, which includes a signed personal cover letter with referral language, Deed of Trust, Promissory Note, Amortization Schedule, HUD—1 Settlement Statement, and Appraisal. In front of each document is a short paragraph explaining the importance of it. She also prepares their closing gifts. The first one is a small maple basket with a gold metal plate that says, "Congratulations from Rose and Michael." The second gift, which is inside the basket, is a brass doorknocker engraved with the clients last name and year they purchased their home.

Rose and I chose these two housewarming gifts for the following reasons. First and foremost, we wanted something of high-quality that would clearly express our appreciation. And second, we wanted the gifts to both greet people and be displayed in the home. Our closing gifts are meant to generate conversation amongst friends, colleagues, and family members who visit the home—to keep our names in front of our clients in a professional way.

The second timeframe of service begins when Rose and I personally deliver the closing book and gifts to the clients' home. On a rare occasion, we will do this at our office if they prefer. We allot time in our business to do this because we realize it is the most intimate moment we will spend with our clients. We understand it is only because of our impressive service in the first timeframe that we can share this special time with them.

This is the *connecting moment* of our business. We've done our best to create the perfect setting: a smooth home loan closing at the title company, excitement on the part of the clients to be in their new home, and the presence of a professional closing book with all of their signed documents. We're ready to make a difference in their lives with our service, and we bear gifts in hand. We want them to know that our service to them is really just beginning, which it is.

We use a script in explaining our service, and to help us master it quickly, we separated our professional transaction management activities from the activities of our personal service. Then, we built the corresponding service for each in sequential order from daily to monthly to quarterly and on to annually, as applicable. The script below is what I tell our clients after I explain their closing book but before I give them their gifts. At long last, I've moved on from meaningless office chatter to meaningful client conversations.

> *Rose and I run our business by referral. We understand that requires a high level of service and that's what we deliver. Our goal is to encourage you to remain clients and confidently allow you to refer family, friends, and colleagues. We hope to achieve our goal by professionally managing your mortgage and providing you a level of personal service that makes a difference. Here's the level of service you can expect from us during the year.*
>
> *We will professionally manage your mortgage by doing the following four things:*
>
> *First, Rose and I watch the mortgage rates daily and when we can lower your monthly mortgage payment without raising your mortgage balance, we'll call you. So as you get mail advertisements about low, low rates and refinance now, just know that we are watching the interest rates daily and you don't need to concern yourself with those types of advertisements. Now, if you see one that's just too good to be true, please call us and we'll gladly explain it to you.*

If at any time during the year you need to take cash out of your home for a home project or a family matter, please let us know and we can help you with it.

We feel it's important on an annual basis to take a few minutes and look at your current family situation and make sure the loan program we have you in is still what's best for your family. Therefore, on the anniversary of your closing, we'll contact you to do an annual mortgage review. If we recommend you change anything, you can always be confident it's what's best for your family.

And lastly, at the beginning of each year, we'll send you a letter reminding you of the tax information you need to provide your tax preparer.

Now for our personal service:

As homeowners, you might one day need the services of other professionals like a CPA, financial planner, or insurance agent. We have partnered with ones who do business like us, and it would be our pleasure to refer one of them if you require their professional services.

Also, if you require any personal services like a family dentist, mechanic, plumber, or chiropractor, please let us know. We have business associates we trust that we can refer.

If at anytime during the year we hear about or come across information that we feel would add value to you, your home, or your wealth, we'll send you an email or call you, as appropriate. The information shared can come from either us or our business partners.

On a monthly basis, we'll send you an email that comes with a letter and a corresponding flyer. Every month will be a different topic, ranging from fun things to do to helpful hints. (Note: when one of these mailings is about one of our business partners' profession, it is functioning as a business partner service process.)

On a quarterly basis, we'll email you a newsletter, which discusses your home and wealth. It provides valuable information about both subjects and will be beneficial to you.

We don't want to just share valuable information; we also love to stay in touch by talking to you. If you don't mind, we will call you every three months to see how things are going and if there's anything we can help you with. Would that be okay? (The answer is always yes.)

We would like to ask one thing of you today. Rose and I are always looking to improve our service, so we would appreciate if you'd take a few minutes and fill out this short survey and send it back to us next week in the pre-addressed, pre-stamped envelope attached to it. (Also on the survey, we ask if they would provide a testimonial, if they know anyone who needs our professional services today, and if they personally require any of our business partner or business associate services. If they answer yes to any of the questions, Rose will immediately follow up with a telephone call. Once more, another business partner service process.) (Note: Rose will also call them if we are marked down in any way. We value these surveys the most because we learn from them, which then helps us improve our service.)

We hope you enjoy our personalized client service, and we look forward to maintaining our relationship with you and helping people you think would benefit from our services.

(Note: Every year we mail our clients a birthday card with a handwritten personalized note and the previously discussed Happy New Year letter, but we don't mention it here. Both of these service items help us over deliver.)

Here are some insightful comments on the script above. First, our service positions us and our business partners in front of our clients throughout the year. Second, if you look at it closely, you'll notice we address four of the five tenets of the client pentagon. The only one we don't talk about concerns client help in acquiring new business partners. We can only do that after we have provided our service over a period of time. Third, we consciously chose to provide a fair amount of our service through email instead of mail. This decision allowed us to cut costs while increasing both our personal efficiency and the delivery speed of our service. (Note: we do mail our Happy New Year letter because we include a business calendar magnet.) Next, our service encourages us to interface with all six traits and ten turning points in some way, at some point. And last, we address the three activities necessary to add clients to our business—we professionally manage the transaction, provide a level of service that makes a difference, and ask for business, written and verbally.

Here is something else we do on these client appointments. We invite our agents to join us—it did take a joint effort to close the transactions. We want them to personally see our service effort to try to build a mini-business with them. They love coming along, and we couldn't imagine doing it without them. Some of them have even started sharing their second timeframe of service during these mutual-client appointments.

These visits are meant to last less than thirty minutes, but they hardly ever do. Somehow we always share personal stories, usually get a tour of the home, and sometimes sit down and break bread. There's nothing better than sitting around the kitchen table in your clients' home sharing good conversation. It's a moment unlike any other. After the visit, we upload acquired personal data into their contact database management record for future use.

Before going any further, think back to the two business partner interview questions: "What is your level of client service before and after the business transaction?" and "How is your business setup so that you can refer business?" Through our service commitment to clients you can see how Rose and I have *positioned* our business to answer both of these questions to any of our business partners and how these two questions reveal a client-centric business.

It took quite a bit of hard work, but we have finally moved to the "see side" of The Look or See Concept. There is at last predictability to our business. And we've removed single-critical business partner failure points from our business, which has created a calming-effect. The emotional result is we have a feeling of independence instead of the silent uneasiness that comes with being dependent.

Here is yet another important insight. It's through our commitment to the second timeframe of client service that we now view a strong market with temptation instead of pure opportunity. Today, a strong market brings us business success instead of market success. Yet once again, service functions in a transformative way.

Let me share with you a subtle feature of our client service. For the past clients who didn't respond to our Starting Anew letter (previously discussed), we continued to *market* to them, on a very limited basis, with our quarterly newsletter that was already going out to our established clients as a service process. The only reason we did this pounce process is it was being sent out for us by another organization at no additional cost or effort to us. Over the years, a few of these *prospective clients* unexpectedly contacted us to help them. It was a predictable low marketing response. But when they did, we provided them our two timeframes of service, making them clients. This situation brings to light an underlying importance of providing service electronically. When you do, you can take advantage of this type of opportunity at little or no additional expense or effort. You have, in essence, brought a *dual purpose* to a single service item—it is serving established clients while marketing to prospective clients. You have flexed a service item beyond its natural use.

This brings us to a recap moment. It is important to take a little bit of time to quickly reiterate the various types of clients who can interface with a powerful referral business. They are just as multidimensional as the business is itself, in that they range from established to prospective clients. Here's how.

First, there are two types of *established clients* you will have in your business. The first, and the most important, is ideal clients. As mentioned earlier, these are your best clients because they have made a personal and professional connection with you and your business. As such, you can use direct referral language with this very loyal group of people. Just below them is your other group of established clients—they have yet to make the dual connection with you and your business, but they are supporting your business with repeat business and referrals. Accordingly, you don't use direct referral language with them. The obvious importance of having both of these types of clients in your business is *they* are helping you start other people on a journey of becoming established clients.

At the other end of the client spectrum is *prospective clients.* The first, and the most important, are those potential clients currently interfacing with some type of pounce process. You are still in the midst of trying to convince them in some way. And well below them are the potential clients like the ones who did not respond to our Starting Anew letter—you are reengaging past clients in some way to try to revive a seemingly lost business opportunity. Rightfully, it's much more difficult to successfully convince these potential clients. The obvious importance of pursuing both of these types of clients in your business is *you* are trying to start people on a journey of becoming established clients.

There's yet one more group of prospective clients who can be a part of a powerful referral business if you so choose. They are, in essence, *transactional business clients* in a powerful referral business. Here's why. They are the clients who you have closed a transaction with, but you decide to only market to them because they didn't quite meet the criteria it takes to enter the second timeframe of service (previously discussed). This type of client falls into a gray area, which makes them prospective clients who are on *probation*. You're going to serve them on a limited basis by providing a portion of your second timeframe of service that you can deliver electronically at little or no additional cost or effort. The duration of this service effort should allow ample time for them to either respond with repeat or referral business or utilize one of your business partners. It's *up to them* to place themselves on a journey of becoming established clients (through their actions they persuade you to start providing the second timeframe of service). If that's the case, formally enter them into the second timeframe of service by explaining and then providing your full service experience. With that said, it's important to reiterate if this is the predominate type of client you have in your business then you are a transactional businessperson who is working hard and spending money. I know that type of businessperson all too well—it was Rose for so many years.

The probation situation discussed above brings to light a possible solution for the peculiar problem insurance agents and financial advisors face during their annual client assessment—they have clients who are not supporting their business, yet they don't want to completely stop serving them in light of the continuing annual income received from the transaction. The potential solution here is to put these clients on an extended probation—market to them on a limited basis. Taking such a step rightfully reduces the service they receive to a minimum effort while hopefully maintaining their recurring income stream.

When you aggressively work the diametrically opposed business opportunities available to you—both established and prospective clients—the end business result is just one thing. And that is, an ever-increasing number of established clients.

Let's get back to our two timeframes of client service today—from beginning to however many more years Rose stays in the mortgage business. It seems rather simple doesn't it, provide service and ask for business. But a lot of thought is occurring just below that *appearance of simplicity*. If you were to illustrate both timeframes of service on a chart, on a timeline, showing the natural progression of client service, the objectives and goals for each timeframe, what each timeframe signifies, who has a need, and what you're responsible to do in each one of them, you would happen upon the *Natural Progression of Client Service* chart below.

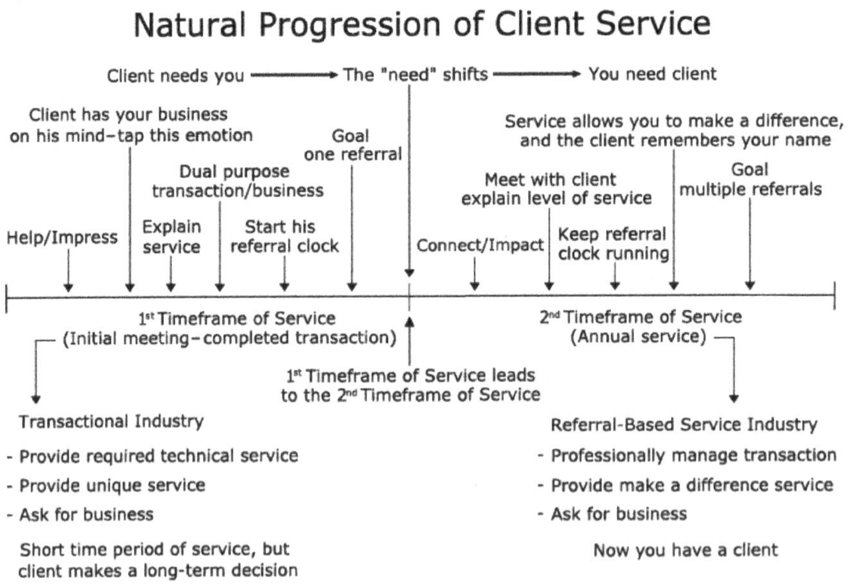

There's no doubt that the client service chart above is a busy one with quite a few details. But it's a busy chart representing a full visual picture of the many aspects of client service that were previously discussed. Hopefully, it's familiar and simplistic to you, in that it just seems the natural thing to do. You are providing service while trying to generate business for yourself and your business partners from the first moment a client enters your business.

And here's the flexibility feature of the client service chart to recognize. It can be utilized to diagnose various business situations. Here's one example. Every now and then the management of an organization will direct their sales force to have a call-a-thon. Such an event encourages business people to call their past clients to see if they can help them or someone they know. It is a caring business activity that always produces results, yet it has to be directed and some salespeople are uncomfortable doing it. So what is the business dynamic driving this management action and what is the reason for the uncomfortable feeling? The chart on the previous page provides the answers when you apply it in a diagnostic way.

When management directs their sales force to conduct a call-a-thon, they are formally recognizing that their businesses stop in the first timeframe of service and they have to encourage them into the second timeframe—the Referral-Based Service Industry. And that's what creates the uneasiness. It's rather uncomfortable for transactional business people to carry out an essential referral-based business activity (ask for business). Why? Their business is based on having brief *client interactions* in the first timeframe of service, not long-term *client relationships* in the second timeframe of service. As such, they are using the telephone to solicit business instead of using it to leverage an explained service experience. It's only natural for them to be timid; take another look at the chart on the previous page again and everything that occurs from the time referral-based business people set out to *help* a client with a transaction, until they *ask him for business* in the second timeframe. It gives you an idea about the scope of work it takes to turn a client telephone call into a conversation instead of a solicitation.

I could delve much deeper into this subject matter if I wanted too. Here's the bottom line. This same type of analysis is possible with various other business situations when you look beyond the words on the chart and apply the concepts behind them.

o

Let me briefly talk about Rose again. As you probably surmised, she values her service, has truly put clients first in her business, and is making a genuine effort to generate referrals for all of her business partners, thereby removing the negative aspects of The Bully-Bully Pulpit Concept. She is obviously in the turning point zone and has clearly passed her tipping point. At long last, Rose has enough new repetitive actions under her belt that the resistance has been overcome and her transactional business legacy has been duly buried. She's no longer a wannabe referral-based businesswoman because she now looks at a business through a full potential lens. And the question, "What did you build?" is now an achievement question for her. As such, she has finally and until the end of her career joined the group of business people who are making the business world more professional. And here's the unseen effect of these changes. They have given me my dignity within the profession. The reasons being: Rose fully embraced the framework I discovered; she became a leader in her business; and she built her business in a way that reflects her individualism.

And now let me for just a moment speak from the heart and the husband point of view. I feel incredibly lucky to have Rose in my life. I have felt that way about her ever since she walked up to me at the Silver Spur Country Club 29 years ago. It was an unimaginable moment. She was the most beautiful woman I'd ever seen (and still is to this day), and I was just an average looking guy who could do a pretty good two-step. There's no other way to say it; I was stunned to be in the moment—she was far more beautiful than I deserved. Beautiful women like Rose always danced with other men, or they were already with a man. What they didn't do was walk up to guys like me at a club. And I was way too shy to walk up to women like her. When I took her hand that night and led her to the dance floor, I knew I would never let it go. I also knew it would be the last night I looked for love. Without even trying, she captured my heart and forever changed my life for the better. When you love someone that much...from the very beginning, you'll do anything you can, for as long as it takes. To now see Rose finally on her journey of building a business, and truly enjoying it, is to know that she has moved from unfulfilled potential to being well on her way to fulfilling her potential as a businesswoman. In doing so, she has made substantial progress when it comes to the following: fulfilling one's potential is not about being more than one can be but, rather, about being the very best one can be. To watch her progressively move across the spectrum of potential in a positive way, to love her as much as I do, and then to know that I had a small part in it...well...I'm sure you know...

A Hurricane Business

Just thinking...

Finally, something is working harder than you.

YOUR WORK IS FINALLY COMPLETE. The countless number of steps you have taken in your business has allowed you to construct the proper framework, and now your ideas fit right over the top of it. When you look at it, though, you don't see one or the other. Instead, what you see is the output of both of them, a powerful referral business. You and your business are now whole. As such, you have successfully compressed business knowledge and ideas into a set of business actions. And that's what it takes, in general terms, to build a powerful referral business—a thorough understanding of the business itself, ideas that reflect your individualism, and an unwavering commitment to the necessary business actions (no matter what they are, how frequently you have to do them, or how difficult they are to do).

So how does it all fit together, and what does it look like visually? It's time to address those two questions by quickly revisiting what's been discussed and putting it all together in a simple visual illustration that shows a hurricane business.

When you visualize a hurricane business, the obvious first thing you notice is the eye. It's the calmest area, and it's right where you and your talent are located. The greatest strength of the storm is the core, where your traits and service processes reside, fanning out from there. The turning points that helped you reach your tipping point permeate throughout the storm. The storm receives its power and rotation from the by-product of consistency and relationships that now encircle it. It maintains its powerful condition by routinely undergoing assessment.

Let's slowly build a hurricane business by first looking at the eye of the storm, which is you and your talent, and then your traits and service processes that make up the core. For purpose of illustration only, you will see some of the concepts associated with service processes. This is merely the first step to building a hurricane business so you'd expect to see a business in development. You've done the early hard work, and now the two essential ingredients of a powerful referral business are in place. If you recall, it is at this point your business is poised for success.

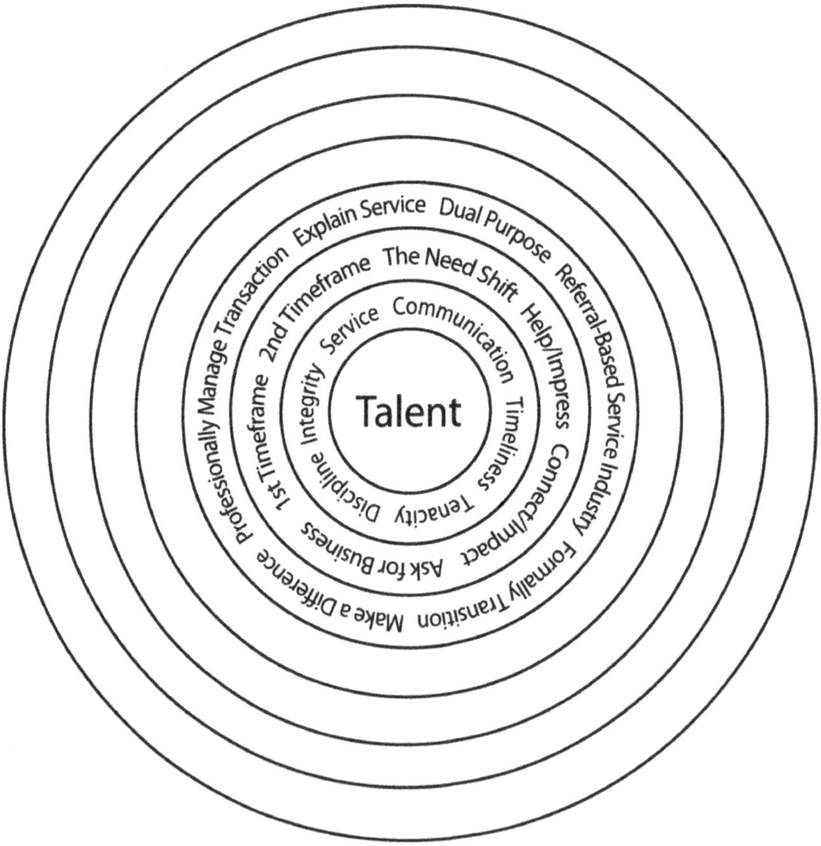

As we move on, it's time to add the turning points. For purpose of illustration only, some of the concepts associated with the turning points are shown. It's during this time you start to see early signs of circulation after passing through your tipping point. When you near the point where you have incorporated all of them, your business is at last on the verge of becoming a hurricane. You have logically moved on from the early hard work to the body of execution work. You now have the three major components of a powerful referral business in place and working together as one: traits, service, and execution strategies. The seminal moment is behind you.

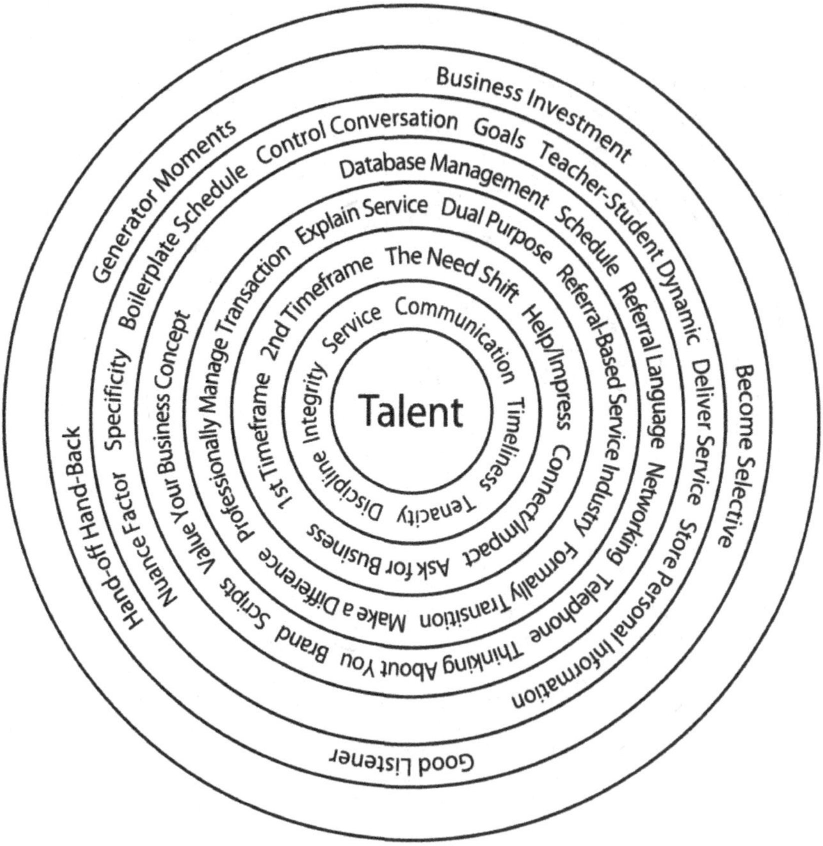

The culmination of everything combined and working together as one brings what is found in a powerful referral business, consistency at the highest level and relationships at every level. Together, they bring your hurricane to life by both encircling it and causing it to rotate. And you've finally created a triangulation-effect between you, clients, and business partners—The Eternal Triangle. You now have the two by-products of a powerful referral business in place, and as such, your business is now working hard for you. At last, you have achieved business efficiency.

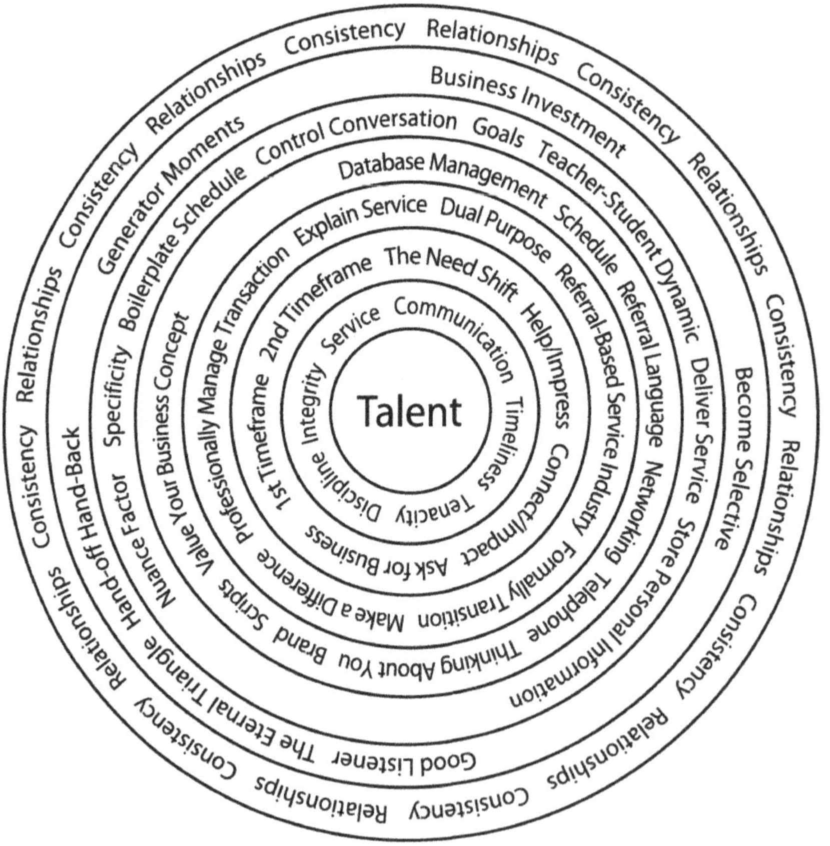

Now that you have built a hurricane business, you must take action to maintain it. You do so by annually assessing the four pillars of a powerful referral business. Failure to do it will eventually lead to a certain weakening and subsequent downgrade. Because you assess different elements of your business (you, service, clients, and business partners), they appear throughout your storm. There is no complacency in you.

There you have it: the framework that makes up a powerful referral business and a hurricane business—from beginning to end. It is a framework based on *methodical complexity*. Now you can clearly see the enormity of a business and the importance of a leverage business model around your talent. An important thing to remember during your journey is to never get wrapped-up in *the comparison game*. It's a guaranteed losing proposition, for there's always somebody better than you. Instead, keep your attention focused on what's important—constructing the framework of a powerful referral business. Worrying about what other people are doing is wasted energy and only takes away from your effort. Why? You are building your business based on your individualism, not someone else's idea of individualism. Here's the bottom line. You now know what to do, so just do it in a way that captures your essence.

And remember, there's no predetermined scale of business associated with a hurricane business; there's only service, repeat business, and referrals. If you recollect, scale of business is a personal choice, for it will reflect either an achieved or desired business result of a working business model. And here's yet one more important point for you to keep in mind. It's not easy to build a powerful referral business. I know that from firsthand experience. For me to suggest otherwise is to be disingenuous. However, I can state with a clear conscious that when you build it, business becomes easy.

And when business gets easy, you'll take vacations. Wherever you go—here's wishing you clear skies and all that comes with it!

The Bowtie

Just thinking…
It's just what it suggests.

I HAVE USED PRACTICALLY EVERY simple geometry shape to describe the different aspects of a powerful referral business—half circle, circle, triangle, pentagon, and decagram. That in itself is surprising to me, given that I was terrible at geometry in high school. As luck would have it, though, these various shapes can be effectively used in a simplistic and illustrative way to help one both solve a difficult problem and illuminate its varied aspects. Not even a powerful referral business can escape the influence of mathematics. And I just used concentric circles to sequentially illustrate a hurricane business. But I have yet to use a shape that captures the layered complexity of the business. Just as it was important to visually see the *methodical complexity,* it's equally important to see the *layered complexity* as well. What's the one shape that can illustrate the many layers of a powerful referral business? It's a shape that naturally wraps things up—a bowtie. I know, another hard to believe moment but true!

In the course of this book's journey, I've talked about a powerful referral business from beginning to end. In doing so, I've taken what appeared to only be a sequential approach, systematically moving from one concept to the next. In an unsuspecting way, I was also sequencing through a powerful referral business in a layered approach as well. To easily see the many layers that make up a powerful referral business, you will use the *Business Bowtie* illustrated on the next page.

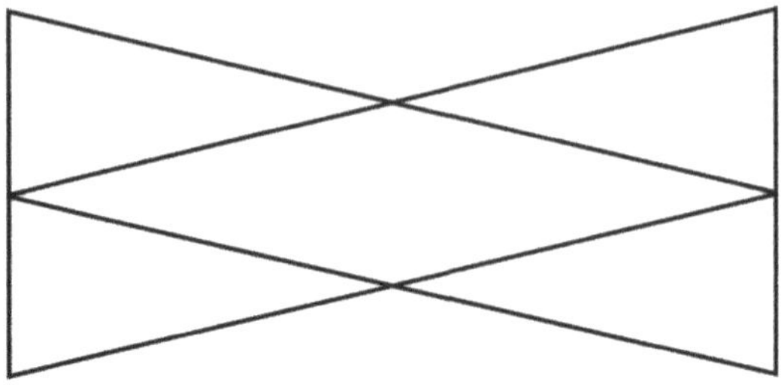

Look at the Business Bowtie again, but this time look beyond the bowtie itself (representing your entire business) and see the geometrical shapes that form it (representing the several layers of your business). When you do, you'll notice the Business Bowtie is made up of three distinct shapes—triangle, parallelogram, and diamond. It's through these shapes that the various layers of a powerful referral business are deftly revealed. It's also through these three shapes that you can start at the beginning of a powerful referral business and sequence through it just like the concepts did. The sage point of each shape is discussed below.

Let's start sequencing through those layers by beginning with the two large triangles. These two triangles reveal the six things I've focused on throughout this book—traits, service, execution, you, clients, and business partners. It's from them that a powerful referral business is built and the many layers revealed. Hopefully, you notice they are the same six things that were in the hourglass—the beginning of the journey.

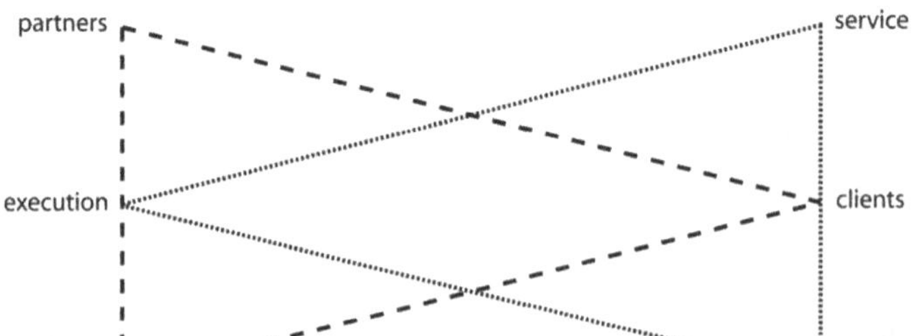

Let's take a closer look at those six words by placing them in four smaller triangles with a specific focus attached to them. What you will now see is two of the triangles are about your business and two of them are about you. What that tells you is a powerful referral business is simply based on a combination of business and human dynamics. Together they create emotion.

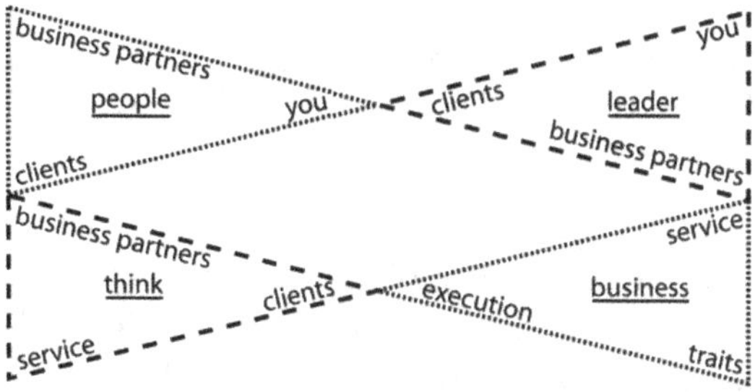

Let's go one step deeper and further breakdown the four triangles by transitioning to a parallelogram that allows us to discuss them in their natural pairs. The first parallelogram below reveals that if you are to have a complete understanding of your business, you have to understand the three major components of your business and the people in your business. Such knowledge is business acumen.

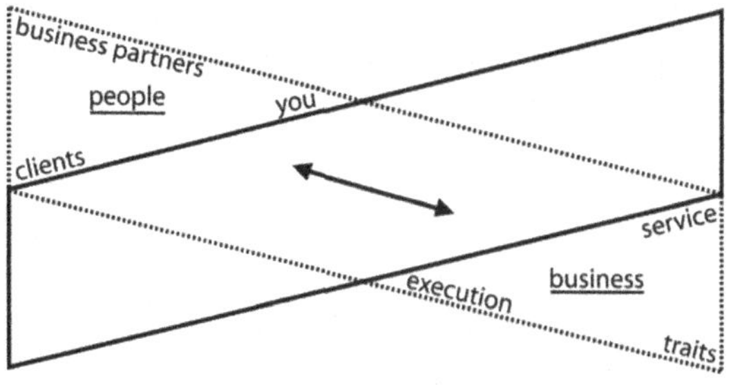

The second parallelogram on the next page reveals that how you think about the people in your business will determine the type of businessperson you are. When you embrace the thought process of service connects clients to your business, which then allows you to hire business partners to serve their likely needs, you become the leader of your business. You have created mutual trust and respect between you, clients, and business partners.

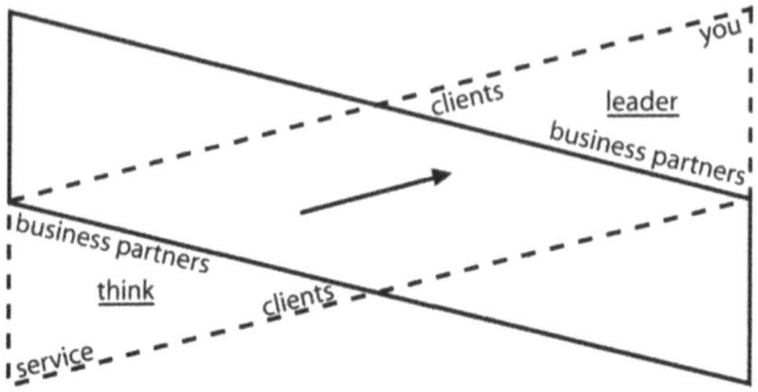

And how about when you look at both parallelograms together? Yes, you also see the bowtie, but what you need to focus on is the arrow pattern in the center. What the crossed arrows below tell you is the way you think about the people in the business (the nexus) determines the traits you adopt, the timeframes of service you provide, and the execution of your business. It also determines what you hope for from clients, what you expect of business partners, and what's required of you. Did you notice the subliminal acronym "HER"—I'm still trying to figure out the hard-to-decode message on that one! When you combine everything, it will lead to you becoming the leader of your business by creating and leveraging client and business partner trust. Once again, never lose sight of the fact that everything flows from how you think about the people in your business. It determines your business actions, the actions of the people in your business, the type of business you have, and the type of businessperson you are.

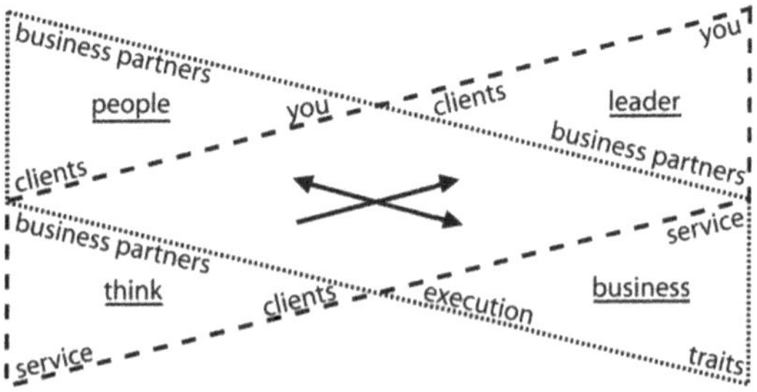

When you compress all of that together, the end product naturally created is the diamond on the next page revealing the four pillars your business is built on—you, service, clients, and business partners. Each one of them brings something completely different to your business that together allows you to build a powerful referral business.

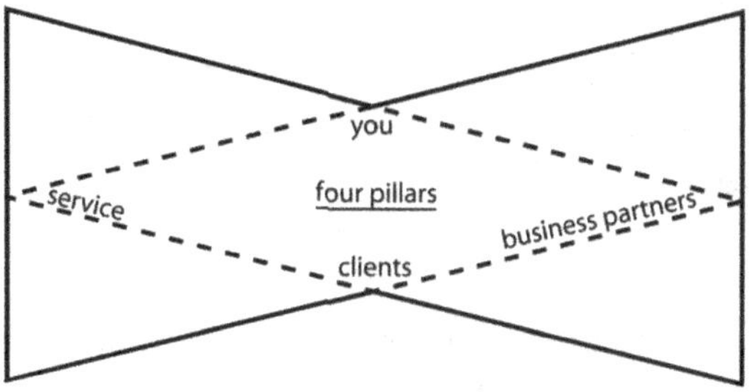

But a business journey is never completed, and therefore, each year you will set time aside to assess the four pillars of your business. You can always improve as a businessperson, and service will constantly be under pressure to change through cutting-edge technology and better ideas. Some clients will make a difference to your business and some will not. Most business partnerships will work (thanks to an interview process), while a few of them will fail for one reason or another. The *controlled evolution* of your business occurs through assessment.

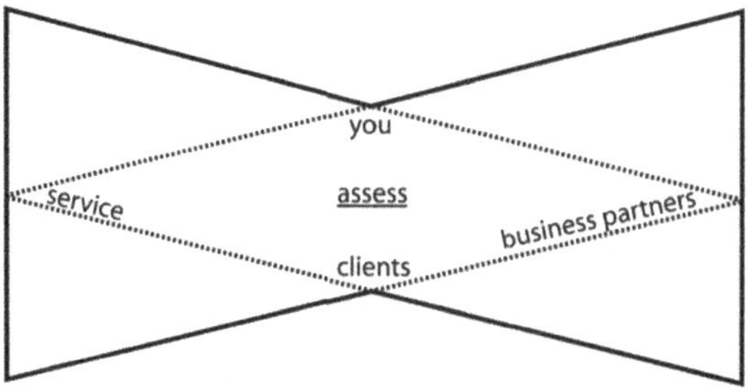

As you look at the Business Bowtie for the last time on the next page, you need to focus your attention on the two diamonds in the middle. You'll notice that they interact with every shape discussed. It just goes to show you they truly are the result of everything discussed. Through the two diamonds you will build and maintain a powerful referral business.

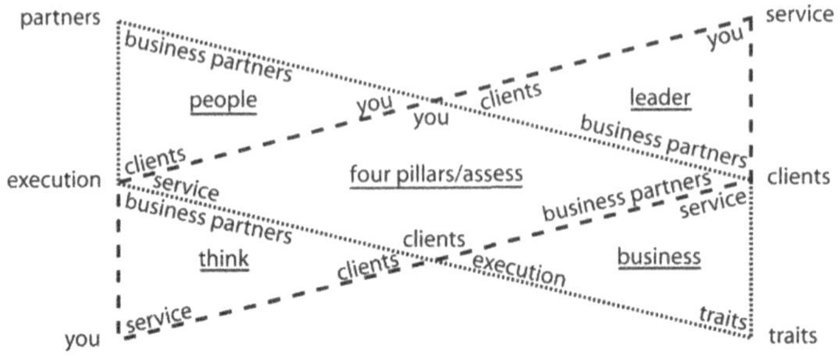

Whether you examine a powerful referral business through a sequenced approach or a layered approach, it all still fits together as one—just like a framework does.

I Have My Fingers Crossed

Just thinking...
Interest is not found in the obvious but, rather,
in the unobvious that makes you want to do the obvious.

AS I NEAR THE END OF THIS BOOK, I hope I met *The Barry Standard* of my life. What's that? It's an out of the ordinary comment from a long-ago conversation that has stuck with me over the years. Many years ago when I was a major on active duty, a young Jamaican man named Barry, who was a civilian defense contractor working at the Air Force base, told me I was like an old country lawyer. He even used the word "slow" with his lawyer reference. He said, "Sir, it isn't that you whine, you just say things in a way that makes people do things they wouldn't otherwise do."

I don't know if that's true or not, but I do hope I have presented convincing arguments for the following three things: the importance of understanding the framework of a business, thinking in Framework Language, and the value of service. Each one of them offers you something different that together makes you a complete businessperson. As such, I have three hopes for you.

First, I hope you realize the importance of emplacing the proper framework around your talent. You see, framework is a choice. As you read this sentence, the existing framework of your business today is determining what you do and subsequently if your business days are spent in business or building a business. That's the telling insight about the framework of your business—it's the mirror moment in business. It will not only reveal you as a businessperson, it will reveal your business actions as well. *There is no more clearer or honest reflection of you as a businessperson then when you look at the framework of your business.*

Second, it is my personal hope that you can now clearly think in Framework Language. That is, you have been fully empowered to successfully tackle the daunting task of building a powerful referral business. You can build it because you have the *acumen answers* (interesting and uninteresting, obvious and unobvious). The value of such sweeping knowledge prevents you from becoming a follower while highly encouraging you to become a leader. Framework Language doesn't tell you what to do. Instead, it tells you how something works through the identification of its major components and then reveals the many influential why concepts within each component. Such empowering knowledge leads to knowing what to do, which then naturally instills the dynamic of thinking to create. The created result is something as unique as a person is individual—a business reflective of you.

My last hope is this book has clearly shown you the value of service. When you make it the premise of your business, you can build a powerful referral business. Service has another important value to recognize, and it directly affects you. Service not only leads to sales, it also leads to *you being in charge.* That's the appealing quality of service—it affects everybody it touches. Where service makes a difference to the people who interface with your business, it makes you responsible. You assume a high level of responsibility throughout your business, for you are no longer in business, you are leading a business. You're in charge of every facet of your business, to include the service you provide, the clients you serve, and the business partners you hire to help you serve your clients. When you build a business based on the premise of service leads to sales, you become a *leader who serves others.* In other words, *The Third Question.*

Not to be overlooked is the fact that it's the core competency of "lead and serve others" that seamlessly threads together business and military into a joint world. And just for a moment, consider the two simple dynamics at work behind this core competency. When you are a leader, you are the best businessperson you can be; and when you serve others, you are the best person you can be. I firmly believe it is the coming together of these two diverse dynamics that creates the moniker, "The most admired businessperson."

And now take just a minute and think about the impact on a company culture if all of the sales force members are leaders who serve others. It creates a powerful alignment. Here's how. There is a continuous leadership thread running through the company—from the CEO to the senior management team, to the mid-level and front line managers, and on to the sales force members. There are leaders at every level of the company; each one empowered with their own unique leadership responsibilities. The end result is a company of leaders. Such a company reminds me of the military—everybody is being challenged to be their best.

The objective of my book was to tell Rose's story in such a manner that it might offer you a *fresh perspective* in the way you look at yourself and the business model you must build around your talent. Your success will not be determined on how hard or long you work but, rather, by the traits you embody, the quality processes you have around your talent, and the strategies you employ to execute your business. Altogether, they will give you the professional consistency and solid relationships that are the hallmarks of a powerful referral business.

It all sounds easy enough, so why is it such a difficult challenge to build a hurricane business? Think back on everything you have read in this book, not one sentence was directed toward discussing a required technical competency—partly because I still don't understand the technical side of the business. Not that it's unimportant. It's obviously very important. In fact, in the pecking order of things, it comes before framework and ideas. It just goes to show you there is another side of your business, the service side, consisting of two concepts working in concert—framework and ideas. If you were to visually think about all three of them together, you would see *the simple architecture of your business* and, once again, see two halves forming a whole as illustrated below.

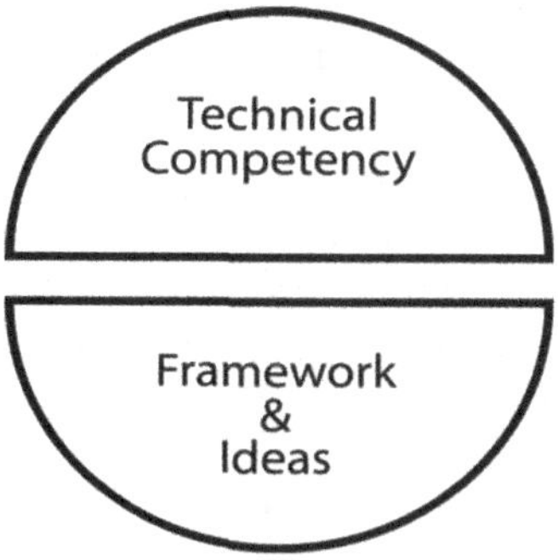

What the two halves above convey is full membership in the Referral-Based Service Industry requires a *Dual Education*. Where the technical education allows you to professionally *conduct* business transactions within your chosen profession, the service education allows you to *generate* repeat business and referrals, putting your technical education to work. *To achieve the business premise of service leads to sales, you have to be equally proficient on both halves of your business.* That's why it truly takes a magnificent effort to build a powerful referral business, you need all three diverse elements—technical competency, framework, and ideas—working seamlessly together as one.

Being proficient on both halves of your business means you've become a professional within a profession. You have total command of both sides of your business (technical and service), and you fully recognize their co-existence and respect their co-dependency. Technical competency by itself is no better than service with technical incompetence; they both lead to a struggled career.

The Referral-Based Service Industry has yet another key quality (besides a Dual Education) to recognize. It becomes a *critical industry* when you consider the *collective responsibility* of the business professionals who are most likely to build a powerful referral business (mortgage loan officers, agents, financial planners, insurance agents, and CPAs). They are a diverse group of professionals who are tightly drawn together by a common purpose—to serve the vital professional needs of a homeowner. Through the accomplishment of their required professional and unique personal service they help a family fulfill its dream of homeownership, protect both its personal and private property, purchase life and other types of insurance, secure its financial future, save for college, maximize its tax deductions, and, yes, even meet its taxation obligation to the government. So much of America's fundamental promise rests in the hands of these five professions. And because business people in the Referral-Based Service Industry advise clients (they have the moral fiber to say, "No" when they can technically say, "Yes"), that promise is safely kept. This high personal standard is an unbending principle of the industry. It's this principle that turns a job into a calling—putting others first.

One of the not-so-obvious but interesting features of a powerful referral business is it's based on a considerable number of *groups of three*. If you look closely at the business, you will see them throughout—that just mentioned on the previous page, the nexus, the full spectrum of service, the major components, fundamental revenue streams, the art of the call, etc. Out of all the groups of three that comprise a powerful referral business, just one stands out above all the rest. That group is the *three guiding principles* (business model, business definition, and business premise). It is from them that a powerful referral business is constructed. They truly are the genesis of everything discussed. As such, the framework draws equally from their nuclear focus. A powerful referral business creates *leverage*, thereby shifting the burden of working hard from the businessperson to the business. Every client and business partner *makes a difference* across the business through two pentagon effects. And it is through an explained first and second timeframe of *service*, along with pounce processes, that *sales* of repeat and referral business are generated.

Here is yet another group of three to be keenly aware of. It is this group that accounts for the struggle of trying to understand a business. Here's how. When you think about a business in *general terms*, it's made up of a *technical* and a *service* side and then *motivational aspects* (attitude, focus, energy, zeal, drive, initiative, etc.). Each one is a *stand alone*, in that they bring to bear a unique capability that makes a business work. Yet, when people speak or write about a business, they tend to mesh all of them together. It's natural to do because they do work as one. However, it's the meshing together of them that *blurs a business* and helps explains why it can be so difficult to learn about a business. A business can be further blurred by adding other relevant miscellaneous information to the mix. Here's the bottom line. To be in complete control when you listen to people speak about or write about a business, you must be able to immediately compartmentalize their comments into one of these three stand alone business dynamics. By doing so, you fully comprehend what you are hearing or reading, thereby determining the true worth of the words. It's just another example of how learning the framework of a business empowers you in yet one more way.

This brings to light the not easily seen *three distinct spectrums of thought* that are steadily advancing business people and their business. The spectrums (framework, ideas, and motivational aspects) are relentlessly being thoughtfully evolved by a large contingent of entrepreneurs and companies committed to this important work. Such work ensures the lasting relevance of each spectrum. When you place them side-by-side and compare them, you realize that each one is a unique and equal area of thought that effortlessly interfaces with the others. In other words, none of them are a panacea. To suggest or believe otherwise is to mislead or be misled. But when they're combined, their common purpose is clearly revealed—to continuously evolve business people and their business in a way that allows both of them to always walk in step with the times. It is these three diverse spectrums of thought that is allowing the proverbial *"can"* to be advanced down the road instead of kicked down the road.

O

If you were to one last time read between the lines of the powerful referral business premise phrase of service leads to sales, here is what you would read this time. Your two timeframes of *service* connects clients to your business, allowing you to hire like-minded business partners to serve their likely needs. Positioning your business to first take care of clients and business partners *leads to sales* of repeat client business, client referrals, and business partnerships where referrals flow back and forth.

The subtlety of the above paragraph is the premise and nexus of a powerful referral business are one in the same. The most basic thought of a business determines the first framework building decision in a business.

Some Final Thoughts

Just thinking for the last time...
It's on to the next project. I have some
ideas I'm working on. See, they are important.

TELLING OUR STORY IN A BOOK has been a very personal journey for me. Along the way I have openly shared our successes and failures, and our strengths and weaknesses. I have candidly revealed our human and business vulnerabilities. What gave me the strength and courage to do it is I believe there are many people like us who want to build a sustainable, successful business based on service, repeat business, and referrals but just aren't quite sure how to do it. We, like most people, are not fully there yet. Rose's management responsibilities, along with inevitable business ups and downs, constantly reminds us that *building a business is based on making progress, not linear progress*. We're okay with that, though, because we now know we're heading there. We couldn't say that in the past.

And Rose's production volume is also heading in a new direction. Wherein the past it was slightly above middle of the pack, it's now in the upper-tier of the company. In fact, Rose was in the top 5% of the loan officers in her region, per the YTD Production Ledger for July 2008. It was the company's last full report. Unfortunately, it closed its doors shortly thereafter (it was a wonderful company). Since then, Rose has moved to a new company and continued her upward movement. Her team's 2009 monthly production numbers consistently placed her at the top of the Loan Officer Ranking Report. In short, she logically moved through the dichotomy of a business, to include hiring an executive assistant and adding a partner. And where is her business model development today when it comes to the Weather or Not Concept? Through the many business and personal changes she has made, her business is now at the tropical storm level. Slowly but steadily, Rose is progressively moving forward in her charted journey of organizational change. (Note: Rose stepped away from her business in 2010 to go to Texas for a year to better help her sister and brothers take care of their mother who is struggling to recover from a terrible car accident in late 2008.)

As my unexpected personal journey of conscious and subconscious thinking (Rose would say maniacal) comes to an end, I have great admiration and respect for just how much of a transformation it takes to move from a transactional to a referral-based businessperson. It's not enough to just make cursory changes. You have to fundamentally change as a businessperson in almost every regard to truly realize the personal and professional success a referral-based business has to offer. The significant difference between the two businesses can be summed up in two words: *conduct* and *generate*. A transactional business conducts transactions with whomever it can, while a referral-based business generates repeat and referral business from selected clients and hired business partners. One business is fraught with vulnerability, the other with growth.

It's so very important for me to acknowledge that my journey of thinking would not have been possible without the incredible *gift of time* Rose gave to me. This is the second untold Rose story in this book to know. The gift of time may not seem like much of a gift on the surface, but I cannot think of any other gift that comes with a greater personal burden to bear. For over a five year period, Rose faithfully answered every type of challenge she faced with determination and grace. She went to the office every day and worked many late nights, while I wrote. She lovingly took care of me and our boys and kept the house up, while I wrote. She put our two oldest sons through college and helped our youngest son enlist in the Air Force, while I wrote. She emotionally and financially supported our family in every conceivable way, while I wrote. And she felt a full range of pressures and stresses associated with work yet somehow found the inner-strength to calmly deal with all of them, while I wrote. When our youngest son went to war in Iraq, she prayed and worried every day, and when he safely returned home, she cried uncontrollably, while I wrote. No matter how tired and exhausted she was the night before, she went to work the next morning, while I wrote. And when her mother was involved in a horrific car crash, she rushed home to Texas to be by her side, while I wrote. All of this burden and she was still unbelievably patient and understanding when I struggled to write. She silently sacrificed her life in numerous other ways, while I wrote. This is the unseen human toll that she quietly and willingly shouldered when she so unselfishly gave me the gift of time through herself. She took a mother's love to a level I had never imagined. I have seen and heard of many beautiful gestures of love in my lifetime, but none can compare to this one. I now know there is no greater expression of love one can give to another then when they give the gift of time. I hope I can do the same for her one day.

Even with everything I said in my heartfelt admission above, it still doesn't capture the raw feeling I carry inside of me every day. It's so very difficult for me to write the following few words, let alone say them to Rose, but it is important to acknowledge the obvious—it has been incredibly unfair the last five years.

In the final analysis, this book was never meant to take an exhaustive review of each subject matter discussed. The intent was to provide the framework of a powerful referral business by touching on the subjects in such a way that the big picture emerged about how it works and why you do things. Such beginning knowledge should empower you to confidently embark on a self-determined business journey. As you do, you should simultaneously embark on a never-ending educational journey as well. For as long as you are making a difference to clients and business partners, you should be learning new things that continuously improves you and your business.

You are highly encouraged to seek out more in-depth analysis and information from various other sources to further develop the several subject matters that were discussed in this book. A leader is always learning and improving. When you fully develop each one, you have, in essence, further strengthened the framework of your business. It just goes to show you again that framework represents the most basic structure of a business. Learning the framework of a powerful referral business begins your *dual journey* of an exciting and fulfilling business career and of thinking while you listen.

There's undoubtedly so much to know about a business that no one person or institution can possibly teach it all. In fact, I am sure you can come up with other subject matters that were not even discussed in this book. What that means is *learning about a business is a collaborative effort from many different sources over many years.* With that said, why turn to framework first? When you learn framework, you not only make sense of your business, you make sense of what other people are saying about a business. That in itself makes it a natural place to start your learning, for it will empower you in multiple ways throughout your career.

Hopefully over the course of this book's many pages I've clearly shown you I'm looking through an *empowering business prism* while probably showing you at times I'm on the edge of crazy. I gladly accept both thoughts if what I shared made sense and is meaningful to you, to the point where you have a new and better way to learn. If I'm lucky, you saw some of your story in Rose's story—I hope so. Her story is that of a kind, honest, hard working transactional businessperson who could be from a number of different professions. And if I'm really lucky, this book's many concepts, along with Rose's story, has provided you answers to some of the struggles and/or challenges you have personally experienced in your business.

So there you have it, everything I know about the framework of a powerful referral business—today. I know there is more to learn, more interconnectivity, more interdependency, more acumen answers, and, therefore, more aha moments. With that said, I hope I have explicitly correlated the inner workings of a powerful referral business to the inner workings of a strong framework.

The real test of a strong framework is that it all fits as one and works together. Some things are stronger than others, but no one thing is strong enough to stand on its own. Its strength is derived from dependency—it is a closed system that is totally dependent on itself, through itself. No matter where you place your hand on the framework, you can trace every single inch of it—something leads to something else, which then leads to something else before eventually starting all over again. *It's a tangle of support that is unequivocally one.* Hopefully I have been able to convincingly show you those exact same qualities with traits, service, execution strategies, and assessment—the framework of a powerful referral business.

The underlying principle at work that guided my journey of discovering a powerful referral business was *The Theory of Framework.* Concisely stated, the theory is a search for the acumen answers that exposes the complexity of a subject matter, which, in turn, reveals the scope of the ideas needed to support it. The theory recognizes that a subject matter with interlocking, interdependent pieces has an underlying framework just waiting to be discovered. It further recognizes that if the subject matter is to achieve its intended function, a full complement of framework and ideas must be present and working seamlessly together as one. Where understanding comes from framework, application comes from ideas. It is understandable application that eventually leads to intended function. Succinctly put, The Theory of Framework is an education uniquely applied to a person's individualism.

Framework is not just limited to a powerful referral business. Every type of business is based on a framework, which represents the most *basic structure* of that business. No matter if the business is transactional, referral, or powerful referral, they all have an interlocking, interdependent framework meant to accomplish a desired business outcome. Regardless of which one you choose to base your business career on, you must understand its framework to reach its full business potential. However, to reach *your* full business potential, there is only one choice.

To help you discover the framework of a transactional and a referral business, you have to look no further than the framework of a powerful referral business. Why? It contains the core business principle that each business is based on. A powerful referral business conducts transactions and earns repeat business and client referrals. Where a transactional business captures the *early moments* of a powerful referral business, a referral business *closely resembles* it. This distinct difference between the two businesses means one framework will be easier to discover than the other. A transactional business will require selectivity with the traits, service, and execution strategies that were discussed. And even then, there will be a different focus applied to some of them. On the contrary, discovering the framework of a referral business will be relatively easy and quite familiar. The only difference from it and a powerful referral business is there's no leveraging of client trust for the benefit of business partners. Therefore, the corresponding business activities that leverage client trust in such a way will be absent.

Just as there is a framework for a transactional and a referral business, there's also a definition and premise for them as well. The definition of a transactional business would be—*both your personal effort and a marketing plan create customer transactions.* Its corresponding premise is *hard work and spending money leads to sales.* And the referral business definition would be—*clients making a difference to a business that is first making a difference to them.* Its resultant premise is *service leads to client sales within the profession.*

Let me take a moment here and provide a quick, insightful analysis of a business. Every type of business (transactional, referral, and powerful referral) is a complex entity with an underlying natural order. It's the *natural order of a business* (traits, service, and execution) that will both simplify the business and lead to the unlocking of its complexity. But before you can do that, you must first establish the nexus, which will determine how the natural order is specifically applied. In the end, the natural order of a business is flexible enough to be applied to all three types of businesses while bringing out the full potential of each one.

I've thoroughly discussed the framework of a powerful referral business, but I have yet to discuss the *influencing aspects* of framework itself, up until now. When the concept of framework is applied in a much broader sense, it can influence decisions at both the management and individual level. Here's an example of each one.

At the management level, it can show if there's complete alignment with a company's sales force mission statement and its education/training program. That is, are they both leveraging the same level of client trust. If there's a misalignment, then framework can help with the corrective action. How? The transparency of framework makes it easy to couple together a personal expectation mission statement and a complementary education/training program (to include mentoring and evaluation) that leads to the desired sales force. It only makes sense that framework could be used in this top down manner. What's applicable to an individual is usually applicable to a group as well. When management applies framework in this broad-based manner, they can create a company culture where each sales force member is building a powerful referral business in his or her individual way while being a leader who serves others.

From an individual standpoint, a broader application of framework can tell if a seminar and/or a coaching program is intended to develop a transactional, referral, or powerful referral businessperson. It'll do one of the three. Knowing this vital information upfront ensures a wise investment of both money and time.

These are just a sampling of some of the important insights that framework can reveal when it's looked at through a *broad lens*. By looking at framework in this way, it can help bring out the best in both a company and an individual.

And here's the underlying insight to be keenly aware of when it comes to both scenarios mentioned above. When management and an individual consider these particular business options, they are addressing their *moral leadership responsibility*. There's no right or wrong answer here; there is only the consciously best answer. It is a decision that has wide and far-reaching impact. It will establish the personally strived for potential, how others are served, and, eventually, economic impact. With that said, here's yet one more bottom line thought for your consideration. The most successful companies and individuals have never played the numbers game. Instead, they have played the *relationship game* that produces numbers. Yet once again, a business provides another substantive either-or choice.

As I near the completion of this book, I have a clearer understanding and a new-found appreciation for the words, education and motivation. It's through these two words that I can account for my long struggle of mentally searching for the acumen answers. As I look back on my journey of near constant thinking, I was highly *motivated* to build a leverage business model around Rose's talent, but because I didn't have a business-building *education* background, my progress was particularly slow. These mitigating circumstances made me once again realize the importance of an education and opened my eyes even wider to the limitation of motivation. Where an education provides *know-how*, motivation creates *energy*. Each one unquestionably has a distinct function, which leads to a natural order between the two of them. If this order gets misconstrued by putting motivation ahead of education, then inevitable consequences are sure to follow. That is, motivation by itself only creates energy, which leads to a long, arduous struggle as I went through. In contrast, motivation directly applied to an education creates *energetic know-how,* which quickly leads to the highly-desired outcome. Education and motivation are both very important, with one clearly in support of the other.

Even though this book has given you an educational approach to a powerful referral business, don't underestimate the challenge ahead. Building a powerful referral business is like raising children. There's excitement when you first start and then the reality kicks in, for you realize just how difficult it is. But you never stop or quit because you know in the end you'll create something that can stand on its own, something that you're proud of, and something that reflects upon you. And when you do, you have achieved what you set out to do. An achievement is not meant to be easy; it is meant to be rewarding.

By taking an *educational approach* to your business, you naturally become a thinker in your business. A sense of liberation comes over you, for it is through thinking that you empower yourself; you improve your decision-making ability; you lead instead of being led; you become independent; you determine your own dignity; and you bring *intellectual thought* to your business and conversations. You have complete confidence in yourself, and you are in command and control of your business.

Intellectual thought is such an empowering concept it is important to briefly expand on it. Let me clearly illustrate its empowering quality by first mentioning and then quickly analyzing a couple of verbal comments that are somewhat common in both the real estate and mortgage professions. When agents say, "I just expect my lenders to close my transactions on time, without any problems," they are choosing control over leverage. It doesn't mean their statement is incorrect, but it does mean their business will never reach its full potential. They are thinking more as an individual than as a businessperson. And when the boss of a mortgage company says, "Our sales force needs to focus on agent relationships," his words are steering his salespeople in a transactional business way that will make them dependent in business. And just like the agents above, the full potential of their business will also be unfulfilled. The application of intellectual thought in this way is almost endless when you truly understand the concept of framework. *Framework makes words matter.* In the end, it's just one of the many attributes that comes with taking an educational approach to a business.

All of this discussion about education takes me back to the first business seminar I attended. I was sitting unnoticed in an audience of hundreds of people, yet I still felt vulnerable. Why? I knew I was an *uneducated* audience member. I didn't understand a business (how and whys), and therefore, I had to take at face value what I heard because I was only able to listen to what was being said. And today when I sit in an audience, I'm an *educated* member. I understand the inner workings of a business, and therefore, I think when I listen, which means I can comprehend the true worth of the words spoken. It is through my own experiences that I realize an audience is just a gathering of uneducated and/or educated people who both want to learn. The only difference between the two of them is they are at different comprehension levels. I have been both.

Here's one last bottom line for you to keep in mind. Just as a college education grows in value over time, the same is true for your business when you take an educational approach to it.

Thinking back to my one and only goal when I joined Rose in her business, *"...to build a business model around Rose's talent that would allow her to realize her full potential as a loan officer."*—I might have gone just a little bit overboard. That's the power of love, sometimes it makes you do unexpected things!

There are numerous different business models you can follow to be successful in business. There's no one right way. With so many different ways to achieve success, why choose the leverage business model of a powerful referral business? I believe it's the one business model that seamlessly blends together four highly-desirable qualities: individualism, leverage, leadership, and service. A powerful referral business allows you to build your business in an individual way that creates the most leverage while being a leader who serves others.

As I approach the end of this book, I'm cognizant of two clear-minded thoughts. First, I realize the exact moment my first cloud appeared in my sky. It was when Mr. Stephen Marshall made the comment, "A lot of loan officers don't get it; it's about the service, not the sale." That was the first moment of my journey. The reason being is it directly spoke to one of my core military values—service. And second, I have a greater appreciation for the kindness and patience the people in the company offered me in my first year. Even though I was in way over my head, and they all knew it, they still treated me with respect and made me feel welcomed. Their actions reminded me of my military days, for they were all professionals.

Although my thinking journey is now behind me, I'm still struggling to be fully comfortable in the business world. Why? I've yet to learn the technical side of the business. With that said, writing this book has been therapeutic, for it showed me that maybe my first year in corporate America wasn't a total loss. It also showed me the Referral-Based Service Industry has the highest standards of any of the service industries. That fact is what makes it a prestigious industry; you can proudly serve and still get paid. In hindsight, maybe that's why I was able to write this book. I'd been doing that type of work for the last 20 years.

I would be remiss if I didn't leave you with one final mad-thought to contemplate, so here it is for your consideration. Over the course of this book, I have shared with you my many thoughts concerning a business. But what would a business tell you if it could speak as well. That's an intriguing question, isn't it? What words of advice would it want to share with you before you begin to work on it? I would venture to say it would probably sound something like this:

> *Some people like to make me seem attractive by saying I'm made up of such things as killer strategies and millionaire secrets, while other people like to oversimplify me by focusing a disproportionate amount of attention on certain aspects of me. In reality, though, I'm just a bunch of common sense with a beginning, middle, and end. You can't learn about me from just one source. To know me well is to learn from many sources over a long period of time. I'm very flexible, for I can be a transactional, referral, or powerful referral business. It is your choice on how you will achieve success. I make no decisions; I only carry out your many decisions. I will succeed or fail based on your actions alone. I will make you work hard in the beginning, but you can eventually shift the burden of working hard from you to me if you so choose. I will naturally allow you to be a follower, but I will greatly challenge you if you want to be a leader. I can be based on making money, but I prefer to be based on providing service, for I can then make a greater difference to you and the people you select to interface with me. I assume no responsibility for my final outcome; that distinction rests solely with you. And I will not stand in the way of your individualism; I will do and be whatever you want. It is you alone who will determine your dignity within the profession. You see, I'm just a reflection of your many decisions and actions. So I ask you today, what type of business framework did you commit to build?*

If you commit to building the framework of a powerful referral business, then the best way to begin is with a *Starting Assessment.* Such an assessment is intended to provide a quick look across the many concepts of a powerful referral business that will identify your current strengths and weaknesses, thereby helping you streamline your effort to build a powerful referral business. It is imperative to mention the importance of being completely honest with yourself during this assessment. If you fudge your answers in any way, you only delay your success because you haven't accepted responsibility for known weaknesses that require attention. Conducting a Starting Assessment is another personal leadership moment.

So how do you develop a Starting Assessment template? If you look closely at the framework discussed, you can glean a set of essence definitions that will allow you to assess yourself across the many *pivotal concepts* of a powerful referral business. Once you identify these definitions, you can assess each one utilizing a *stop-light approach:* Green means you're fully doing the activity. Yellow means you're partially doing the activity. And red means you're not doing the activity at all.

When I first did this type of assessment for Rose, there was far more red and yellow than green. It was an expected visual outcome because a transactional and a powerful referral business are opposing ways of business. The chosen psychology of her business, business partners over clients, was clearly reverberating throughout her assessment. So much so, it vividly revealed the sweeping changes she would have to make as a businesswoman if she was to successfully transform her business. The framework of Rose's (tropical depression) business had been exposed for the very first time.

Not only was the framework of Rose's business exposed, but she could see exactly where she was in her business model development as it related to a powerful referral business. If you recall, determining business model development is the first framework question. By reviewing her Starting Assessment, we clearly knew two things: precisely where our business development effort stood, and the specific areas we needed to focus on. We finally had the all important, yet elusive, two reference points it takes to move a business forward in a methodical and efficient manner.

(Note: For your convenience, both a Starting Assessment template and a corresponding set of essence definitions have already been developed and are freely available at the iFrameworks website. Also, if you'd like, you can view Rose's Starting Assessment there.)

Now that you have read everything, it's time for one more hand-off, and this one doesn't require a hand-back. A business has always been willing and ready to hand you the reins of leadership. A powerful referral business places those reins in your hands. So confidently grab them, never let them go, and never look back. GIDDY UP!

I'm sure someone, somewhere, once said, "You first write what you know." I now know firsthand there's absolute truth to that statement. As I ponder one last time what I have written, I realize that's all I did in this book. I simply wrote about what I was most comfortable and familiar with by applying leadership and service to a business. I've long since moved on from the United States Air Force, but it's quite obvious its values will always be a part of me.

And when I look back over the business journey Rose has traveled, it can be summed up in just two words—paradigm shift. In the past, Rose was a businesswoman who learned by business activity; she took a training approach to her business; and she was a follower. She was a glowing representative for the transactional industry—honest and hard working. And today, she learns by studying a business model; she's taken an educational approach to her business; and she's a leader. In every case, she has taken an opposing way to her past. As I stated earlier in this book, these days she is a proud member of the Referral-Based Service Industry—she is still honest, but now her business is starting to work hard for her. Her business journey truly has been a paradigm shift—she now works in a different industry then when I started writing this book.

There's one last thing I learned on my long, thoughtful journey. I now understand the dynamics behind critical-thinking. It is a combination of the conscious and subconscious minds that constitute critical-thinking. Where the conscious mind can be turned on and turned off (for example, typing at a computer, taking a thoughtful walk, or even thinking in the shower), the subconscious mind is ignited by a passion for something or a love for someone. Together, the two minds maximize the thinking capacity of the brain.

With that said, it is the incessant running of the subconscious mind that makes critical-thinking possible. While it is constantly trying to solve the problem like a supercomputer (silently crunching), it is continuously filtering everything (verbal, visual, and written) from the surrounding environment to aid that process. Such acute consciousness can spark a multitude of outcomes—thought in a different direction, further development of an early thought, enhancement of a developed thought, a finishing touch on a supposed completed thought, adding a new thought to develop, figuring out an interconnectivity between thoughts, etc. The outcome of this is the thinking ability of the mind is greatly expanded.

The subconscious mind is working in yet another interesting way. Not only is it the most intense aspect of critical-thinking (because it is driven by emotion), it is predominantly where "the most original thinking" occurs. The reason being is random ideas are intermittently firing across the mind (just like shooting stars)—these thoughts emerge that quickly and expectedly stay that briefly. Most of them will quickly flame out, but a few of them will maintain their brilliance. It is, in essence, a mental exercise of massive failure with very little success. However, it is this spontaneous mental exercise that eventually produces the most original thought. An example is the Business Bowtie concept. The random idea that came to me was two isosceles triangles turned on their sides and overlapped (don't ask me where it came from). In time, this shape revealed the many layers of a powerful referral business. Another example of a random idea out of nowhere was associating the acronym "M.A.D." with the phrase, make a difference. This crude thought eventually led to the development of the MAD, M.A.D. Service concept.

Here is my interpretation of critical-thinking: When the subconscious mind is fully engaged (in all the ways discussed), along with the conscious mind, the mental capability of the brain is pushed to its very limit of thinking and creativity. The combined effect will take a person on a journey of discovery he or she could have never imagined possible. I know it did for me...but my head really hurts!

Before departing ways, there's one last tidbit of information to share with you. During my college days, my nickname was *Breezeman.* I have wondered on occasion, during the writing of this book, if it was my destiny to write a business book based on weather...nah!

…maybe

Bud,

It's only appropriate that this book ends where it started, with you. Just you being your beautiful self has once again, in yet another way, inspired me to give my best. It was your presence alone that sustained me on a long and wondrous journey of unimaginable discovery. I now know how to accomplish the goal that was so easily stated while being so intellectually challenging to solve. It just goes to show you, when love is the motivator, anything is possible. And boy do I LOVE YOU!

Michael